Confrontation of Courage

Six young Kiowa braves sat on their horses, calmly watching her. All were naked to the waist. Their heavy black hair hung in thick braids, interwoven with rawhide and strips of ermine. All wore bone chestplates and copper bracelets.

Isabel pulled her team to a halt. Moving slowly to hide her racing heart, she raised her right hand, palm forward, in greeting.

One by one the Indians guided their horses down the slope toward her and formed a semicircle, blocking her path.

"You come here all alone and you no scared? Maybe we scalp you." The leader's face was solemn.

The banks of the dry wash screened Isabel and the six Indian men from the outside world. She was truly at their mercy.

"I think maybe we scalp you now," the leader signed. He prodded his horse forward. A knife appeared in his left hand. He snatched the Winchester from his lap and placed the end of the barrel against Isabel's head. She heard the click of the hammer as it was cocked.

Isabel went completely numb. Every thought went out of her brain. The roaring in her ears grew into a crescendo as she awaited the fatal bullet. Cold chills shot up her spine. She closed her eyes and prepared to die. . . .

Light on the Mountain

Leonard Sanders

This they tell, and
whether it happened so
or not I do not know;
but if you think about it,
you can see that it is
true.

> BLACK ELK,
> *Black Elk Speaks*

BANTAM BOOKS
TORONTO · NEW YORK · LONDON · SYDNEY · AUCKLAND

LIGHT ON THE MOUNTAIN
A Bantam Book / January 1987

Permission for use of Wind Songs, dance chants, and Death Songs was graciously granted by Maurice Boyd. First published in his three-volume series, *Kiowa Voices* (Texas Christian University Press), the material was translated by James Auchiah, Kiowa elder.

ISBN 0-553-25817-6

Published simultaneously in the United States and Canada

PRINTED IN THE UNITED STATES OF AMERICA

KR   0 9 8 7 6 5 4 3 2 1

For Florene

Acknowledgments

With gratitude to Susan M. Eltscher, director of The American Baptist-Samuel Colgate Historical Library in Rochester, N.Y., her staff, and the library, for preserving and making available Isabel Crawford's diaries;

George Younkin, blood brother to the Kiowas and retired archival director of the Federal Records and Archives Center in Fort Worth, Texas;

Maurice Boyd, author of the superb, profusely illustrated three-volume series *Kiowa Voices*, published by Texas Christian University Press in Fort Worth, and director of the *Kiowa Voices* research project, sponsored jointly by the National Endowment for the Humanities and Texas Christian University;

Dr. Paul Parham, director of the Mary Couts Burnett Library at TCU, and Jan Ferguson, director of the Interlibrary Loan Department.

I also extend heartfelt thanks to Kiowa friends and acquaintances of my boyhood and collegiate years, and to my hosts at long-ago Kiowa powwows near Saddle and Rainy Mountains. They provided insights that have granted me deep appreciation of the Kiowa tribal mystery.

Leonard Sanders
Fort Worth, 1986

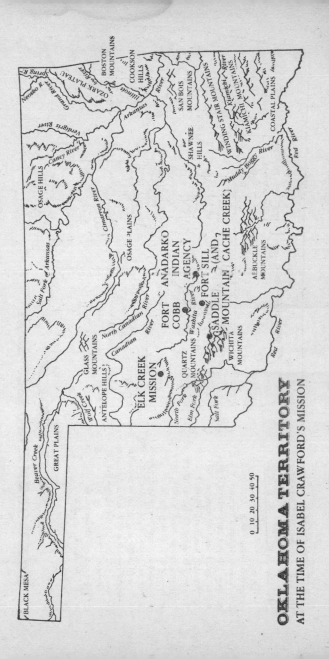

OKLAHOMA TERRITORY
AT THE TIME OF ISABEL CRAWFORD'S MISSION

0 10 20 30 40 50

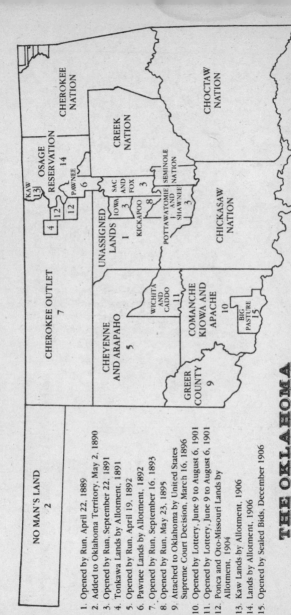

THE OKLAHOMA
LAND OPENINGS 1889-1906

1. Opened by Run, April 22, 1889
2. Added to Oklahoma Territory, May 2, 1890
3. Opened by Run, September 22, 1891
4. Tonkawa Lands by Allotment, 1891
5. Opened by Run, April 19, 1892
6. Pawnee Lands by Allotment, 1892
7. Opened by Run, September 16, 1893
8. Opened by Run, May 23, 1895
9. Attached to Oklahoma by United States
   Supreme Court Decision, March 16, 1896
10. Opened by Lottery, June 9 to August 6, 1901
11. Opened by Lottery, June 9 to August 6, 1901
12. Ponca and Oto-Missouri Lands by
    Allotment, 1904
13. Kaw Lands by Allotment, 1906
14. Lands by Allotment, 1906
15. Opened by Sealed Bids, December 1906

BOOK ONE
The Reservation

The Indian races are melting in the presence of European civilization like snow in the rays of the sun. . . .

ALEXIS DE TOCQUEVILLE,
Democracy in America,
1835

The great leaders were gone; the mighty power of the Kiowas and Comanches was broken; the buffalo they had tried to save had vanished. It had all happened in less than ten years.

DEE BROWN, *Bury My Heart at Wounded Knee*

Chapter One

Thunder and lightning persisted through most of the night, but in the hour before dawn the storm ended. Isabel awoke to a profound silence. Reluctant to abandon sleep, she lay motionless, leisurely assembling the loose, broken images of a dream. She had been with her father, traveling somewhere, but she could not recapture details. Only the warm comfort of his presence remained. Burrowing into the soft blankets, Isabel basked in the lingering illusion.

Then the cat jumped from the bed. A moment later he meowed at the side door, demanding to go out.

Reality returned in a rush.

This was the day.

Isabel sat up, savoring a stir of excitement.

Moving quietly, she eased out of bed and pulled a quilted Watteau robe over her flannel nightgown. Not bothering to light a lamp, careful not to awaken Sister Everts, she twisted her long hair into a loose chignon, then slipped bare feet into her heavy, vulcanized gum boots, opened the door for the cat, and followed him outside, onto the porch.

Far to the east, the last flickers of lightning were fading away. Overhead, stars shimmered through trailing wisps of overcast. The angle of the Big Dipper confirmed that night was ending.

Prodded by a growing restlessness, impatient for the day to begin, she snuggled deeper into her robe against the penetrating chill and walked down the slope, away from the cluster of mission buildings.

The nightlong downpour had left the ground soft and yielding. In the wide meadow below the mission she sank to her ankles in mud and struggled with each step to pull her boots free. Amused by her own awkwardness, she turned toward higher ground. Finding firmer soil, she raised the hem of her robe, kicked high, and sent clumps of red loam flying. She enjoyed a moment of private, sporting pride in how much higher she could kick mud than when she came to Elk Creek three years ago.

She approached the creek, now a raging torrent, and stopped, awed by its overnight metamorphosis. At this spot she often had hopped across a clear, calm, peaceful stream, aided only by stepping-stones. Now foaming waters lapped over the banks and edged into the surrounding prairie.

First light was spreading across the eastern horizon. At her feet, she could see that tender green shoots of buffalo grass had pushed bravely through winter's dead thatch. Isabel knelt and ran her palm over the damp, spongy turf. She looked up. Rain-soaked sprigs of spiderwort, purple paintbrush, and wild foxglove awaited the sun. Around her, every sagebrush and sharp spine of prickly pear sparkled with raindrop jewels. Relishing her rare moment of privacy, Isabel walked carefully beside the swollen creek. At the edge of the woods she stopped to absorb the solitude, the regeneration around her.

Time seemed suspended, awaiting the sunrise.

She glanced back toward the unpainted mission buildings, gray and drab in the languid, moist air. Beyond, on the slopes of the upper meadow, the encamped Arapahos and Southern Cheyennes were stirring. Woodsmoke hung low over the tipis. Horses grazed listlessly in nearby pastures. From a distance came the lonesome call of a mourning dove.

She remembered the thrill of her first glimpse of the mission three long years ago, how strange and exotic it had seemed, and the heady sense of adventure that had possessed her.

So much had happened since that day. Now, common sense and intuition told her it was time to move on.

She must put friendships, loyalties, her own commitment to the test.

Familiar anxieties assailed her in this moment of tranquillity.

Was she undertaking too large a burden, as Miss Burdette and the Home Mission Board in Chicago seemed to think?

Was she truly too ambitious, as Sister Everts suggested?

Was it sinful to want her own mission, as Brother Clouse implied?

She had asked herself those questions many times. She had prayed for answers.

Thus far, she had received no sign.

She examined the low-hanging limb of an elm. The buds were bone hard, on the verge of leaf.

An ear-shattering "Thwack!" "Thwack!" sounded above her. Startled, Isabel looked up. At first she saw only bare, wintry branches. Then, cautiously, a mockingbird peeked from behind a crotch. Its beak opened, and Isabel saw its throat move in song.

For a moment she wished she had brought her conversation tube. But experience had taught her that she would not be able to hear the bird even under the best of circumstances. The heavy doses of quinine given her by doctors when she was sixteen had weakened her hearing, and left a constant roaring in her ears. Too few of the pleasurable sounds of the everyday world could penetrate the ceaseless cacophony generated in her own head. As far as her ears were concerned, all birds that twittered and chirruped did so in vain. Among them, she could hear only the low-pitched calls of mourning doves, the seasonal honking of wild geese, the gobble of turkeys, the clucking and crowing of chickens, and the baritone hooting of owls.

Yet memories lingered. On occasion sounds arose unbidden from the depths of her childhood to fill in the silences. As Isabel watched the bird's beak open and close, and its throat move in song, she imagined an excellent imitation of a robin filling the air: "Cheerily . . . cheerily . . . cheerup!"

She laughed aloud.

Now she could not only read lips, she had progressed to reading beaks!

On her laughter, the bird flew.

Watching the mockingbird arc into distant trees, Isabel was beguiled by a tantalizing thought: If her religion were a bit more mystical, she might proclaim the song of the mockingbird a clear-cut sign.

And even from the most practical standpoint, perhaps it was.

All fall and winter she had told Sister Everts that with the coming of spring, she would begin her mission to the Kiowas.

Yesterday, the last of the necessary papers had arrived with the mail from Fort Supply.

Today, in the wake of the rain, the meadow teemed with the first solid signs of spring.

Isabel turned to face the sunrise.

Gold, vermilion, and purple-blue shafts blossomed from the dapple-clouded horizon until the entire sky was ablaze.

Isabel stood rejoicing in the beauty of the earth. Time slipped by. Only after the passage of many minutes was she able to drag her mud-burdened feet across the wet clay and meadow grasses.

With renewed resolution for the battle ahead, she hurried up the slope toward the mission.

"I'll be going tomorrow or the next day," Isabel said, standing in the doorway to the kitchen. "The wind has already turned back to the southwest. The ground will dry quickly."

Sister Everts refused to look at her. A rattle of pans was the only reply.

"I'll write often," Isabel promised. "It isn't as if I were going to the moon."

Sister Everts jammed more wood into the cookstove.

Isabel could not suppress a smile.

Today Sister Everts seemed to be the deaf one.

Returning to the bedroom, Isabel tucked in the blankets and folded the comforter. As she placed her boots in a corner to dry, she again glanced through the doorway to the kitchen.

Sister Everts stood at the stove, eyes closed, lips trembling, tears coursing down her cheeks.

Isabel shook her head in dismay.

The argument had raged all winter and still was no closer to peace.

Today would be slow torture.

She swept the bedroom, pushed the dust and mud out the side door, and hurriedly cleaned the porch and steps.

The sun had climbed above the low bank of clouds in the east. Indians were gathering at the church door for morning worship and a visit to the missionary barrel. A few were draped from neck to moccasins in government blankets, but most now wore citizen clothes. Isabel's nose was assailed by their smoky, unwashed stench. She had never grown accustomed to it.

She set aside the broom and reluctantly returned to the

kitchen. Sister Everts gave the biscuits one last turn in the flour, arranged them in a pan, and slid it into the oven, keeping her face averted the whole time. Isabel walked past her and poured milk and last night's scraps into the cat's dish. As she held the cat back from the stream of milk, she felt the vibrations of his vigorous purring, even though she could not hear it. She rubbed his lush black pelt.

"I'm glad we're not all struck dumb this morning, Othello," she said.

After washing her hands, she made coffee and scrambled six eggs, her daily contribution to breakfast.

With the meal ready, Isabel and Sister Everts took their places at the table. Sister Everts said grace. Only then did she look up at Isabel through red-rimmed eyes.

"Brother Clouse won't *let* you go," she said.

Isabel did not know how to answer. She had anticipated strong opposition from Brother Clouse once he became convinced she truly was going. For months he had taken her plans lightly, making it plain he considered them mere idle dreams.

Today he would have to deal with them.

Sister Everts dug deep into the loose folds of her Mother Hubbard for a handkerchief. "Belle, I don't understand why you insist on doing this. You'll be killed! I just know it!"

Isabel much preferred heated argument to tears. She remained silent while she determined the best tack to take.

During the past five years she and Sister Everts had shared so much. Throughout their two years in the Baptist Missionary Training School they routinely had walked together into the depths of Chicago's Black Hole. Armed only with Bibles, they had ministered to prostitutes, drunks, and worse. That sordid tenement district between Van Buren and Twelfth streets, and from State Street south to the river, had contained four hundred high-licensed saloons, five hundred houses of prostitution, widespread gambling and crime, and some of the most miserable poverty in America. Almost daily she and Sister Everts had been frightened out of their wits. On rarer occasions they had been transported to tears by experiences almost beyond human emotion, and rewarded by a few sublime victories.

On their graduation, the Mission Board had sent them as a team into this raw land that since had become Oklahoma Territory.

For three years they had served as missionaries to the Arapaho and Southern Cheyennes. Now the Cheyenne-Arapaho reservation was gone, absorbed into yet another "land rush" by the ever-encroaching whites. The Indians had received their own allotments and now lived in some semblance of civilization, with government-built houses, plows, and livestock.

Isabel and Sister Everts had shared the five most trying years of their lives. Yet their minds remained worlds apart.

Sister Everts began crying openly, her breakfast forgotten. Big tears escaped her handkerchief and dripped off her chin. Her soft copper hair, still limp from the rain, lay in small, close ringlets. Her wide, round eyes and soaring brows lent her an expression of constant surprise, an impression enhanced by tiny pointed ears and a pixie nose. It was always easy for Isabel to imagine her as a vulnerable child in times of tearful distress. The passing decades and her taxing experiences had not brought complete maturity.

Isabel was moved to a final effort. She pointed to the window, to the Indians at the mission door. "Look out there, Sister. What do you see? Nothing but churchgoing Christians. We've been ministering to converts the past two years! My work here is done! Anyone with barely enough sense to come in out of the rain is fully capable of handing out clothes and blankets."

Sister Everts dabbed at her eyes. "But Belle! What about the little ones? How can they ever hope to function in the white man's world if we don't teach them English? Don't you worry about that?"

Isabel buttered a hot biscuit before she answered.

"With the reservation gone, there surely will be territorial schools here before long," she said. "The Indians can learn along with the white children. And if you'll remember, I've never pretended to be a schoolteacher. When I joined the Society, I pledged to take the Word of Christ to the heathen races, wherever I was sent. Remember Odysseus? After his voyages? He was told to put an oar on his shoulder and to walk inland until he found a place where there was no one who knew what it was. That's exactly what I shall do. I will travel into Kiowa country until I find a place where no one ever heard of Jesus Christ. There I shall set to work."

"But the Kiowas are *wild* Indians!"

"All the more reason I should go among them. Please stop crying. I can't understand you when you mumble."

Sister Everts lowered her gaze. "You'll be alone! They may take advantage of you!"

Isabel supposed that fear resided permanently in every woman's head. She had rarely been able to keep it completely subdued in her own.

"Remember what Ellen Foster said at the Woman's Congress? *Be a woman, and you can be anything you want to be.*' The Kiowas may be savages, but they are also human. I'm convinced that a basic core of decency exists in everyone, no matter how savage. I'm confident that if you approach a savage in a womanly way, he will respond with respect."

Sister Everts looked doubtful. "I wouldn't want to depend on it."

Isabel gestured impatiently. "Eat your eggs before they're cold."

Sister Everts managed a few more bites. She rose from the table, stacked her dishes, and placed them in the dishpan. "Brother Clouse won't allow this," she said again. "Surely you know he loves you. Sometimes I think he cares more about you than his wife, the church, or anything."

Isabel was shocked to the soles of her feet. "Sister! What a thing to say!"

"It's true! We all think so!"

Abruptly, Sister Everts fled the room. The front door slammed behind her.

Isabel, shaken by Sister Everts's declaration, gathered the rest of the dishes and cleaned the table. Lifting the tea kettle from the stove, she scalded the dishes and washed and rinsed them, hurrying to avoid her thoughts.

She finished restoring the kitchen to order just as the mission bell across the courtyard tolled for morning worship.

Brother Clouse's gaze fixed on Isabel from the moment she entered the chapel.

Clearly Sister Everts had spread the word.

Isabel gathered the folds of her Mother Hubbard and made her way toward the front. The sanctuary was a third filled with Arapaho and Southern Cheyennes, along with a sprinkling of Comanches and Wichitas. Most sat leaning forward, uncomfortable on the hardwood pews. Many of the men held on their knees the wide-brimmed black hats that lately had become the fashion among them. The women wore loose-fitting dresses in every color of the rainbow, gleaned from past visits to the missionary barrel.

Sister Everts sat at the pump organ, her nervous, restless hands arranging and rearranging sheet music. She did not look up or acknowledge Isabel's presence.

Brother Clouse stood in the pulpit. He was a big man, well over six feet tall, thick through the shoulders and chest. He had light, thinning hair; a high forehead; and a round, open, florid face. His eyes were pale blue and prominent, his mouth filled with large, slightly protruding teeth. He was not a convincing speaker. He brought few converts to the altar by persuasion; rather, he overwhelmed them with his goodness.

Isabel dreaded her coming confrontation with him. His unwavering righteousness was far more effective than logic.

He nodded a greeting as she stepped onto the platform to take her place beside him. Raising his hymnal, he spoke in the shout he habitually used with the Indians, as if the language barrier might be overcome through sheer volume. Isabel had no need of the conversation tube dangling from her neck.

"First we shall sing that fine old hymn 'Washed in the Blood of the Lamb.' "

Isabel cringed inwardly. She had never thought the hymn suitable for savage ears. Moving her hands and arms rapidly, she conveyed in Plains Indian sign language the essence of Brother Clouse's words, ending with a gesture that directed everyone to stand.

After a prelude of furious pedal-pumping to fill the bellows, Sister Everts attacked the keyboard and took the lead in her loud, clear soprano. Isabel joined in, signing the meaning of each verse, exaggerating the pronunciation of each syllable. Most of the Indians did not know the words. The few who did, made a valiant effort. Isabel, Brother Clouse, and Sister Everts persisted to the close of the third stanza.

As the hymn ended, Isabel motioned the congregation to be seated.

Beside her, Brother Clouse shouted, "Then Jesus called His disciples unto Him, and He said, 'I have compassion on the multitude.' "

As Clouse read from the Book of Matthew, Isabel battled to reduce the story of the loaves and fishes and the feeding of the four thousand to the limitations of sign language and to terms the Indians would understand. Clouse's rather florid speech emerged starkly simplified: "Jesus, people on trail three days. Nothing to eat. No food in bad land. Jesus said not tell people go away hungry. No strength to go back to tipis."

As she relayed the essence of Brother Clouse's sermon, telling how Jesus divided seven loaves of bread and a few fishes to feed four thousand men, and the women and children who were with them, a murmur of amazement swept through the congregation. The Indians had heard that Jesus had raised people from the dead, turned water into red grape juice, walked on water, and made blind men to see.

This was something new.

Isabel never felt comfortable describing the miracles to Indians before they had acquired a sufficient understanding of Christ's purpose on earth. Brother Clouse often made Jesus sound like a trickster, no different from those in the Indians' own folk tales. As always, Isabel slipped her own commentary into the story, explaining that Jesus could do these things only because He was the Son of God. She loved telling the Jesus stories, loved making the sign for His blessed name: right forefinger to left palm, left forefinger to right palm, signifying how He was nailed to the cross.

The sign language, born of necessity to solve the babel of Indian tongues on the Plains, was often far more eloquent than mere words, despite its structural shortcomings. For instance, the phrase "I think" or "I believe" was conveyed by placing the right palm over the heart, then moving the hand out and down, meaning literally "This comes from the heart," or perhaps, "This is plucked from my heart." The word "good" was signed by drawing the right hand across the chest, palm down, to signify "on a level with the heart."

For the past three years Isabel had specialized in the Indian sign language, working from books by Captain Clark of the U.S. Army and Brother Hadley, a Plains missionary. She had honed her skill among the various tribes and had become so adept that often she found herself thinking in sign language. Gradually she had acquired a vocabulary of more than eight hundred words.

With the knowledge that someday she would be totally deaf, she also had explored European and American sign languages. But the Indian version was far more eloquent and complete.

After another hymn and a brief prayer, Brother Clouse ended morning worship.

The Indians rose from the benches and moved out the side door toward the storehouse. There they stood in small groups, debating the story of the loaves and fishes in their various languages. Isabel hurried through them to open the missionary barrels and boxes recently received from Chicago.

The morning work went rapidly. Isabel and Sister Everts matched donated clothing and new owners, arbitrarily settling occasional disputes over choice items. Most of the Indian women favored loose, flowery, flowing dresses. The men were partial to colorful shirts and sturdy trousers of any description. The children were especially delighted with a selection of sailor suits contributed by a Chicago department store after customers spurned them at any price. The markdown tags were still attached.

Sister Everts avoided direct contact with Isabel throughout the morning, preferring to clown with the children and maintain an artificial gaiety.

After the Indians drifted away, Isabel uncovered her own long-hoarded cache in a corner of the storeroom. She stood for a moment gazing at it. The pile of material had been assembled with much effort and sacrifice over more than a year. She knew the source of every item. The sturdy shovel and pickax had come from her brother Hugh in the new state of North Dakota, along with considerable advice on camping in the wild. The tent was a gift from her sister Emily and brother-in-law, John Firstbrook, in Toronto. The folding cot, bedding, and a large supply of canned goods were donations from her sister Fanny and her brother-in-law, the Reverend Mr. William H. Cline, and his tiny Baptist congregation on the frontier of western Manitoba. Isabel's mother had forwarded from Toronto a set of collapsible tin cups, along with the Case pocket knife Isabel's father had carried from her earliest memory to the day of his death. Miss Mary Burdette of the Women's American Baptist Home Mission Society in Chicago had squirreled away the ten missionary boxes and barrels of clothing to help Isabel start her new mission. The sidesaddle had been a gift from her father on her sixteenth birthday, no small expenditure for a rural pastor. The big Bible and two large boxes of books came from his library.

Isabel carried the goods outside and began loading her wagon, purchased with money from the sale of her paintings.

She worked leisurely, aware she must wait a day or two for the ground to dry before starting her trip.

She had planned every inch of space so thoroughly that actual stowage seemed anticlimactic. She fitted her tent, clothing, tools, and missionary supplies and equipment into the forward end of the wagon. Her precious books and side-saddle went into the center, where they would be most protected from harm. Near the endgate she placed grain for the horses, canned goods, boxes of dried food, and bedding.

She was wrestling the heavy canvas cover over the wagon hoops when Brother Clouse emerged from the rectory and strode straight toward her.

Sister Everts trailed meekly in his wake.

Clouse placed a hand on the wagon box and glanced at her arrangement of the load. His cheeks and ears were blotched red, whether from anger or some other high emotion, she could not tell.

He looked up at her and spoke in a voice curiously gruff and strained. "Sister Crawford, I thought you'd long ago abandoned this crazy scheme. You can unload this wagon. I'm not about to grant you permission to drive off to your death."

Isabel was ready for him. She had been assembling her argument for weeks. She sank onto a missionary box and looked at the pastor. Beads of perspiration stood on his forehead and across his upper lip. His strict formality never allowed him to remove his often uncomfortable black frock coat and vest in public.

Isabel felt some regret at keeping much of her plan secret from him. She had done so in the hope of avoiding unpleasantness. At the moment, her calculated reticence seemed furtive and disloyal. She swept off her sunbonnet, pushed back her hair, and smiled down from her high perch. "Brother Clouse, perhaps I should remind you. I'm not here under the auspices of the church. In the strictest sense, your permission is not required."

It was only a partial truth. Although she took her orders from the Woman's American Baptist Home Mission Society at 4026 Grand Boulevard in Chicago, the board would never act against the wishes of the church. Isabel knew she stood on shaky ground.

Clouse wiped at his lips and forehead with the back of his hand. "Sister, I promise you that if you go, I'll send word to

Colonel Baldwin. He'll send troops and move you off the reservation."

Isabel understood for the first time that her secrecy might not have been wise in fundamental ways. Clouse had no inkling of the time and effort she had put into her planning. He had no reason to think of her mission as other than a fanciful dream. She tried to keep her tone reasonable. "Brother Clouse, I have a letter from Secretary of the Interior David R. Francis, granting me permission to move onto the Kiowa-Comanche Reservation to do my work. I hardly think Colonel Baldwin will countermand the Secretary's wishes."

Clouse stared at her in surprise. "How did you manage that?"

"I simply wrote to him, explaining what I want to do."

Clouse slowly shook his head. "Sister, don't you realize that you're going where you're not wanted? Washington does not have the last word. The Kiowas *themselves* have barred white people from their reservation. *They'll* move you off, probably at the point of a Winchester."

Isabel played her trump card. "Chief Domot himself has invited me onto the reservation."

Clouse made a short, barking sound that could have been either a laugh or an exclamation of despair. "Domot? That old reprobate is no chief! And he's certainly not a Christian. How could he be, with two or three wives? Surely you misunderstood him. Why would he invite you?"

Thrown off guard, Isabel felt her argument faltering. She had assumed that Domot was a chief. He'd certainly acted like one. "I don't know *why* he invited me. But he did."

Clouse leaned over the endgate and spoke more intimately. "Sister, it's *you* I'm thinking of! You don't have any idea of the danger! Those Kiowas are *wild* Indians!"

Isabel had never understood the reasoning behind common classification of Indian tribes. The Choctaws, Creeks, and Seminoles in Indian Territory to the east were listed among the five "civilized" tribes, presumably because they to some degree had been farmers when the whites first encountered them, as differentiated from the "wild" tribes, who hunted.

Yet, early in the century, those "farmers" had given the U.S. Army some of the bloodiest battles in its history.

The labeling was inexact. The Cheyennes had farmed on the shores of the Great Lakes until, driven westward by whites, they became hunters on the Great Plains and were then considered "wild" Indians. Their principal chief, Black Kettle, sought peace for decades and found none. Colonel Chivington had massacred Black Kettle's village at Sand Creek in Colorado. Custer had slaughtered the remnants of Black Kettle's people on the Washita River, only a few miles from where Isabel stood. Not many survived. Now the Southern Cheyennes were judged "tame" by default. Already their treaty-protected reservation was gone, and both the Arapaho and Southern Cheyennes were being speedily assimilated into the territory's white culture.

In contrast, the Kiowas and Comanches had fought desperately from beginning to end and were the last of the "wild" Plains Indians to be subdued. Now they and a few surviving Apaches were restricted to an extensive reservation straddling the Wichita Mountains in the southwestern corner of Oklahoma Territory. There they were still battling fiercely to retain their tribal identities.

"I know the Kiowas are different," she said.

"I don't think you understand *how* different. A few years ago your good friend Domot was murdering and scalping whites all the way from the Cimarron to the Rio Grande. He's nothing but a bloodthirsty old savage. Most of the Kiowas at Saddle Mountain are just like him. They're the worst in the whole territory."

Isabel remembered the tall, dignified, almost genteel old Indian. Clouse's description did not fit.

"Domot?"

Clouse nodded emphatically. "Sister, I have never mentioned some of the things those Indians have done because I felt they were too indecent for a woman's ears. But I'll tell you right now what kind of Indians you'll find at Saddle Mountain. Maybe it'll save your life. Big Tree lives over toward Rainy Mountain, but he runs with Domot and that bunch at Saddle Mountain. Big Tree once roasted a teamster alive. Spitted him on a wagon wheel over a slow fire like a side of beef. Big Tree and some others were sent to a prison in Texas, but after a time they let him out. I don't know why. Odlepaugh lives on Saddle Mountain Creek, not far from Domot. Odlepaugh made scalping raids into Texas long after they drove the tribe onto the reservation. Domot rode with him. And there's Loki Mo-keen, a Mexican renegade, probably the lowest, meanest man who ever walked this earth. On one raid into Texas, Mo-keen picked up a white baby by its heels and bashed its brains out against a stone fireplace. That's a fact."

For a moment Isabel thought she would be sick. She cupped a palm over her mouth to still her rising gorge.

She thought of the large, imposing Indian who had been with Domot on the day he had invited her to come and live at Saddle Mountain. The big man had called himself Loki Mo-keen.

She said the first thing that came to mind. "I don't believe it."

"Then don't take my word for it. Ask Colonel Baldwin. It's all in Army records. Loki Mo-keen and Odlepaugh attacked a house filled with women and children on Elm Creek of the Brazos, down in Texas not far from Fort Belknap, in the fall of '64. The women were butchered alive—slashed to ribbons. Some of the children were killed on the spot. Some were taken captive. The Army has reason to believe one or two of them are still being held prisoners on the reservation. Others say they were tortured to death years ago. No one knows."

Isabel saw her well-made plans falling into disarray. Had she been hopelessly naïve? Was her dream of a mission truly impossible?

Apparently chastened by her stricken face, Clouse paused. "I'm sorry to be so blunt. But it's for your own good."

Isabel thought again of Domot and Loki Mo-keen. She had accepted without question her impression that they were among the honored elders of the tribe.

"The government has tried for years to civilize the Kiowas," Clouse went on. "But those savages have resisted every effort. Now they've taken up the Ghost Dance. I know that some people think the Ghost Dance is just another Indian religion, but it's far more than that. They get crazy drunk on cactus buttons, dance themselves into a frenzy, and make plans to kill all the whites in the territory. One of these days they'll try to do exactly that. I haven't mentioned this to you or to Sister Everts because I've never felt we were in any danger here. But if you go onto Kiowa land to live, there's no telling what may happen to you. Matters over there are building closer every day toward another Wounded Knee uprising."

Isabel felt a cold chill along her spine. Five winters ago more than one hundred fifty Sioux and two dozen soldiers had been killed on the Pine Ridge Reservation in South

Dakota after the government banned the Ghost Dance and attempted to arrest the principal chiefs. She had heard the rumors that the Ghost Dance was being practiced on the Kiowa reservation, but she had placed little credence in the reports.

Had she been wrong?

From the first she had known that in moving onto the reservation she would suffer at times—from loneliness and deprivation, if nothing else. But she had never dreamed that she might be in actual danger. She loosened the neck of her shirtwaist and took comfort in the warmth of the sun.

For a brief moment she almost succumbed to doubt. She was tempted to retreat, accept Clouse's argument, and continue her peaceful life at Elk Creek.

Then she remembered the thousands of Christians who had died for their faith, as chronicled in her copy of *Foxe's Book of English Martyrs*.

She thought of her father, who had devoted his entire life to spreading the gospel into new, raw lands.

Had he ever questioned God's call?

Had he ever retreated one inch?

He had not.

She had been taught a precept at the missionary training school; she spoke it aloud:

"The greater the sinner, the more fertile the ground for the seeds of the gospel."

Clouse moved, and for a moment Isabel thought he was reaching for her hand. Instead, he gripped the endgate of the wagon. "Sister Crawford, your work is here, where you're needed. Let a *man* go onto that reservation. A man who is equal to the task."

The exact division between the authority of the church and the Woman's American Baptist Home Mission Society was a delicate matter. Isabel chose her words with care. "Brother Clouse, we were taught in training school that God calls women as well as men. Not to go into all the world and *preach* the gospel, but to go into all the world to *teach* it in a simple, womanly way. That is precisely what I propose to do."

Clouse's abrupt laugh was humorless. "A woman's gentleness will have no effect whatsoever on those savages. Those poor women Loki Mo-keen and Odlepaugh murdered would tell you that if they could."

Isabel placed a hand on his arm. She spoke softly, hoping he would see that her words came from the heart. "Brother Clouse, I now regret I haven't been entirely honest with you. I've been cowardly, knowing how strongly you would oppose my going. But please try to understand. I'm convinced that God intends that I do more than hand out clothing from a missionary barrel. I'm needed far more on that reservation than I am needed here. Everything you've said only confirms that."

Clouse spread his arms in a gesture of despair. "But how do you expect to manage? This old wagon is falling apart. Even if it holds together, that mismatched team of yours probably can't pull it through the rough country between here and the reservation. And if you *should* reach Saddle Mountain, you'll be helpless. You don't know one word of Kiowa. The Indians won't allow a house to be built on the reservation. You won't survive the first winter in a tent. Besides, you're too tiny to do all the heavy work required. I don't know how you manage even to harness that team. And consider this: you'll be alone, maybe two days' hard journey from any other white person. If you land in a difficult situation, you can't expect help from the Army or anyone else."

"In time, after I am established, the mission board will send a sister to help me," Isabel said. "I won't always be alone."

Clouse shook his head. "That may be months, years away. Don't you understand? You're not equipped for an undertaking of this magnitude."

His hands, resting on the endgate of the wagon, were trembling. Isabel did not want to leave him so upset. She sought to lighten the moment. "To the contrary, Brother Clouse, I couldn't be better prepared. I have a cast-iron constitution, a Scot's determination, more than a measure of Irish nonsense, the Divine call, and the power of the Holy Spirit. I spent two years in training school studying under Miss Burdette, and I've had three years here with you. I'll never be more ready. Besides, I've been authorized by the Mission Board to hire an interpreter."

"What if you can't find one?"

"Then I'll make do with sign language."

Clouse spoke with such earnestness that his voice quavered. "Sister, this is the worst possible time for you to go onto that reservation. And not just because of the Ghost

Dance. Colonel Baldwin is extremely worried over the Jerome misunderstanding. Trouble may erupt any day. If fighting breaks out, you'll be caught right in the middle."

Isabel knew about the dispute over the Jerome Agreement. The treaty, now awaiting approval by the U.S. Senate, would start the process for opening the Kiowa-Comanche-Apache Reservation to white settlers. The Kiowas believed they had been cheated.

"That's in God's hands," Isabel said.

Clouse looked at her with an intensity she found disturbing. "Sister, I know you've had disappointments in life. But that is no reason to set yourself up as a martyr."

For a moment Isabel thought Clouse was referring to her initial fury over being sent to Oklahoma Territory rather than to some place more exotic, like China or India.

Then she understood his meaning and felt heat flood to her face.

His remark was the first indication that he—or anyone—was privy to certain details of her personal life.

"I know of no disappointments," she said firmly.

Clouse saw that he had overstepped. After an awkward pause, he spoke softly, almost apologetically. "Sister, I'm begging you. At least wait a while, until this Jerome matter is settled."

"I can't," Isabel said. "I will need the whole spring and summer to build a congregation, and to erect some sort of shelter before cold weather comes again next fall."

Clouse stepped back, one hand still on the wagon. He lowered his head and studied the ground for a moment. At last he looked up and met her gaze. "Sister Crawford, if there were any way I could prevent your going, I would do so. But I can't rope and tie you. I suppose I can only give you my blessings. And my prayers."

Isabel smiled to hide her own growing doubts. "Thank you, Brother Clouse. I'll need them."

Abruptly he turned and strode away.

Isabel sat for several minutes, fighting the apprehensions Clouse had raised within her.

Then, with fresh determination, she finished loading the wagon.

Chapter Two

Isabel pulled her team to a halt at the bend of the river, on a strip of flat, dry sand a dozen steps from clear water. The river, running narrow and shallow, rippled gently over graveled shoals. A curve of high red clay bluffs guarded the approach from the north and east. To the south and west, salt cedars completed the circle, screening the site from the outside world.

Isabel stepped down from the wagon, confident she would not find a better place to camp.

Jeremiah the horse, ever eager to please, nuzzled her as she stripped off his harness. Jonah the mule, as troublesome as ever, tried twice to bite, and as she unhooked the trace chains he threatened her with a raised hind hoof.

Isabel had purchased Jonah for ten dollars from a disillusioned white settler who had abandoned his claim in the territory and returned to Missouri. The settler said he no longer needed the mule, but after her first attempt to work the animal in harness, Isabel suspected the man had other motivations.

Sister Everts had named Jonah after witnessing that debacle. "What could be more appropriate?" she asked. "When the Lord told Jonah to go in one direction, he promptly went in the other."

Isabel had bought Jeremiah from an Arapaho who found the horse hopelessly entangled in a length of wire, and starving. The poor animal was covered with harness sores and whip scars and was lame from festering cuts on his forelegs. Isabel had nursed him back to health, but a life of harsh treatment had left even deeper scars. For a long time he started at the slightest unexpected sound and trembled at the touch of harness. "He's just like the prophet Jeremiah, always expecting the worst," Sister Everts had said. The name stuck. Isabel had spent a year soothing his nerves before he was comfortable in harness.

After feeding them grain from a shallow bucket, Isabel fastened hobbles to their forelegs and turned them loose. Immediately Jonah set out for higher ground, traveling with the peculiar hop he had learned in an attempt to defeat the hobbles. Jeremiah lingered near the wagon until Isabel drove him through the salt cedars to grassland beyond the riverbank.

She gathered dry driftwood amid lengthening shadows and built her fire in the lee of the wagon. After spreading a canvas wagon sheet, she warmed her pot of stew, a farewell gift from Brother Clouse's wife. Isabel ate slowly, watching killdeers at play along the sandbars. Nighthawks darted and swooped low over the salt cedars, harvesting their own supper. An owl took up station somewhere upstream and offered a few soft, tentative hoots. As the sun sank behind a lone cottonwood, Isabel finished her supper with coffee and a piece of the apple pie Sister Everts had baked especially for her journey.

Dusk slowly faded into night. Isabel sprawled luxuriously on her bedroll while her campfire died to glowing embers. Overhead, the stars seemed alive, endless. From a distance came the howling of wolves, occasional hoots from the owl.

Isabel felt immense satisfaction. Her first day of travel had gone well. Despite trouble with Jonah, she had covered almost twenty miles. She was certain she was now past the former boundaries of the Cheyenne-Arapaho Reservation. All day she had driven south on the old Western Cattle Trail, blazed two decades ago by Texas drovers on their way to the Kansas markets. The route had taken her many miles west of where she wanted to go, but Brother Clouse had insisted that this longer, indirect course would be easier. Tomorrow she would leave the well-marked wagon track and turn southeast toward the Kiowa-Comanche-Apache Reservation. Traveling would become much more difficult. Every dry wash would present a challenge, and she knew she might have to search for hours to find safe crossing at each of the many creeks.

In the afterglow of the fire, she sat lost in thoughts of the future as she combed and braided her hair, and gently massaged the rose-scented cream, sent by her mother, into her face, neck, and arms. What her wind-dried, thirsty pores did not absorb during the night, she would bathe away in the morning with warmed water and soap.

Stretched full length on her bed, she looked up at the stars and reflected back upon the memory of her departure from the mission. Indians had come from all over the former reservation to tell her good-bye. Some had cried. She had been surprised and touched.

She flushed with embarrassment as she thought of Brother Clouse's remark about her "disappointment in life."

How had he known?

Was her "disappointment in life" common gossip?

If so, the busybodies did not have the full story. She wished she could tell them that the "disappointment" was not as great as they assumed.

During her girlhood, her future had seemed so simple. In the small Canadian village where she was reared, young ladies carefully selected husbands on the basis of honesty and industry, married, and busied themselves with the rearing of children.

No woman ever seem to consider any other course, and Isabel had been unaware that any other way of life existed.

When Fenton Hopper came into her life in her seventeenth year, their future seemed predestined. Young Mr. Hopper was handsome, gentle, polite, and quite a catch. At twenty-six, he already had six hundred forty acres under cultivation. He was ambitious. Everyone said he "would make something of himself."

At first their marriage had been delayed by her lingering illness. She almost died of an unexplained fever. The doctors dictated that she remain abed on a diet of milk and quinine, and there she had stayed six months.

Later, as she slowly regained her strength, the engagement became a comfortable habit, Fenton almost like a brother. He spent far more time in the Crawford parlor discussing theology with her father than paying court to her. She came to regard him as a convenient escort, someone to hold the future at bay.

In truth, she had looked ahead to marriage in blind panic. She could not envision herself pinned down to a life of drudgery as a farm wife.

One of her first Sunday school teachers, Belle Hatch, had become a missionary to India. Isabel had grown up idolizing the woman. On rare occasions through the years, her letters were read in church as she sought contributions from the congregation for her various projects. In India, she adopted and educated a native boy who eventually became a doctor, and together they had founded a hospital for lepers.

Isabel could not think of anything grander, more exotic.

She dreamed of becoming a missionary, but from her home on the wheat plains, such a life seemed beyond reach.

She once wrote Belle Hatch, offering her services. Although she watched the mail eagerly for months, she did not receive a reply.

By the time Isabel reached maturity she had learned from books that a few women did manage to lead lives of romance, drama, ambition, dedication, sacrifice. And the more she read, the greater grew her dread of marriage.

Fenton apparently sensed her growing reluctance, and gradually their relationship cooled. But as their engagement entered its third year, community and parental pressures forced the issue. A date was set.

Four weeks before the wedding day, with preparations almost complete and Isabel torn by premonitions of disaster, Fenton had eloped with a flaxen-haired sixteen-year-old.

But Isabel refused to permit his abandonment and her own self-doubt to defeat her.

The elopement had ignited a community scandal. Although Isabel was devastated, the blow was more to her pride than to her dreams. It was an embarrassment that would not go away. Everyone felt compelled to express compassion at length, and at every opportunity.

Yet her anger at Fenton had been intermingled with guilt, for she felt that she should have tried harder to breathe some life into their relationship.

At twenty-one, Isabel found herself far down the road toward becoming an "old maid." All of her friends were married and busy with their own families. The community was virtually devoid of eligible men—even assuming she would want one.

Then she heard a talk by Miss Mary G. Burdette of the Woman's American Baptist Home Mission Society. Miss Burdette was touring churches in the Dakota Territory, seeking candidates for the training school.

That day changed Isabel's life. At last she saw her own chance for romance, drama, dedication, meaningful sacrifice, exotic travel. She spent the next three years earning her tuition for training school. She taught art, sold paintings, and gave pantomime performances and violin concerts until at last she had the money she needed.

Her two years in Chicago had been eye-openers. She had seen the best humanity had to offer: great teachers and thinkers during the two years of the World's Columbian Exposition. She also had seen the worst: the filth, squalor, and degradation of Chicago's Black Hole.

Her three years at Elk Creek taught her even more. But the time had arrived to move on, to renew her sense of accomplishment and adventure.

At her present snail's pace, she expected to reach the site of her proposed mission in two more days.

The moon rose, filling the river bottom with a soft light. The sand beneath her bedroll was warm and comfortable against the cool spring night. Lulled by the tranquil setting, Isabel slept.

She awoke to a roar, an earth-shaking rumble. She sat up, listening, trying to sort out the sounds.

The ground beneath her bedroll seemed to be vibrating. The night air was charged with tension.

Upstream, a wall of water materialized in the moonlight, swept around the bend of the river, and bore down upon her.

Scrambling to her feet, she attempted to gather her bedroll. She was too late. The first surge sent her tumbling end over end, completely under water, battling for her life. She fought her way to the surface and tried to stand. The sand beneath her seemed to churn. She could not find footing. Half-strangled, she grabbed frantically at salt cedars to keep from being swept farther downstream. Sticks, branches, and large tree limbs dashed against her. There was no time to pray, or even to think. Crying out, she tumbled, helpless, until she found a secure handhold among the cedars.

She clung to a thin sapling, her mind numb. Branches and debris dashed against her, threatening to jar her loose and again send her downstream. Half drowned, she kept her grip through a battering that seemed interminable.

At last the water settled into a swift, thigh-deep current. Cautiously, still in danger of being swept off her feet at any moment, Isabel made her way to shore. Kneeling, she retched into the sand, losing most of the water she had swallowed, and her supper with it. She rose, weak and shaky, surprised to find she had no broken bones. Scratches and bruises stung all over her body.

By moonlight she walked upstream through the brush until she found her campsite.

Her wagon had been turned around by the current but remained upright. Isabel waded to it and peered inside. Although water still flowed over the axles, the wagon box and its contents seemed intact.

She tried to devise some way of moving the wagon out of the river. But the tongue and doubletree were under water. She knew she would never be able to coax Jonah and Jeremiah into the swiftly moving current and make them stand to be hitched. Reluctantly, she climbed into the wagon and waited for daybreak.

Dawn revealed a scene of great desolation. The water level had dropped, but her bedroll, coffee pot, and most of her cooking utensils were gone. No sign remained of her campfire. The entire river bottom was overspread with mud and woody debris.

Too late, Isabel remembered stories of the sudden headrises in this part of the country. A heavy rain sixty, eighty, even a hundred miles away could send a flood of water downstream. She had been disarmed by the cloudless sky. Pitching her camp in the riverbed had been both naïve and foolish. A thunderstorm far out in Texas had almost drowned her.

Exhausted, bedraggled, and miserable, she examined the countless abrasions on her arms, legs, and hands.

Her slat bonnet was gone with the bedroll. Soon the early morning sun beat down on her head unmercifully. The soaking had left sand and grit beneath her clothes, clinging to her skin. Her whole body itched. She considered making an attempt at a bath, but the river was too muddy.

Almost half of each wheel of the wagon was buried in sand. Isabel considered saddling Jeremiah and going for help. Most of the land to the west was under lease to Texas ranches and covered with great herds of cattle. She was sure she could find some cowboys within a day's ride. But seeking help on her second day away from the mission would set a poor precedent.

She chastised herself with the thought she was not exactly a helpless woman.

She removed her long-handled shovel from the wagon, tied her skirts knee-high, and set to work, making sand fly.

By noon she had uncovered the wheels, wagon tongue, doubletree, and singletrees. She wrestled tree limbs and

debris aside and cleared a path to firmer ground. Suddenly
aware she had forgotten breakfast, she lingered long enough
to eat cold biscuits and honey, then set out in search of Jonah
and Jeremiah.

She found them almost a mile upstream. After removing
their hobbles, she led them back to the wagon. As the sun
grew oppressive, she began to regret the loss of her bonnet.
Her still damp skirts flopped about her legs.

Fortunately she had formed the habit of stowing harness
behind the dashboard of the wagon. It was dry. Moving
cautiously, ever wary of Jonah's hooves and teeth, she harnessed
the team.

For an hour or more her prospects seemed hopeless.
Jeremiah did not have the strength to pull the wagon up the
slippery slope alone, and Jonah was not inclined to help.
Driven to the limits of exasperation, she at last took the whip
to Jonah. She lashed his backside furiously, wanting with
every stroke to relieve herself in tears. Thus encouraged,
Jonah laid back his ears and reluctantly shouldered his share
of the load. Slowly the wagon eased out of the riverbed.

A few miles farther downstream, Isabel checked her map
and turned toward the southeast, away from the old cattle
trail. Soon the bald granite dome of Headquarters Mountain,
the westernmost peak of the Wichita Range, appeared on the
horizon to the southwest, and she knew she was on her
planned course.

The wagon wheels began to screech in a raucous sym-
phony. Isabel knew that the river current had carried away
her axle grease, but she did not know how to remove the
wheels and repack the hubs. She could only hope that by
traveling slowly, resting often to allow the axles to cool, she
might reach Saddle Mountain before the wheels fell off.

All afternoon she traveled southeast. The cacophony grew
in volume. Despite her discomfort, Isabel regained her high
humor. She wished that Brother Clouse could have seen her
flaying the mule.

Too tiny, indeed!

That night she camped on high ground near a large creek.
Although the stream did not appear on her map, it flowed
toward the east, apparently a tributary to the Washita.

On reflection, Isabel realized that perhaps she should be
grateful for her near-disaster. Nothing essential had been
lost. She missed her bedroll and bonnet, but she had a good

ground cloth and blankets and could make do. She now had more confidence in her ability to handle crises. Also, she had earned Jonah's respect. Now she had only to raise her whip and he plunged into his harness as if his very life depended upon it.

After supper, with the team grazing hobbled and tethered, she removed her shoes and cautiously waded into the clear, thigh-deep creek. She bathed her sunburned face and neck in the cool, soothing water. Loosening her clothing, she bounced and splashed until all the sand and grit she had acquired in the North Fork of Red River were gone. Emboldened by the success of the experiment, she filled her palm with soft soap from the wagon and washed her hair. After darkness she hung her Mother Hubbard on the side of the wagon to dry.

The bath did wonders for her spirits. Wrapped in two blankets atop her canvas ground cloth, she slept soundly throughout the night.

By midmorning of the following day the stubby knobs of the Wichitas came into view far to the south. Few of the mountains rose more than a thousand feet from base to summit, but as the only variations on the horizon, they dominated the rolling plains. By late afternoon, Isabel could identify the most prominent—Rainy Mountain, Saddle Mountain, Baker Peak.

She turned toward Saddle Mountain as her worries mounted. Jeremiah was limping from his old wounds, and her wagon wheels had begun to wobble. She drove even slower, and with greater caution.

That night she camped beside a small creek. Although encircled by a cottonwood grove, she did not build a fire, for she estimated that she had entered the Kiowa-Comanche-Apache Reservation. She hoped to find Domot and enlist his support before other Indians drove her off their land.

The next morning Jonah again turned troublesome. Unless Isabel brandished the whip, he sulked in his harness and allowed poor crippled Jeremiah to take the full load. Isabel battled Jonah almost constantly.

Just before noon, crossing a rugged dry wash, Jonah dropped so far back in the traces that his singletree dragged the ground. Thus preoccupied, and vexed with him, Isabel became oblivious of her surroundings until a slight movement on the creekbank caught her attention.

She glanced up.

Six young Kiowa braves sat on their horses, calmly watching her.

All were naked to the waist. Their heavy black hair hung in thick braids, interwoven with rawhide and strips of ermine. All wore bone chestplates and copper bracelets.

Each carried a rifle.

Isabel pulled her team to a halt. Moving slowly to hide her racing heart, she raised her right hand, palm forward, in a greeting.

One by one the Indians guided their horses down the slope toward her and formed a semicircle, blocking her path. One pointed to Isabel's horse and mule and said something in Kiowa.

The other Indians laughed.

For the first time, Isabel fully realized her plight. She was alone, at least twenty miles inside the reservation, a hard day's ride from any other white person. She had not the slightest doubt that the men barring her way were total savages, unlike any other Indians she ever had known.

She forced a smile, as if sharing the joke about her mismatched team.

Inwardly, she shrank from their strong, wild odors, their vermin-covered, unwashed bodies.

One Indian rode forward and reined in close to her wagon. Even in her terror Isabel saw that he was a magnificent specimen. Lean, and perhaps more than six feet in height, he sat erect on his horse, his sinewy muscles at play as he shifted his rifle to balance across his lap. An eagle feather, his only headdress, rippled in the breeze. His nose was large, his face heavily boned and angular. With his long, bare legs dangling, he seemed almost totally nude. Isabel kept her gaze on his face. He solemnly returned her greeting, his impassive brown eyes unwavering.

He raised his right hand shoulder high, palm forward, fingers spread, and wiggled it in the "question" sign that could mean "what?" "where?" "why?" or "when?" He pointed to Isabel, then raised his closed fist to his mouth and brought the fist forward, forefinger extended, in the "talk" or "called" sign. Without conscious thought Isabel understood his literal meaning: "Question you called?"

"Isabel," she said aloud. "Isabel Crawford." She pointed in the direction of Saddle Mountain and signed. "I come to live among you, to tell you about Jesus."

The other braves laughed. Their leader did not smile. His graceful arms and hands spoke effortlessly. He repeated the question sign, pointed to Isabel, made the Jesus sign, then the hair-combing gesture for a woman. Again his meaning was clear: "You Jesus woman?"

Isabel hesitated. A Jesus man was a preacher. She did not wish to confuse them. "No," she signed, "not a Jesus woman. I come to tell you about Jesus, to help you to find the white man's road."

He pointed to the conversation tube hanging from her neck. "Why you carry little bugle? Maybe you blow it and call the soldiers to come chase us."

Isabel forced herself to join in the laughter. "Not bugle," she explained. She put her palms close to her ears, moved them in a small circle to indicate deafness, and followed quickly with the thumb-and-forefinger sign for "little." She raised the metal tube and demonstrated its use.

The Indian leader was intrigued. He put out a hand and gestured for it. Isabel slipped the gold chain over her head and handed the tube to him.

He put the small end to his right ear and said something in Kiowa to another Indian, who answered. The leader listened through the tube, smiled, and handed it back to Isabel.

"You do not need a bugle," he signed. "Your wagon makes more noise than many bugles."

Feeling foolish, Isabel again joined in the laughter. "I do not have far to go," she signed. "I will get there."

The leader's hands and arms moved in smooth rhythm. "You come here all alone and you no scared? Maybe we scalp you."

His face was solemn. Isabel glanced at the other Indians. Now not one was smiling.

The banks of the dry wash screened Isabel and the six Indian men from the outside world. She was truly at their mercy.

"I think maybe we scalp you now," the leader signed. He prodded his horse forward. A knife appeared in his left hand. He snatched the Winchester from his lap and placed the end of the barrel against Isabel's head. She heard the snick of the hammer as it was cocked.

Isabel went completely numb. Every thought went out of her brain. The roaring in her ears grew into a crescendo as she awaited the fatal bullet. Cold chills shot up her spine. She closed her eyes and prepared to die.

The moment seemed to stretch into eternity, and yet the expected bullet did not come.

Isabel opened her eyes. The Indian was still holding the rifle against her head. His face remained expressionless.

Moving slowly so the Indian would not think she was reaching for the gun, Isabel began to sign. "The Great Father travels with me. Maybe I die right now, as you say. But this I know: The Great Father will take care of me. I am not afraid."

The Kiowas sat in silence, watching her. Isabel waited, her temples pounding with each beat of her heart.

Then the Indians laughed.

The leader lowered the rifle, pointed the barrel into the air, and pulled the trigger. The hammer snapped on an empty chamber. He replaced the knife in its sheath, cradled the rifle across his lap, and gave Isabel a knowing smile.

She assumed she was the victim of a prank.

But she was not sure.

The leader placed a thumb to his chest. "Red Eagle," he said aloud. He reached up with his long arm and shook her hand so vigorously that Isabel almost toppled from the wagon.

The name was familiar. Red Eagle was a rather famous horse thief. The Army had difficulty keeping him on the reservation.

"I have heard of Red Eagle," she signed. "Maybe this is a good time to start my Jesus talk."

Again the other Kiowas laughed. Red Eagle offered only a slight frown. "Walk softly, Jesus woman," he signed. "The last Jesus man to come to our camp ran away like a rabbit. You walk a dangerous road. Maybe some other Indian scalp you."

He backed his horse. Turning away, the six mounted Indians crossed the dry wash, broke into a gentle trot, and rode toward a rank grove of elm and post oak.

For a moment Isabel felt faint. She sat trying to collect her wits, too weak to lift the reins. After several minutes the Indians reappeared in the distance, driving a small herd of horses at a rapid gait across the open prairie.

Isabel began to shake uncontrollably.

Brother Clouse had been right.

The Indians could have killed her, or worse, and no one would have known. Her screams would have been futile.

They could have plundered her wagon, burned it, and buried her in a shallow grave, with no one the wiser.

Briefly she considered returning to the Elk Creek Mission.

Then she thought of her five years of preparation, her long struggle to obtain permission, the confidence the Mission Board had placed in her.

Whatever happened, she could not turn back.

She took up the reins, threatened Jonah with the whip, and resumed her journey toward the Wichita Range, now dark and brooding on the southern horizon.

From the moment Isabel drove into the lush meadow on Saddle Mountain Creek she knew she had found the perfect site for her mission. The small, clear stream flowed gently in a semicircle at one end of the glade, nurturing huge cottonwood, elm, and pecan trees. Nestled into the base of Saddle Mountain, the meadow was flat and blanketed with shortgrass and wildflowers. The mountain rose to the south and west. Huge pink granite boulders along the heights were rounded and heavily weathered.

Isabel examined the site and made plans. Here beside the stream she would pitch her tent. Across the meadow, in a natural amphitheater formed by boulders, she would build her brush arbor. Eventually she would raise her chapel in the middle of the glade, facing north, overlooking the distant broad sweep of the Washita River valley.

She wished she could notify Domot that she had arrived. But she did not know how to find him. She felt she should not mingle with the Indians until it was clear that she had Domot's support and could be introduced properly among the tribe.

More pressing was the need to establish her permanent camp. She set to work, deciding that Domot would hear of her arrival and come to welcome her.

She wrestled the tent from the wagon, struggling under its bulk and weight. By raising one pole at a time, she managed to tighten the stays. Gradually the tent took shape. By sundown it was fully erect, secured by large stakes driven deep into the ground with the flat of her ax.

As darkness gathered, she lit a lantern and unloaded her wagon. She stored the food and missionary boxes carefully at the back of the tent. After feeding and hobbling the team, she was near exhaustion. Yet much remained to be done. She gathered firewood and fixed a makeshift supper. Afterward, she washed her cookware and tin dishes in the creek. Beside the stream she worked up a cold-water lather and washed a few pieces of clothing as best she could and draped each garment on a low-hanging limb.

On impulse, she knelt again beside the stream with her treasured little creamer, one of the few pieces that had been kept as a souvenir when her parents' wedding presents were sold to pay their way to America. After the death of her father, it had been passed on to her. She had happened upon it in one of the boxes as she rummaged for supper. As the moonlit water flowed into the translucent mouth of the creamer, she could see the faint outline of the tiny blue pattern against the white china. With weariness pressing against her eyes, she found, in the dim half light, a few spikes of early-blooming grasses, which she placed into the pitcher. She set it on the wooden box beside her cot and studied it for a moment, then slipped hurriedly into her nightgown.

The night wind sent a chill into the tent. She settled beneath the blanket and reveled in its warmth and the refuge from the night.

Isabel had to smile as sleep drew near.

She was beginning to feel content that she had made a bold start. Not even the clamor of the wolves on the nearby mountain could disturb her growing sense of peace.

She awoke hours later amid inky blackness and fierce, horrendous grunts. She sat up, still half asleep, in what seemed to be the grip of a nightmare.

Again came loud snorts close beside her tent, terrifyingly real. A heavy form lunged against the canvas. The fabric ripped. Isabel was sitting, frozen, wondering what to do, when her cot rose, tilted, and tumbled over. She put out a hand to block her fall and felt a dark, furry mass charging across the floor of her tent. Sonorous gruntings came from all around.

Too late, she remembered that there were bears in the Wichitas.

The tent was filled with the creatures.

Screaming, clad only in her nightshirt, she scrambled out of the tent and fled into the night.

In mindless panic she ran headlong into the creek. Gasping, sobbing, stumbling painfully over submerged stones with her bare feet, she struggled across the knee-deep stream and sought protection in the trees.

Slowly she regained her breath. Hunkered beside a tree trunk, she looked back.

The moon had long since set. By starlight she could see that her tent was down. Dark shapes lumbered about her camp.

The night air was cool, her thin shift soaked. Isabel sat on the ground and shivered, too frightened to make a sound. Slowly a layer of clouds formed, shrouding the sky. Soon she could no longer see the animals.

The night seemed endless. Toward morning she slept from sheer exhaustion.

With daylight and the first glimpse of her camp, she began to cry in frustration. Her mission supplies—so painstakingly assembled over more than a year—lay trampled and scattered.

Still barefoot, she waded the creek and wandered through the debris.

The tent rested flat on the ground, ripped in a dozen places. Canned fruits and vegetables littered her campsite, some torn asunder by massive jaws. Teeth marks were plain on the soiled tins. Her undergarments, washed and hung so carefully the night before, were now in shreds, stamped into the dirt.

And there, perhaps most eloquent of all, lay her shattered whimsy of the night before, the delicate little creamer in pieces, the few small wilted flowers almost indistinguishable in the surrounding grasses. It was a cruel rebuke.

Brushing aside tears, Isabel gathered the fragments and tied them in a handkerchief. She then searched through the wreckage until she found the precious books she had not packed away: her Bible, Shakespeare's *Tragedies*, *Foxe's Book of English Martyrs*, Captain Clark's *Indian Sign Language*, and Lewis F. Hadley's *Sign Talk*. The cover of Shakespeare was torn at one corner. The Bible and *Foxe's* had survived unscathed. The sign-language texts were safe in their oilskins. Isabel carefully placed the books back in the wagon.

She hunted until she found a relatively unsoiled dress. After slipping it over her head, she wriggled out of her wet nightgown.

Driven by the white heat of anger, she struggled for an hour and again raised the tent. Holes gaped on the top and sides.

The memory of her clean, spotless tent—so lovingly given and so beautiful the evening before—started her sobbing again. She could not help it.

For a time she did not even try to stop.

Toward noon, still sniffling, she set to work, making one pile of the hopelessly damaged goods, and another of what yet might be salvaged.

When she had finished, the pile possibly worth saving was pitifully small. She put the unbroken tins of food into a missionary box and was dragging it toward the tent when a man's voice spoke behind her.

"Hang your food in the trees. They can't reach it there."

Startled, Isabel turned.

A wagon and team had driven within a few feet of her. For a moment she stood speechless. She could not imagine being caught so unaware.

High on the wagon sat an Indian man and woman. Two children—a boy and a girl—stood in the bed of the wagon, shyly looking down at Isabel. The woman held a baby and cradleboard on her lap. Three yellow hounds sniffed their way through the pile of ruined food. They seemed more curious than hungry.

The man wore citizen clothing—a black suit, white shirt open at the neck, heavy brogans, and a broad-brimmed black hat. Most strange was his hair, coal black and lush, trimmed just short of shoulder length, as if in uncomfortable compromise between the style of the white man and the long braids of the Kiowas. He was a shade darker than most of the Plains Indians, and his skin seemed of a slightly different texture. Isabel wondered if he were a Mexican, or possibly a Frenchman, who had married an Indian woman to claim a tribal headright. She had heard of such instances. He was of more than medium height and solidly built, with a large, powerful chest and wide shoulders. Isabel assumed the couple to be in their late twenties or early thirties.

And he had spoken to her in perfect English!

The woman was small, not much larger than Isabel. Her hair, long, straight, and loose in the Kiowa fashion, was softer and lighter than that of most Indians. Her features were delicate, her eyes warm and intelligent.

Isabel was fully aware of the spectacle she herself must pose. She was barefoot, in a torn dress covered with grass stains, her hair uncombed. The skin on her forehead, nose, cheeks, and neck had blistered from three days without a bonnet, peeled, and blistered again.

The man pointed toward the nearest cottonwood. "I'll show you how to hang your food in the trees so they can't reach it."

Isabel had been thrown hopelessly off stride and said the first thing that came to mind. "Can't bears climb trees?"

"Not bears. Pigs."

He had a rich baritone voice, strong and masculine. Isabel shook her head. "Bears. I felt their fur."

He pointed to the ground. "Bears don't leave pointy little tracks like that. Pigs do. They are Odlepaugh's pigs." He pointed toward the mountain. "Odlepaugh lives over that way."

Isabel remembered Brother Clouse's claim that Odlepaugh had been among the war party that had butchered the women in Texas. Struggling to regain her poise, she reached up to shake hands. "I'm Isabel Crawford. I have come from the Baptist Mission on Elk Creek to live among you, to spread the gospel of Jesus."

The man's grip was calm and firm, not abrupt and painful, like that of most Indians. Isabel was most impressed by his eyes. Calm and observant, they had that rare lustrous, brown-on-brown depth sometimes encountered among Indians. "I am Lucius Ben Aitsan," he said. "This is my wife, Mabel. My son Amos. My daughter Jessie. And this is little Sarah."

The boy was about nine or ten, the girl a year or two younger. The baby appeared to be only a few months old. The two older children kept stealing curious glances at Isabel. Each time she attempted to smile at them, they shyly lowered their gazes and looked away. Their mother sat motionless and silent on the wagon seat, her face as serene and finely chiseled as a Greek statue. Isabel assumed she did not speak English, and signed a greeting. It was returned.

Aitsan wrapped the reins around the brake lever and stepped from the wagon. "We will help you."

He took charge in an effortless manner Isabel admired. Grabbing a shovel from his wagon, he sent Amos and Jessie to bury the spoiled goods away from camp. With a length of rope, he showed Isabel how to suspend her food between two tree limbs so it easily could be raised and lowered, yet kept safe.

Isabel's sewing kit had survived. With a few brief words of Kiowa, Aitsan put his wife to mending the tent.

Within two hours the camp was restored to a pale imitation of its former order and tranquillity.

"My horses are gone," Isabel said. "I hope they weren't stolen."

"They are grazing on the side of the mountain," Aitsan said. "Amos will bring them down."

His accent seemed eastern, almost professorial. Only an occasional hesitation in search of the right word, his economy of speech, and his infrequent lapse into Indian phraseology revealed that English was not his native tongue. Isabel's curiosity caused her to commit a tactical error. "Where did you learn to speak English so well?"

She regretted her words the moment they left her mouth. Indians did not like personal questions. If she had learned nothing else during her three years among them, she had learned that.

Aitsan's eyes narrowed slightly. He did not answer for a moment. "Carlisle Indian School," he said.

In that instant Isabel understood much about him. Years ago the government had sent a small number of intelligent Indian children to be educated at the Pennsylvania boarding school, on the assumption that someday they would lead their tribes onto the white man's road.

Instead, most had returned to their tribes neither fish nor fowl. They lived somewhere between two cultures, unable to function well in either.

Isabel saw a way to soften her rudeness. "Mr. Aitsan, you may be a godsend. I'm authorized to pay twelve dollars and fifty cents a month for an interpreter. Would you be kind enough to help me in my work here?"

Again Aitsan did not answer immediately. He stood watching his son drive Isabel's horses down the side of the mountain. "I'll think about it," he said.

"You would be needed only for an hour or two, perhaps three or four nights a week. And, of course, on Sunday mornings."

Aitsan's broad face was impassive. From his silence, Isabel understood that the time had come to change the subject. "Why doesn't Mr. Odlepaugh keep his hogs penned?"

Aitsan considered the question at length. "He does not want them around his tipi. They make stink."

Isabel laughed. "Then why did he buy them?"

Aitsan hesitated, as if deciding how much to reveal. "He

did not buy them. Several years ago the government tried to turn the Kiowas into pig farmers. They gave every family some pigs. Most of us killed and ate them to get rid of them. We did not like the meat. Odlepaugh turned his pigs loose. Now they run wild on the mountain. Sometimes they come down and cause trouble."

Isabel remembered her terror, the wreckage of her camp. "They're a menace. Why doesn't someone do something about them?"

Aitsan studied her. "Odlepaugh won't let anyone shoot them. He says they have a right to live, the same as we do."

Isabel was momentarily confused. Had not Brother Clouse said Odlepaugh was a murderer, an incorrigible savage who valued life not at all?

Again Isabel tactfully changed the subject. "Won't you and your family stay for supper?" she asked. "Perhaps I can resurrect something from this disaster."

Aitsan gave a brief nod. Isabel set to work. But it was quiet, efficient Mabel who performed miracles. Hanging her baby and cradleboard on a tent pole, she sent her two older children to gather more wood. She built a fire and soon turned a few potatoes, some ears of corn, and a tin of beef into a delicious meal.

Afterward, Isabel and Mabel scoured the pans in the creek by twilight while Aitsan put his horses back into the traces. By the time the dishes were done, he was waiting on the wagon seat.

Aitsan took the baby in his arms while his wife climbed up beside him. Isabel thanked them profusely for their help, then decided to make a candid appeal.

"Mr. Domot invited me onto the reservation. But I've not yet seen him. Could you possibly get word to him that I have arrived?"

Aitsan was silent for a moment. "Domot and my father, Loki Mo-keen, have contracted as freighters for the Army. They are in Kansas. They will not be back for about two weeks."

Isabel hoped her shock did not show on her face.

Aitsan was the son of Mexican renegade Loki Mo-keen—the baby-killer, a known leader of the Ghost Dance movement.

The fact was confirmed by Aitsan's swarthy complexion.

He was half Mexican.

"Then I suppose I'll just have to wait until they return,"

she managed to say. "I was hoping he would introduce me to the families on this part of the reservation."

Aitsan looked down at her. "Miss Crawford, I think I should tell you this: There has been much hot talk about you in council. Some of the Kiowas want to move you off the reservation."

Isabel was not certain she had heard correctly. "Hot talk? About me?"

Aitsan nodded. "Red Eagle spoke for you. He said he tried to scare you off the reservation, but you made your heart brave and did not run. He told the council you have a Kiowa heart."

Isabel could not suppress a laugh. "I don't know how he could believe that. I was frightened out of my wits."

Aitsan gave her the bare wisp of a smile. "A woman all alone and not scared of six Kiowa braves would be a"—he searched for the right word—"how do you say . . . ?" He made a fist, put the clenched fingers to his forehead and rubbed in a small circle, signifying a brain in a whirl.

"A crazy person. An idiot. A fool."

"A fool," Aitsan agreed. "There have been many hot words about you. Red Eagle said the council should wait until Domot and Mo-keen come back from Kansas before they do anything. I do not know what will happen."

"Thank you for telling me."

Aitsan nodded, slapped the reins against the rumps of his horses, and drove off.

Isabel held her lantern high and waved to the children until they disappeared into the darkness.

Not until later did it occur to her to wonder what stand Aitsan had taken on the issue.

Remembering a trick her father had used to keep marauding weasels out of the hen house, Isabel lit three lanterns and spaced them in trees so their flickering glow covered the surrounding glade. With cord, stakes, and empty tin cans filled with pebbles, she constructed a warning system encircling her tent. Once all was in readiness, she arranged her campaign desk under the canopy of the tent and began a long letter to the Mission Board.

A large, sturdy club rested against her knee.

She did not know how she would get the letter to the

agency for mailing, but it most certainly could not be sent if it were not first written.

The pigs arrived a few minutes after the moon disappeared over the mountain. She first heard their grunting in the darkness outside her circle of light, then the clank of a tin can behind her tent.

Swinging her club with both hands, she waded into the pack and dealt one of the brutes a solid blow on the snout. He ran squealing into the darkness.

His companions eluded her and circled the tent.

She found it impossible to defend all fronts. While she held a half dozen at bay in the meadow, others ripped the canvas walls and penetrated from the rear.

Shouting, Isabel ran inside and flailed away until the squealing pigs retreated into the shadows.

In the wake of the skirmish, her folding desk lay on the ground, the ink spilled, her papers scattered.

Her tin can warning system had been rendered useless.

Isabel changed her tactics.

After moving one lantern into the tent, she cleared her cot and other obstacles from the walls. Club poised, she waited until the slightest movement of canvas betrayed an inquisitive snout.

Then she struck.

The battle continued throughout the night.

At dawn, exhausted, she at last surrendered to the inevitable and returned her goods to the wagon. She folded the tent, dragged it to the wagon, and wormed it over the endgate. She spread her blankets on top of the load and managed two or three hours of sleep.

She awoke furious at herself. If she had moved into the wagon earlier, the pigs could have rooted wherever they pleased.

Other matters were far more important than her own comfort.

She must confront the Kiowas with a *fait accompli* by the time Domot and Loki Mo-keen returned from Kansas.

After a hurried breakfast she picked up her ax, walked into the distant woods, and began toppling tall willow saplings. By noon her muscles ached almost intolerably. Her palms blistered and split. By sundown she was so tired she could hardly move. After a cold supper, she collapsed on top of the wagon box.

Only once during the night was she awakened by the pigs as they grunted and foraged under the wagon. Unable to find the food, they soon went away.

The following morning she harnessed Jonah and dragged her felled saplings into the clearing. That afternoon, she trimmed them into long poles.

The next day she dug deep postholes with her shovel and pickax and began the erection of her brush arbor in the boulder-lined amphitheater.

As she worked, Indians occasionally came to watch. At first she caught only brief glimpses of curious faces peering from behind distant tree trunks, or from among the pink granite boulders along the slopes of the mountain. But as the arbor took shape, entire families paused in their wagons across the meadow. Isabel made the greeting sign and invited them closer to talk, but none approached. All turned away and moved on, as if they had important business elsewhere.

Once a tall, magnificent warrior astride a handsome paint rode close by the arbor. Although Isabel signed a greeting, he did not respond.

She assumed he was her nearest neighbor, Odlepaugh.

By the end of the second week she had finished the arbor. She then cut and shaped logs. Harnessing Jonah, she dragged them to the arbor and arranged seats for her future congregation. She stacked three empty Arbuckle coffee boxes and nailed them together to serve as her pulpit.

The days passed. Driven by restless energy, she kept busy. She washed all the pig-soiled mission clothing in the creek and hung each garment on a bush to dry. The spectacle of the glade draped in Joseph's-coat colors lured more Indians to pause and stare.

Fortunately, no rain fell. Isabel knew her luck would not hold. The spring storm season was at hand. The wagon would offer little protection from high winds and hailstones so common in the region.

Cutting more poles, she fashioned a crude framework for the wagon box and spread her tent over it. The improvised shelter was far from handsome. But it was snug and the best she could do.

One evening, under the cover of a series of shifts, she waded into the creek, scrubbed herself until her skin burned, and washed her hair. Her small, nimble body presented new, unfamiliar angularities. With the washcloth, she found more bones than any one person ought to have. Her family would be dismayed at the skinny wraith she was becoming, with so much hard labor and so little time even to think of nourishment.

She had proposed to teach God's word in a *womanly* way. How could she "be" a woman if she lost all vestiges of womanly form?

She resolved that when she had accomplished her most pressing goals, she would turn her attention to cooking, making rich stews and gravies, corn puddings, and crusty pies.

As a matter of fact, she thought, as she sent a stream of water coursing down her back, once she had her mission in operation, she would make fritters for breakfast every morning of the world. Maybe she would have time to go out and look for wild plums, and if supplies permitted, she would make jelly for her bread.

She splashed about for several minutes to rinse away every trace of soap, and stepped from the stream to stand upon dry grass. Refreshed and enlivened down to her now-prominent bones, she tossed her head, flinging a shower of water into the bushes. The brief bath sent her spirits soaring.

Late the next afternoon, as she gathered firewood, she saw horses and riders approaching from downstream. Alarmed, she retreated into the trees, ax in hand.

In single file, six cavalry troopers rode into her camp. Isabel emerged from hiding and, idiot-like, raised her hand in an Indian greeting.

A tall, lanky officer dismounted and handed his reins to one of his men. Removing his hat, he wiped his brow with a red bandana and walked toward Isabel.

"Good day, ma'am," he said. "I'm Lieutenant Ryan. We got word a white woman was camped on the reservation. I was sent to tell you that white people are required to stay off Indian land."

"I have the government's permission to be here. I was invited onto the reservation by the Indians."

Ryan studied her camp, casually taking in everything with one glance. "In that case, I'm expected to examine your papers."

Isabel went to her wagon and returned with the precious bundle. She showed him the letter from the Secretary of the Interior, her commission from the American Baptist Mission Board, and the certificate from the U.S. Bureau of Indian Affairs, all granting her permission to establish a mission.

Ryan signaled to his men. They dismounted and led their horses to the creek for water.

The lieutenant spent several minutes studying her documents. As he refolded them, he gestured toward her wagon. "Are you really living here all alone?"

Isabel smiled and nodded.

"Meaning no disrespect, ma'am. I don't think you're aware of the danger. I've fought Indians for more than twenty years—Sioux, Blackfeet, Nez Perce, Cheyennes, Utes, Apaches, the whole lot. I was on the Texas High Plains with Colonel Mackenzie clear through the Kiowa and Comanche campaigns. And I can tell you a fact: These Kiowas are the meanest Indians alive. When it comes to fighting, they've got no quitting sense. You could take six ordinary Apaches, two run-of-the-mill Comanches, and a whole tribe of Blackfeet, and they probably wouldn't add up to one good Kiowa warrior. Speaking for myself, I wouldn't think of spending a night out here alone."

"The Indians have been very kind to me."

"That's the way they are to your face. But most of them would sneak up on you in the dark and lift your hair without blinking an eye. Miss Crawford, I'm advising you in the strongest way I know how. Get off this reservation as quick as you can."

Isabel managed to retain her smile. "Not unless you force me off."

Ryan shook his head. "I regret to say I can't do that. Every 'i' is dotted and every 't' crossed on your papers. I can only warn you. Since I haven't changed your mind, I'll speak more plainly. A good-looking woman like you would be a powerful temptation for some savage Indian with no more sense of right and wrong than a barnyard animal. Do I make my meaning clear?"

Isabel felt warmth rushing to her face. "I'm here to *teach* the Indians moral principles."

Ryan's gaze lingered on her. "I hope you do, ma'am." Again he signaled to his men, who returned to their saddles. "We'd stay and give you at least one night's protection, but we're out looking for some stolen horses. You wouldn't have happened to see some young Indian bucks driving a herd of Texas mares, would you?"

Isabel hesitated. Red Eagle had spoken for her in council.

"I've only been on the reservation a little more than two weeks," she said.

Ryan swung into his saddle, adjusted his reins, and gave her a quick salute. "Well, if you do see them, please send us word."

Isabel watched the soldiers ride away, consoling her conscience with the thought that she had not lied.

She simply had not told the whole truth.

Chapter Three

Three yellow dogs trotted out of the trees and circled Isabel, sniffing the ground and wagging their tails. A moment later a rumbling wagon came into view. Domot, Loki Mo-keen, and Aitsan sat high on the spring seat, as dignified as if they were aboard the finest English carriage. Isabel covered the three small catfish she was cleaning, placed the pan out of harm's way, and stood waiting as Aitsan drove into her camp.

From their serious demeanors, she was certain they had come to tell her she must leave the reservation. She waved a welcome despite her sinking heart.

Aitsan pulled his team to a halt and locked the brake lever. Domot solemnly returned her greeting.

As Mo-keen stepped from the wagon, Isabel was impressed once again by his unusual size. He was even wider through the shoulders and chest than his son. Although in his late fifties or early sixties, he moved with the ease of a much younger man. His braids, as thick as Isabel's wrists, were interwoven with rawhide. The skin of his face was as gnarled as the bark of an oak. His eyes, dark brown and fathomless, glanced at her and moved on, offering no hint of whether she was of the slightest interest to him.

Domot was far less complicated. His countenance was more open, his eyes more receptive. Like Mo-keen and Aitsan, he wore citizen's clothing—a black suit, white shirt, brogans, and black hat. He signed that he was glad to see she had come to the reservation.

"This is my father, Loki Mo-keen," Aitsan said in English.

Mo-keen acknowledged her presence with a bare nod, giving no indication that he remembered meeting her at Elk Creek. Isabel made the welcome-to-my-tipi sign.

The Indians loved ceremony. Isabel was determined to provide them with an example of her own. "I was about to brew some tea. I've made molasses tea cake. Would you three join me?"

Aitsan conveyed the invitation in Kiowa, then helped her spread a canvas wagon sheet on the ground. The men sat on it, legs folded Indian fashion, before her small fire, leaving a place for her between Domot and Aitsan.

While the kettle heated, Isabel cut and served the cake. She poured with deliberation, using four of the seven china teacups that had escaped the attention of Odlepaugh's pigs. Then she settled back on the wagon sheet and carefully arranged her skirts.

Domot and Mo-keen followed her lead in handling the teacups and cake. They seemed curious about the tea but were too polite to ask what it was. They obviously liked the cake, eating with the communal silence that seemed to be their custom.

Isabel was grateful for the occasion to offer her hospitality, even though her guests may have arrived with bad news. She found a quiet satisfaction in presiding over one small ritual of civility.

Covertly, she studied the men. Aitsan was still a mystery to her. He was unlike any other Indian she had ever known. When not translating, he sat quietly, dominating even the older men with his sheer presence. He remained watchful and guarded, never revealing himself through the slightest word or gesture.

In the way of the Indians, the subject of the visit was not raised until Mo-keen put his empty cup and saucer on the wagon sheet, arranged himself in a more erect position, and began a long, formal speech that was meaningless to Isabel. His deep, resonant voice carried over the glade, the rise and fall of the melodious Kiowa language as appealing as a song.

When Mo-keen finished, his son offered a literal interpretation.

"My father, Loki Mo-keen, says it is true that Domot asked you to come here to tell the Kiowas about Jesus. But this has caused much trouble. When the soldiers brought us here, the Kiowa council agreed not to allow any white persons on the reservation. Some of the Kiowas here at Saddle Mountain have heard a little talk about Jesus. They now say they want to hear more. The mission at Rainy Mountain is too far away for them to go every Jesus day. Now the Kiowas here at Saddle Mountain cannot agree. Some want to hear more about Jesus. Others do not want any Jesus talk here at all. They want you to leave the reservation. Many hot words have been spoken. We have come to listen to your words. We will take them with us to the Kiowa council fire."

Isabel was relieved to learn that the final decision had not yet been made. "I will be happy to answer any questions," she said.

As Aitsan interpreted her words, Mo-keen sat in silence, casting analytic glances at her. Domot sat quietly listening, taking no part.

Mo-keen spoke again, and Aitsan translated. "What can Jesus do for the Kiowas?"

Isabel answered automatically; she did not need time to think. "Jesus offers salvation, a life everlasting."

Aitsan encountered some difficulty in translation, apparently over the word "salvation." Father and son talked back and forth for several minutes in Kiowa. Isabel waited until the problem was resolved.

"Are you big-water or little water?" Mo-keen asked.

Isabel sighed in exasperation. Methodist and Baptist preachers had confused the Indians with their different views on the ceremony of baptism—Methodist by sprinkling, Baptist by total immersion.

"Big-water," she said. "Baptist."

Mo-keen frowned as he formed his next question. Isabel was certain she knew what it would be, and when the translation came, she was not surprised.

"The Jesus man at Anadarko is little-water. The Jesus man at Rainy Mountain is big-water. Why do Jesus men say different things? How can we know what is true?"

"The Jesus men agree on all the *important* things," she said. "They disagree only on little things. Jesus spoke His message clear and simple. It was the men who came after

Him who added different interpretations and made matters difficult."

Again Aitsan spent several minutes in translation.

"Will you have the Jesus eat here at Saddle Mountain?" Mo-keen asked.

Isabel had ceased to be shocked by the directness of Indian speech. She considered his question carefully.

She did not want to place Holy Communion beyond reach.

Once she had organized her church, she believed her isolated congregation could receive Holy Communion from its duly elected deacons. The church would not be required to wait until a minister was assigned.

Isabel made the "yes" sign to Mo-keen and added, "But not now. Perhaps in the far-ahead time."

Mo-keen stared for a time at Saddle Mountain, apparently lost in thought. Then he again launched into a formal speech, pausing occasionally to listen with care to the translation, as if checking its accuracy.

"Domot has told me he thinks you have a good heart. My son Aitsan says the same thing. I have listened to your words and looked upon your face. I also believe that this may be so. But hear my words and think hard about them. A Kiowa is not like a white man. The Great Father put him on this earth to be a Kiowa, not a white man. A Kiowa and his religion are one and the same thing. His thoughts toward the Great Father, the earth, are something he lives and breathes through every moment of every day."

Isabel nodded in agreement. She thrilled to hear her own views expressed so eloquently. "That's the way it should be," she said.

Mo-keen listened to the interpretation, then made the "no" sign several times.

"That is not the road of the white man. All of my life I have watched the white man. When I was a boy, before I became a Kiowa, I was taught about Jesus. When my son Aitsan went to the white man's schools, he learned to walk the white man's road. He has told me about his life there. When he came back here, he rode for five winters with the Army as a sergeant of scouts. I visited him many times at the Army camps. Always I have watched the white man. This is a thing I know to be true. I have seen this with my own eyes. The white man thinks of Jesus only on Jesus day. On other days he does not think of Jesus or the Great Father at all unless he mashes a finger, or loses at cards, or someone makes him angry."

Isabel felt cornered by Mo-keen's argument; she had said as much herself many times.

"You've seen poor examples," she said.

Mo-keen nodded. "I ask you this: Can the Indian walk the Jesus road better than the white man?"

"I'm sorry to say that he probably can. If the Indian takes Jesus into his heart and works hard, he probably will be a better Christian than many white men who call themselves Christians."

Again Mo-keen lapsed into a troubled silence. He sat looking into the distance for several minutes.

"We are told now to do this and to do that so we will be more like the white man. Today the Kiowa makes a pale shadow on the earth. I also know this is true: If the Kiowa is turned into a white man and throws away all his Kiowa things, he will not make a shadow at all."

Isabel did not know what to say. She felt overwhelmed by the battering of Mo-keen's unwavering logic.

She forced herself to remember who was speaking—the baby-killer who, through his Ghost Dance, asked his god every day to kill all white men.

Who would have expected such eloquence and abstract reasoning from a complete savage?

After a long pause, Mo-keen resumed speaking. "The Kiowa grandfathers walked the Sun Dance road. Many Kiowas alive today once walked that road. It was a good road. When the white soldiers brought us onto this reservation, they told us we could have any religion we wanted. But later they came with big guns and stopped the Sun Dance. They told us the Kiowas must not walk that road. Now the Kiowas have thrown away many Kiowa things. The Sun Dance no longer works for us. Some Kiowas want to turn back to this road of our grandfathers. Others say they can see that the world has changed, that all the old roads are gone. That is why some Kiowas are looking at the Jesus road."

Isabel had read much about the Sun Dance; it was typical of primitive religion, with rituals of self-purification, idol worship, fasting, self-torture, and other acts designed to induce hallucinations the Indians believed to be of a spiritual nature.

If she expected to turn the Indians away from such practices, she first must gain their trust.

"I have been told that some Kiowas are walking the cactus button road and the Ghost Dance road," she said. "You can tell the council that I have no quarrel with the Kiowas who have chosen those roads. If I thought the cactus button would bring me one step closer to the Great Father, you would see me chewing cactus night and day, spines and all. If I thought I could get closer to the Great Father by dancing, I would dance the rest of my life without stopping. But the Bible and prayer are all I need. That is all anyone needs. I will teach this road to those who will listen. I believe the Kiowas soon will see that it is the best road, and we will all walk it together."

Isabel thought she saw a silent exchange between Domot and Mo-keen the moment Aitsan translated her knowledge of the cactus buttons and the Ghost Dance, but she was not sure. The three men talked for a time in Kiowa before Aitsan translated.

"My father, Loki Mo-keen, says that five winters ago the white soldiers shot many Sioux because of the Ghost Dance. It is not a thing that we should talk about."

Isabel refused to allow the matter to be shunted aside. She spoke emphatically. "Mr. Aitsan, if I am to remain on the reservation, we *must* talk about it. I cannot live among you and do my work unless I am trusted not to run to the agent or to Fort Sill with every bit of gossip. Surely you understand that. Please tell your father, and all the others, that I am here only to do my work."

After her words were translated, Mo-keen spoke again. "You have spoken true words: Some Kiowas hunt visions with the medicine button. They say that road is the one we should walk. They say the medicine buttons will tell us what to do. Many Kiowas have listened to the Jesus talk at Rainy Mountain and other places. They say maybe we should walk the white man's Jesus road. We must decide what to do quick. But we must be careful. This I know: If the Kiowas choose the wrong road now, the Kiowas will go under. Each Kiowa is hunting the right road as hard as he can. Not long ago our medicine had great power. Now our power is gone and we are dying."

Isabel was moved. She had assumed she would find spiritual hunger on the reservation. Mo-keen's words suggested it might be even greater than she thought.

"There is power in Jesus Christ," she said. "That is the greatest power there is, because it comes from the Great Father."

Mo-keen studied her closely. "You are a man-hearted woman," he said after a time. "That is a rare thing. I believe you can see Indians as human beings, and that is an even more rare thing for a white person. But you cannot live among us. There is much hot talk about the Jerome paper that we signed. Maybe there will be heaped-up trouble here at Saddle Mountain. Maybe we will fight again. I do not know. You must go back to Elk Creek."

Isabel glanced at Domot. He had not spoken a word. "Mr. Domot, do you also think I should return to Elk Creek?"

Domot did not answer immediately. Throughout the conversation he had deferred to Mo-keen. But now his voice conveyed firmness and conviction.

"I hold my words here in my heart so I will have them when I need them in council. But I will tell you what I think: I have two wives, so I cannot walk the Jesus road. I have done many bad things in my life. When I die, maybe I will go to the bad place the Jesus men talk about. That does not matter. All of my life I have seen only trouble. The bad place will not be a new thing for me. I have listened to the Jesus men at Rainy Mountain and Elk Creek and I have thought about their words. They say Jesus is the big chief of Peace. That is good. I want peace in the days I have left on this earth. I want to see peace for my children and my grandchildren. If the Jesus road will help them live with the white man, then I want them to get on it quick. Already we Indians are way-behind on the Jesus road. The little Jesus woman has been busy here. She has made us a good place to listen to her Jesus talk. I think we should hear what she has to say about Jesus before we tell her what she must do."

Mo-keen pointed to Isabel's makeshift shelter over the wagon and spoke to Domot. Aitsan interpreted for Isabel. "The Jesus woman cannot live in her wagon. Big winds will come and blow away that little cloth and maybe the Jesus woman with it. Big hailstones will fall and hurt her. Before the first deep snow she will die of the cold."

"I can build a shelter before winter," Isabel intervened. "Something very small."

Mo-keen made the "no" sign. "The council agreed not to allow a white-man house on the reservation. Some Kiowas kicked hard when the council allowed my son Aitsan to put up his small house. If you stay here you will make heaped-up trouble."

"Mr. Mo-keen, I was sent here to *help* the Kiowas," Isabel said. "I'm willing to do anything the council wishes. What harm could I possibly cause?"

Mo-keen replied slowly. "After the white man brought us here, some white chiefs in Washington decided they would turn us into melon farmers. They gave us melon seeds and told us how to plant them. We were surprised how quick the melons grew. No one told us how to eat them. We ate them green and our stomachs became scared. Many Kiowas died of the melon sickness. After the great Kiowa chief Satanta died in the Texas jail, I took his wife, Zoam-tey, and his son Odlepaugh into my tipi. Zoam-tey was the mother of my son Aitsan. She died of the melon sickness. She died because some white chiefs far away who never saw a Kiowa Indian tried to make the Kiowas into melon farmers."

Isabel tried to take in what he was saying. If Odlepaugh and Aitsan had the same mother, they were half brothers, a fact that Aitsan had neglected to mention. Odlepaugh was the son of Satanta—White Bear—sentenced to a Texas prison for the Warren wagon-train massacre. Satanta the father and Odlepaugh the son both had participated in the roasting alive of the teamster.

Brother Clouse was right; she certainly had landed in the thick of it.

"I'm sorry about your wife, Mr. Mo-keen." She looked from one to the other. "And your mother, Mr. Aitsan. But I don't understand. What has this to do with my Jesus talks?"

"Hear me," Mo-keen said. "A good heart can do bad things. I think you should go back to Elk Creek quick."

Isabel shook her head emphatically. "I can't do that. Not unless you send me away. I spent five years learning how best to tell the Kiowas about Jesus. My mission council depends upon me. Besides, I've made a covenant with the Great Father."

Aitsan stopped in his translation. "Covenant?"

"A pact. A holy agreement. A bond. A promise."

Aitsan finished the translation. Mo-keen frowned. "We will think on your words, and talk again in council."

He rose and walked toward the wagon. Domot and Aitsan followed in his wake.

Isabel hurried after them, her muscles aching from sitting rigid so long on the ground. "May I speak to your council?"

Mo-keen paused to hear the translation, then answered with the "no" gesture, adding in sign language, "You cannot catch horses by running into the herd."

The three men climbed into the wagon, waved good-bye, and drove back over the hill.

That night, as if in fulfillment of Mo-keen's prophecy, dark clouds rolled in from the west, and rain poured in torrents. Isabel crawled into her tiny shelter and trembled as wind lashed the trees along the creek and brilliant lightning sent thunder reverberating along the mountainside.

The night seemed endless.

At first light she assessed the damage. Most of the brush on her arbor was gone, but the framework remained intact. Jonah and Jeremiah appeared none the worse for wear. The wagon shelter had failed to shed all of the deluge. Her bedding and the mission goods were soaked.

She spent the next two days drying her supplies, cutting brush, and repairing her arbor. Her uncertain future on the reservation was never far from mind, and her nights were plagued by doubt.

Late on the third day, Aitsan, Domot, and Loki Mo-keen returned. As they drove into her camp, Isabel could not determine from their expressionless faces what the council had decided. Again she served molasses cake and tea.

After he finished eating, Mo-keen spoke, pausing at the end of every sentence for translation so there would be no misunderstanding. "We have talked long and hard in council. Domot, Red Eagle, and others have spoken for you. I have told you what I think. Many Kiowas say you must go off the reservation. Others say we should keep our ears open and hear everything these days. Maybe this is so. Here is what we decided: We will come and listen to one Jesus talk. We will think hard about what we hear. Then we will talk again in council and decide what to do."

Isabel understood. Her reprieve was only temporary.

On the basis of a single Jesus talk, she would be judged.

She would need all the help she could muster.

She turned to Aitsan. "Have you considered serving as my interpreter?"

A veil seemed to settle over his face, as if he were withdrawing into himself, establishing a vast distance between his thoughts and the world around him. "If the council decides you may stay on the reservation, I will help you find someone." Isabel could not fathom his refusal, but at least she now knew better than to ask his reasons.

Her battle seemed to be at a dead end. She felt truly discouraged. She would not be able to sway Mo-keen and her other opponents with a single talk—and certainly not if confined to the limitations of sign language.

But she was left with no alternative.

"All right. I will give a Jesus talk here tomorrow night at the arbor. I hope everyone within riding distance of Saddle Mountain will come."

After Aitsan conveyed her words, the three men rose, shook her hand formally, and climbed into the wagon. Once again they drove back over the hill, the yellow hounds trotting along as escorts.

In the glow of four flickering lanterns, Isabel signed the theme of her talk. "Strait is the gate, and narrow is the way, which leadeth unto life, and few there be that find it."

She progressed slowly, frequently repeating phrases and resorting to alternate expressions for clarity. She was determined not to coddle her prospective congregation. She warned the Indians that becoming Christians would not be easy, that although Jesus had promised that baptism would wash away all of their bad roads, they would be tempted to pick them up again. She stressed that being a Christian would mean fighting hard battles every day of their lives.

She could not have asked for an audience more attentive. Domot and Loki Mo-keen sat in the front row, along with other members of the tribal council. In the center sat Taboodle, almost a hundred years old, clearly accorded the position of honor.

On the log behind them sat Aitsan and his family, and Kokom and his wife, Pope-bah. At the back sat Spotted Horse; his wife, Hattie; Papedone with his wife, Sapemah; Odlepaugh and his wife, Ananthy; and Hunting Horse and his wife, Beathomah. Isabel had made a special effort to remember names as she was introduced, but there were more than fifty. She could not remember all this first—and maybe last—time.

She completed her short talk, outlining the basic tenets of the Christian faith.

"Are there any Christians here?" she asked.

Every head went down.

"Are any of you thinking hard about walking the Jesus road?"

Many hands went up.

Among them were those of Aitsan, Pope-bah, Spotted Horse, Hunting Horse, Heenkey, and Papedone.

Isabel was elated. She had not expected such an impressive response. Also, Aitsan's raised hand was the first solid indication he might be on her side. For some reason she could not define, this boosted her spirits immensely.

"An open heart is the first step on the Jesus road," she signed.

Then she made a tactical error. "Are there questions you would like to ask of me?"

Spotted Horse was the first. He rose to his towering height, and his long arms moved with a balletlike precision. "Does the Bible say that every Indian is to get a tiny little piece of land and a plow? I have tried to work the fields like the government man told us to do. But plowing makes my heart hit hard. I do not like it. My hands and my feet are strong, but my heart is sick for the long-ago time. I think hunting is the road the Kiowas should walk. If a Christian must plow the land, I do not want to walk the Jesus road."

Carefully, Isabel explained that the size of the land allotments had been decided by the white chiefs at a big council in Washington and had nothing to do with Jesus and the Bible. But she added: "In the Bible it is written that by the sweat of our face we shall earn our bread. If your heart did not hit, you would be dead. Life is not easy. When you are as anxious to save your soul as you are to save your body, come to me and I will teach you that it is impossible to save both. Your heart will always be sick until your soul is saved."

Odlepaugh rose. Until tonight, Isabel had seen him only from a distance. He was taller by a head than his half brother Lucius, leaner, and longer-limbed. But most arresting was his face. Most Indians conveyed a calm dignity with their eyes. Odlepaugh's were open, less guarded. He moved, spoke, and looked upon the world with a nervous intensity. He was handsome in the high-cheekbone cast of the Kiowas, but a faint scar across his upper lip lent his mouth a quizzical expression.

"You are a small woman," he signed. "But strong and healthy. You make a man's eyes happy. Why are you not married, making babies? Why you come here to live without a man?"

Isabel's mind froze. She knew that the emotional impact of the question was reflected in her face, but she was helpless to do anything about it. She also recognized the hostility embedded in the question; Indians were rude only by calculation. Signing her answer firmly, she tried to keep her anger hidden. "That is a long story. I do not like to tell it, and it is not for the ears of strangers. In the far-ahead time, when we know each other like brothers and sisters, maybe I will tell that story to you. But not now."

Old Taboodle stirred. He rose shakily, gathered his blankets, and slowly began signing. He was so old and wrinkled that the whole history of the human race seemed to be written in his ancient face. Isabel prepared herself for a profound question.

"Why is it that some white men have no hair on top and others have a heap on their chins?"

Isabel almost laughed aloud. But not a single member of the congregation even smiled.

Taking her cue from the congregation, Isabel treated the question with equal seriousness. "Most white men are descended from many tribes. They have grandfathers in many countries. That is why some white men are different from others."

Hunting Horse rose with a question. "Why do they send us a Jesus woman? At Rainy Mountain they have a Jesus man."

For a moment Isabel stood immobile, confounded, her hands frozen and clasped before her.

The answer was beyond sign language. She glanced at Aitsan in silent pleading. His face remained impassive.

Hesitantly, she signed her answer. "I did not come here to do the work of a man. Men work at big things, and when they stop, they sit down. That is the road of a man. Women work at many little things, and their work is never done. That is the road of a woman. In Jesus work it is the same. A Jesus man preaches, builds Jesus houses, and does big things. A Jesus woman meets in little circles of people to tell Jesus stories, pray, find food and clothing for those who need them,

and help in many small things. In a great city on a big lake far
to the north and east of here are many, many women who
wash clothes, sew, and work hard to make money so I can
come here and tell you about Jesus. They also send us food
and clothing. They have sent me here to help you to find the
Jesus road, the white man's road."

A long silence followed while her explanation was absorbed.
Then Loki Mo-keen stood. All eyes turned toward him, and
Isabel felt tension spread through the congregation.

Clearly her trial was only beginning.

Mo-keen's powerful arms moved in short, flowing movements. Isabel had no difficulty in following their meaning.

"When I was a young man we had plenty of buffalo. We
made our tipis, our clothes, our bedding from the hides.
All-the-time we had plenty to eat and the dogs were never
hungry. Twenty-two winters ago the white soldiers came and
they shot and shot and shot and killed and killed and killed
big and little, taking the skins and leaving the meat to rot. In
seven winters the buffalo were all gone and today we Kiowas
are poor and hungry. White men are kill-crazy. The buffalo
they kill, kill, kill. Indians they kill, kill, kill. They killed
Jesus, too. Why do they do these things? Why? Why? Why?"

He continued to make the "question" sign, his broad right
hand wiggling in front of his shoulder, keeping the question
hanging in the air.

Isabel felt transported beyond her capabilities.

All through training school she had been taught the simple
themes she must convey to savages. No one ever had suggested to her that those savages might possess their own
rather startling perceptions.

The man they called a baby-killer had just asked a question
of hopeless complexity. And her answer might determine her
future at Saddle Mountain.

She signed her reply slowly, allowing herself time to think.
"White men are not perfect, not even those who work hard to
stay on the Jesus road. Only one man among all the men who
ever lived on this earth was perfect. That is why we must try
to be like Him. That is why the Jesus road is so difficult.
White men have done many, many bad things. Sometimes
they have even done bad things in His name. The Indians
have done many bad things, too. But if we could all live like
Jesus, there would be no bad things. There would be no
killing, no wars. We would all live in peace."

Mo-keen seemed to consider the answer at length. Then his arms and hands moved. "I think the Kiowas and the Jesus people pray to the same Great Father. We call Him *Dom-oye-alm-daw-k'hee.*"

He spoke the name aloud. A murmur of approval swept through the congregation. Mo-keen held up a hand for silence and continued.

"*Dom-oye-alm-daw-k'hee* made the Kiowa grandfathers and put them on this earth. He also made the stars, the grass, and the trees. He made the buffalo. Maybe He also made the white man. Maybe He gave the white man the Bible road. But the Indian cannot read the white man's talking paper. So He gave the Indian the dance road. I ask you: Does the Kiowa have to throw away the dance road to take up the Bible road?"

On impulse, Isabel resolved to say exactly what she thought, and pray that her stated policy never reached the Home Mission Board in Chicago. "The Kiowa is a beautiful human being. Mo-keen speaks the truth. God made the Kiowa the way he is, and perhaps we should not question God's purpose. The Kiowa can walk the Jesus road without throwing away his Kiowa things. This is what I think."

As Mo-keen returned to his seat, Aitsan rose. He signed his words for the benefit of the congregation and gave Isabel a literal translation in English.

"In the white man's school they taught me to read the white man's talking paper. A few days ago a white man said in the *Chickasha Express* that all full-blood Indians should be sent to some other country. He made funny of us. He said other countries might welcome us, because Indians are first-class in a shooting match, or at a game of monte, or in making a full hand at loafing. He said that in making two spears of grass grow where one grew before, we are a failure. He said the government should buy our land and herd us to some other country. He said we have been pests and scabs long enough. I ask you: How can we hope to walk the white man's road when white men say things like this about us?"

Anger flooded through Isabel unbidden. For a moment she lost her composure. Hot tears came to her eyes. She signed her answer in vicious chops. "If I had that white man here now I would hit him. I would have to ask Jesus to forgive me, but that white man should be whipped. The things he says will never happen. He only says these things because he thinks they make him a big man. But they show everyone that he is a little man."

She paused, appalled that she had lost control of herself so completely. How could she expect to teach these people if their straightforward questions made her break into tears and respond in irrational anger?

In training school, Miss Burdette repeatedly had stressed that a missionary should never reveal strong emotion before the simpler races. And now she had made a spectacle of herself on this first—and perhaps the last—night.

She forced herself to make a calm, reasonable summation.

"The Kiowas should not worry about the foolish words of small men. These small men are like flies on a horse. They can make us angry, but they cannot hurt us."

Aitsan glanced at his family, at the congregation. Again he spoke to Isabel in English, and to the congregation in sign language, interspersed with brief passages in Kiowa. It was a virtuoso performance.

"I have listened to the hot words in the Kiowa council about the Jesus talks, and I have not spoken. I was away from the reservation for many years, and some of you think I am no longer a Kiowa. That hurts me here." He put a hand over his heart. "At the white man's school they tried to make me into a white man. They cut my hair, gave me white man's clothes, and gave me a white man's name. But I still have a Kiowa heart and a Kiowa brain. I still think as a Kiowa. I speak now because I see that the council fires of the Kiowas are growing cold. Soon we will be left in darkness, and each of us will have to find his own way in the world. Already, some of us are going off in different directions, away from the council fires. Some of us have gone to Anadarko to listen to the little-water Jesus man. Some of us have gone to the big-water church at Rainy Mountain to listen to the Jesus man there. Some of us have liked what we have heard about Jesus. Now Domot has asked Miss Crawford to come onto the reservation to tell us more. Some Kiowas think we only need new visions. They have taken up the cactus button road of the Comanche Chief Quanah Parker. They say that if we stay long enough in the sweat lodges, and eat enough of the magic buttons, a vision will come to us and tell us what to do. Maybe this is so. I do not know. Some Kiowas have taken up the Ghost Dance road of Wovoka the Paiute, who says he is the Indian Jesus. Some Kiowas went across the high mountains to the west to listen to his words. They came back saying different things, and we cannot agree. Some said he is a false Jesus because when they found him he was sick in bed and his feet were dirty. Others say his words are true, and that if we dance enough and pray enough, all Kiowas in the world beyond this one will come back in a great spirit army and drive the white man out of our land with tornadoes, lightning, hailstones, earthquakes, and prairie fires, and that when this happens, the buffalo will come back out of the ground where they are hiding. Maybe this is so. I do not know. I have seen so many strange things in this world that nothing surprises me anymore. But this I know: The Kiowas I see today are not the Kiowas I saw when I was a child. Before the Army drove us onto this reservation, no one told us what to do. Any man who told a Kiowa what to do would find himself full of arrows before he drew another breath. Now everyone tells us what to do. The Kiowas have been turned this way and that way until we are dizzy. Our chiefs are all gone, and we cannot agree on anything. I am worn out from all the talk. My stomach jumps day and night like a rabbit in a sack. I think it is time the Kiowas decided what road they want to walk and take it up quick."

A rumble of agreement came from the congregation. Isabel thought she saw a hint of approval in Mo-keen's heavily lidded eyes.

Aitsan turned and spoke directly to Isabel. "I would like to hear the thoughts of the Jesus woman on this. Miss Crawford, you have come to Indian country from a place far away, to talk us into taking up the Jesus road. Why did you come here? Why do you want the Kiowas to take up the Jesus road?"

The congregation sat alert, expectant, awaiting her answer. Isabel sensed that she must not equivocate. She might anger some, but she must take that chance. She sensed that if ever an audience wanted honesty, this one did. She signed with care, so no one would mistake her words.

"Your first question is easy to answer. Jesus said that those who believe in Him should go out into all the world and spread His message. I believe in Jesus. So I am here. The second question is more difficult. But you have asked me, so I will tell you what I think. The Kiowas cannot go back. The old ways are gone, along with the buffalo. In four more winters we will be starting another hundred winters on the white man's calendar. Right or wrong, the Kiowas have signed the Jerome Agreement. White settlers will be coming to claim the land you have signed away. The question of who owns the land to the west of the reservation also will be answered soon. Whatever the white councils in Washington decide about that land, you can be sure the Indians will be the losers, for they have no voice in those councils. North, south, east, and west, the whites will swarm in to take up all this land. They will be as thick as a village of prairie dogs. Somewhere in all of this, the Kiowa must find his place quick. I believe the Ghost Dance and the cactus button are false roads. They will lead the Kiowa farther from the white man's world and deeper into trouble. The next hundred winters on the white man's calendar will bring many problems for the white man, too. His way of life is also changing fast. He also is afraid of all the new things. He has little time to listen to the troubles of the Indian. The time ahead will be difficult for all of us, but most especially for the Kiowa. He will need spiritual strength—strong medicine—to live through this bad time. I know he will find the necessary strength on the Jesus road. I doubt he will find it anywhere else."

Isabel was keenly aware of the deep hush in the arbor. The Kiowas stared up at her, curious and fervent in their earnest searching. The covert gaze, still new to her, seemed to probe her soul. She felt so utterly small before this collective presence. Throughout her long speech Aitsan had remained standing, concentrating on her words with an intensity unique in her experience.

His questions had revealed the extent of the complexities she faced. Her dream was beginning to look more than ever out of reach, towering far above her. She was beset with a sense of futility. Her burden of responsibility suddenly seemed unbearable. Here she stood, at this awesome ford in the life road of the Kiowas, making what might be seen as a pathetic bid, coming from a skinny little Jesus woman.

Her mission was perhaps seconds away from a decision that would affect everyone in the arbor.

To blazes with her skin and bones, her paltry limitations!

She lifted her chin, and her cool gray eyes locked on Aitsan. She applied herself to making her voice firm and filled with conviction.

"And Mr. Aitsan, you might consider this: The Jesus road

may be the *only* common meeting ground for the Indian to live in peace and brotherhood with the white man."

Aitsan frowned and looked away. He seemed deeply disturbed. After a moment, he again signed to her, this time not bothering to translate. "You say the Kiowa cannot go back. He must go forward. Is there nothing ahead for the Kiowa but the white man's road?"

Isabel answered with all the power of her conviction. "The Kiowa must learn to walk the white man's road as well as any white man. Only then will he make his voice heard in the white man's council. When that day comes, the white man will honor him as a Kiowa, not as a pale shadow of the white man. That is what I think."

A profound silence fell. At last, Mo-keen rose and signaled that the questions had ended. He turned to Isabel. His hands moved slowly and deliberately. "Maybe you have spoken true words. We will think hard about them."

Isabel returned to her coffee box pulpit and, with a sense of relief she could not have explained, signed to her congregation. "Let us pray, each on his own road."

Isabel left her camp and set out to climb Saddle Mountain in the relative coolness of early morning. Three days had passed and still she had received no word. She was restless and worried. No doubt her complete candor had made many enemies among the Ghost Dance and cactus button Indians.

By following the creek upstream, she found its source amid large, moss-covered boulders and seeping springs. Despite the growing warmth of the day, the canyon was cool and the ground moist. Isabel stopped to catch her breath. She drank from the clear running water and found it delicious. Above her, the jumble of huge stones seemed delicately balanced, ready to roll down the mountain upon her. But appearances were deceiving. Clearly the boulders had weathered in place. Most apparently had not moved in thousands upon thousands of years.

Choosing her way carefully, she moved steadily upward among them.

The climb was easier than she had expected. Skinniness had its rewards. She could not remember being so light on her feet. She made her way from boulder to boulder, as if walking up giant steps, ever higher. Breathless, perspiring, she was not aware she was near her goal until she was struck by the cool, crisp breeze blowing across the mountaintop. After making her way up the last few hundred feet in a cautious crouch, the long folds of her blue-and-yellow calico dress held aside as she moved, she found herself on the cantle of Saddle Mountain.

Walking leisurely along the ridge, she reached the pommel within an hour.

The view was breathtaking.

To the northwest was Rainy Mountain, dark and brooding, long the spiritual home of the Kiowas. To the southwest was Baker Peak, bright in the early-morning sun. Mount Scott rose far to the southeast. Beyond it, unseen, was Fort Sill.

With her view from the mountaintop, Isabel easily could understand why the Indians were so upset. With only a little help from her imagination, the entire countryside seemed to be in turmoil in every direction, as far as the eye could see.

To the north lay the heavily wooded valley of the Washita, easily traced by its belt of lush greenery. Beyond, all the way to Kansas, the Indian reservations had been opened to white settlement in a series of gigantic land rushes. Seven years earlier, the "unassigned lands" of the Seminole and Creek preserves had been thrown open to white settlers in a giant "run." Four years later, a hundred thousand white men had raced to claim six million acres in the Cherokee Outlet. Since then, one by one, the Sac and Fox, Iowa, Kaw, Ponca, Oto, Wichita, Kiowa-Apache, Potawatomi-Shawnee, Cheyenne and Arapaho, Pawnee, Tonkawa, Osage, and Kickapoo domains had vanished under a series of human onslaughts.

Many of the settlers who swarmed to claim those lands were no less exotic than the tribes they replaced. Poles, Czechs, Lithuanians, and other European immigrants founded their own communities, wore their own costumes, spoke their own languages. Freed slaves from the Old South formed enclaves, seeking a belated share of the American dream. Strange religious sects arrived from the East, from Europe, from all over the world. People of diverse political and sociological persuasions established tight communal centers to practice their beliefs. Murderers, robbers, thieves, and debtors poured in from other states, some seeking a fresh start, others seeking new victims.

Oklahoma Territory was a raw, rugged, unshaped land teeming with life and confusion.

To the east, beyond Fort Sill, lay the sovereign, separate

Indian Nations of the Chickasaws, Creeks, Cherokees, and Choctaws, beleaguered under constant white efforts to meld them into a territorial government. To the south, in rolling grasslands stretching away to the Red River was the bulk of the Kiowa-Comanche-Apache Reservation, most of it now signed away under the Jerome Agreement. Bordering the reservation to the west was a large block of disputed land, covering hundreds of thousands of acres between the Prairie Dog Town Fork and the North Fork of the Red River. The area had been claimed, settled, and organized by Texans as Greer County. The government had declared Prairie Dog Town Fork as the boundary and sent troops to clear the area of settlers, pending a ruling by the U.S. Supreme Court. The county—larger than many eastern states—was still open range, grazed by Texas cattle.

No matter how the high court ruled, Greer County soon would be thrown open to white settlement.

Only a little more imagination was required to see this landscape as it had been a few years ago, when it was known only to the Kiowas, the Comanches, and a few other nomadic Indian tribes.

At the time of Isabel's birth thirty-one years ago, a hundred million buffalo still roamed these rolling plains.

Twenty-two years ago, Colonel Ranald S. Mackenzie's relentless war against the Kiowas and Comanches had climaxed in a series of battles. Now Mackenzie was dead of brain fever—living his final years as a raving lunatic, some said—and the Kiowas and Comanches were wards of the government, penned on their reservation like cattle in a corral, beleaguered, confused, half starved.

Tears came to Isabel's eyes.

Never had she dreamed that the problems of the Indians would be so complex, so *human*.

The next few years would bring even more drastic changes to the country that now lay before her—and to the Kiowas.

Perhaps their sufferings had only begun.

Kneeling on the mountaintop, Isabel prayed aloud:

"Dearest Lord, please grant me the strength of dedication to Your service that You granted to my father. Please use me in any way that I best may serve Your heavenly kingdom. Please help me see what needs to be done and grant me the strength to do it. Please accord me with the wisdom and power to guide these people aright. Most of all, I ask that

You show me the way to be a *teacher* but never a *preacher*. Already You have made me see that guidance, not correction, is most needed here."

From the moment Aitsan, Domot, and Loki Mo-keen drove down the hill and into her camp, Isabel knew they had bad news.

Not one would meet her gaze.

She invited them to sit on the wagon sheet, poured coffee, and served tapioca pudding. Aitsan and Domot seemed to be enveloped in gloom. Mo-keen was his usual stoic self. Isabel waited patiently while they ate in silence.

At last Aitsan spoke in English, not bothering to sign for Domot and Mo-keen. "Many of the Kiowas want to hear your Jesus talks. But there is a trouble that will not walk away. The council has decided that you must move off the reservation."

Isabel was devastated. Although she had feared the worst, she had not really expected it. A moment passed before she could reply. "What is that trouble?"

"You cannot live through the winter in your wagon. And you cannot build a house here."

Isabel felt a surge of hope. "It doesn't matter. I can survive somehow."

Aitsan shook his head. "You would freeze."

Isabel busied herself by refilling their dishes with pudding. She would *not* allow herself to be driven away simply because she did not have a place of her own.

She had been thinking of a possible solution in case the decision went against her.

"I can move down across the Washita, off the reservation. I'll saddle my horse and ride back here two or three times a week to give my Jesus talks."

Aitsan looked at her. "That is a half day's ride each way."

"I know that."

Aitsan said something in Kiowa to Domot and Mo-keen. The two older men seemed disturbed by Isabel's suggestion. They talked for a time in Kiowa. Then Mo-keen answered Isabel, flopping his right hand in the "no" sign.

Aitsan translated. "My father says that in the winter, when the wolves are hungry, they will eat you. He says the white men who have settled along that part of the Washita are bad. They drink whiskey, rob people, and shoot off their pistols for no reason. They would hurt you."

"I'm not afraid of them. Or the wolves," Isabel said.

Again Aitsan spoke in Kiowa. Aitsan and Mo-keen exchanged sharp words for several minutes.

After a brief silence, Aitsan translated. "He says you cannot do this. The council will not give you permission. They would ask the Army to keep you off the reservation before they would allow you to be hurt."

Struck by the complete ridiculousness of the situation, Isabel shook her head and laughed. Brother Clouse, Sister Everts, Lieutenant Ryan, the Mission Board, her family, even some of the Cheyennes had warned her of danger from the Kiowas. They had tried to stop her in order to protect her from the Indians.

Now the Indians were finding it necessary to protect her from the whites.

She had never felt so frustrated, so helpless. "I only want a place to lay my head. That's all I ask."

Aitsan did not answer. He seemed preoccupied, troubled. Again he withdrew into himself, shutting out the world. He stared into the distance, his eyes veiled and unseeing. Isabel resisted a silly impulse to wave a hand in front of his face and ask, "Mr. Aitsan, are you in there?"

She had seldom felt so comfortable with anyone on such brief acquaintance. In many respects he reminded her of her father—in his studious nature, in his seriousness.

The three Indians sat a long time in silence.

At last Aitsan raised a hand and pointed. "My tipi is over there about a mile. The Kiowa council let me build a little house with two rooms. In one we sleep. The other is a kitchen. In summer my wife cooks in a tipi. You can come and live with us and sleep in the kitchen."

Isabel was appalled. She remembered the filth and vermin among the Indians at Elk Creek. There she at least had been able to keep her distance. Whenever conditions became absolutely intolerable—as they often did—she could always find relief in her own quarters.

Never in all her planning for her own mission had she considered that she might have to take up the life of the Indians, sharing their fleas, lice, and bedbugs. The constant training school admonition against "going native" came to mind.

Yet Aitsan's invitation offered a solution. And it revealed an unexpected willingness on his part to help her.

She could not reject those exciting possibilities lightly.

She spoke to hide her indecision.

"I couldn't impose on you in that way, Mr. Aitsan. It would be too much of a burden on you and your family."

He spoke quietly but firmly. "It is the only way for you to stay on the reservation."

Isabel covertly studied him. His shoulder-length hair, his dark suit were clean. Perhaps he had learned some basic hygiene at the white man's school. And she had been favorably impressed by his wife.

The Aitsans appeared to be a cut above most Indians. Aitsan's offer might be a godsend.

But many questions remained. She must have answers before she could make her decision.

"Mr. Aitsan, I appreciate your offer. I know the sacrifice involved in taking a complete stranger into your home. Forgive me, but I must ask. Why are you doing this?"

Aitsan frowned, and for a moment Isabel thought that again she had gone too far. But when he spoke, his voice was gentle. "While I was a scout with the Army at Fort Sill, I interpreted for the Catholic church there. Later I interpreted for the Methodist Church in Anadarko. All the Indians here at Saddle Mountain know I have heard many wise talks. They come to me all-the-time with questions I cannot answer. I want to help them."

Isabel could not hide her surprise, her excitement over the revelation. "And this is the first time you've mentioned it! Did you receive instruction? Were you baptized? Why didn't you speak up when I asked at the arbor if there were any Christians present?"

Aitsan gave her his calm, quiet look before answering. "Two years ago Brother Weeks at Anadarko sprinkled some water on me and said I was a Christian. But I did not feel different."

"Some conversions are immediate," she explained. "Others may take years to come to full flower."

Aitsan seemed not to have heard. "All the time I interpreted for the churches, I hid the wise words of the Jesus men in my heart. Brother Methvin of the Methodist Church gave me a Bible. I have spent much time reading it and thinking hard about it. I now believe the Jesus road may be the right one for the Kiowas. But I don't know. I think the Kiowas should hear your Jesus talks."

Isabel was overjoyed. She could hardly contain her enthusiasm. "Mr. Aitsan, I'm *sure* the Jesus road is the right one. If I were not convinced of this, I wouldn't be here."

"There are many words in the Bible I do not know," Aitsan went on. "I prayed to the Great Father to send a Jesus man here to Saddle Mountain so I could learn. When He sent a Jesus woman, I did not like it. I thought maybe He was making funny with me. But now I think maybe when He sent you, He knew what He was doing."

Isabel closed her mouth. She sensed the time had arrived for *her* to remain silent for once.

Mo-keen and Domot had been sitting patiently through the exchange. Mo-keen spoke briefly to Aitsan in Kiowa. From his inflection, he seemed to be asking a question.

Clearly he was not pleased with Aitsan's answer. He replied angrily.

The two men argued. Rising from the wagon sheet, they strode off, still talking. They stopped at the bank of the creek. Soon their debate turned into a shouting match.

Domot seemed embarrassed. He gazed down at the wagon sheet and would not look at Isabel.

She touched his knee to gain his attention. "I don't want to cause trouble between them," she signed.

"This is not a new thing," Domot signed back. He glanced to make certain neither Aitsan nor Mo-keen was watching, and explained. "Mo-keen has been talking his son away from the Jesus road and onto the Ghost Dance road. He thinks that if you go to live with Aitsan, you will keep him on the Jesus road."

Isabel groaned.

Out of the frying pan and into the fire.

Aitsan and Mo-keen continued to storm at each other in Kiowa for several minutes.

As they returned, Isabel rose to meet them. "I do not want to cause trouble between you," she signed.

Mo-keen answered with abrupt gestures "If you go to live in the house of my son, the Kiowas will kick hard. There will be heaped-up trouble. They will abuse my son."

To prevent misunderstanding, he repeatedly pointed to his son's chest with the gesture for *abuse*, *scold*, or *throw lies*.

"It is my home," Aitsan said to Isabel in English. "I can invite anyone into it I want."

Mo-keen turned and walked toward the wagon.

Aitsan resumed his seat.

Mo-keen stood at the wagon with his back to them.

Isabel lowered herself into a sitting position on the wagon sheet. "Mr. Aitsan, if my moving into your home will make some of the Indians angry and cause even more division within the tribe, then it will serve no purpose."

"Only the Ghost Dance people will kick," Aitsan said. "Many Indians want to hear your Jesus talks."

One question remained: "What about the job of interpreter? Will you take it?"

Aitsan looked away. "I will try to find someone."

Isabel was exasperated. He had interpreted for the Catholics, the Methodists. Why not for her? "Mr. Aitsan, why are you so reluctant to accept the job, when you have been so helpful to me in other ways? You said you have experience. Surely a few hours of translation each week would not be as difficult as taking me into your own home."

Aitsan studied the motionless figure of Mo-keen beside the wagon for a time before he answered. "Translation is a hard thing to do," he said. "Words do not have the same meaning in both languages. The thoughts are different. There is no way to make them true."

"You can convey the general idea. That's all I want."

Aitsan would not meet her gaze. "When the government men came from Washington to talk about the Jerome Agreement, the son of Satank translated. His name was Joshua Given, and he was my best friend. We left the reservation together as boys and went away to Carlisle. When he translated at the Jerome talks, he did not understand all the government words. He made mistakes. The Kiowas thought they were leasing land, the same as they have done for years with the Texas ranchers. They put their marks on the white man's paper. Now the Kiowa lands are given to white men because of that mistake. A curse was put on Joshua Given. He died from it. On the day that happened, I said I would translate no more forever."

Isabel could not allow such a pagan belief to pass. "Mr. Aitsan, a person can't be killed by a curse. Surely you don't believe that!"

Aitsan glanced at her. "Miss Crawford, that is one way of death for a Kiowa. Every Kiowa walks his own road, maybe more than a white man. But he cannot live without the tribe. When the tribe throws him away, he dies."

"Mr. Aitsan, that is pure superstition!"

"No, it is true," he insisted. "When I was a boy, Kicking Bird gave the white soldiers the names of the Kiowas in the big fight at the agency. As the soldiers put Maman'-te into a wagon to take him to prison in Florida, Kicking Bird rode up on a gray horse. I was there. I heard Maman'-te tell Kicking Bird he would die for what he had done. And before the sun rose on another day, Kicking Bird was dead. The medicine curse is a serious thing, Miss Crawford. Don't make funny with it."

Domot guessed the subject from the names mentioned. He solemnly signed to Isabel that Kicking Bird and Joshua Given truly had been killed by bad spirits.

Isabel dropped the matter for concerns more immediate. "Mr. Aitsan, you know the limitations of sign language. If I'm to be of full benefit to the Kiowas, I must have an interpreter. Can't you see that you would be performing an invaluable service, not only for me, but for all the Kiowas?"

Again Aitsan frowned. "If I speak the wrong words, more Kiowas will make bad mistakes."

Isabel knew she needed Aitsan's complete cooperation. Living in an Indian home would be as strange as taking up residence on a distant planet. Brother Clouse and the Home Mission Board would be apoplectic at the mere thought.

She must have help communicating with the Indians. The only alternative was to return to Elk Creek in failure.

"Mr. Aitsan, I'll make a covenant with you," she said. "My board in Chicago sends me money to run a mission. I would expect to make contributions of food and clothing to your family. I'm an able-bodied woman, accustomed to hard work. I would expect to help your wife about the house. I've taught school. I would be happy to work with you, to further your already remarkable grasp of the English language, to help you to read your Bible and to understand it. I would be pleased to teach your children, to give them a start toward an education. All I ask in return is that you serve as my interpreter for an hour each Sunday morning, and again for an hour, only two or three nights a week. I will also pay you twelve dollars and fifty cents a month."

Isabel knew he would be tempted. Food was always in short supply among the Indians. Often the government rations were late. And opportunities to earn money were rare.

He did not answer for several minutes. When he spoke, his

hesitation conveyed his reluctance. "I will interpret for you, Miss Crawford. But only if I can put the English words in the Kiowa way."

Isabel understood. He was proposing to provide only a literal translation, retaining a sense of the Kiowa meaning and sentence structure, rather than attempt proper English.

"That would be agreeable."

"And I will not speak my own thoughts. I will speak only the words you tell me to say."

Isabel nodded her acceptance. She did not expect Aitsan to enter into the services.

Aitsan, Isabel, and Domot rose and walked across the glade to Mo-keen and the wagon. Aitsan and Mo-keen exchanged words. Mo-keen glared at Isabel with all the amenity of a thundercloud.

Isabel sensed that this was not the time to retreat.

"I know you are opposed to my staying," she signed. "When you told me about the melons, I understood. I promise you I will not be another burden to the Kiowas. This comes from my heart: If I see that I am causing more trouble among the Kiowas, I will leave the reservation."

Mo-keen spoke rapidly to Aitsan in Kiowa.

Aitsan interpreted.

"He said thank you for the coffee and the pudding. And he asks you to pardon us if we are careful. He said you should understand this: It is the white man who has made us so."

Chapter Four

Aitsan and his son Amos arrived late in the afternoon, riding double and bareback on a large paint horse, flanked by the yellow dogs. Isabel sat waiting on a log beside her loaded wagon, resting after having spent the entire day repacking her goods and tidying the campground.

For once Aitsan seemed in good spirits. He laughed as he swung Amos to earth. He dismounted and stood beside the horse, joshing and teasing the boy in Kiowa. He turned to Isabel. Already he habitually faced her when he spoke so she could read his lips, a consideration rare in her experience.

"We are having a big eat tonight to welcome you to my home," he said. "All the Saddle Mountain Kiowas will be there."

Isabel tried to hide her dismay. She would have preferred to arrive at Aitsan's home quietly. It seemed God did not want her to do anything in a corner.

From her Cheyenne adventures, she knew that a "big eat" meant a nightlong celebration. She was thankful that she had taken time for a quick sponge bath in the creek and to change into a clean Mother Hubbard. Of muslin, it was deep blue, a color becoming to her, but also sensible because it was dark enough not to show every smudge and grass stain.

"You shouldn't have gone to so much trouble," she told him. "But I'm honored."

He sent Amos to bring in her team. For a time he occupied himself with a length of rope, tying a wagon sheet securely over her load and testing the result. He stepped off the wagon and puttered around it, tightening the endgate rods, chocking the sideboards solidly against their straps.

"If there is trouble tonight, it will be a Kiowa thing. It will have nothing to do with you."

Isabel wondered exactly what he meant by "trouble." It could be anything from harsh words to a shooting.

"But it *will* be about me," she said.

Worry lines etched his forehead, but he did not answer. After a moment, he pointed toward the mountain. "Amos found your horses quick."

As Isabel looked up, Amos waved from the side of the mountain. Apparently confident of his control over the animals, he had removed the hobbles and carried them looped over his shoulders. Jonah frisked down the mountainside well ahead of the boy, kicking his heels high every few bounds, his ears laid back in mulish complaint. Jeremiah trotted along behind Jonah, head low, more cautious on the steep trail. Amos kept pace close behind them, leaping effortlessly from boulder to boulder.

As the horses drew near, Aitsan took a lariat from the wagon and moved out to intercept them.

Within minutes he harnessed the team. He handled Jonah with a firmness that brooked no nonsense. He even disdained the mule's hooves as he latched the trace chains.

Dusk was gathering rapidly as they left Isabel's camp. A full moon hung suspended over Saddle Mountain. Amos rode the paint, moving on ahead with the dogs. He guided the horse effortlessly at a fast trot with only a skimpy rope halter. Soon he was out of sight, apparently eager to reach the celebration well ahead of the wagon. Isabel clung to the spring seat as Aitsan drove over the hill and through a rugged, boulder-studded ravine. Two days before, Aitsan had removed the wheels, inserted shims, and packed the hubs with grease. The wagon now moved as if it were brand new.

Throughout the drive Aitsan remained silent, occasionally snapping the reins against Jonah's flank to keep him pulling his share of the load.

Isabel felt the beat of the drum before she was fully conscious of the sound. It came low and persistent on the night air, mingling with the moonlight; the mountain; the rumbling of the wagon; the fireflies rising from cactus, sage, and mesquite.

Riding beside Aitsan toward his home, listening to the primordial beat of the drum, Isabel felt she was being transported back to some primitive time on earth. She had not felt so totally alive since the first day she arrived at Elk Creek.

As they topped the last rise, Aitsan's home came into view. Around a huge fire more than a hundred Indians stood in welcome.

Isabel's breath stopped in sheer surprise.

Every single Indian was in full costume.

It was as if all that was drab and mundane in the world had been magically transformed. The bright colors seemed endless in their variety.

She thought of how dull she must look in her shapeless old Mother Hubbard.

As Aitsan drove the wagon into the yard, the drum shifted into a strange double beat. The Indians turned to face her and began a chant: "Hey-yeah-yeah-yeah! Hey-yeah-yeah-yeah!"

Aitsan's wife, Mabel, stood a few steps in front of the group. She wore a beaded buckskin dress gaily emblazoned in red, yellow, and blue designs. Aitsan leaped to the ground and helped Isabel from the wagon. The chanting stopped.

The drumbeat continued. Mabel approached Isabel, her gaze downcast in her habitual shyness. She spoke in English.

"Miss Crawford, I am so glad you have come to live in my house that I cannot say it."

Not expecting anything half so grand, Isabel was taken unaware by a rush of emotion. She brushed aside quick tears and embraced Mabel.

Amos and his sister Jessie came running through the crowd. Both were in costume, their faces painted in bright primary colors. Amos wore lavishly decorated buckskin, and a crown of eagle feathers tied under his chin with a black string. Jessie's little fringed and beaded dress was knee-length. Her high-shanked moccasins were trimmed with red and blue beads and silver buttons.

Isabel knelt and hugged the children.

The crowd fell back.

"We will show you your new home," Aitsan said.

Like everything else in Aitsan's life, his home was a compromise between two worlds.

In front of the house stood two large tipis and a brush arbor, an arrangement typical of every Indian "home" in the territory. Beyond lay a post oak corral, feed troughs, and clapboard sheds identical to those of the white homesteaders. Near the brush arbor a side of beef turned on a spit over a glowing bed of coals. Wagons, tents, saddle horses, dogs, and Indians littered the landscape as far as Isabel could see into the night.

The house was hardly more than a chicken coop, a faithful copy of the frontier shelters white settlers were erecting all over the territory. Isabel followed Mabel inside. The small front room was lit by a single lamp. The rough plank floor was bare of furniture, save two ladder-back, cane-bottom chairs, and a long bare-plank table against the far wall that held the lamp, stacks of enameled tin "graniteware" dishes, a water bucket, and a single dipper. The ceiling was so low that Aitsan walked with his head bent.

He picked up the lamp and gestured toward the far wall. "We will put your cot over there."

Isabel followed Aitsan and Mabel into the other room. It was no larger. A big family bed lay on the floor. Assorted clothing, draped from nails, decorated all four walls. The floor was covered with dirt and mud tracked in from the yard, the corral, and places Isabel did not dare speculate upon.

She wondered how she could possibly survive stuffed into this tiny place with a family of Indians. With children, dogs, and Indians underfoot, how would she ever manage all the correspondence required in running a mission, begging money, urging donations, and keeping dozens of church congregations interested and involved?

Surely she would be able to make other arrangements before winter. She consoled herself with that thought.

"It's very nice," she said.

Aitsan's smile danced among the shadows in the moving lamplight as he guided her back into the front room. "Mabel will take you out to the tipi."

As Isabel and Mabel emerged from the house, Loki Mo-keen and Domot were rolling back the flaps of the nearest tipi. They continued with their work until a full third of the covering was tucked aside, exposing the interior. The walls were decorated with artfully arranged bunches of beaded eagle feathers, buckskin dresses, bows, arrows, painted war shields, rifles and revolvers, and blankets that rivaled Joseph's coat of many colors.

Mabel led Isabel to a seat of honor near a small fire at the center of the tipi. Mo-keen, Domot, Taboodle, Red Eagle, Odlepaugh, and other Indians seated themselves around the fire with great decorum, in a pecking order Isabel could not fathom. Nor could she read Mo-keen's impassive expression. He sat staring straight ahead, as if contemplating some great problem.

Red Eagle signed to her without smiling, "Tonight we scalp you."

Isabel laughed aloud at his dry humor.

A few minutes later Aitsan entered the tipi, so changed in appearance that Isabel almost failed to recognize him. His face was painted red and yellow. He wore fringed buckskin leggings and a long white shirt painted with bright red-and-blue tipis, stars, and buffalo. An ornate beaded belt with blue and yellow designs encircled his waist. Strips of beaver bound his hair into abbreviated braids. He took his seat beside her.

The tipi quickly filled with Indians. The rest gathered close outside.

Aitsan spoke to Isabel. "Miss Crawford, would you ask the Great Father to bless our food?"

The drum had not stopped. It seemed to anticipate Isabel's every heartbeat. As she groped for words, a delightful thought intruded: She would have a wonderful story for her report to the Home Mission Board. Surely few missionaries from the Chicago society had prayed under more exotic conditions.

She pushed the distraction aside and concentrated on her prayer.

"Dear Father in heaven: Please bless our food, and help us to do thy work here on earth so that we may earn our place in heaven. Please help us to learn more about Jesus. And as the Kiowas have welcomed me into their hearts this night, may You welcome them someday into Your kingdom. This I pray in Jesus's name. Amen."

Aitsan spoke a few short, terse commands in Kiowa. Stacks of graniteware cups and plates were passed. Large handfuls of knives, forks, and spoons made the rounds. Tin pails filled with sizzling beef followed, accompanied by an abundance of pinto beans and canned peaches. Amos, Jessie, and other children moved about the tipi, pouring coffee.

Isabel had gone all day without food. She was famished. The beans and beef were especially delicious.

The Kiowas ate with enthusiasm and little talk.

Isabel sat savoring the variety of food flavors. Thrilled by the spectacle around her, she almost forgot that her Mother Hubbard seemed a paltry smudge against such brilliance. But as she sipped the fragrant, robust coffee, she felt high color rising to her cheeks, a warmth in her eyes.

She had not felt so giddy since the parties of her school days in Ontario. She was filled with a heady sense of well-being. Surely this communion of spirit was fertile ground for the work ahead.

When the meal was completed, each diner stacked his or her own dishes and they were passed back to the tipi entrance, where they were whisked away. Soap, pans of water, and flour-sack towels were circulated.

Isabel was amused and impressed. The entire dinner had been served from beginning to end without a single step by the host or hostess.

Aitsan added wood to the fire at the center of the tipi. Standing beside it, he began to speak in Kiowa. His tone and expression remained deeply serious. He spoke for several minutes, his rich baritone in complete harmony with the steady beat of the unseen drum.

From behind Isabel came a stir of male voices raised in obvious dissent.

Aitsan gestured for silence and for a time talked over them.

The voices of protest would not be denied. At least a dozen Indians began yelling at Aitsan. Others, apparently siding with Aitsan, shouted them down.

The atmosphere inside of the tipi became bedlam.

Not a single Indian would meet Isabel's gaze, confirming that she was the subject of the quarrel.

As she sat wondering what to do, Mo-keen rose to his feet, his face a thundercloud. He raised a hand, pointed, and barked several words in Kiowa.

The tempest was stilled. Only the beat of the drum continued on the night air.

From behind Isabel came sounds of movement and subdued mutterings. Against her will, she turned to look.

Several Indians were leaving the tipi. Among them were Little Robe, Amonstake, Pie-gad, and Paudlekeah. At her Jesus talk they had been introduced as powerful men of the tribe.

She glanced at Aitsan, searching for any sign of emotion. His soft brown eyes revealed nothing.

She wished she could tell him that she would sleep out in the woods on the bare ground before she would bring more pain to him, his family, and the Kiowas. But the tension in the tipi remained at high pitch. She sensed that she should not intervene.

Slowly the rumble of departing wagons died away. Mo-keen spoke angrily to Aitsan and abruptly sat down.

Aitsan resumed his talk. At last he looked down at Isabel and spoke to her in English: "Many here want to say words of welcome to you. I will translate for them."

Isabel hesitated. She could not pretend that the dispute never happened. Whatever the consequence, she could not remain on the reservation under false colors.

"Mr. Aitsan, I thank you for this marvelous reception. But I meant what I told your father. If my presence here is the cause of more trouble among the Kiowas, I will move off the reservation tonight."

Aitsan glanced toward his father before answering. "This is the cause of the trouble: I told the Ghost Dance people they must put all their hot words behind them and cut off all bad thoughts about the Jesus talks, because most of us want to hear them. I said that while you are living in my house, you are the same as a Kiowa, and they must think of you as my sister."

Isabel's eyes filled with emotion. She doubted that any welcoming speech would top that.

Mo-keen sat watching the byplay. It was his scolding that had sent the dissidents on their way.

"What did your father say to them?"

"He told them they dishonored all Kiowas by causing trouble tonight in my tipi. He told them that if they could not welcome you into the home of his son, they should leave."

The other Indians sat motionless, gazes downcast, waiting. Isabel studied them, seeking to sense their mood. They now seemed withdrawn, distant.

The dispute appeared to be more a matter of honor than a defense of her presence on the reservation. In the wake of all the pain and suffering the Kiowas had endured—and all they had yet to face—she should not burden them further.

Not only had she brought dissension and division among the Kiowas, she also had placed Aitsan and his family firmly in the middle of the trouble. And they were her best friends on the reservation.

"Mr. Aitsan, my Jesus talks will be meaningless if they are awash in ill feelings. You may make the announcement now. Tomorrow I will move my camp across the Washita. I can ride back to the reservation two or three times a week to give my Jesus talks. I think that will be the best course for the Kiowas, and especially for you and your family."

Aitsan held up a hand, palm outward. "Miss Crawford, listen to what these people have to say to you. Then if you still want to go, I will tell them."

He nodded to Ah-to-mah. She rose, smoothed her dress, and came to stand in front of Isabel. She spoke, and Aitsan translated. "I am glad you have come here to give your Jesus talks. Our horses are poor and we cannot go the seventeen miles to Rainy Mountain to hear the Jesus man there. Sometimes we want to pray to Jesus, but we do not know Him. I will come to your Jesus talks and listen hard."

Isabel thanked her and shook her hand.

Ananthy, the wife of Odlepaugh, was next. She was a tall woman with a sad and beautiful face. Tall and of fragile appearance, she was as gracefully muscled and strong as a Thoroughbred.

Ananthy spoke quietly, her voice musical with the lilting tones, the rising and falling pitches of the language.

Aitsan translated her words.

"When I heard about the Jesus road I did not think it was for me, because I knew I was mean and cranky. I did not think Jesus was looking for that kind of people. I still do not know much about Jesus. But I have been to the white man's Jesus house at Rainy Mountain four times. Each time when I left, I was like a bird up in the sky that comes down to drink. I do not know why you have come to live among us poor Kiowas, but I am glad you are here. I hope we can build a Jesus house here so I can take a good long drink of sweet living water often and feel better."

Isabel opened her mouth to reply but found she had no words. Instead she rose and hugged the woman.

Next, Spotted Horse stepped up and shook Isabel's hand vigorously. "No white Jesus man ever sat down with us. One Jesus woman all alone among Indians and not scared! You trust us. This is good."

Kokom held Isabel's hand and spoke briefly. "We thank you for coming. We will listen to your words and think hard. Maybe the Jesus road is for us. I do not know. Our thank-you to Jesus is still way-ahead."

"I am forty-five years old," said a husky, gloriously painted brave named Ah-mot-ah-ah. "All of my life I have followed every crossroad I came to. I heard about the Bible and the Jesus days. The Jesus man at Anadarko told me that the Great Father loves me, but I do not see how this is so. When the Jesus man said the Great Father gave His Son to save me, I was ashamed, because I did not know what he was talking about. I do not know now. I am glad you came here. I want to hear everything about Jesus and think hard."

A big Indian the whites called Smokey stood before Isabel with a wide smile. She had seen him several times at Elk Creek. His nose was huge, and deep laugh lines gave his face considerable character. "You will be the first Jesus woman to live at Saddle Mountain," he said, his eyes bright with amusement. "We are all great gamblers and hard drinkers here. You have much work to do."

An older Indian named Tone-gah-gah spoke in soft, hesitant tones: "I can remember away back, to the long-ago times. Our grandfathers were very wicked, fighting white people and other tribes. When I was a young man I never heard one word about Jesus. When I heard that a Jesus woman was here, I rode over the mountain to see Aitsan to see if it was true. I went to the brush arbor to hear the Jesus talk, and I keep the words here in my heart. I was surprised that the Jesus woman was so little. Maybe the Kiowas on the other side of the mountain will laugh at me, but I don't care. I want to know about this other life in heaven. I am glad you have come here to tell us about it."

An even more ancient Indian came forward. Aitsan introduced him as Queototi. His eyes were clouded and pale. "I am an old man," he said. "I have done a lot of work for the devil, and he gave me bullets for it. I carry them in my body yet. My wife has gone over to that other world, and now I am sad and I cry a lot. I am like a worm on a tree that feels around for something to take hold of, and when he finds it, he jumps over. I search and search and search, and I find nothing. Maybe your Jesus talks will give me something to hold on to."

Isabel could not contain her tears.

Never had she heard spiritual hunger so beautifully described—not in her father's congregations, not in Chicago's Black Hole, not during her three years at Elk Creek.

Her earlier decision was abandoned in that moment. Wild horses could not drag her off the reservation until she found this man comfort.

Lacking a handkerchief, she blotted her cheeks with the loose sleeves of her Mother Hubbard. She reached for Aitsan's arm. "Tell Mr. Queototi I am sure Jesus will give him something to hold on to."

A tall, unusually handsome Indian with a broad face, wide mouth, and beautiful hands stepped forward to tower over Isabel. He stood with the trail of his gorgeous blankets draped over a forearm, Roman style. Isabel remembered him from her first Jesus talk, and recalled his name—Tonemoh—even before Aitsan spoke it aloud.

Tonemoh began a formal speech.

"A few years ago the Kiowas sent my brother Ahpeatone and some others beyond the high mountains to the west. They told him to look upon the Paiute who said he was Jesus come back to earth to kill all the whites and to return the buffalo to us. My brother Ahpeatone looked at him one time and came right back here and told us that the Ghost Dance was one big lie. He told me, 'Tonemoh, I have visited many,

many tribes. I have tried all the religions of the Indians. They are short. None of them leads all the way through.' He told me, 'Tonemoh, I think maybe the Jesus road is the one true road. I think it goes all the way through. I have two wives and cannot put my feet on it. But I want you to look for it till you find it and pick it up quick.' I have thought hard about what my brother said, for he was a smart Indian. Now I am happy you have come here to make Jesus talks, because I want to look at the Jesus road and see if it is for me."

One by one, forty-two Indians came forward to offer their words of welcome, their reasons for wanting to hear her Jesus talks. Throughout, Isabel battled to keep her emotions under control.

She would do her best to convey the words of the Indians to the Mission Board, and the sincerity of the welcome she had received from them. But words could not possibly describe the sadness, the desolation she saw in their eyes.

It was Pope-bah, the wife of Kokom, who shattered her poise completely for the remainder of the night.

"I am so glad you have come to live among us that I am ashamed I have nothing to give you to make your heart happy," Pope-bah said. "When you write to your mother, tell her we love her because she did not keep you at home."

Isabel was emotionally undone. She had called these people savages! In her unthinking arrogance, she had assumed that months, perhaps years of preparation would be required before most of the Indians could comprehend Christianity.

But surely anyone capable of understanding a mother's love in giving a daughter would understand a Father's love in giving a Son.

Isabel wept for a time before she could compose herself sufficiently to respond. At last she stood and faced the group. Aitsan interpreted her words.

"Every day I have prayed to the Great Father, hoping that I was doing the right thing in coming here. I have had many doubts. I often thought about going back to Elk Creek, or maybe across the Washita. But now your wonderful welcome tonight has convinced me that I did the right thing in coming to the reservation. I will remember this night and what you have said. I will keep your words in my heart and treasure them always."

After she took her seat, Aitsan gestured toward the entrance of the tipi. "Now Amos wants to welcome you to our home with a Rabbit Dance."

With much encouragement from the adults, Amos walked to the center of the tipi. He wore a shirt and leggings of yellow buckskin with white fringes. His hair was woven with beaver fur into long braids under his crown of eagle feathers. A multicolored sash encircled his waist, and a beaded band hung over one shoulder, crossing his chest. Here and there, medallions had been sewn into the costume. He stood with utter seriousness, knees bent, one moccasin tapping the earth as if absorbing the beat of the drum. Slowly he put his hands to his ears. With two fingers of each hand extended, he began a series of hops that were for all the world like those of a rabbit.

Isabel clasped her hands in delight. Around her the Kiowas began a chant she assumed to be lyrics, telling the story of the rabbit.

Aitsan spoke into Isabel's conversation tube, translating:

Dance and be happy,
Dance and be happy,
Let your ears wave back and forth,
And up and down,
Because that is the way we Rabbits dance.

The performance continued several minutes, as stylized as a ballet. When it ended, there was no applause. But shouted comments and smiling faces assured Amos that he had performed well.

Isabel took his hands in hers. "That was not only the first Rabbit Dance I've ever seen. I'll bet it will be the best I'll ever see."

Aitsan translated. Grinning, Amos ducked his head shyly and backed away.

"In the old days, the Rabbit Society was the first step on the road toward becoming a warrior," Aitsan told Isabel. "Young Rabbits were taught how to shoot arrows, ride horses, run, swim, track animals—all the things he would do as a warrior. In six or eight years, after he had learned all of these things, he would be taken into the *adaltoyup*—the Young Wild Sheep—and he would ride on raids. When he proved his manhood, he would be taken into a warrior society. Now there are no warrior societies. Not even the Young Sheep. The little Rabbits have nothing ahead of them."

"Were you a Rabbit?" Isabel asked.

She would have loved to see Aitsan, with his ever-serious expression, hopping about as a boy.

Aitsan nodded. "And a Young Sheep. We were driven onto the reservation before I became a warrior."

Again the drumbeat altered slightly in tone. Aitsan gestured for Isabel to reverse her seated position. As she turned, she experienced a moment of disorientation.

The space in front of the tipi was magically converted into a stage as a dance circle formed. The tipi, only moments before the backdrop for Amos, now became choice seating for the dances, with its walls serving as a shell to capture the beat of the drum, the chants of the dancers. Isabel marveled over the ingenuity.

The reverberations of the drum deepened, and more than a dozen dancers began to move. Each wore buckskin leggings, a red breechclout, and a black blanket wrapped around the waist. Their moccasins were beaded with colorful designs. Silver bells bobbed on the toes; Isabel would have given a king's ransom to have heard them, but their sound was too high for her hearing. Long buckskin streamers trailed from the heels of every moccasin. Most of the Indians wore two strings of beads crisscrossed, one red, one silver. Each dancer was crowned with a headdress of porcupine quills arranged in a narrow strip from front to back and topped by a single eagle feather. Each carried a red and blue blanket draped across the shoulders. In the left hand each held an eagle feather, and in the right a brightly painted gourd rattle.

Isabel now saw why the drum so dominated the night. It was huge. Six or eight men were seated around it, beating the rhythm, chanting with each stroke. The sound seemed to rise out of the earth itself. The steady beat throbbed in her mind, throughout her body.

"That is the thunder drum," Aitsan said. "When you hear thunder in the Wichitas, you will remember it."

"I'm sure I shall," Isabel said. "What is this dance? What is its meaning?"

Aitsan hesitated. "It is called the *goon-gah*. It was given to the *Tiah-pah*—a Kiowa warrior society—a long time ago. It tells this story: A warrior was lost. As he hunted for his tribe, he heard beautiful singing. He looked over a hill, and there was a red wolf with a gourd in his paw, dancing. The warrior watched the dance and listened to the words of the song. When the red wolf had ended the dance, he looked at the warrior and told him in Kiowa that he was giving that dance to the Kiowa people. He said the dance would remain with the Kiowas as long as they lived on the face of the earth. When the *goon-gah* is done right, it takes a long time. There are opening ceremonies. Many stories have been added to it. Tonight the dancers are doing only a little of it, because the songs are good, and they like to do them."

Later the tempo changed, and women joined in the dance. The chanting became more melodious, with lilting inflections. Isabel assumed from the expressions that the lyrics were more playful. She asked Aitsan.

"*Gomda dawgyah,*" he said. "Wind songs." He watched the dancers for a time, as if deciding on a way to explain. "In the long-ago time, the grandmothers sang for their grandsons, away on the warpath. They wanted them to be brave, and to do brave things, so they would win a good woman when they returned." The first and middle fingers of his right hand tapped the beat into his left palm as he translated a verse:

The land is wide.
When man travels upon it
He will never reach the end.
But because there is a prize offered
To test a man to go as far as he dares,
He goes because he wants to discover his limits.

The dances, chants, and songs continued for hours.

Isabel sat as if under a spell. Exhausted, emotionally spent, she was too captivated to go to bed. Never in all her life had she been so completely charmed, so totally enthralled.

After midnight, prudence won. She rose and said good night.

"Amos has set up your bed," Aitsan said. "It is ready for you."

Alone in the dark house, Isabel removed her dress, donned her nightgown, and slipped between the blankets.

After more than a month of living in a wagon box, the canvas cot felt heavenly.

She remained awake for a time, listening to the drum, the chants, wondering what lay ahead for her, for the Kiowas.

Obviously her presence had deepened serious rifts within the tribe. This she regretted. But she knew now that she belonged on the reservation. There was much work to be done here.

Chapter Five

Twenty-seven Indians sat patiently in the yard, awaiting supper. The day had been sweltering, and now the late-afternoon shadows from Saddle Mountain offered only slight relief. Faint from the heat, Isabel peeled another dozen potatoes and added them to the pot.

"That's all," she signed to Mabel. "If any more Indians come, they will go away hungry."

Mabel smiled, sank to the floor, and began to feed the baby. Amos, Jessie, and a half dozen of their friends tore through the house, fleeing in mock terror from one of the yellow pups. A hen stuck her head in the door, spied some dried beans Isabel had dropped, and gathered her feet to hop over the sill. Isabel crossed the room and shooed her and the rest of the surviving chickens away from the door.

Only three laying hens were left of the eighteen—and the lone "Mr. Hen"—which Lucius had brought home from Kansas six weeks ago. Heat and pox had accounted for six and wolves for the rest.

With signs, Isabel asked Mabel to watch the stew and see that it did not boil over. She then went into the bedroom, where Pope-bah sat on the floor beside her daughter Montahahty, who was just entering the first stages of labor.

Isabel made the question sign.

"I think the baby will not come out for a long time," Pope-bah replied. "My way-behind little one is very sick. The baby hides. He does not want to come out."

Isabel knelt beside Montahahty and bathed her angelic face with a damp rag. It was the only comfort she could offer. Hardly more than a child herself, Montahahty lay with eyes shut, teeth clenched against the pain.

This would be her third baby. The last two had died in infancy.

Isabel placed both hands on Montahahty's stomach. The baby seemed to be in the right position, but she could not be certain. Isabel thought Pope-bah was probably correct: Chances were that Montahahty would not enter serious labor for several hours yet.

Isabel bathed the young mother's face and comforted her for a while before returning to the kitchen.

Testing the potatoes with a fork, Isabel determined that the stew was done. She moved the pot to the serving table and crossed to the door.

"Chuck!" she called into the yard.

It was the one word of English every Indian knew. They quickly formed a line at the door. The eldest assumed places at the head of the line. Immediately behind were the council chiefs, and thereafter the remainder of the men. The women quietly went to the end of the line to form their own pecking order.

Isabel stood in the doorway of the stifling shack and said grace. She spoke the words in English, and signed them for the benefit of the Indians.

One by one the Indians entered. Each picked up a granite-ware plate. Mabel helped serve the food. Carrying heaped-up plates, the Indians filed back into the yard and sat cross-legged under the brush arbor. They adeptly balanced the plates on their laps as they ate.

Isabel and Mabel moved among them, pouring coffee and tea from large pots.

When Isabel returned to the kitchen and brought out the three chocolate cakes, a murmur of surprise swept through the males under the arbor. Isabel heard grumblings of dissatisfaction.

The men were unhappy she had hidden the cakes. They much preferred to eat sweets first.

"Whites always walk the sly road," Odlepaugh signed to her.

Isabel did not know if he were joking, but she could not suppress her anger. She had spent all afternoon cooking for them.

"Indians always walk the softest road they can find," she signed back. "That is why they are sinking into the ground."

Odlepaugh did not reply. But more angry mutterings came from the group, calculatedly too low for Isabel to hear the words, even if she understood Kiowa.

She returned to the house, picked up a cloth and towel, and stole away to the creek for the one brief interval of privacy in her daily routine.

Smaller than Saddle Mountain Creek, the tiny branch that coursed through the Aitsan pasture remained dry much of the year. But the mountain served as a giant sponge. For weeks, even months after heavy rains, moisture seeped from the base of the mountain, sending a trickle down the tiny creek. Isabel had found a spot curtained by trees and heavy brush. She thought of it as her own. The Indians seemed to respect her need to be alone for a few minutes each evening.

She was hot and tired after a long day of cooking for the Indians. Lucius, Domot, and Mo-keen were away from the reservation again, fulfilling a freight contract with the Army. Tonight she must give her Jesus talk in sign language—an extra burden that always sapped her remaining energy.

She wet her cloth and bathed as well as she could under the circumstances. Removing shoes and stockings, she sat on a low boulder and soaked her feet, relishing that simple luxury.

It was the first time she had relaxed for a moment since well before daylight.

Miss Burdette and the Mission Board had questioned her tactic of cooking for the Indians. But missions all over the world used food for bait, and after a long exchange of letters, she had convinced the Board. Her budget had been increased to accommodate the additional expenses.

The plan seemed to be working. At least thirty or forty Indians came each evening to eat and to hear her Jesus talk. Isabel had created a captive audience. But sometimes she wondered how long she could endure the extra work.

During her two months with Mabel and Lucius Ben Aitsan, she had fallen so quickly into a routine that now it seemed no other world existed.

No day was ever long enough. Each morning she awoke

and hurried to complete her toilet before the Aitsans stirred. She overcame the lack of privacy with tricks learned in girl-hood during long Canadian winters, when the entire family dressed and undressed around a roaring fire. Her mother had taught her how to change from nightgown to daywear without exposing any part of the body. Merely by slipping arms from the sleeves of a nightgown, a loose tent could be created under which to work. At bedtime, the process was reversed.

Indians began arriving with daylight and waited under the arbor for handouts. Twice each day she opened the mission stores in the spare Aitsan tipi and dispensed clothing. The missionary barrel had been popular, drawing Indians from the far corners of the reservation.

Throughout the day she doctored cuts, and administered basic remedies to the sick.

In the mornings she conducted English classes for adults. In the afternoons she taught the younger children. Both groups already had moved through the alphabet and were constructing simple sentences from standard missionary dog-cat-horse drawings.

In the evenings she gave her Jesus talks under the Aitsan brush arbor. Slowly she was working her way through the Book of Luke.

Each day held a sameness that taxed her spirits.

The hot, dry wind that persisted throughout the summer months almost seemed a living thing. Often she felt it would blow away what sanity she had managed to preserve.

Surrounded by humans, she was beset by loneliness.

There now seemed little hope the Mission Board would ever send a sister-companion. At the moment there were no facilities.

Aside from Lucius, Isabel had no one to talk with. Mabel understood some English, but how much, Isabel was never able to determine.

"She is afraid she will make a funny mistake," Lucius explained one evening. "So she does not speak at all."

Isabel was disappointed with her own progress in Kiowa. She had found it a most difficult language. Sign language remained her chief means of communication.

The problem of dirt, filth, and vermin around her defied solution. No matter how hard she scrubbed, dust was every-where. Flies from the stables were a constant menace. The Indians were hosts to fleas, ticks, and body lice. Covered with parasites, every Indian was a tribe unto himself. Isabel had showed them how to eradicate the pests with turpentine or coal oil. But her efforts had aroused little interest. The bedding in most tipis was infested with bedbugs. Isabel had tried to convince the Indians that the vermin could be eliminated, but they seemed to prefer to scratch.

She had worked to establish a measure of sanitation about the house but had received absolutely no cooperation. Mabel possessed a sweet, pliable disposition, but she remained blind to the very conditions Isabel found so disturbing. Amos and Jessie were sent out daily to gather cowchips and horse apples. The dried dung was used as cooking fuel, and the cloying odor never went away.

Snakes, scorpions, centipedes, and spiders were even more prevalent at Saddle Mountain than they had been at Elk Creek. Lucius insisted that the rattlesnakes were harmless if one did not foolishly crowd them. The Indians did not seem concerned that everyone saw rattlers almost every day, usually scurrying under rocks or into brush. The children played outdoors, and no one worried about them. In fact, Amos and his friends sometimes made a game of catching rattlers by the tail and popping their heads off by swinging them like a whip. When Isabel expressed her horror, and her fear for the children, Lucius had merely laughed and said he had done the same as a boy.

After three years in the territory, she had learned to live with scorpions; one never donned shoes or clothing until after a thorough shaking. Centipedes were her special aversion. They seemed to lurk beneath every rock and stick. Although not dangerous, their stings were extremely painful.

Both Mabel and Lucius resisted any discussion of personal matters. Isabel had managed to convince Lucius to call her "Sister Crawford" or plain "Sister" and now addressed him as "Lucius" instead of "Mr. Aitsan," but any suggestion of intimacy stopped there. Little private information was volunteered. Isabel had lived with them six weeks before she learned that Mabel was Domot's baby sister.

Lucius had neglected to mention the fact.

And Domot had never given the slightest indication that he and Lucius were brothers-in-law.

The discoveries further convinced Isabel that the tribal structure was intricate and that she had much to learn. Family ties appeared stronger than those among most whites. Yet tribal and council loyalties often intervened, even in close blood relationships. The social arrangement posed a mystery Isabel longed to explore.

But she had little time for such matters.

From the time she awoke in the morning until she tumbled into her cot at night, she worked. Mostly, she cooked.

During her first two months with the Aitsans, no meal had been served with fewer than nine at the table or brush arbor. On one memorable evening, thirty-five Indians from the other side of the mountain had descended like a cloud of locusts, devouring everything in sight. Impromptu visits seemed customary among the Kiowas, and guests took care to arrive just before mealtime. Government rations had been skimpy in recent weeks. Isabel could not in good conscience turn anyone away.

During the past four weeks she had sent Lucius to Anadarko for supplies three times. Now her funds were running low.

She had written long letters to the Mission Board, explaining the situation. Miss Burdette had replied that money was short, and Isabel simply must make do for a while.

Isabel was discouraged. She did not know how long she could keep her makeshift mission operating.

The Indians absorbed her Jesus talks like sponges—and did nothing. After two months she had no converts and was no closer to building a church than on the day she arrived. Her grand plans for a mission now seemed ridiculous when she faced the fact that she was living amid squalor in a two-room shack with a family of Indians.

Nothing in training school—not even her work in the Black Hole of Chicago—had prepared her for such a miserable existence.

Often she went a week or more without a change of clothes.

Within the short space of a few weeks, she had committed the unpardonable in missionary work. She had descended to the standard of the Indians instead of bringing them up to hers.

Isabel moved about the yard in the deepening dusk, lighting lanterns around the brush arbor.

Her dark mood and exhaustion pushed her to a talk she had been considering for weeks.

Tonight she would set Luke and the spiritual aside for the moment and offer a theme more practical.

For weeks she had delivered nothing but tranquil talks, disturbing no one. She felt it high time to stir her little congregation to its foundation.

She waited until the Indians were settled and she had their undivided attention. She stood on a coffee box platform under the Aitsan arbor, facing them. Summer moths circled the lanterns and sent shadows dancing.

"The Great Father has watched you sit day after day, doing nothing but eating and talking," she signed. "He does not look down upon you with happy eyes. If he had made the road for you to eat and talk and nothing else, he would have given you no hands, no legs, and no feet. He would have given you only a mouth and a big chuck-bag. The Great Father put hands and feet on you for you to use."

By the silence and frozen faces, Isabel knew the Indians were offended, but at the moment, she was past caring.

"I have heard much bad talk from you because the government is late again with the rations. I now speak the truth: My heart does not cry for you. The Indian should not sit and wait for the white man to bring his chuck. He should look to himself and to the Great Father."

A disgruntled murmur swept through the congregation. Isabel ignored it and continued her theme: "When you plant corn, the Great Father sends the sun and the rain to make it grow. He does the hard part. You should try to please Him, and do your part. He could send the women-with-wings to plow for you, but He does not. How could we show Him we love Him if the women-with-wings did everything for us? All of you who plowed today made His heart glad. All of you who sat on your hind ends and did nothing made Him sad."

Odlepaugh rose to his full height and furiously made the "cut it off" sign.

Isabel folded her arms and waited.

Odlepaugh spoke in Kiowa and signed for Isabel's benefit.

"In the long-ago time, the Great Father gave Indians the land where we now stand, and all the land in every direction. He put the buffalo on this land so the Indian did not have to work. The Indian only had to hunt the buffalo. Before white men came we were happy all the time and seldom got mad. Now we cannot eat white-man food. We have no Indian food. When we are hungry we get mad quick and want to fight."

A murmur of agreement came from the men around him. Odlepaugh went on as if he had not heard.

"Old Odlepaugh was a great war chief in the long-ago time. My father, Satanta, gave me his name. When Old Odlepaugh got mad he bit the noses off his wives. He bit the noses off three of them and turned them loose. He was the greatest warrior who ever walked this earth. When we went on the warpath with him, we rode till the food gave out and then we ate our horses and kept on going. We were looking for just one thing: white men. When we found them, we fought them hard. The white men took our land and put us on this little ground. Now there is talk that they are coming to take all that is left and move us over again. I have heard the Jesus man at Rainy Mountain. He said we are to forgive our enemies. I cannot. But I can no longer fight. The old roads are passing away, and none is left for the Indian. The Jesus man at Rainy Mountain said Jesus will come back to earth soon, put the sheep Christians on one side, the goat Christians on the other, and burn up this world. I think Jesus is wise. I think that is what should be done. Jesus cannot do it quick enough for me."

Again a murmur of agreement swept through the congregation. Isabel rapidly signed her reply:

"If you think that, then you should get on the Jesus road at a high lope. I don't know when Jesus is coming again. Men have been waiting nineteen hundred winters. Maybe He will come next week. Maybe He will not come in our lives. But when He comes, all of you should be on His road. If Jesus comes and you are not on His road, He will throw you away. If you are on His road, He will take you where there is no more hungry and no more crying. That He promises you."

Odlepaugh again made the "cut it off" sign. "If the Jesus road is heaped-up great, why did the white soldiers not tell us about it when they drove us to the reservation? Why? Why? I will tell you. I think the Jesus road was made only for the white man, not for the Indian."

Isabel signed without thinking: "If you think that, you are a foolish man."

Odlepaugh stared at her for a long moment. Then, with dignity, he turned and walked toward the horse corral.

A buzz of excited voices arose from the seated Indians.

Only then did Isabel remember that the sign for "foolish"

was the same as for "crazy"—but quickly followed by the sign for "little."

She had forgotten to add the diminutive.

She had called Odlepaugh crazy.

Few insults were greater to an Indian.

She considered running after him, but communication would be impossible in the dark.

After a moment, she heard his horse trot away into the night.

She ended her talk with some thoughts from Luke, and a prayer.

Returning to the house, she found Montahahty in labor. While waiting, Isabel washed and scoured the stove and swept the kitchen. By the time she had finished, the Indians were gone from the yard. Mabel put the children to bed in her cot in the front room.

Isabel, Pope-bah, and Mabel began their long vigil.

Two hours before dawn, Montahahty delivered a baby girl.

The infant was underweight, perhaps a month premature, but healthy. Isabel helped Pope-bah and Mabel clean both mother and child. Then Isabel returned to the front room, blew out the lamp, and sank onto a blanket in the corner, fully clothed.

Her humiliation was complete. She had managed to insult one of the most influential Indians on the reservation. In doing so, she also had insulted Lucius, who had shown her every kindness, even to taking her into his own home and telling everyone she was the same as his sister.

Isabel burned with shame.

But she was too exhausted to cry herself to sleep.

On his way home, Lucius stopped by the Anadarko agency for the mail. There were three letters: two from Miss Burdette, and one from Isabel's sister Fanny.

Isabel ripped open the letters from Miss Burdette, hoping that the Home Board at least had sent a little money.

The first letter was personal:

June 6, 1896

Dearest Belle,

I write briefly to urge you to keep us more fully informed as to your situation there on the reservation. We recently received a most urgent appeal for information about you from our good friend and ardent supporter, Pastor Clouse at the Elk Creek Mission. At that time, he had received no news of you in more than a month and was quite beside himself with worry. Fortunately, your first letter from the reservation arrived in the next few days, and we were able to assure him you were safe and well—at least as of that writing.

I realize you are busy and that your work there is most difficult. But please remember that we and others who love you are concerned for your safety and that only a few minutes of your time would help to put our minds at ease. Also please remember that *reports* from our missions are necessary to continue the heartfelt support we now enjoy from so many. All of us cannot go into the field; we at home participate only when you share your experiences with us.

I am sorry that more funds will not be forthcoming in the foreseeable future. Be careful of your money, for I don't know when you will get more. The churches and circles are slow in sending their offerings, and the bank has shut down on us. We can only pray that the national economy will alleviate these conditions soon.

Yours in Christ,
Mary G. Burdette

The second letter, dated four days later, was couched in Miss Burdette's formal, official style:

Dear Sister Crawford:

At a meeting of the Executive Board held yesterday, the ladies voted to allow you to remain at Saddle Mountain only *as long as it is safe and prudent* and to continue your allowance of $12.50 per month for an interpreter.

Many of the board expressed concern for your safety in the light of correspondence we have entertained from the Pastor at the Elk Creek Mission and from the Commandant at Fort Sill. We understand from these communications that the situation with the Indians there is very unsettled in relation to some of their savage practices and because of dispute over land distribution.

In continuing your charter at Saddle Mountain, we are relying on your good judgment. Please do not fail us in this regard.

Yours in Christ,
Mary G. Burdette

Isabel sank to the bare plank floor of the Aitsan home with the letters resting in her lap.

In her reports to the Mission Board, she had not exactly lied about her situation at Saddle Mountain, but she certainly had put the best face on truth. Moreover, she had overspent her budget recklessly, trying to make up for the short rations from the government.

Was she supposed to allow the Indians to starve?

She had assumed that she was not.

Now the possibility existed that she would starve along with them.

Also, she had described at length the enthusiastic response accorded her Jesus talks without mentioning that, as yet, not a single Indian had come forward to receive Christ.

Somehow she must convince the board that more financial support was needed, despite her lack of success.

Upset by Miss Burdette's letters, she almost put aside the letter from Fanny, with the intention of reading it later. Her sister habitually wrote at length, including elaborate descriptions of the weather, crops, her garden, her husband's sermons, and local church work.

Still thinking about her depleted funds, Isabel opened the envelope.

When a single page fell out, she knew instantly that something was wrong. Then she picked up the envelope and saw the Toronto postmark.

Fanny lived in western Manitoba.

Alarmed, Isabel hurriedly scanned the letter:

Dearest Belle:

When I heard from Mother that she was feeling poor, I decided right away to come to visit because, as you know, Mother never complained, not in her entire life. I thank God that I came, for I found her in the hospital, and Jack and Emily beside themselves with worry!

Now Mother is somewhat better, but it seems she simply cannot recover her strength, and I am worried about her. She is back home with Jack and Emily, and I will stay here as long as I am able. The doctors do not know if it is her heart or her lungs, but sometimes she cannot catch her breath. She has had several spells that have frightened us.

Belle, I know your work there is important, but if you can come even for a short stay, I think you should do so. I do believe it may be your last chance to see your mother in this world.

I will close now, as I want to get this letter into the post today, so it will get to you as soon as possible. Inform me if you can come, for I know that news would cheer Mother more than anything.

All My Love,
Fanny

Lucius entered the house, carrying more supplies. He stopped in the middle of the room and waited until she looked at him. "Something wrong?"

Isabel glanced at her cot, the few scraps of clothing on the walls. Aside from Jonah, Jeremiah, and the wagon, it was all she owned in the world. Her words tumbled out almost impetuously.

"My mother is sick. My sister thinks she may be dying."

Lucius sank down beside her. He did not respond immediately; Indians were not given to platitudes.

"I should go to Canada before it's too late," Isabel went on. "But I don't see how I can. This little dab of supplies took the last of the mission money. Miss Burdette has written that it will be a while before she can send more."

Lucius seemed settled into his position on the floor beside her, but Isabel was pressed to carry on so he would not feel he was infringing on her privacy.

To think aloud to him came easy. He never diffused her thoughts with mere words. Sometimes it was as if he were someone she had always known, like a brother, perhaps. In some ways he already was as close to her as her brother Hugh.

"How far is it to Toronto?" he asked.

Despite his Carlisle education, he was still vague on geography beyond the places he had seen.

"It takes almost a week by train."

"Maybe Colonel Baldwin would give you money."

Isabel shook her head. "He has no funds for such purposes."

They sat for a time in silence.

"Next month the Kiowas will get some grass money," Lucius said. "Those who come to hear your Jesus talks will share their grass money with you."

Isabel was touched. The Indians badly needed what little cash they received. "I couldn't allow them to do that. I'll wait a while and see. Maybe my mother is not as ill as my sister believes."

"I will talk to my father, Loki Mo-keen. He may think of something to do."

The mention of his family reminded Isabel of her insult to Odlepaugh. "I wish you had been here last night for the Jesus talk. It did not go well."

"I heard."

"I didn't intend to call Odlepaugh crazy. I made a mistake."

Lucius studied her for a moment before answering. When he spoke, his gentle voice softened his words. "I told you that translation can cause much trouble. If you had been a man, Odlepaugh would have killed you. He is very dangerous when he is mad."

"I want to go over to his tipi. I want to tell him I did not mean it."

Lucius frowned. "We will go. But you must let me talk to him first. He is very mad."

Worried about her mother, her continuing failure to reach the Indians, the unending poverty around her, Isabel gave way to a moment of complete despair. "Now I understand why Solomon asked for wisdom instead of riches or honor. I seem to be doing more harm than good here. The Indians come to eat and listen, but they're not interested in pledging their hearts."

"They are listening," Lucius said. "They are thinking hard. You must give them more time."

"When I first came to the reservation, I thought that by now I would be surrounded by converts and well along toward the building of a church. What vanity! I have just offended one of the most important men in the tribe. How

can the Indians have any respect for me, for my teachings, if
I do such foolish things?"

Lucius spoke so quietly Isabel almost did not hear him.
"He may be your first convert."

Isabel could not hide her disbelief. "Odlepaugh? What
makes you think so?"

"Of all the Kiowas, he is most troubled by your Jesus
talks."

Far in the distance, on the flat land along the Washita, dust
devils formed, raising brown spirals against the blue horizon.
After moving along the ground for several minutes, they fell
apart and disappeared, leaving only a splotch of dust in the
air. As Lucius drove along the trail at the foot of the mountain, Isabel watched three whirlwinds, miles apart, drifting
across the plain. No rain had fallen in weeks. The grass,
weeds, and withered stalks of wildflowers seemed lifeless.
Heat shimmers rose from the scorched earth. Grasshoppers
fled in waves ahead of the wagon. The sun beat down unmercifully. Isabel wished that she had taken the time to make
herself a slat sunbonnet. She had been so busy since coming
to the reservation that she had not bothered. Now she was
almost as dark as any Indian.

Lucius raised a hand and pointed. "That's Odlepaugh's
place."

It was a typical Indian layout, with three clustered tipis
and the inevitable brush arbor. Isabel had seen it from a
distance the day she climbed the mountain, but at close
range it was more impressive. The tipis were brightly decorated with painted designs. Colorful blankets were airing on
pole frames. Odlepaugh sat alone in the shade of the arbor, a
rifle across his lap.

He did not make a sign of welcome or greeting.

"I will talk to him," Lucius said.

Isabel remained on the wagon seat while the two brothers
conferred. After several minutes, Lucius returned. "He's still
mad. But I think he will hear you."

He helped Isabel from the wagon. As she approached
Odlepaugh, Isabel made the "I am ashamed" sign, repeatedly
crisscrossing her open palms just in front of her face, as if
hiding behind a blanket.

Odlepaugh ignored the gesture. He motioned for her to sit
on a blanket facing him. Lucius sat down beside her.

Isabel spoke in English, pausing frequently to allow Lucius time to translate.

"I am sorry for what I said. I did not mean to say it. I hope you understand that I used the wrong sign. You have every reason to be angry. You have every right to bite off my nose if you want. I would not feel more ashamed if you did."

Odlepaugh listened without visible emotion. He sat for several minutes in silence, then spoke at length before Lucius translated.

"My heart grew hot because of what you said about the Kiowas all-the-time sitting on their hind-ends and doing nothing. I love my tribe. I have fought for my tribe against the white soldiers, Texans, Mexican soldiers, Blackfeet, Tonkawas, Utes. I would fight again tomorrow. My heart always grows hot when I hear bad words about the Kiowas. But now I have thought about your words. I think maybe they are true. The government ration is making the Kiowa weak. Every time the ration is late, the Kiowas cry like children and do not know what to do. If the government food does not come, they go hungry. I do not know if the white chiefs in Washington planned this as a way to drive the Kiowas into the ground, but it is happening. You have opened my eyes. Maybe I will open yours a little: The plow is not a good thing for the Kiowa. The plow is not his road. But you spoke true words when you said that the Kiowa should not sit around on his hind-end. The Kiowa is the greatest warrior in the world. He must take up new weapons."

"You are a chief," Isabel pointed out. "You can take the Kiowas onto the white man's road."

Odlepaugh snorted. He glanced at Lucius, sharing his amusement. Odlepaugh explained. "In the long-ago time, when my father, Satanta, was a chief, the Kiowas camped and moved together. Every band had a strong chief. Now we are scattered like the wind. Today there are no chiefs."

Isabel took the plunge. "If Odlepaugh walked the Jesus road, most of the Kiowas would follow him."

Odlepaugh shook his head and made the "no" sign. "I now think the Kiowas cannot walk the Jesus road. I have heard your talks. We have done too many things Jesus would not like. I think if Jesus saw the Kiowas coming, He would close His tipi flap and keep them out."

"Jesus will forgive terrible things you have done," Isabel told him. "When you are baptized, all of your bad roads are washed away. The Jesus road is closed only for those with two or three wives."

"You speak too quick," Odlepaugh said. "You do not know what the Kiowas have done."

"Tell me," Isabel challenged. "And I will tell you what Jesus would say."

Odlepaugh looked at her for a long moment and said something to Lucius, who answered sharply. The two brothers argued for several minutes. Isabel assumed that Lucius was insisting that Odlepaugh could trust her with tribal secrets.

Odlepaugh resumed speaking to her, pausing every few sentences for translation.

"Make your ears strong. I will tell you some of the things I have done. In the long-ago time, I went with my father, Satanta, and some others to hit a wagon train in Texas. We killed many white men. I do not remember now how many. The soldiers came and put my father in jail. I am told he was the first Indian anywhere to be put in jail under the white-man law. After he was there a long time, he got mad and jumped out a window and was killed. It is the Kiowa road that when someone is killed like that, a son or a brother will go on the warpath and take scalps to make everything even. Comahty, Honeyme-a-daw, White Buffalo, Apole, Paudlekeah, Papedone, and a few others now dead went with me a long way off, to where some white people lived. We hid along the river till we saw three men coming. We jumped out and killed two. The other one got away. We scalped the two and left the bodies in the road to scare other white people coming along. Later we put the scalps on a long pole and danced. My heart was happy because I got even about my father. This is one thing I did."

"That was a terrible thing," Isabel agreed. "But Jesus would forgive you if you were truly sorry and would never do it again."

Odlepaugh remained silent for several minutes. "If the white people make me mad enough, maybe I will do it again," he said thoughtfully. "I do not know. It is the Indian road to get even. I heard the Jesus man in the little-water Jesus house at Anadarko. He said God says not to get even, that He will take care of all that when He ends this world and burns it up. Do they say the same in the big-water Jesus house?"

Isabel nodded. "The Lord said, 'Vengeance is mine.' All

Christians agree that baptism washes away all sins. They differ only on the ceremony, and that is not as important as what is in your heart."

Odlepaugh's wife, Ananthy, came out of a tipi and sat on the ground a respectable distance away. Isabel had not painted or sketched for years, but she now wished she had the time for a portrait of Ananthy's sad, beautiful face.

Someday perhaps she would find the time.

The sun had slipped over Saddle Mountain, placing Odlepaugh's tipis in shade. Isabel sat watching three hawks circle over the pommel of the mountain.

Again Odlepaugh spoke to her.

"Another time, we went on the warpath. We hid along a river in Texas and soon a white man in a little buggy came along. We jumped out and took off his hair. The man had a leather bag, and we cut it to pieces and scattered the letters everywhere. We did not know what money was then. Some of us later rolled the money with tobacco and smoked it. Old Odlepaugh put some on his shield and it was buried with him. I could tell you many, many stories. I think Jesus would be scared to have me in His house."

"I'm sure many sinners far worse than you have been welcomed with open arms."

Odlepaugh sat for a time in silent contemplation. Then he spoke again.

"Not a long time ago, we could see ahead to what was coming. Sometimes we had troubles. Maybe we would be hungry. Maybe Blackfeet would come and we would have to fight them. But we had no troubles we could not make right. Now I see ahead nothing but darkness. I spoke at the Jerome council and told the others not to sign the paper, but no one would listen to me. Now after a while there will be no more grass money. I do not know what will happen. You have come to live among us. You have taken up our troubles. I think this is good. Do not think any more about the hot words between us. They are gone like smoke on the wind. Sometimes I get mad quick. But my hot thoughts do not live long. That is my road. Everyone will tell you this about me."

On the way home, Lucius remained quiet. He did not speak of their visit until they had topped the last rise and were descending the slope to the Aitsan place. His words were thoughtful.

"When I was a little boy, Odlepaugh was the greatest

warrior in our tribe. He always went into the center of every battle and he was never scratched. Now he is like an eagle with the tail feathers gone. It is a sad thing to see."

Isabel did not answer, but she basked in the warmth of the small confidence.

It was the first time Lucius had shared his private world with her.

Chapter Six

The large wagon trundled into the Aitsan yard just as Isabel finished snapping the last of the string beans. The sun was not yet an hour high. Amos and Jessie halted their play under the arbor and stood gaping. Lucius came from the horse corral, closing the gate behind him.

The wagon was a huge prairie schooner of a type rarely seen in the territory, with rear wheels fully six feet in diameter. It was pulled by four big draft horses with hooves the size of gallon buckets. An Indian man and woman sat at the front under a soaring canvas cover. The woman held a child in her lap.

As the man pulled the horses to a halt, Lucius raised a hand and spoke to them in Kiowa.

The man answered at length, gesturing toward the house.

Lucius replied briefly and motioned to Isabel. She walked into the yard and approached the wagon.

"This is Pauahty—Walking Buffalo," Lucius said. "He lives to the east of here, near Cut Throat Gap. This is his wife, Aupkauty. Their little girl Ella is dying. Pauahty said they heard that a Jesus woman had come here to live with me. They have brought her to you."

Pauahty stepped down from the wagon. He was tall, light-complexioned, and slight of build. His gorgeous red blanket hung in graceful folds, lending him a regal appearance. His thick braids were interwoven with beaver fur, and he wore a chestplate of polished bone. His wife was also tall, and very thin. She handed the little girl to Pauahty, who passed her to Isabel.

Loosely wrapped in a blanket of brilliant yellow, green, blue, and black, the child seemed to be about five years of age. She was skeletal and as weightless as a kitten. She was fighting for every breath, her tiny face drawn into a taut frown of suffering. As she held the child, Isabel felt the desperation of the struggle taking place in her arms.

She put a palm to the child's forehead and knew that the situation was beyond her capabilities.

"Lucius, this baby's burning up with fever. We must get her to a doctor."

Lucius's face showed nothing. "It is consumption. They know she is dying. They have come here to ask you to bury her."

Isabel looked down into the child's hot almond eyes. With the tips of her fingers she traced the lines of the taut, angelic face. Indian children often were exceptionally beautiful and little Ella was a heartbreakingly excellent example.

Already the sun was sweltering. The child would not survive the day-long journey to a doctor. Even if she reached Fort Sill alive, proper treatment would be difficult to obtain. Good doctors were rare in the territory. Indian babies—especially female Indian babies—were not accorded high priority in the white man's world.

Pauahty spoke in Kiowa. Lucius waited until he had finished before translating. "He said he and his wife are not Christians. But they have heard that Jesus takes dead children straight to a place where there is no more hungry and no more crying."

"Tell him they heard right."

She carried the child into the shade of the arbor and sent Amos and Jessie for a bucket of water and wet cloths. While Lucius and Pauahty unloaded long poles from the wagon, Isabel bathed the child's face and upper body with wind-cooled towels. As soon as the Pauahty tipi was erected beside the arbor, she took little Ella inside, placed her on a blanket, and knelt beside her.

"She's unconscious," she told Lucius. "It's a wonder she's not into convulsions. Tell her parents I will give her quinine to bring the fever down. Maybe we can ease her suffering."

In the silent, mysterious way of the Indians, the news of the baby's crisis quickly spread across the Saddle Mountain portion of the reservation. By noon forty or fifty Kiowas sat in a death vigil in the yard.

Isabel spent the remainder of the day tending to the dying child. Hour after hour she bathed the wasted, fevered little body, waiting for the inevitable. Pauahty and Aupkauty sat on the other side of the child, stoically watching as she fought for life. A tiny pup, the child's playmate, lay against the wall of the tipi and whimpered incessantly.

By sundown more than a hundred Indians had gathered. Mabel, Ananthy, Pope-bah, and other Indian women prepared the last of the missionary food and served it to the throng. The Indians ate by lanternlight.

Little Ella's battle continued on into the night. After the outside lanterns were extinguished, a few of the Indians slept, curling up in their blankets. Most remained awake, sitting quietly in the darkness.

A single lantern burned in the tipi. Hour after hour Isabel agonized with every rasping breath, praying one moment for the struggle to cease, praying in the next that it would not. The dreadful heaving of the tiny lungs, the pitiful whining of the pup, the stolid faces of the grieving parents, the hiss of the lantern blended into a night of unrelenting torture.

A few minutes after dawn the frail, emaciated body shuddered twice and the breathing stopped. Isabel felt for a pulse. The beat faltered and vanished beneath her fingertips. The dark almond eyes remained open, unseeing.

In that moment, Isabel felt only relief.

"She's gone," she whispered. She made the sign for death—right forefinger passing beneath the extended left hand—literally signifying "gone under."

The mother threw back her head and howled—a screech more animal than human. The sound shattered the stillness and sent chills through Isabel's marrow. She reached to comfort the woman, but Aupkauty fought free and, still shrieking, fled from the tipi.

The father sat staring at his dead child. He began to rock slowly back and forth, chanting in Kiowa, pounding his knees with clenched fists.

Slowly a chorus of wails arose around the tipi and built to an ear-splitting crescendo as every Kiowa on the place joined the parents in mourning. Isabel's heart froze. Never in her life had she heard anything so primeval—not even the howling of wolves.

The keening went on and on, growing in volume.

Isabel's concern shifted from the child to the mother. Folding a blanket over the small, still form she went into the yard.

Aupkauty stood by a front wheel of the wagon. Isabel hurried toward her, making her way through seated, wailing Indians. In the faint light of early dawn, Isabel first thought the woman stood gripping the wagon wheel for support and that the rhythmic movements of her body were the wrackings of uncontrollable grief.

Then Isabel saw the knife.

The mother's left hand rested on the iron rim of the wheel. She was hacking at the forefinger.

"*Hawnay!*" Isabel yelled. "*Hawnay!*" She stumbled across seated Indians and seized Aupkauty's wrist. The woman tried to push her away. Isabel kept her hold and attempted to seize the knife. As they struggled, blood from the slashed hand coursed across Isabel's arms. She felt drops splash on her ankles.

Then her own wrists were caught in an unyielding grip.

Lucius spoke in her ear: "Leave her alone."

"She's out of her head!" Isabel shouted. "Stop her!"

Lucius pulled Isabel backward. She lost her hold on Aupkauty. The woman resumed her attack on the nearly severed index finger. It fell into the dirt.

Isabel's stomach churned. So nauseated she could hardly stand, furious over the manhandling, she tried to break away from Lucius. He kept his hold on her wrists.

"Why didn't you stop her?" she shouted.

Lucius shook her twice, violently. He spoke in a voice tinged with anger. "You said we could keep our Kiowa things. This is a Kiowa thing."

Isabel's queasiness was absorbed by her fury. "It's plain savagery! I've never heard of anything so primitive!"

"It is the Kiowa road."

Isabel managed to rip her hands free. "The Kiowa road! That's all I've heard since I came here. Does it never occur to you that some of your tribal practices are revolting to the civilized mind? You of all Kiowas should be able to see that!"

Lucius looked at her for a moment without reply. His expression was calm. "This is not a bad thing to do. Today the pain helps to take away the hurt in the heart. In the far-ahead time Aupkauty will never forget the baby she lost. The cut-off finger will always remind her. That is good."

Pauahty came toward them, walking tall and stately, oblivious of the tears streaming down his face. He spoke at length to Lucius in Kiowa.

"Pauahty said if we will make the coffin, he and his wife will prepare the body for burial."

Still shaken from her anger, her loss of self-control, Isabel forced her thoughts away from Aupkauty and the bleeding stump.

What was done could not be helped. Now, practical matters demanded attention: Temperatures would soar to a hundred degrees or more before noon. The child must be buried without delay.

"What will we use for a coffin?" she asked.

Lucius thought for a moment. "The chip box."

Isabel was appalled. "Lucius! It's filthy!"

"It is the only wooden box big enough. We do not have time to make one."

Isabel went into the kitchen and dumped the dried cowchips and horse apples from the box. Carrying it to the creek, she scrubbed the bare wood thoroughly with lye soap. Rummaging in the missionary barrels in the spare tipi, she found an old white muslin skirt.

Hurriedly she lined the interior of the makeshift coffin.

The result was crude, but she could think of no way to improve upon it. With a piece of charcoal, she painstakingly wrote across the lid:

NOT DEAD, BUT LIVING WITH JESUS

She carried the box out to the tipi. The body, already prepared, lay on an arrangement of blankets.

Isabel stared, unable for a moment to believe her own eyes.

In death, little Ella seemed more lifelike than during her final hours on earth.

Dressed in bright yellow buckskin, the body lay on a cream-colored shawl bordered with scarlet roses. A dozen twists of red and blue beads encircled the tiny neck and rested on the chest. A profusion of bracelets and rings covered fingers and wrists.

Little Ella's hair and face were tinted the shade of autumn

leaves. Cheeks, ears, the center line of her hair, and lips were painted crimson. Her eyes remained open. Her lips were parted, as if about to speak.

Lucius gently lifted the body and placed it in the chip box.

With her left hand now bound in a bloody cloth, Aupkauty used the other to arrange rubber and leather dolls and a play set of dishes around her child.

Pauahty picked up the whining pup. Isabel foresaw what was about to happen.

She opened her mouth to voice a frantic protest.

Lightning-quick, Lucius grabbed her wrist and shot her a warning glance.

Holding the pup in one broad hand, Pauahty stuck the slim blade of a knife into its heart. With a single, plaintive yip, the pup died. Pauahty wrapped it in a red cloth and placed it at the child's feet.

Lucius nailed the coffin shut. He then carried it out to the arbor and placed it across two sawhorses Amos had brought from the corral.

Isabel went into the house for her Bible. By the time she returned, the Indians had gathered around the coffin.

Seldom had she ever felt so inadequate. After a long, taxing day, she had gone the entire night without food or sleep. Her eyes felt puffed and swollen. There was no time to comb her hair or even to wash her face.

For a moment she could see herself as her family, the women in Chicago might see her. She had not removed her grimy old Mother Hubbard in more than a week. A month had passed since an honest bath. Her skin was hopelessly dried by summer wind, browned by the scorching sun. Day after day of hard work had removed every spare ounce from her body.

She doubted that her own mother would recognize her.

The Indians fell silent as she stood over the coffin, Bible in hand. She spoke from memory. Lucius translated.

"I am the resurrection and the life. . . ."

Christ's comforting words from the Book of John came without effort, seared into her heart from so many sad occasions. She quoted the Twenty-third Psalm: "The Lord is my shepherd; I shall not want . . ."

She concluded the service with a prayer: "Dear sweet Jesus, we thank You for ending little Ella's suffering. We ask

You to take her straight into your heart and that she shall abide there forever. Amen."

The coffin was placed at the tailgate of the Pauahty wagon. Isabel and the Indians followed in a long procession as it was driven to the foot of the mountain.

Sweating in the August heat, Lucius and the other men dug the grave. Isabel offered another prayer. The men lowered the coffin on a blanket and covered the grave.

Spreading over the open field, the mourners gathered stones. Isabel helped place them on the grave to protect little Ella's body from the wolves.

By the time the work was done and the procession returned to the house, the grieving parents had whacked off their hair, slashed their breasts, and set fire to their tipi. The coals were still burning, the smoke acrid on the heated air.

The couple stood in middle of the Aitsan yard, wailing in anguish, blood coursing down their bodies and soaking their clothes.

When they spied Isabel, they came running with the exaggerated stagger of drunks and the emotionally distraught. They seized her hands and babbled away in Kiowa. Isabel battled to keep from showing her revulsion.

"They are thanking you for sending their baby to Jesus," Lucius said.

Isabel suddenly was burdened by questions never covered at the training school. Should Christ's teachings be intermingled with such pagan practices? How far should she go in urging the Kiowas to abandon their barbaric ways?

She looked at the Pauahtys and spoke to Lucius for translation. "Tell them we will pray for little Ella. Tell them they are welcome to come to our Jesus talks."

The Pauahtys climbed into their wagon and drove away. Slowly the mourners dispersed. Lucius brought a shovel and hoe from the sheds out by the corral and began scooping up the coals from the burned tipi. Isabel used an old, worn-out broom and helped him clean the entire yard.

As she worked, the emotional turmoil of the past two days began to ferment. She did not have to close her eyes to see the agony in the beautiful face of the child as she fought in vain for life. Isabel at last gave way to tears.

"Lucius, do you realize we buried that baby in a stinking chip box? I'll never forgive myself."

Lucius glanced toward the house, where Amos and Jessie

had resumed their play with the pups around the stoop. He leaned on his shovel and gazed at the mountain. "The chip box does not matter," he said quietly. "After the finest coffin is dust, that old mountain will still be the same. The grass will still grow. It is what we feel here that matters."

He placed a hand over his heart.

Again Isabel was struck by the hopeless inconsistency. The Kiowas could be so intelligent and humane one moment, so vicious and primitive the next.

She felt that even if she lived among them twenty years, she would not understand them.

Lucius worked several minutes in silence. "I think we gave little Ella a very fine good-bye," he said. "It's the first time I've seen the Kiowas truly satisfied with anything since the Army drove us onto the reservation."

Little Ella was the first. As word of Christ's love of children spread, Indians came from all over the reservation, Kiowas, Comanches, Apaches, bringing their dead and dying babies to be buried.

During the next two months, Isabel buried twenty-six.

Returning from the creek with a basket of laundry, Isabel heard loud voices from beyond the sheds at the corral. Not wishing to intrude, she circled around through the trees.

She emerged closer than she expected.

Loki Mo-keen and Lucius were locked in furious argument. When they saw her, they broke off their shouting match and turned away. Isabel gave no indication she had heard. She walked on toward the house. A few minutes later, Mo-keen rode off on his horse.

Carrying his rifle, Lucius walked across the pasture toward the mountain.

Isabel built a fire in the yard, then set up her ironing board in the front room. She showed Amos how to throw the thumb latch on the handle to pick up a hot iron. She began work, with Amos and Jessie running relay from the yard with freshly heated irons.

As she worked, Isabel thought back over the months, searching for insight into the rift between father and son. Mo-keen had seldom visited the Aitsan home in all the time she had lived there. She had never attached much importance to this fact. But in light of the argument she had overheard, she wondered. Was Mo-keen still angry because Lucius had invited her into his home?

Isabel had to consider the possibility.

She recalled three earlier instances when heated debates suddenly flared between Lucius and his father.

Afterward, Lucius never mentioned them.

Isabel doubted he ever would tell her the source of the trouble. If it did concern her, he would forever do his best to protect her from it.

Mabel came into the room to start supper.

Isabel put the iron on its rack and signed to Mabel. "Lucius and Mo-keen had another bad argument today."

Mabel nodded, smiled, and said nothing. There was not an ounce of deceit in Mabel's innocent nature. But she would walk barefoot across hot coals to avoid unpleasantness. Isabel tried again.

"Is the trouble over me?"

Mabel quickly looked away, which in itself was an answer.

Isabel waited until she again had Mabel's attention. "I told Mo-keen I would leave the reservation if I caused more trouble. Why won't they come to me with it? Why are they keeping it from me?"

Mabel glanced about the room as if seeking some place to hide. She signed her answer hesitantly. "It is the Ghost Dance people who are making the trouble."

Isabel kept pushing. "Are they still abusing Lucius because of me?"

Wavering, Mabel nodded yes.

Furious that she had been excluded from knowledge of this, Isabel signed rapidly. "I will stop it. I will go and talk to the Ghost Dance people. I will not allow them to abuse Lucius because I am living here."

Mabel shook her head as she made the "no" sign. "There is another thing."

Again she paused, as if trying to decide how much to tell. "Lucius is trying to stop the Ghost Dance," she signed. "He says they do not know what they are doing. He says they are working with . . ." She frowned and made her index and middle finger into a "V," spiraling down from above, quickly followed by the "throw it away" sign.

She looked at Isabel dubiously.

"Bad spirits," Isabel said, nodding to show she understood.

"Lucius is right," she added. "The Ghost Dance people may be calling up bad spirits."

Mabel began to sign rapidly, eager to impart information now that the barrier had been broken. "Lucius told the Ghost Dancers that if they do not stop the dancing, the white soldiers will come and shoot them. He said it would be the same as with the Sioux six winters ago."

Isabel felt her pulse quicken. Lucius spoke the truth.

"What did the Ghost Dance people say to that?" she asked.

"They said that if the soldiers come here, the Ghost Dance people will fight."

Shaken to the core, Isabel stood speechless.

All of this had taken place right under her nose.

Why had Lucius not confided in her?

Mabel went on nervously, her arms moving in a frantic ballet. "Six summers ago the Kiowas went to the Washita for a Sun Dance. The white soldiers came from Fort Sill and told them to stop quick. The Indians picked up their rifles and said they would fight. Lucius was a scout with the white soldiers then. He left the soldiers and went to the Kiowas and told them that the white soldiers had big guns—guns that fire many, many bullets in a single breath. He told them the white soldiers would kill them all. He pushed them with his talk until they went home. That was the last Sun Dance. Many Indians did not like what Lucius did that day. They have not forgotten."

Isabel thought of Lucius in his soldier suit, riding out alone, speaking eloquently to the people he loved, begging them not to fight.

He no doubt had risked court-martial, dismissal, or worse.

And he had been rewarded with the hatred of many of his people.

He seemed destined to be trapped forever between two worlds.

Chapter Seven

"This I have learned from your Jesus talks," said Pope-bah. "You told us the Great Father made man first, then woman. I think maybe that is why women are still way-behind."

Isabel laughed, and even Lucius smiled in his translation. It was a clever play on words.

"That's good," Isabel said. "Now, the rest of you. Just tell me your thoughts on our Jesus talks. Have they helped you?"

The night was cool, with a hint of frost in the air. Sixty-six Indians were seated before her, the largest attendance since early spring. Even Mo-keen, Little Robe, and some of the Ghost Dance people had come.

Isabel's elation over the turnout was dampened by lingering guilt. She knew that for many present, her Jesus talk was not the principal attraction.

One night in late summer, in a rare mood, she read *Ali Baba and the Forty Thieves*, mostly for the benefit of the children. But the adults also sat mesmerized as Lucius interpreted the narrative.

Afterward the Indians talked so much about Ali Baba and his "strong medicine" of "open sesame" that Isabel grew concerned, fearing they might confuse *Ali Baba* with her Bible teachings.

She confided her worry to Lucius.

He replied he felt certain the Kiowas would understand that it was just a story. "In the long-ago time the teller of stories was an important person in the tribe," he explained. "When I was a boy, old Taboodle was the story-teller. Every night we listened to him. Many of them were about Saynday, who was very smart, like Ali Baba. That is one of the things the Kiowas have lost in coming to the reservation."

In the wake of the reading of *Ali Baba*, the size of Isabel's congregation grew. The Indians had let it be known they wished to hear more such stories.

Trapped, Isabel had fallen into the practice of telling a brief story, usually something to illustrate the point of her Jesus talk. She loved to read and tell the stories because they brought back memories of her childhood. After exhausting her childhood repertoire, she resorted to her volume of Shakespeare.

"Anyone else?" she asked. "Anyone who has been helped by our Jesus talks?"

Hattie rose and held up a hand. Isabel nodded to her. Hattie spoke hesitantly in Kiowa. Lucius interpreted.

"Ever since we were driven onto the reservation, I have wished I had been born in the long-ago time. I have now more than thirty winters. I do not know how many, but I remember the warpath and the buffalo. I remember when the Kiowas went around fighting and taking scalps. Once they brought a black man's scalp home and put it in a tree. I was so scared I could not sleep. Now the world is different. The old roads are passing away. For a long time I was sad because of this. Now I am not happy, but I am not sad. I think the Jesus talks have made me this way."

"Very good, Hattie. Any of you men? Come on. It is the women who are supposed to be way-behind!"

Dangerous Bear lumbered to his feet. "Not long ago, I was mad all the time. Now I have listened to many Jesus talks. I am not mad so much anymore. Last night my wife left the meat in the fire too long and it got hard. It made my teeth tired. I got mad. Then I remembered the Jesus talks and I was not mad anymore."

"Good, good," Isabel said.

Akometo spoke. "A long time ago, we did not know about Jesus days. Now on Jesus days I get up early and wash myself all over. I comb my hair and clean myself from my head to my feet. When I am through I ask Jesus to look at me. Then I sit down and think Jesus till it is time to get the horses."

Long Horn was next. "When you told us Jesus wanted us to forgive our enemies, I thought of Paudlekeah right off. My heart is turned against him and I cannot fix it myself. Once I went up to him to shake hands. I got so mad I could not do it. I am still trying. I think that after a little while I will be able to talk to him and the bad will go out of my heart."

"I hope so, Mr. Long Horn," Isabel said. "You are truly working at it in the Christian spirit. Anyone else?"

Keapetate spoke a few words in Kiowa. Before Lucius could interpret, the entire congregation erupted in laughter. Isabel waited until Lucius could make himself heard.

"Keapetate says she likes the stories best."

Isabel joined in the laughter. "Which was your favorite?" she asked Keapetate.

"Sinbad. He was very smart when he got the old man off his back by getting him drunk."

"Caesar," said Dangerous Bear. "He was a strong, wise chief. They should not have killed him on the way to council."

"What about Hamlet?" Isabel asked.

The Kiowas groaned. Isabel smiled. The Indians had grown exasperated waiting for Hamlet to kill Claudius.

Odlepaugh spoke. "If Hamlet had been a Kiowa warrior, he would have been left behind with the women."

"I wanted to hear more about Lady Macbeth," said Pope-bah. "I think she was right in wanting many things for her husband. But she did not know the right road to do it. I like the way she washed and washed and could not get the blood off her hands, because the blood was not there. It was in her head."

"That is a good story," Isabel agreed. "And that is the way a bad sin works on us. We cannot rub it out. Only Jesus can make it go away."

Mo-keen rose and stood for a moment before speaking. "I will tell you a story you will see in your sleep."

The congregation fell silent. Isabel felt tension in the air. She glanced at Lucius. He had interpreted his father's words without inflection, but his eyes had narrowed slightly—whether in anger or wariness, she could not discern. The Indians were usually perceptive to nuances. Apparently they detected challenge in Mo-keen's manner.

"Go ahead," Isabel said. "I would like to hear your story."

Mo-keen fixed his dark, fathomless eyes upon her and began speaking. "From the first day the Jesus woman came here, I saw in her face that she has heard a bad thing about me. The white soldiers tell this bad thing. It is not true. I will tell the Jesus woman the true story. Close your ears if you do not want to hear the truth."

"My ears are open," Isabel signed.

"In the long-ago time when I was a young man, the Comanche chief Little Buffalo came and told us that the white soldiers were at war with each other and that the soldiers were gone from the forts in Texas.

"So I took up the war road with Little Buffalo and maybe seventy or eighty other Kiowas and Comanches. We hit the Texans hard along the river the Mexicans call the Brazos de Dios. Many white families were living there along a creek. Aperian Crow and I led an attack on one of the houses. There was no one there but some women and a few children. Some of them were black. We had never seen a black person up to that time and we did not know what to think.

"It is not the Kiowa road to fight with women, but a woman came to the door with a gun and shot at us, so we killed and scalped her. Then we went into the house and took captives. We found one little girl under the bed. We burned the house and took this little girl and about six other captives with us. Many of them also were children. We rode for two days and nights without stopping, changing horses on the run. Some of the captives could not keep up, so we killed them.

"We took twelve scalps on that ride and brought back many horses and captives and much plunder. All of us came back without a scratch, so we danced the Scalp Dance and were happy. Some of the women captives would not cook for us. Later we traded them to Mexicans for cornbread.

"Not long after that the white soldiers said that while Aperian Crow and I were in the house, we took a white boy baby by its heels and hit its head against a rock until the brains fell out. That is not true. I think maybe the baby was under the bed and we did not see it. Sometimes when a body is put into a fire the brains cook and swell up and make the skull break into little pieces. I think maybe that is why the white soldiers found the baby's head all broken. Aperian Crow is dead now. But the Great Father knows that what I say is true."

Again, there was a deep silence in the arbor. Isabel wondered at Mo-keen's motives in telling the story.

Granted, he wanted to set the record straight. But he also might be informing her that the Kiowas had their own standard of conduct, their own relationship with God, and needed none of her moralizing from Shakespeare and the Bible.

Or he still might be attempting to scare her off the reservation. "You are right, Mr. Mo-keen," she said. "That is a story I will see in my sleep. Let us pray."

In late October, ration day again was delayed. Under the terms of the Medicine Lodge and other treaties, the Kiowas were to receive an allocation of beef, bacon, sugar, coffee, flour, baking soda, soap, and tobacco every other Friday.

The government seldom kept its promise.

Six weeks had passed without distribution of food, and Isabel's meager mission stores had long since been exhausted. All over the reservation, Kiowas were hungry. Some had eaten their cattle, others their horses.

In early November word came that food was on the way. But confusion reigned over the distribution point. At first it was said that rations would be dispensed at Rainy Mountain, as had happened in the past. Rumors also persisted that everyone would have to travel to Fort Sill, twenty-five miles to the east, or to Fort Cobb, almost thirty miles in another direction.

Domot and Kokom rode to the agency to see if a decision had been made. On their way home they stopped and talked to Lucius in the yard.

"It will be at the Anadarko agency," Lucius told Isabel upon his return to the house. "You should come with us. The Indians will have full chuck bags again. There will be dances and horse races."

Isabel was tempted. She had not received a letter from her mother since September, and not a word from Chicago since early October. Letters might be waiting in Anadarko. Also, she was hungry. For the past two weeks she and the Aitsans had subsisted mostly on rabbits and the harvest from a handful of beans she had planted down by the creek.

"I would feel so conspicuous," she said.

"It is cold." Lucius pointed out. "All the Indians will be in blankets. You can wrap yourself in one. You will look like an Indian."

"I really shouldn't go," she said. "I have so much work to do. I'm way behind in my letters. But I truly think I *need* a holiday."

The next morning Isabel and the Aitsans set out before dawn. All day they drove northeast against a cold north wind.

That night they camped along the upper reaches of Cache Creek.

Just before noon on the following day they arrived at the Anadarko agency.

At least a thousand Indians were already in camp on the distribution grounds east of town. More were arriving every minute. Isabel had never seen such a spectacle. Tipis and tents covered the entire landscape. Smoke from hundreds of campfires laced the pale blue sky.

Lucius drove the Aitsan wagon and team onto the grounds, skillfully weaving among pedestrians, dogs, horses, and tipis. A powerful stench filled the air. Lucius and Mabel seemed not to notice. Isabel wished she had brought a handkerchief dabbed in Florida water, a precaution that sometimes helped.

Lucius stopped the wagon between two tipis. "We will camp here," he said. He unharnessed the team and pulled the poles for the tipi from the wagon. But he did not turn his hand to help further.

Setting up the tipi was woman's work.

"I must find Odlepaugh," he told Isabel. "We will give Colonel Baldwin some hot words about the late ration."

He strode away. Amos and Jessie joined other Indian children in racing among the tipis and tents in an elaborate game Isabel was unable to fathom.

Pope-bah, Ananthy, and Hattie came to help with the tipi. Soon the job was done. Mabel placed the baby inside on a blanket, then built a fire from dead wood Amos and Jessie had gathered on the long drive from Saddle Mountain.

At sunset the thunder drum began its beat. While Isabel brought her journal up to date, Mabel prepared a pot of stew for supper.

Lucius and Odlepaugh returned tired and upset. Their meeting with the agent had not gone well.

After changing into tribal costume, Lucius and Odlepaugh seated themselves Indian fashion before the fire and opened their blankets to catch the heat.

Behind an artfully draped quilt, Mabel changed into her beaded buckskin dress. Soon the tipi was filled with Kiowas in native costume. Domot, Heenkey, Tonemoh, Smokey, Spotted Horse, and Akometo came to hear the news, and for a time the men talked in Kiowa. Their tones were angry, and Isabel gathered that their patience with the government ration system was near exhaustion.

Isabel wished she had not come. She felt terribly out of place. She was certain she was the only white person in the encampment. The constant beat of the thunder drum intensified her growing sense of estrangement.

Little Robe, Red Eagle, Amon, and Gahbein came by to hear about the meeting with the agent. As she watched them, Isabel began to notice the unusual deference accorded Little Robe. She had seen him only two or three times since the welcoming "big eat" Lucius and Mabel had given her when she first moved into their home. Little Robe had been one of the Ghost Dancers who had departed after the dispute that night.

Older than the men around him, except perhaps Domot, Little Robe was in his middle or late sixties. His hair was cut just below the left ear, and he wore a single braid on the right in the fashion of the older Kiowa men. His face was weathered but his eyes were sharp and alert, taking in everything at a glance. In her rare meetings with him, he had been neither friendly nor unfriendly. Mostly he ignored her, as he did tonight.

During the past few months Isabel had gathered the impression that he was steadily gaining power in council. Now she wondered how much of that influence could be attributed to his leadership in the Ghost Dance movement.

Although Odlepaugh might be right in his claim that the tribe now "had no chiefs," Little Robe clearly was rising to ascendancy in the Saddle Mountain community.

Lucius did not speak to her until the visitors had gone.

"The ration will start in the morning," he said. "Colonel Baldwin said he will make the ration days easier for everybody. He said that if Washington approves, he will make little agencies for us at Saddle Mountain, Binger, Rainy Mountain, and Fort Sill."

"When?"

"He said he was not sure."

"That probably means never."

Lucius nodded. "We told him we were tired of promises. Our talk with him was very hot. Some of the Kiowas and Comanches may go to Washington to complain."

Isabel knew a better solution. Indians on the farthest reaches of the reservation traveled three or four days every other week to draw rations. If they would put that much energy into growing crops, they would be free of the white man's shortcomings.

"What about the mail?" she asked.

"Colonel Baldwin did not know you would be here. He did not bring it from town. I will go get it tomorrow."

Isabel told Lucius and Mabel she had decided not to attend the dancing. They raised their hands and made signs of closing their ears to such talk.

Mabel produced a brilliant crimson and cream blanket, draped it over Isabel's shoulders, and signed that she had brought it along especially for Isabel to wear. She showed Isabel how to gather folds over her head to make a hood, and held up a small mirror so Isabel could examine the results.

Isabel had to admit that with her sun-bronzed skin and her now-prominent cheekbones, she did indeed look mightily like an Indian.

Thus encouraged, she followed Lucius and Mabel through a maze of wagons, horses, and tipis toward the sound of the drum.

At the center of the encampment hundreds of Indians sat on the ground, watching the dancers. Out in the clearing more than a hundred warriors stepped and whirled in time to the drum. Around Isabel the crowd chanted, the volume growing with each beat. Even shy, self-conscious Mabel became animated, clapping her hands and chanting as loudly as anyone.

The dancers wore a costume Isabel had not seen before. Except for bone breastplates, they were naked to the waist. Each trailed a long red cape and carried a lance in his right hand. A black shawl encircled each at the middle. An ornate porcupine-quill roach decorated each head. Bells danced on their moccasins. Every leg was covered in black. As they stomped and whirled, the one-two beat of the drum grew as sharp as cannon shots. The dancers lunged and parried frantically with the lances, as if engaged in a desperate battle.

"These are the Koitsenko—the Black Legs," Lucius said into Isabel's ear trumpet. "They are the last warrior society."

He waited until a chant ended, then explained further.

"The dance tells of a battle that happened in the long-ago time. Some Kiowa warriors met a big bunch from another tribe. The Kiowas were outnumbered, so they hid in tall grass. The other Indians set the grass on fire. The Kiowas did not run out. They knew that if they were taken, the other

Indians would find where the rest of the Kiowas were camped. So they stayed in the burning grass and fought until the other Indians went away. When the Kiowas came back to the village, their legs were burned black. Today the Koitsenko still paint their legs black to remember that bravery.

"Everything the Koitsenko wear comes from their many battles. The red cape makes everyone remember a fight with Mexicans. A warrior called Goolhaee saw a Mexican officer wearing a pretty red cape. Goolhaee wanted it. He rode alone through the Mexican Army, killed the officer, and took his cape. It was the bravest thing anyone had ever seen. He scared the Mexicans, and they lost the fight. The lance is for Pawtawdle, a warrior the whites called Poor Buffalo. In a fight, he put a sash around his neck and pushed a lance through it and into the ground to show that he would not retreat. He died there. They are now singing his death song."

As the crowd chanted, Lucius translated a verse:

All brave men must die sometime.
The Koitsenko must die, too;
It is a great honor to die in battle.

"The Kiowas all love stories of bravery and death songs," Lucius said between chants. "You remember that when the soldiers were taking the father of Joshua and Frank Given— Satank—to Texas with Big Tree to stand trial, he attacked the soldiers with a knife so they would have to kill him. Before he did that, he stood up and sang his death song. The Koitsenko are singing it now."

Even though I live now,
I will not live forever.
Only the Sun and the Earth remain forever.

"Now they are singing the death song of Satanta, Odlepaugh's father:"

No matter where I fall in battle,
Do not mourn for me,
For I will not know it.
Somewhere in some far-off land
My body will be devoured by wolves,
But I will not know it.

"And this is the death song of Ghee-ale. He was killed in the big mountains far to the west many years ago, shot in the stomach by white soldiers. The Kiowas with him knew that he was dying. He knew it, too. He told them to leave him some water and food, that they must ride on and keep ahead of the white soldiers. Before they rode away, he sang his death song:"

> Now I am ready to go,
> I hear my comrades calling me
> Over on the other side.
> I am going to join them.

The chants, songs, and dances continued for hours. After a time Lucius seemed to grow restless. He left for a while, and later Isabel saw him among the dancers.

Isabel noticed that the women took care to remain "way-behind" and did not dance in the way of the men.

Isabel felt suspended in time. The thunder drum, the ritual dances, the chants seemed so primeval. Yet the spectacle held strange appeal to her senses.

When Lucius returned a long time later, everyone was repeating a single verse. Isabel asked its meaning.

Lucius thought for a moment and shook his head. "The words cannot be made the same."

"Try," Isabel urged.

Lucius frowned in concentration and made the translation. Isabel committed the verse to memory:

> We, the old chiefs, are looking down;
> We leave you these songs and this dance
> For you to preserve.

Mabel shook Isabel awake and signed rapidly. "The ration has started. We must go take a place in line."

Isabel had lain down fully clothed. She rolled from beneath the blankets and without so much as washing her face followed Mabel out into a frigid morning and a sharp north wind.

Under a gray, leaden sky they joined the hundreds of women on their way to the agency buildings. It seemed that all color had vanished with the night. Again the women huddled beneath drab government blankets.

Despite the cold, some were barefoot.

The women formed a long line three or four abreast in front of a large clapboard warehouse. As early arrivals, Isabel and Mabel earned a place in the front portion of the line. After a long wait, a Dutch door was opened, and the white men inside began handing out the rations. Each woman's name was checked carefully against the agency list.

Although the line moved slowly, the women stood with infinite patience. More than a dozen dogs circled around, barking.

As the first women received their rations and turned away, Isabel gasped in disbelief. The women ripped open the sacks and poured flour onto the ground. They then folded and saved the cloth sacks. The bacon they tossed to the dogs.

Isabel was horrified.

With the rations six weeks behind schedule, these people had been on the verge of starvation!

She grabbed Mabel's arm. "Tell everybody to keep the flour," she signed. "I will teach them how to use it."

Pope-bah and Hattie were only a few feet ahead in the line. Mabel spoke to them in Kiowa. They shook their heads and made the "bad" and "throw it away" signs to Isabel.

"You seem to like my sweet cakes," Isabel signed back. "You like my bread. Where do you think those cakes and bread come from? If you will keep the flour, I will teach you the flour road."

Half convinced, the women agreed to keep the flour. Pope-bah and Hattie told their neighbors. Word spread up and down the line.

"Save the bacon, too," Isabel added. "I know your men do not like to eat it. But they will like it with their beans."

As Mabel stepped up to the door, drew the rations, and the names of the Aitsan family were checked off the list, Isabel stood to one side, waiting.

One of the white men glanced at her in idle curiosity but made no comment.

Isabel was amused.

For the first time among whites, she had passed as an Indian. The man had looked, and seen exactly what he expected to see—an Indian woman freezing beneath a thin government blanket.

She helped Mabel carry the Aitsan ration back to the tipi.

When they arrived, Lucius waited before the fire. One glance told Isabel that his mood was as gray as the day.

He answered her questions reluctantly, and she did not hear the full story until after breakfast was cooked and eaten. He had attempted to obtain a freight contract with the Army. The government man had told him that he probably would not be needed until spring.

Isabel saw deep disappointment in his eyes, and perhaps a little fear. When the Jerome Agreement went into effect, the grass payments would probably cease. Money would be in even shorter supply among the Kiowas.

The distribution of beef began that afternoon in a spirit of great excitement, with the entire encampment crowded around post oak corrals east of town.

For an hour or more the men rode through the penned cattle, bickering over which animal they would receive. About a third were gaunt Longhorns. The remainder were of mixed lineage among the stubbier Shorthorn breeds. The Indians much preferred the tough, stringy meat of the Longhorn. They said it more resembled that of the buffalo.

Argument and chaos prevailed while the men made their selections. Finally the animals were tagged and driven into smaller corrals leading to the chutes.

One by one steers were released and pursued by beef chiefs on horseback in a pathetic imitation of the hunting of buffalo. The crowd cheered as each animal was shot neatly through the lungs.

Soon dead and dying animals dotted the prairie.

On signal, the women swarmed onto the killing ground with butcher knives. In the cold and wind, Isabel would not have believed it possible, but clouds of flies appeared as if by magic. Dogs bounded around in packs, respectfully keeping their distance, awaiting their share of the feast.

Searching among the carcasses, Isabel and Mabel soon found the small Shorthorn steer bearing the Aitsan tag.

As Isabel waved a blanket, fighting off flies, she marveled over tiny Mabel's expertise in carving the animal. After slitting open the carcass, she quickly dumped the intestines onto the ground and tossed the offal to the dogs. Deftly she removed the tongue, liver, heart, gall bladder, and pancreas— all considered choice delicacies by the Kiowas. Rump, ribs, and shoulders were separated into manageable portions. By the time Lucius drove the wagon onto the field, the meat was ready for loading.

A party atmosphere prevailed throughout the remainder of the afternoon. Mabel, Pope-bah, Hattie, and Ananthy built a large communal fire in an open space in front of the tipis. There they cooked the most perishable portions of meat and hung others to be cured in the smoke. While the women worked, chattering away in Kiowa, the men sat around the fire, eating raw liver dipped in gall from the animal bladders.

Isabel could not contain her disgust. She signed that if the uncooked liver did not make them fatally ill, they at least were making her sick to her stomach.

The men seemed to think it a good joke.

"The gall from the white man's steer is like water," Odlepaugh signed. "In the long-ago days, the gall from the buffalo was strong. It made the Kiowas strong."

Isabel was writing a letter to her sister Fanny when Mabel, Pope-bah, Hattie, and Ananthy came into the tipi to pack away the meat. All were crying. Pope-bah and Hattie were hugging and comforting each other.

Alarmed, Isabel caught Mabel's sleeve. "What is wrong?" she asked.

"It is the singing, dancing, and storytelling," she signed. "Ration day is a little like the long-ago time, when everyone worked and camped together. Ration day makes everyone cry."

Isabel turned back to her letter. Clearly, civilization was not the answer to everything.

While Odlepaugh and the other men went away to gamble, Lucius saddled a horse and rode into town for the mail. He returned just before dark.

From the moment Isabel saw his face she knew he was the bearer of bad news.

He handed her three letters. Two were from Chicago. The third was a bright yellow Western Union envelope. Isabel ripped it open and read four brief lines:

DEAREST BELLE COMMA YOUR MOTHER PASSED AWAY THIS MORNING STOP LAST WORDS AND THOUGHTS OF YOU STOP EXPECT TO CONDUCT SERVICES SATURDAY UNLESS YOU CAN COME HOME STOP PLEASE ADVISE STOP

Isabel looked at the date.

The telegram was two weeks old!

It had been in the Anadarko post office all that time! No one from the agency had picked up her mail and sent it to her on the reservation; the people at Western Union, fully aware of the contents, had made no effort to see that the message reached her. The sheer callousness was beyond belief!

Blindly, Isabel rose from her desk and walked away from the tipi—away from the noise, the smells, and the constant, wearing presence of the Indians. She found a quiet spot behind the wagon, where she was partially shielded by a neighboring tipi. Lowering her head to the wagon box, she waited for tears to come. But she was beyond any such relief.

She would never see her mother again in this world.

Self-recrimination assailed her. Somehow she should have gone home before it was too late. She could have found a way. Brother Clouse, Sister Everts, someone would have lent her the money.

Sinking to the wagon tongue, she thought of the clean, open spaces of Canada, the prairies of Dakota, the neat and comfortable homes she had known there, the warmth of family and friends.

What was she doing on this God-forsaken Indian reservation?

Suddenly the world around her seemed horrid. She had not a single taste in common with it. She was certain she lived in the most miserable corner of what must be the most decrepit place on the face of the earth.

She had left home, all the people who loved her.

For this!

At last tears came.

As she wept, she faced facts she had long denied:

She lacked the strength of mind necessary for missionary work. She could endure sickness, filth, hunger, discomfort, exposure to the elements. But no longer could she abide the loneliness.

For five months she had not looked upon another white face.

And the first civilized person she had seen in all those months had not even recognized her as a white woman.

Except for her brief exchanges with Lucius and an occasional word from Mabel, she never heard English, save the parroted phrases in her classes.

Sometimes she now caught herself thinking *constantly* in sign language!

No longer could she ignore another fact: Her mission had failed.

Despite all the promises in her letters to the Mission Board, all the extra supplies she had managed to obtain, all the money she had begged and spent, she had not found a single convert.

Her grand plans for a church now seemed no more than childish fantasies.

Torn by grief, she saw herself in the clear light of reality: She was penniless, living in complete squalor in an Indian shack, deluding herself that by her superior example, she would be able to raise the Kiowas above their station.

Some example!

She had never felt more depressed. There was only one thing to do: She would admit defeat, resign her commission, and go back to civilization.

With the decision made, Isabel surrendered to complete desolation. She wept uncontrollably, not caring if she never stopped.

Suddenly a blood-curdling wail rose behind her.

Startled, Isabel looked up.

Domot came striding across the dry grass, jabbering in Kiowa, his long, powerful arms churning in sign language: "Poor little Jesus woman. Your mother dead! Your heart all broken into little pieces!"

Before Isabel could move, he seized her in a crushing hug. His filthy blanket enveloped her. His long, greasy braids brushed her cheek. For a moment she could not breathe. Isabel struggled, but he held her fast. His unwashed stench burned her nostrils. Revulsion swept through her like a fever. She pounded at his chest, thinking she would die in the next moment of absolute horror if he did not free her.

Then Domot's hot tears fell on her neck.

And in that moment a new kind of love was born.

The old savage was grieving—for her!

In one sublime instant, Isabel was consumed by a new state of grace. Instinctively she knew her world would never be the same. She had been swept up in a spiritual conversion as powerful as baptism.

A sweet, perfect calm settled over her. She put her arms around Domot's waist and hugged him.

Domot had invited her onto the reservation, fought for her in council. He fully understood that he was destined never to walk the Jesus road because he had two wives. Yet no one had worked harder for her mission.

He might be an old savage who had lifted many scalps. He stank to high heaven. But under that leathery old hide he had been moved by pure human compassion and love to share her grief.

Isabel tightened her hold on his waist.

They remained for an interminable time embraced, gently weeping.

Chapter Eight

"The bread medicine works night and day," Isabel signed to her cooking class. "If you will put a cloth over it and leave it on the back of the stove or any place warm, it will work while you are sleeping and be ready when you make biscuits the next morning."

"How can it do that?" asked Hattie.

Isabel answered without considering the consequences. "Little bugs inside it do the work."

A murmur of dismay rippled through the group.

Instantly Isabel regretted mentioning details.

All morning they had been crowded into Mabel's small kitchen while a fierce blue norther howled outside. The children had been sent into the other room to play. Repeatedly Isabel had been appalled by the women's ignorance of basic culinary arts. Until coming onto the reservation they had cooked in buffalo stomachs. Although most now owned pans and skillets, they did not possess enough basic kitchen skills to prepare the variety of food available in the white man's world.

"The little bugs are so tiny that you cannot see them," she explained, only making matters worse.

The women groaned, shook their heads, and grimaced to show their disgust.

"I do not want to use the bread medicine," Hattie quickly signed. "If my husband ate it and someone told him about the little bugs he would kill me."

"If you cannot see them, how do you know they are there?" Ananthy asked.

Isabel did not know the sign for "telescope," or even if one existed. She pantomimed looking through her conversation tube and signed, "Have you seen the glass that brings far-off things up close?"

Pope-bah had. She said the word in Kiowa. The other women seemed to understand.

"Two hundred winters ago, a smart white man made a glass that would look at little things and make them big. If we had his glass here, we could see the little bugs."

"I do not want to see them," Hattie signed.

The other women nodded and made sounds of agreement. In too deep to retreat, Isabel pushed on.

Perhaps before the twentieth century arrived, she might be able to bring these Indians into the nineteenth.

"The tiny little bugs live all around us," she signed. "They are called *germs*." She spoke the word aloud. "The little bread medicine bugs are good. A white man named Louis Pasteur showed that they work for us. So we must keep them. He also found that other little bugs bring much sickness. So we must fight to kill them, and throw them away, to protect our families."

The women spoke animatedly to each other in Kiowa. Isabel waited.

"How do we kill the bad little bugs?" asked Pope-bah.

"With soap and water. Hot water is best. White people boil their dirty clothes to kill the little bugs in them. They scrub their houses, and they scrub themselves."

Mabel seldom entered into the discussions, but now her shyness was forgotten under the duress of a burning question.

"Is that why white people sometimes call us 'dirty Indians'? Is that why white people do not want to come near us? Are they afraid of the little bugs on us?"

With regret Isabel remembered that she herself had avoided

personal contact with the Cheyennes and Arapaho when possible.

Had they noticed?

Mabel's soft brown eyes searched her face, seeking the answer.

Isabel decided that the full truth would serve best.

"White people have many reasons for not mixing with Indians," she signed. "Some are afraid because they know Indians have lifted many scalps. Some do not know how to talk to people who do not speak English. They are a little ashamed. But it is also true that with many white people, the tiny little bugs are the reason."

The women said no more. Preoccupied with her baking demonstration, Isabel did not notice that they were profoundly disturbed.

Late that afternoon Lucius returned from the grass money payment at Rainy Mountain.

On the following morning he would not speak to her. Isabel recognized telltale signs that he was angry. Tight little wrinkles gathered at the corners of his mouth, and lowered eyebrows made his eyes even more deep-set.

Isabel tried once to speak to him. He stalked away and avoided her the remainder of the day.

She could not imagine what she had done.

Two days later, after supper, he lingered in the kitchen while she cleaned the table. In the next room Mabel sang a Kiowa lullaby as she put little Sarah to bed.

"Mabel said you called the Kiowas dirty," Lucius said.

In that instant Isabel knew. At first she was relieved. The incident hardly seemed serious. At times she had said much worse. She tried to explain. "Lucius, I only said it in passing. I was telling the women about the bread medicine. They asked questions, so I told them about germs—the good and the bad. Mabel asked me if that was why some whites did not like Indians. I could not tell her a lie. It's true. You know it's true. By white standards, some of the Kiowas *are* dirty."

For a moment Isabel wondered if he were about to hit her. His face turned deep red. His fists clenched. His voice rose.

"Do you forget I have been in the white man's big towns? I have seen white people living like *pigs*."

"So have I," Isabel said. "That's just my point. There are people of every race who don't know better. We should want the Kiowas to be above that."

"The women told their husbands what you said. The men are very hot."

"I'm sorry I have made the men angry," she said. "But Lucius, just look around you. Not a single Kiowa family owns an outhouse. Everyone makes dirty wherever they happen to be. Some Kiowas don't keep themselves or their children clean. Their tipis are filthy. Their clothes are crusted with grime. They put on a shirt or dress and wear it until it falls off. They never throw anything away, and the trash piles up. Most of them have fleas, bedbugs, head lice."

He opened his mouth to speak. She held up a hand to stop him. "I know what you're about to say: so do many white people. And you're right. But you must understand. When white people see lice on an Indian, they say that is the Indian road. Afterward they avoid all Indians. Lucius, I only speak the truth. If I've made everyone angry, I can't help it."

Lucius turned away without answering, went into the bedroom, and closed the door.

When she awoke the next morning, he was gone.

Unable to contain her curiosity, she questioned Mabel. "Where has Lucius gone?"

Mabel signed that she did not know. But after a moment she added, "Sometimes he goes into the mountains to think hard."

Lucius was gone five days.

When he returned, he no longer seemed angry, only morose. He still would not talk with her. He spent most of his time out by the corrals, staring into the distance.

As November progressed, the north wind calmed. A bright sun brought unseasonable warmth to Saddle Mountain—the first decent weather in a month. Isabel recovered from a bout with the grippe and felt much better.

She sent out word that she would give a Jesus talk.

"In the long-ago time, a man was going from one place to another. Some bad men robbed him, beat him, and threw him in a ditch. They left him for dead."

Isabel's small congregation listened with complete attention. The lanterns made the Aitsan arbor an island of light in the surrounding darkness. Isabel hurried to complete her talk, for with nightfall the chilling cold was rapidly returning.

"The next man who came along the road looked at the man who had been robbed and did not stop," she went on. "An-

other man came along and he did not stop, either. But the
third man looked down at the robbed man and his heart hurt.
He stopped and fixed the robbed man's wounds. He took the
robbed man to a place where he could rest until he was
well."

Isabel paused a moment to allow her congregation time to
absorb the story.

"Many winters later, when Jesus told those with him that
we must love our neighbors the same as we love ourselves,
someone asked Him what He meant by the word 'neighbor.'
As an answer, Jesus told this story and asked which of the
three men on that road loved his neighbor, the two who did
not stop, or the one who did?"

The Indians remained so quiet that Isabel was not certain
they understood. "What do you think about this man?" she
asked. "What do you think about this story that Jesus told?"

For a moment there was no sound except the hiss of the
lanterns, the rustle of cold wind through the dried twigs of
the brush arbor.

Pope-bah hesitantly raised her hand. "I think the third
man did the right thing. He was very brave. The robbers
could have come back and killed him."

Odlepaugh's voice rose in quick comment. Lucius did not
translate his brother's remark. A strained silence fell over the
congregation.

Isabel waited a moment. "Lucius, what did Oldepaugh
say?"

Lucius would not meet her gaze. "He said maybe the first
two men thought the man in the ditch was a dirty Kiowa.
That was why they passed him by."

Isabel stood stunned. The entire congregation was looking
down as if ashamed, yet casting quick glances at her to see
what she would do.

She stepped off her little platform, walked to Odlepaugh,
and took one of his big hands between her own.

"Odlepaugh, you of all people know that is not what is in
my heart toward the Kiowas. Mabel asked me if some white
people feel that way about Indians. I said they did, and I told
her why. You know what I say is true. Some Kiowas are not
as clean as they should be."

Oldepaugh spat a Kiowa word and jerked his hand free. A
discordant chorus arose from the congregation.

Oldepaugh shouted over all of them. "What you say is not

true. My wife, Ananthy, cleans our tipis every day. I do not
have fleas or lice. I do not think I have the little bugs you
cannot see, either."

All the Indians began shouting, apparently trying to say
they also did not have fleas or lice or the little bugs, either.
But Lucius could not interpret for everyone at once.

The din continued until Lucius raised his hands for silence.
He began to speak in Kiowa, halting with each sentence to
translate into English for Isabel.

"When I told the Jesus woman I would interpret for her, I
said I would say only her words. I said I would not speak for
myself. Now I speak for myself."

Isabel marveled at the immediate effect of his commanding
presence. The entire congregation had hushed.

"When Mabel told me what the Jesus woman said, my
blood turned hot. Now I have thought long and hard about it
and I believe the Jesus woman is right."

Again shouting erupted. Again Lucius raised his hands for
silence.

"I will tell you what the old people have forgotten and the
young do not know. When our camp got dirty in the long-ago
time, we moved to some other place. When we came back
many winters later, the rain and the wind had cleaned everything for us. Now we make dirty in the same place all the
time and we don't know how to clean it."

He continued in a softer voice. "What the Jesus woman
told us about the little bugs is true. I heard about them in the
white man's school. Maybe we need to know more about
them. Maybe the tiny bugs are why many of our children are
sick all the time and more than half our babies die in their
first winter."

Again he paused. There was not a woman in the congregation
who had not lost at least one baby.

"The whites tell us that when the Jerome Agreement is
approved in Washington, we must pick a place to live the rest
of our lives. On this place our children will live, and maybe
our children's children, too. The whites say the place we
choose will be ours forever, and maybe this is so. The whites
have pushed and pushed the Kiowas. They must stop pushing
somewhere. Maybe the Jerome Agreement is where they will
stop. We must learn to live on this place we choose because
we may have to live on it until we die. The Jesus woman is
here to help us. We must listen to her. She gives us the

truth. She never gives us sugar water. I, Lucius Ben Aitsan, have spoken."

He folded his arms.

A buzz of discussion erupted. Isabel made no move to interfere. This was one issue they would have to resolve for themselves.

Pope-bah raised a hand. She spoke, and Lucius interpreted. "The Jesus woman told us about the bread medicine road. I have tried it and it is good. My husband, Kokom, says it is good. I now think maybe she is right about the dirty road. We must get off it quick. I do not care about the white people. They can make funny about us and think and say whatever they want. I think the Kiowas should walk the clean road because it is the right road. The Jesus woman is very smart. She can teach us the clean road. I think we ought to get on it quick. I am not scared of hard work."

Hattie spoke next. "I have buried three babies. My heart still cries for them. Sometimes I wake up in the night crying and I do not know why until I remember. Our grandfathers told us that the Caddos all died quick of a sickness. I do not want this to happen to the Kiowas. I think we should walk the clean road quick."

Isabel resumed control of the meeting. "I am glad you all feel this way. You know that I am not talking about all Kiowas but only some of them. It will not take much work to be cleaner than most white people. I will teach you what you need to know. Let us pray."

The first ice storm struck in early December. High winds toppled several trees along the creek. The water bucket froze in the kitchen despite a fire Lucius kept burning through the night. Sleet and snow continued to fall intermittently through the next three days, closing all trails and wagon routes. No one could travel to the agency for ration day.

On the morning the blizzard ended, Isabel pulled on her red gum boots and walked out of the house and into a world magically changed. Saddle Mountain towered above her like a massive confection, the bare tips of boulders peeking through the snow like chocolate drops in ice cream. Below the corrals, the whiteness stretched away to the Washita Valley, and beyond, as far as the eye could see.

Lucius pushed his way through the drifts to feed the live-stock. Isabel followed his footsteps in the snow. At the corral,

Jeremiah nuzzled her until she almost lost her footing, and even Jonah seemed glad to see her.

"Snowbound!" she said to Lucius. "This makes me so homesick for Canada. It seems to me I spent half my childhood snowed-in. We never worried. I don't think we have to worry now. We have plenty of food. Let's plan a good, old-fashioned Christmas."

Lucius resisted her high spirits. "I hope the snow does not last that long. Some of the Indians need to draw rations."

That afternoon Isabel introduced Amos and Jessie to the delights of snow ice cream. She taught them how to mix sugar and vanilla in the right proportions in a tin cup before dumping in a handful of snow. With deft stirring, delicious ice cream could be coaxed into existence precious moments before the whole mess melted. Mabel joined in the fun and proved to be the most adept. Baby Sarah was fed a few spoonfuls and cooed her enthusiasm.

By lamplight that evening, Isabel told the story of Dickens's *Christmas Carol*, with Lucius repeating her words in Kiowa. After the story, Amos and Jessie were determined to have a Christmas tree.

The next morning Isabel led them to the foot of the mountain, where they found and cut a small evergreen. They carried it back to the house and spent the afternoon decorating it. Isabel showed them how to pop and string corn, and to make stars and candles from cardboard. They capped the day by building a snowman in the yard and ganging up on Lucius in a snowball fight.

Isabel thoroughly enjoyed the day. Amos and Jessie were rare, precious children, and she regretted that she had been too busy to spend much time with them. Isabel could see how much they had grown since she first arrived on the reservation. Amos was rapidly losing his childish ways and acquiring the solemnity of his father. Clearly Amos believed the sun rose and set on Lucius, for he studied and aped his every gesture. Amos was an unusually handsome boy, with a lean, strong body; crisp black hair; and deep-set, intelligent eyes. Jessie had inherited her mother's beauty, with high, well-chiseled cheekbones; a wide, expressive mouth; strong chin; and sparkling eyes. She also had inherited her father's self-confidence and unusual power of concentration.

Baby Sarah was pampered by everyone and accepted it as

her natural due. She was good-natured to a fault and usually gained her way with laughter and a heartwinning smile.

Although the nights remained cold throughout the next week, the sun returned each short day, bringing a partial thaw. Most of the Indians were able to drive to the agency for rations. Lucius and Mo-keen made the trip and returned with six barrels of mission goods, a stack of mail to be answered, and three boxes addressed to Isabel—Christmas gifts from her brother and sisters.

Isabel forced herself to wait until Christmas to open the boxes, but she had no doubt what they contained. Her family knew that nothing pleased her more than books.

On Christmas morning, all three Aitsan children found gifts under the tree. Isabel and Mabel had collaborated on a rag doll for Jessie, and her father had bought her a set of play dishes at a store in Anadarko.

Isabel had put aside a baseball and glove from the missionary barrel for Amos. Lucius gave him a knife with a deer bone handle made in the long-ago time by his great-grandfather Heap-of-Bears.

For Little Sarah, the missionary barrel contributed a baby bonnet and bib, and a toy dog that rolled on wheels. Mabel had made her two small dresses from flour sacks, dyeing the cloth with intricate designs and stitching tiny blue and yellow flowers all over. Lucius gave her a tiny china doll with Indian features.

Mabel received a sewing kit containing a selection of colorful thread from Isabel, and a turquoise comb and brush set from Lucius.

Among the mission goods, Isabel had found a red wool coat that fit Lucius perfectly. Mabel gave him a wide, beaded snakeskin belt she had made to go with his big silver buckle.

Opening her own gifts, Isabel felt blessed. Amos and Jessie had made her a bookmark of tooled leather. Mabel and Lucius had made her a beaded and painted buckskin dress so she no longer would feel "different" at big eats and powwows.

And as she uncrated the books from her brother and sisters, she could not hold back tears of joy.

She could see the care each of her family had taken in choosing the books, deciding which titles were exactly right, and she could imagine the loving conspiracy among them to guard against duplication.

Loki Mo-keen, Oldepaugh and Ananthy, Kokom and Pope-bah, and every other Indian within five miles arrived for Christmas dinner. Twenty-seven adults crowded into the small room for rabbit pot pie, pinto beans, stewed dried apples, cranberries, bread, currant buns, tea and coffee, and tapioca pudding. The children were served in the bedroom.

A second storm arrived on New Year's Day, ushering in 1897 with a strong north wind that piled snow into high drifts. The following days remained heavily overcast with intervals of sleet. The nights were awesomely cold. From her memories of Canadian winters, Isabel estimated that the early-morning temperatures were well below zero.

Despite a roaring fire in the stove, cold penetrated the house. First Mabel, then the children became feverish. Isabel put them to bed and kept a huge pot of potato soup warm on the stove—the only liquid diet she could devise with the materials at hand.

"We should keep them as warm as possible," she told Lucius. "We can take turns tending the fire."

Instead, Isabel and Lucius fell into the habit of sitting up most of the night, reading, talking, and caring for the sick.

Although they had worked together closely for months, it was during these long evenings of forced intimacy that a special bond began to grow between them.

Through the nights they shared the lamplight before the wood stove, Lucius with his Bible and dictionary, occasionally asking questions, Isabel writing letters, reading her new books, working on her journals.

She quickly discovered that during his six years of hard study, he had absorbed the Bible with remarkable comprehension.

One evening he admitted he preferred the Old to the New Testament because it reminded him of his childhood.

"It seems different, but if you think hard, it is much the same. The people in the Bible traveled over the land in small tribes, just as the Kiowas did. Their prophets told what would happen in the far-ahead time. The Kiowa medicine men did the same. The people in the Bible went off to themselves, went a long time without food, and searched for visions. When they received a vision, they lived by it all of their lives much like the Kiowas in the long-ago time. The people in the Bible talked to God, and He answered them. This happened to some Kiowas. The people in the Bible had tribal laws they had worked out with God. They had ceremonies, animal sacrifice. That was much like the Kiowas used the buffalo in the Sun Dance. All of it is much like the Kiowas."

"Some white people think the Indians may be the lost tribes of Israel," she told him. "They say the Indians became lost about two thousand years ago and somehow found their way into this country."

Lucius frowned in doubt. Then he laughed at a new thought. "In the long-ago time a band of Kiowas went off hunting and did not come back. Maybe they found their way to the Holy Land and became Jews."

Isabel smiled.

"I think my father also preferred the Old Testament. He said the Book of Job contains the sum of man's religious experience."

Lucius nodded. "Job was like a Kiowa. He suffered and suffered and did not know why. God quit talking to him. God no longer talks to the Kiowas."

"Yet Job kept his faith," Isabel pointed out.

Lucius frowned, searching for words. "It is not easy. The Kiowas still believe in God, even after all that has happened to them. But now they are hungry and sick. Like Job, they see their children suffer and die, and they do not know why. God will not tell them. After many years, God talked to Job. Why won't God talk to the Kiowas?"

"Lucius, maybe God *has* spoken to us, through Job. Remember? God asked Job: *Where wast thou when I laid the foundations of the earth?* My father always said God was telling Job that some things surpass human understanding. In the end, God rewarded Job for keeping his faith and chastised Job's friends for losing theirs. Maybe that is the way it will be with the Kiowas."

"I hope I live to see it."

"Maybe you will. I hope someday to introduce you to a great man, Dr. Robert J. Burdette. He is the brother of Miss Burdette, the lady who runs our Home Mission Society in Chicago. Dr. Burdette is one of the greatest religious thinkers alive today. I'm sure he would be interested in the parallels you have observed between the Kiowas and the ancient Jews. I doubt anyone else has thought about them."

Lucius pointed to his Bible. "They are there."

As the feeling of intimacy grew, night after night, Isabel was thrilled with the insight she gained into his nature, but he still remained reticent about his personal life. One evening, Isabel determined to learn more.

"Lucius, I wonder if you realize what a fine mind you have," she said. "Few white Christians have studied the Bible so thoroughly. It is absolutely remarkable that you've accomplished all this by yourself, with no one to guide you. I've met several Carlisle graduates. None has bothered to go beyond what he learned there. Why did you go on? What drove you?"

Isabel thought at first that he would not answer. He put more wood into the stove. Then she saw that he had taken her question seriously.

"I don't know," he said. "I have *always* wanted to learn more, from the time I was little. When they told us at Carlisle we had studied enough and had to go back to the reservation, I did not want to go. After we were sent back from the school, most of the Indians threw away their books. I kept mine. I read them over and over until they fell into pieces. When Brother Methvin gave me the Bible, I was happy because I had a new book to read."

"Lucius, you are a natural-born scholar. That's a wonderful, priceless thing. And yet I know so little about you, even after all these months."

Lucius sat looking at her. The soft light of the kerosene lamp lent depth to his eyes, and the shadows strengthened the firm character lines around his mouth.

"What do you want to know?"

"Everything. Your boyhood. How you came to go to Carlisle. How you and Mabel met and fell in love. All the things a good friend comes to know in the course of time."

Lucius continued to study her. "I don't know many things about you."

Isabel laughed. "All right. If you will tell me about you, I will tell you about me."

Lucius smiled. "We have a covenant. What do you want to know first?"

"The things that made you what you are."

Lucius spoke hesitantly. "I don't know what I am. Until I had eight winters, I thought I would grow up to be a Kiowa warrior. Everyone thought that was what I would be. At Carlisle they gave me a white name and tried to make me into a white man, but they could not do it. I have my father's Mexican blood, my mother's Kiowa blood. I have a name that is part white, part Indian. I have pieces of all this inside me. I feel that I am a Kiowa, but some people think I am no longer a Kiowa. I do not know what I am."

Isabel sensed his discomfort. She changed the subject. "Who gave you your white name?"

Lucius smiled. "Captain Pratt. He was in charge when the Army took the chiefs to prison in Florida. He could have been mean to us. But he was not. He told the chiefs they could make arrows and other Indian things and sell them to the white people there. The chiefs made much money while they were in prison. Later Captain Pratt took two Kiowa boys, Charley Buffalo and Chad-dle-ty, and two Cheyenne boys to see President Hayes in Washington. He told the President that a special school was needed for Indians. That was the start of Carlisle Indian School. Captain Pratt gave us white names. He said he would give me the name of his good friend, Lucius Ben Stuart, but I told him I did not want to throw away my Indian name. He said, 'All right, we will call you Lucius Ben Aitsan.' That is the way that happened."

Isabel realized she did not know the meaning of the word *aitsan*. Every Indian name was descriptive, and some translated easily into English. The word *odlepaugh*, for instance, meant "buffalo bird."

"What does *aitsan* mean?"

"The words in English are not the same as the word in Kiowa. The closest, maybe, is 'kills him on the sly.' "

Isabel continued to look at him questioningly. Lucius laughed.

"Yes, there is a story to it. On the night I was born it was very cold. My grandfather Heap-of-Bears saw a Blackfoot Indian hiding across the river. The Blackfoot was on his way to visit the Cheyennes. My grandfather called to him in Cheyenne words. The Blackfoot thought it was his friends calling to him, and so he started across the river. When he got to the middle of the river, my grandfather shot him because they were long-time enemies. All the Kiowas thought my grandfather was very smart to trick the Blackfoot that way. They said they thought I would be very smart, too. So they named me Aitsan."

"Maybe it was prophetic. You *are* smart."

"I have all of these things inside me. Indian things, white things. They are all mixed up."

"Maybe you are a better man for it."

Lucius thought for a moment, then shook his head. "No. I do not think it makes me better. A man should be hard, of one piece, like my father, Loki Mo-keen. He is the same man the soldiers drove onto the reservation. He has had to change his life, but he has not changed inside. I have. Most Kiowas have."

He remained silent for several minutes. When he spoke, his voice was softer. "When I was four, I learned to shoot with the bow and arrow, and the rifle. When I was six, my father brought home a buffalo calf and tied it to a tree. He showed me where to shoot for a clean kill, and I killed it. We had a big eat. I had my own little tipi, a white dog with a red spot on top, and a little donkey. When we moved, the donkey carried my tipi and the little white dog. I was seven the winter the soldiers trapped us in the Palo Duro Canyon. We called it A-go-ta-pa-a, Chinaberry Creek. The day the soldiers caught us was cold and rainy. Loki Mo-keen put me behind some bushes and told me to stay there. But I could see everything. I heard much noise and shooting. The warriors were yelling their war cries, and the soldiers were shouting and blowing bugles. Horses were running everywhere, and I was scared I would be stomped into the ground. The Kiowas fought hard that day. Maybe we would have whipped the soldiers, but they cut us off from our horses. Then the soldiers shot all our horses, more than a thousand. It was a terrible thing to see. The bones are there today on the floor of the canyon. When I think about it, I can still hear the horses screaming as the soldiers shot them."

Lucius closed his eyes for a moment, then went on. "The Kiowa warriors would have chosen that day to die if the women and children had not been there. The soldiers were all around us, and it would have been easy. But the warriors remembered the fight on the Washita six winters before, when Custer and his soldiers killed all the women and children, too. So the Kiowas put down their rifles. The soldiers herded us east to the reservation like cattle. We walked all the way. More than a hundred and eighty miles. A big snow fell and we were very cold. Few of us had blankets. Some did not have moccasins. Many had only a few clothes. Loki Mo-keen carried me much of the way."

Lucius frowned, lost in his memories. "It does not seem possible, but I was younger then than Amos is now. When we came to Fort Sill we were all worn out and very hungry, but they put us in a stone corral and kept us there. They threw raw meat to us like we were animals. I was very scared. After a few days the chiefs were chained and put into wagons to be taken to prison in Florida. Lone Wolf, Maman'-te, Biako, Goho—all the great chiefs were taken away, along with many Comanches and a few Apaches. Everyone cried and we were sad a long time. First the government tried to make the Kiowas into sheepherders. Then they wanted to teach us to farm. A few Kiowas tried. Others stood around and made funny of those who plowed. Then came the melon sickness and my mother died. My father loved me the same but a man cannot take care of a child."

Lucius seemed to lose the thread of his story. For a time there was only the howling of the wind.

Isabel did not know if he intended to go on. She waited patiently. After a time, Lucius resumed his story.

"When I was nine, Mr. Thomas Beatty came and started a school in a tent on Cache Creek. He was a Quaker. He had pictures of animals and things. He said the names in English and we tried to say the words. But that did not last long. My father came and took me home. Many Kiowas believed then that if we looked at the pictures too much, we would die quick like the Caddos. Later, when I was fourteen, there was a school at Fort Sill and I wanted to go. My father said no, but I wore him down. I learned the ABC's and to spell 'cat,' 'dog,' 'cow,' 'boy,' and a few other words. The teacher there said I was very smart. So the next summer, when Agent Hunt wanted names to go away to Carlisle, Joshua Given and I gave ours one day when my father was out hunting horses. When he heard, he said he would kill himself if I went. But I said, 'I'm going anyhow.' Agent Hunt said he would take care of my father and not to worry about him. When I rode away in the wagon, my father cried hard. Eleven of us went that day. Hunting Horse came in with his little sister and said, 'I love my little sister, but I want to send her to school.' I felt sorry for her because she was so little and so scared. I never thought then that I would marry her. I did not know I loved her until we were finished at school and we were on the train coming home."

"And then you became a soldier?"

Lucius nodded. "For six years I was an Army scout. Most of the time we patrolled the reservations north of here, trying to keep the white men out until the openings."

"The Boomers and the Sooners," Isabel said.

Boomers attempted to settle on land before it was legally opened. Sooners sneaked in ahead of the opening and remained hidden until the appointed hour, then emerged to stake choice claims.

"Yes, the Boomers and the Sooners," Lucius said. "Now you know about me. I do not know about you. Remember, we have a covenant."

Isabel smiled. "I assure you, there's nothing about me half so fascinating. You have the poor end of the bargain. Besides, it is almost morning. We should sleep. I will tell you my story tonight."

The mood lingered throughout the day. While Isabel tended to the sick, Lucius went out to feed the livestock and to chop more wood. The day was cold and gray, and by late afternoon more snow was falling.

Lucius returned to the house worried. "Some of the Indians will be running out of food. They will not be able to get to the agency to draw rations."

Isabel had lost track of time. Counting back, she realized that the last distribution of food had come in mid-December.

With the storms, no one had been to the agency in more than three weeks.

"Surely this awful weather will not hold," she said. "Maybe Domot and Mo-keen will be able to bring supplies with their big freight wagons."

Lucius frowned. "If the snow does not melt quick, it will have to be done with pack horses. Many Indians will be hungry before long."

Isabel thought of the forty-mile trip to the Anadarko agency. It had been difficult, even under the best of conditions. Horses would be battling chest-high drifts all the way.

"If the situation grows much worse, maybe the Army will learn of it and rush food out from Fort Sill," she said. "Surely they won't allow the Indians to starve."

Lucius gave her an amused glance and did not answer.

"My parents were born in Ireland," Isabel began. "I will tell you their story first, because I think it quite wonderful."

The hour was late. The night was cold and wind howled under the eaves. Isabel and Lucius had draped blankets over their shoulders against the drafts.

"On my father's side, the Crawfords were well-to-do, strict

Presbyterians," Isabel said. "My father was made to study the Bible for at least an hour every day."

She smiled, remembering what happened next.

"The Bible study was his undoing. Reading about John the Baptist, he became convinced of error in Presbyterian orthodoxy. He started attending a Baptist church, and soon he was baptized. When his family learned of it, he was turned out of his home, and cut off from his inheritance. He was never allowed to sleep in his father's house again."

Lucius made an unintelligible sound. "I could never do that to Amos."

Isabel attempted to explain. "You must understand the times in which this happened. Religion had been the cause of much trouble in England and Ireland. Many hot words had been said. Many people had been killed. Anyway, my father was fourteen and penniless. A great man named Alexander Carson took him into his home and prepared him for a university education. My father earned his way through Stepney College, an almost impossible thing to do in that time and place. While he was a student, he met my mother, and they fell in love. Her family were Episcopalians, and you can imagine their reaction when they learned she wanted to marry a Baptist. And a poor one at that! But my father won them over. They had a grand wedding. My mother's family was very well-to-do, and there were many presents."

Isabel thought of the little blue china creamer, a casualty of the pigs when she first came to the reservation. As far as she knew, that had been the last of the wedding gifts.

"After a long time, my father was ordained, but there were few Baptists in that place, and not many opportunities for a preacher. When he saw that conditions were not about to improve, he decided to come to America."

She wished she could convey to Lucius the many difficulties that decision entailed, but his perception was limited. She could offer him only a glimpse.

"The ocean voyage was very long—more than three thousand miles—and very expensive. By then Father and Mother had two babies, my sisters Emily and Fanny. They sold their wedding gifts, almost everything they owned, to pay the passage. They landed in Toronto with no money at all. My father searched until he found a little village west of there called Cheltenham, where they needed a preacher. It was there that my brother Hugh and I were born."

Lucius reached for his dictionary, which contained maps. Isabel showed him the approximate location of Cheltenham, and he made a small "x" on the map in pencil.

"I was a late baby," Isabel went on. "My father was almost fifty years old when I was born. When I was about three, he was invited to teach at the Baptist seminary in Woodstock, a few miles southwest of Cheltenham, near Toronto. There I grew up." She showed him on the map.

"We had a nice, big house in Woodstock. I don't remember the earlier years when there was little money. My father was very strict. On the Sabbath all our dolls and toys were put away and we couldn't sing or whistle. Every night my father went over our schoolwork with us. At nine o'clock he rang a little bell, and for thirty minutes we discussed the significance of what we had learned. Then he rang the bell again, and it was bedtime. My mother taught us music and French, with lessons every day except Sunday and no excuses. Our church was heavily involved in mission work. When the missionaries returned from the field, they told us about their lives. I knew when I was a little girl that was what I wanted to do. But I never dreamed it would really happen. Then when I was sixteen, my father decided to go into western Canada and start another seminary."

Again she bent over the map. "He established it here, west of Winnipeg, at a little place called Rapid City. The railroad was supposed to come through there, but it came through Brandon instead and left us rather remote. Not that it mattered. After a time, the Canadian Baptists decided one seminary was enough and ordered Father to close his. So we moved here, into Dakota Territory, to a little town called St. Thomas."

She pointed and waited until he marked the map.

"By then my older sisters were married, so I was left in Canada to close the seminary. I became ill from overwork, and that was when I was given the quinine that took my hearing."

She did not want Lucius to suspect what a tremendous disappointment that move had been for her father, in stepping down from director of a seminary to be pastor of a small rural church.

"We remained in St. Thomas six years. In many ways they were our happiest. Then my father lost his pastorship. And he could find no other."

She could not hold back tears at the memory. "After a lifetime of service in the church, he was seventy-one years old and without a cent to his name."

Isabel wiped her eyes and forced herself to finish the story. "He and Mother went to live with my sister in Toronto. About that time, I was engaged to be married. But just before our marriage, the man ran off with another woman."

Again Lucius made an unintelligible sound deep in his throat. "That man was crazy."

Isabel felt his reaction was sincere and not just simple courtesy. But she did not want to sail under false colors.

"Maybe it wasn't entirely his fault. I think maybe he sensed that I really did not want to marry him." She hesitated, seeking a way to explain. "At that time and place, there was a plain road every young woman was expected to walk. She married, had children. We didn't know another road. I didn't want to take it up, but I didn't know what else to do. So in a way the man did me a favor."

"He also did the Kiowas a favor," Lucius said. "But it was a bad thing to do to you."

"It was all for the best," Isabel insisted, moved by his intensity. "Maybe the Lord helped. Not long after, I heard Miss Burdette speak, and I learned how to become a missionary. I was accepted and attended Training School. I applied for citizenship in this country and received it." She laughed and spread her hands. "And here I am."

Lucius reached for her hand and took it in his own. Gently he pressed her palm to his chest, over his heart. He looked at her in the soft lamplight, his eyes conveying a tenderness she had seldom known. When he spoke, his voice was husky with emotion. "I am very, very glad you are here. You are the best thing that has happened to me."

Warmth spread through her. She gazed into his eyes, lost in the moment. Her other hand seemed to rise of its own volition and traced his cheek, the firm line of his chin.

He pulled her to him, and his strong arms went around her. Isabel surrendered to his embrace, burying her face in his broad shoulder. His strong hands caressed her back, her arms, her hair. Passions long ignored took full possession of her.

In the next room, Amos coughed.

Isabel awoke to the danger as if from a dream.

She pushed away and shook her head.

Cold reason returned in a rush. Lulled by the warmth of the stove on a winter night, disarmed by their shared intimacy, she had allowed matters to go too far.

Mabel was within earshot in the next room.

She might even be awake, listening.

Kiowa women were accustomed in the long-ago time to sharing their husbands with other wives.

Had Mabel expected something like this to happen?

The situation was impossible. Even if Lucius were not a married man with three children, there were inescapable differences. She had learned to love Lucius as deeply as anyone she had ever known, and felt an almost overpowering physical and intellectual attraction to him.

But he had his family, his responsibility to his people.

She had her work, her commitment.

Not the barest whisper of scandal should ever be breathed. The matter must be laid to rest, stopped, right here and now.

Lucius sat motionless, his face a study in uncertainty.

With quick common sense, Isabel understood that she must make her position plain. Unresolved, the impulsive incident would forever remain an awkwardness between them.

She reached for his hand.

"I'm glad I'm here, too, Lucius," she said. "You and Mabel are two of the dearest people I have ever known."

She squeezed his hand, picked up her book, and the spell ended. Crossing to her cot, she closed the blanket partition, signaling that she was preparing to retire for the night.

She lay down fully clothed. A few minutes later, Lucius carried the lamp into the bedroom.

Isabel remained awake in the darkness, listening to the wind under the eaves.

Their embrace had struck her to the heart—a magic, transcendent encounter that would never be far from her mind.

But she knew it was one she must never risk again.

Before the norther faded, another snowstorm struck. Lucius said he had never known such a winter.

One morning Domot and Little Robe rode into the yard, exhausted and half frozen. They thawed by the fire, talking animatedly with Lucius. Isabel served them hot beef stew and waited patiently for the translation. At last it came.

"Domot and Little Robe went to Anadarko to draw rations," Lucius said. "Colonel Baldwin told them snow has stopped trains all over the country. The agency has no food at all."

Isabel simply had to sit down.

The possibilities were terrifying. She had never considered for a moment that the supplies would not be available once the storms lifted.

The rations were now a full month overdue.

"Little Robe and Domot said nearly everyone was out of food when they left home," Lucius went on. "They have been gone a week. The agent told them a train was due at Paul's Valley, and he expected supplies from there. So they waited two days. Then the talking wire said the train was stopped in Kansas by snow."

Paul's Valley, the closest siding on the new railroad, was sixty miles beyond the agency. Telegraph wires had been completed from there to both Fort Sill and the Anadarko agency.

"How are the roads?"

"Little Robe said the snow is very bad. He said he wanted to turn back at Cache Creek, but Domot was worried about his family and would not stop. Little Robe said they almost killed their horses."

Isabel thought ahead to the worst.

Unless conditions improved, supplies probably could not be hauled from the railroad. The telegraph lines might fail at any moment. Something had to be done quickly.

"First we need to know the true situation," she told Lucius. "Once we learn, we can send for help."

Within the hour Lucius saddled his strongest horse and rode away with Domot and Little Robe.

Isabel and Mabel fretted helplessly as more snow fell during the night. It had not stopped by midmorning when Lucius returned so frozen he could scarcely talk.

"I rode all the way around Saddle Mountain," he said. "Everyone is hungry. Sickness is everywhere. I do not know what to do."

While he thawed by the fire, Isabel set up her campaign desk and spread her writing material. She wrote hurriedly, for once not worrying about neatness or syntax.

When she had finished, she gave the letters to Lucius, along with the last of the money from Miss Burdette.

"Lucius, we must let the outside world know what is happening here. Go to the telegraph office in Anadarko.

Send this message to these two congressmen. They are friends of Dr. Burdette. They may be able to do something in Washington. Send this message to Miss Burdette and wait for a reply. It may take two or three days. She may have to borrow money from a bank. But she will send it. When the money comes, buy food and medicine in the citizen stores in Anadarko. You can use Jonah and Jeremiah to bring everything back. If you have any trouble at the telegraph office, or anywhere, go see Brother Methvin. I'm sure he will help you. This note is for Colonel Baldwin. It explains everything we are doing, so he will not be surprised when hot words come back to him from Washington."

Lucius saddled the horses and rode away in the swirling snow.

Isabel knew what she had to do.

She struggled into her red gum boots and several layers of the warmest clothing she could find. She did not know if she had the strength. But if she did not try, she would never be able to face herself in the mirror again.

She spread a blanket on her cot and began piling food and medicine on it.

Mabel began signing frantically. "You can't go out in this storm. Lucius has taken the horses. You will die in the snow."

"We must do what we can," Isabel answered. "We don't have much food left, but we can share. I will be back before Lucius returns."

She set out walking in the driving snow, carrying the blanket filled with food and medicine on her back.

With Saddle Mountain obscured, she worried about keeping her sense of direction. The cold soon penetrated her clothing, and before she had gone a mile her feet, hands, and face were numb.

All trails were obscured. For hours she moved from one landmark to the next, concentrating on keeping to a straight line. She kept looking in vain for the dry wash where the trail turned, but she could not find it. Nothing seemed remotely familiar. Ahead of her, as far as she could see in the blinding storm, were only drifts of driven snow.

Fighting down panic, she stopped and tried to restore calm reason. Belatedly she understood that the dry wash she sought was probably drifted level, and she was now past it.

She considered turning back. But with her tracks already

erased by wind and snow, one direction seemed as safe as another.

Moving on, she found a stand of trees she thought she recognized. Barren of leaves and ghostly in the snow, they appeared different. But trees were not abundant in the region. It could hardly be a case of mistaken identity. Correcting her course, she turned southward.

She came upon the Kokom tipis unexpectedly. One moment she was pushing her way through the snow, uncertain as to her exact location, and in the next the tipis appeared magically in her path.

The Kokom place was so quiet she first feared they were all dead. Then she saw faint wisps of smoke rising from the ventilation hole at the top of the nearest tipi. She called to them.

Pope-bah unlatched the flap. She had lost so much weight that Isabel hardly recognized her. As she came forward, she wheezed with every breath.

"We are all sick," she signed. "I think maybe we are dying like the Caddos."

Isabel followed Pope-bah into the tipi. It was dark and cold, with heat and light coming only from a small fire. Isabel found a lamp and started to light it. Pope-bah stopped her, signing that there was no medicine water for the lamp. Isabel went outside, found more wood, and built up the fire.

Kokom tried to sit up and assume his role as host, but he was out of his head with fever. Isabel pushed him back onto his bed and signed that he was to lie still and rest.

She examined the children. Fanny, Bessie, Blanche, and Wesley all were in the throes of pneumonia. By placing her ear to their chests, she could hear fluid rattling in their lungs.

For a time Isabel sat warming her hands and catching her breath, momentarily paralyzed by a growing sense of inadequacy.

She had no medical training, and only a few patent tonics and salves, all probably worthless.

But it was plain that she was the only healthy person on the place.

And at least she could cook.

Opening two tins, she made a pot of beef broth. The children were too weak to sit up, so she fed them one by one.

By the time she finished, darkness had fallen on the short day. She dispensed the medicines she had with little faith in their effectiveness. The children retained the food. Isabel found a measure of hope in that.

She spent the night tending to the Kokoms, catnapping only at rare intervals.

The next morning Pope-bah awoke much improved. She helped Isabel make a beef stew and warm a loaf of bread. After breakfast, Kokom and the children also seemed stronger.

Isabel felt too tired to go on, but her way had been made easier. The snow had stopped and Saddle Mountain again was plainly visible. At least she would not get lost.

"I must go to the Spotted Horse tipi," she signed to Pope-bah. "Lucius said they are very hungry. Little Robert is heaped-up sick. I will leave you some food here. We will bring more soon."

She set out through the ice and snow and walked the two miles to the Spotted Horse tipi.

The brush arbor in the yard had collapsed under an accumulation of snow. The compound seemed deserted. But on Isabel's call, Hattie came out of a tipi and embraced her. Hattie's eyes were bright with fever, her face taut with worry.

"My baby is sick," she signed.

"I have brought medicine and a little food," Isabel told her. "We will make soup. Lucius has gone to the agency for help. We will do what we can."

Isabel showed Hattie how to prepare beef broth. The baby's lungs were full of fluid, but Isabel knew there was nothing more she could do. Either the baby would, or would not, get well.

It was in God's hands.

"I must take food to others," she signed.

That afternoon she visited the Heenkey and Odlepaugh tipis. At each she found hunger and sickness. That night, with her food and medicine exhausted, she turned back home.

"You cannot go in the dark," Ananthy signed. "You will get lost in the snow and freeze."

"There will be some light from the moon," Isabel answered. "I will be able to see the mountain. I must be there when Lucius returns."

The moon was partially hidden behind a pale overcast. The landscape around her was vague, indistinct. But the way grew more familiar with every mile.

She was high on a spur of the mountain when she saw the

first dark form following her. At first she thought she had imagined it. But looking behind her, she saw other movements.

Her heart lurched as she realized that the shadows were wolves, stalking her. In panic she broke into a run. The shadows kept pace, moving out to flank her on each side.

Caution broke through her terror.

If she fell, the animals would attack.

She slowed to a fast walk. The wolves came closer. She could see their eyes and teeth glistening in the moonlight.

Stopping, she dug beneath the snow for stones. After gathering a handful, she began throwing them and shouting.

The wolves retreated.

Emboldened, Isabel walked on. The wolves continued to follow, but at a safer distance.

She had always heard that wolves attack only the weak. As she passed a thicket of underbrush, she selected a big stick.

She walked on, occasionally looking back.

The wolves slunk along behind her, dodging from side to side, their tails between their legs.

Isabel laughed. They were nothing more than a pack of cowardly dogs.

Shouldering her stick, she began to sing at the top of her voice:

Onward, Christian so-old-jers,
Marching as to warrrr . . .

She continued to sing, stepping in cadence, as she passed her brush arbor, her old campground.

From time to time she glanced back. The wolves had fallen farther behind.

For a time she was seized by uncontrollable laughter.

Clearly the wolves did not know what to make of her.

Many people had that trouble.

In the still night air, Isabel heard the awful wailing even before the Aitsan home came into view.

Alarmed, she quickened her step. As she topped the last hill, she saw that the Aitsan yard was filled with wagons, horses, and tipis.

From the house came a mournful chorus that sent shivers up her spine.

She hurried to the house and pushed open the door.

The floor was almost covered with Indians.

Mabel was in a corner tucking blankets around a small, still form. Sepemah sat wailing beside the child, rocking back and forth in her misery.

Isabel crossed the room and knelt beside the baby. Almost all breath had ceased. The infant certainly would die within the hour.

Isabel counted twenty-two Indians on the floor, all sick, many probably dying.

Sepemah's husband, Papedone, signed to her. "My way-behind little one is dying quick. The Great Father is kind. He knows there is no food, and too many in my tipi."

Isabel had no answer for him.

Would the trials of Job never end?

She shed her boots and excess clothing, then went from patient to patient around the room, checking the condition of each. She found that as ever, the old and the young were most seriously afflicted. Two elderly men and three more children probably would not last the night.

In all, thirty-nine Kiowas had descended upon the Aitsan household.

"Some of the children have not eaten for days," Mabel signed. "What can we do?"

The Aitsan calf had been butchered in the fall, and—after a month without rations—the cow had followed in December. Isabel now considered the possibility of butchering a horse. Several teams had been placed in the corral. But the animals had wintered hard and were little more than skin and bones. They would provide little nourishment. Jonah and Jeremiah were fleshier, but Lucius had taken them along to bring back supplies.

"We can only make everyone as comfortable as possible and wait for Lucius," she signed.

The Papedone baby was the first to die. Isabel sent two of the men out to her wagon to empty a missionary box and to reshape it as a coffin. She carried the small body out to the storage tipi. Moving barrels and boxes aside, she turned the tipi into a temporary morgue.

She then organized a rotation schedule to keep the fire going and the sick tended.

All through the night she and Mabel bathed fevered faces and cleaned emaciated bodies. Diarrhea was rampant. The odors in the small room were almost beyond human tolerance. The constant chorus of steniorous breathing, the groans of the suffering helped to turn the house into a torture chamber.

Dawn brought no relief. The cries of the hungry children only added to the din.

The morning passed and Lucius did not come. As she worked, tending to the sick, Isabel worried.

She remembered the blinding snow on the day he left, and her own difficulty in keeping her direction even on familiar ground.

Her fear for Lucius's safety began to shove all other concerns aside.

In early afternoon Cct-in-paut died, ending his century and more on earth. His body was carried to the storage tipi. Isabel went out to pray over him.

She wept in helpless fury with the knowledge that he had not eaten during his last four days of life.

Just before dark, Loki Mo-keen drove into the yard, leaped from his wagon, and strode angrily into the house. His eyes searched the crowd for Mabel. At the moment she was in the next room, feeding little Sarah.

"Where is my son?" Mo-keen signed to Isabel.

"He went to the agency three days ago for food," she signed.

"In the storm?"

Isabel raised a forefinger and dropped it in the "yes" sign.

"He may be dead, lying somewhere in the snow," Mo-keen signed.

Isabel did not answer.

Her own fear continued to grow by the hour.

Mabel came into the room and talked to Mo-keen in Kiowa. She explained to Isabel in signs that Mo-keen, freighting for the Army, had been trapped at Fort Sill by the last storm. He had not known there had been no rations for six weeks.

"I will go to Anadarko in my wagon," he signed to Isabel. "I will take my rifle. I will use it to get food at the white man stores. I will bring that food back here."

Isabel made the "no" sign emphatically. "If that was the right road, I would pick up a rifle and go with you. That is the wrong road. You will find only trouble on it. I have sent a talking wire letter to the white chiefs in Washington, telling them what is happening here. They will find food for us. Lucius will need help hauling it back here."

Mo-keen made a circle of the room, talking to the Indian men. He then saddled a horse and rode away to tell Domot and Odlepaugh to bring their wagons.

Shortly after midnight, Mo-keen, Odlepaugh, and Domot set out for Anadarko. Mo-keen signed that they had strong horses and would take turns breaking trail.

Lucius arrived late the next afternoon, walking, the three horses burdened under full loads.

"I had to wait for the money from Miss Burdette," he said. "The owners at the stores did not believe I would get it."

Lucius also brought a telegram from one of the congressmen.

WIRE CONCERNING KIOWA SITUATION ARRIVED LAST NIGHT STOP BE ADVISED COMMISSIONER OF INDIAN AFFAIRS ISSUED INSTRUCTIONS TODAY THAT IF RATION NOT IN HAND COMMA SHORTFALL TO BE DISTRIBUTED IMMEDIATELY FROM ARMY SUPPLIES FORT SILL STOP PLEASE KEEP ME INFORMED STOP

Lucius said he met Mo-keen, Domot, and Odlepaugh near Cache Creek. He told them about the requisitioning and gave them what was left of the mission money.

Isabel and Mabel opened cans and heated big pots of soup. "Do not overeat," Isabel warned the Indians. "Your chuck bags have shrunk. They can hold only a little at a time. This food is not to be wasted."

The nourishment came too late for some. Two more baby girls breathed their last, and early in the evening old Challinone died. He had spent his last years near Big Tree Crossing, between Saddle and Rainy mountains.

His body was moved into the storage tent.

Exhausted, Lucius slept a few hours. At dawn Gahbein, Heenkey, Long Horn, and Lucius went to the foot of the mountain to dig graves. The boards from Isabel's wagon box were used to make coffins.

Before the graves were completed, Big Tree arrived. He had heard that his boyhood friend Challinone was bad sick. When told he had come too late, he began to weep. He held the hand of his dead friend and made a long speech in Kiowa. His oration set off an orgy of grief throughout the Aitsan compound.

"What did he say?" Isabel asked Lucius.

"He talked about how he and Challinone played together as children. He told about their days on the war road and how they have worked together to try to save the Kiowas. He said they were baptized at the Rainy Mountain church on the same day, and that since they are both Christians, they will soon meet in the other world."

Isabel followed the Indians to the graveyard and conducted the services, so tired that she hardly knew what she was saying. Challinone's Bible was placed beneath his head, his medicine bag at his feet.

He had told his friends he did not want to hand down the old religion to his children, that they must find a new road.

After the funeral services, Lucius harnessed his team. "I will take a small ration to every family," he said. "Maybe that will keep some of the sick alive until Mo-keen brings back the government issue."

"I'll go with you and do what I can for the sick," Isabel said.

Lucius and Isabel traveled for seven days and nights, visiting every family in that part of the reservation. At every tipi the story was the same—hunger and sickness, and sometimes death.

One evening, tending the sick in a tipi on the far side of the mountain, Isabel lifted her lamp, turned to get a bottle of cough syrup from her pack, and came face to face with a white woman.

Startled, Isabel spoke in English. "Hello. I'm Isabel Crawford. I don't believe we've met."

The woman turned and fled into the night. Isabel looked out just in time to see the flap close on an adjoining tipi.

Quickly Lucius was at her side. "You must never tell anyone you saw that woman."

"Lucius! She's white! What is she doing here?"

Lucius held her gaze. "She is a Kiowa."

"But her eyes are gray! Maybe blue! I couldn't tell in this light. Her hair is as fair as mine!"

"She is a Kiowa," Lucius said again. "Her name is Say-haye-do-hole. She is the wife of Goombi. She does not speak one word of English."

"But her skin is so light! She *must* be one of the captives the Army believes is still held on the reservation!"

All the Indians in the tipi were following the discussion. Although they did not understand the words, their eyes were alive with concern.

"Say-haye-do-hole has lived as a Kiowa more than thirty

years," Lucius said quietly. "She has nine children, many grandchildren. All are Kiowas. She does not want to leave them. When the soldiers come here she stays hidden. When she must go to the fort or agency, she stains her skin with walnut juice. She is afraid that if the Army learns she is here, they will take her away from her husband, Goombi, and her children."

"At least we could let her white family know!"

Lucius shook his head. "She was two years old when she was taken. She does not remember her white family. Would they want her back now?"

Isabel did not answer. Lucius was right. Say-haye-do-hole would find no place in the white world.

Isabel knelt again beside the sick child.

"That is Say-haye-do-hole's daughter Minnie," Lucius said.

Isabel gave the child a teaspoonful of cough syrup. The child was nine or ten years of age. Now that Isabel knew, she could see evidence of white ancestry in the child's lighter complexion and finer hair. She wiped the girl's face with a damp towel and was rewarded with a smile.

Isabel easily could understand Say-haye-do-hole's plight.

"You can tell the Goombi family that I will keep their secret safe," she said to Lucius.

The bad weather continued through February. Many families were unable to go to the agency to draw rations.

Lucius and Isabel continued to travel throughout the Saddle Mountain region of the reservation, tending to the sick, burying the dead. It seemed that everywhere they went, Loki Mo-keen had been there, delivering life-saving supplies.

Isabel expressed her admiration for Mo-keen's dedication and tenacity.

"He is a very strong man," Lucius said. "One time Hunting Horse was caught in quicksand in the Red River during a flood. My father went to him, pulled him from the quicksand, and swam the river with Hunting Horse on his back. The Kiowas call Loki Mo-keen 'Man of Iron.' "

The memory seemed to plunge Lucius into a reflective mood. That evening, as they drove by moonlight to help another family, Lucius talked about his father.

"When I was at Carlisle, there was a man there who spoke two languages, and because of that everyone said he was very smart. He had papers hanging on his walls, showing how smart he was. Sometimes white men tell me I am smart because I speak two languages. But my father, Loki Mokeen, speaks six languages—Kiowa, Comanche, Ute, Spanish, Cheyenne, and Arapaho. He also knows some Sioux, and he can make himself understood with the Blackfeet, Osage, and Apache. When he speaks in Kiowa, it is like Shakespeare in English. In the long-ago time Indians rode for days to hear him speak in council. He spoke for the Kiowas at Medicine Lodge. He is the keeper of the Tai-may, the sacred medicine bundle. A Kiowa can be given no greater honor by the tribe. And with my own ears I have heard the white soldiers at Fort Sill call him an old savage. Why is that? Why do they say such things when they do not know anything about him?"

With a heavy heart, Isabel remembered that only a few months ago she had said the same, not just of Loki Mo-keen but also of all Indians.

"Ignorance, Lucius," she said. "Plain ignorance."

"At Fort Sill I heard two officers talking. I was in a wagon and they did not know I was there. One of the officers said to the other one, who had not seen Indians before, 'You notice how all these Indians are shifty-eyed? They won't look you in the eye. You can't trust them.' What he did not know is this. Indians do not think it is polite to look hard at anyone. You do not stare at anyone unless you want to fight him. That is why Indians never look anyone in the eye. Sometimes I think white men do not *want* to know these things about Indians."

Recalling her own similar thoughts, Isabel was ashamed.

"You're right, Lucius," she said. "Not wanting to know is part of the ignorance."

By the last days of February, the crisis had not ended. Wagons continued to arrive at the Aitsan home, bringing the dead and dying to be buried in the cemetery started by little Ella Pauahty. Less than a year old, the cemetery was spreading steadily along the base of the mountain.

In all, fifty-six Kiowas died that winter of disease, exposure, and starvation.

Isabel was moved beyond pity.

She emerged from the ordeal consumed by an anger contrary to every Christian concept she had been taught. She could not pray away her fury over the fact that unfeeling, complacent Christians had done this to their fellow human beings.

Late one night she confided in Lucius. "When I first came onto the reservation, Red Eagle said I had a Kiowa heart. That meant nothing to me then. Now, after living through this winter, I truly feel that at heart I am a Kiowa."

Chapter Nine

"What happened here this past winter must never, ever happen again," Isabel said. "There is absolutely no excuse for it. This spring we will plant gardens everywhere. We will plant food crops—oats and wheat, sorghum and sugarcane, corn and potatoes. I will teach you how. When the food is harvested, it must be put away for winter—canned, preserved, and stored—so it will not rot. I will show you the canning road. No Kiowa must ever starve again, not while he stands on the Great Father's good green earth that grows so many wonderful things."

Lucius translated her words to the fifty or more Indians jammed into the Aitsan home. Wind and rain pounded on the roof in the final throes of a cold, damp norther. Although supposed to be a meeting of Isabel's cooking class, the group contained as many men as women.

"You must save your grass money for seed," she went on. "You must plan *now* what you will plant and *where* you will plant it. When it is time to plant, you will be so busy you cannot think. You must do your thinking now."

Pope-bah raised a hand. "What will we plant in our gardens?"

Isabel laughed. "Get ready for your mouths to water. We will plant beans of all kinds—butter beans, Kentucky Wonder beans, pinto beans, October beans, speckled beans. I'll show you how to cook them. We'll plant peas—black-eyed peas, lady peas, whippoorwill peas, early June peas. Irish potatoes and sweet potatoes. Lettuce, cabbage, radishes, onions, beets, shallots, tomatoes, cucumbers, squash, cushaw, okra, peppers, turnip greens, mustard greens, beets! Pumpkins and watermelons. Cantaloupe and muskmelons."

"I am not a rabbit," said Odlepaugh. "I cannot eat those things."

"Of course you can. Not everyone likes everything. You must find what is good for you. We will try different ways of cooking and find something you like. A fine garden will provide food all year round. Some of the food must be eaten when it is harvested. Some must be cooked and preserved. You *must* plan ahead. As you plant popcorn, think of how much fun you and your children will have popping it on cold winter nights. As you plant goobers, think of how you will sit by the fire and eat them all winter long. Not only will you have food, it also will be good food."

"Not as good as food from the buffalo," said Odlepaugh.

"You might try raising buffalo, but I doubt you will be successful," Isabel answered. "A better prospect would be chickens and turkeys. They will give you eggs that can be cooked in many good ways. A chicken or a turkey is walking chuck. If all else fails, you can always kill and eat him."

"Lucius tried to raise chickens, and the wolves ate them," Odlepaugh pointed out. "They ate my pigs. Chickens and pigs are walking chuck for the wolves."

"Then you must trap and kill the wolves," Isabel said. "Nothing must take food out of the mouths of your family."

"I think we should take up the garden and chicken roads quick," said Pope-bah. "I would like to have all this good food when we need it."

"Those roads are not easy," Isabel warned. "The women and children must work hard in the gardens. You may have to carry water from the creek to make the plants grow. The men must work hard in the fields. No one likes to plow, but it must be done. There will be trouble. Wind and hail will come and kill some of your plants. The chickens and turkeys get sick, sometimes from the little bugs, sometimes from big bugs. They can be killed not only by wolves, but also by hawks, skunks, weasels, and maybe your dogs, so you must build tight fences and little houses to protect them. And they must be fed and watered every day."

"The Ghost Dance people will kick if we put up little houses," said Heenkey.

"Let them. The Ghost Dance people will change their minds when they see you sit down to a chicken dinner with all the trimmings. They will see that you are on the right road. They will see that you will never have to depend on the government issue ever again."

"I think we must take up the planting and the chicken roads," said Heenkey. "This earth belongs to Jesus, and we are here to work it for Him. He gives us everything to work with, and if we don't go ahead, we are lazy. If a man goes past my place and sees it not growing anything he will go around and say, 'Look at Heenkey. He does not do anything, and all the Great Father has given him is wasted.' I do not like the plow. But if I have heaped-up food in my tipi, I will not have to wait all hungry for the agent to tell me when to come get chuck. These are wise roads. The Jesus woman is right. Pope-bah is right. We must take them up quick."

"And you must build houses for yourselves, no matter how hard the Ghost Dance people kick," Isabel went on. "The government built houses for the Cheyennes and the Arapaho. I'm sure they would build houses for the Kiowas if they were asked."

"They have tried to build houses for us," Lucius said. "The Kiowa council told them we do not want white-man houses."

"Why not?" Isabel demanded. "I have been in your tipis. They are freezing cold. You told me I could not survive a winter under a canvas cover in my wagon. What is the difference?"

Odlepaugh spoke. "There is no power in a white man's house. A tipi is round, as it should be. Look at the world and think hard. Everything you see is round—trees, bird nests, prairie dog holes, the moon, the sky. Only the white man lives in a box with sharp corners. A box does not have the power of a circle."

"The white man's house may have no power, but at least it is warm," Isabel answered. "Your families will not freeze. I don't understand how the Kiowas survived in the long-ago time."

"We slept under buffalo hides and they were warm," Odlepaugh explained. "When we made our tipis of buffalo hides, they could be tied to the ground with pegs and they would not rot. Canvas rots quick where it hits the ground. Wind blows through the little holes. That is why our tipis are cold."

"Then you have no choice," Isabel told him. "I doubt you will find any more buffalo hides. Unless you can find something better than canvas, you must use wood or stone if you do not want your families to freeze. I have told you the Kiowas can keep many Kiowa things. But I think this is one that must be thrown away. If the Ghost Dance people dance back the buffalo, then you will have your buffalo hides again. But if I were you, I would not wait until that happens. I think the Kiowa must take up the white-man-house road if he does not want to freeze, and he must take it up quick."

Isabel's opinion was greeted by a long silence.

At last Mo-keen spoke. "Maybe that is the road for my children," he said. "But I cannot change. I will live in a tipi until the day I die."

In a few short weeks, the gray overcasts and frigid winds of February and early March yielded to clear skies and warm, sunny days, and spring arrived with its deliverance.

In some ways it seemed impossible to Isabel that she had now lived among the Kiowas for a full year. Engrossed in her work, she had allowed the months to fly past without even attempting some of her most important goals. She still had no converts. She was no closer to erecting a church than on the first day she arrived.

Yet much had been accomplished. She truly felt that she at last had convinced the Saddle Mountain Kiowas that they must fend for themselves. Through her Jesus talks, she had given them a fundamental understanding of Christianity. She had established herself in the community.

While she could scarcely believe she had been at Saddle Mountain a year, in other ways it seemed she had lived there forever.

In late March she took the Indians into the meadow below the Aitsan house and showed them how to select ground for planting.

"You must pick a place that is not so low that water will stand, nor so high that water will run off quick. This patch is level, with good, dark soil. It will do."

With the help of Lucius, she showed the men how best to prepare the ground for spring wheat, oats, corn, peanuts, and potatoes. With sand and pebbles she demonstrated the way to broadcast the wheat and oats, how to drop the corn and peanuts into neat rows, and described the best methods to plant the potato eyes in little hills. She drew pictures of the "stone boats" used by white farmers to clear their land of stones and small boulders. She introduced them to a posthole digger and illustrated the proper construction of a barbed-wire fence.

"You must keep cattle and horses out of your fields," she told them. "They can destroy your crops almost as quick as a hailstorm."

As the threat of late frost faded, theory was put into practice. With Jonah and a simple walking plow, Lucius turned the earth in long furrows, preparing it for planting. In his wake came a crowd of Indians—men, women, and children—observing and discussing.

Once Lucius finished planting, the other Indians began work in their own fields. Isabel saddled Jeremiah and rode from place to place, helping to select the proper ground. As the seeds sprouted, she repeated the process, showing the Indians how to distinguish between seedlings and weeds. She demonstrated the use of the hoe in ridding the row crops of unwanted plants.

Then she spoke to the women.

"You must pick a place close to your tipi, for a garden requires almost constant care," Isabel warned. "You will be working on it every spare minute. But a garden is fun. You can *see* the food growing."

By early June the fields and gardens were flourishing, and Isabel was filled with a satisfying sense of accomplishment.

Then one afternoon Domot returned from the agency and brought Isabel's mail. Lucius was in the field, plowing. Mabel and the children were working in the garden. Isabel carried the letters to an old stump beneath the arbor and examined the envelopes.

Amid a bundle of correspondence from missionary societies across the country was a single letter from Miss Burdette.

Isabel opened it, never suspecting for a moment the gravity of its contents.

June 14, 1897

Dear Sister Crawford:

I can hardly gather the courage to write this letter, but I must. Yesterday at a meeting of the Executive Board, the ladies re-examined your situation there at Saddle Mountain. Everyone spoke in the most complimentary terms of your dedication in caring for the *physical* well-being of the

Indians. We are fully aware of the excellent work you have done in this regard.

However, the *spiritual* well-being of the Indians remains of our utmost concern. You have been at Saddle Mountain a year, and it is our understanding that the only converts are those who were living there when you arrived. The expenses of your mission this past winter were *tremendous* and have put our treasury in arrears for the first time since it was founded. While we recognize that many lives were saved through your mission last winter, I and the ladies feel the Society has been doing the government's work, to the neglect of our own.

Therefore, it is the decision of the Executive Board that you should return to the Home office, perhaps with the objective of re-examining your commitment. While we hold every sympathy with the sad plight of the Indians, our mission has ever been to bring more souls to salvation in Christ's everlasting glory. We must keep this goal before us always.

                                        Mary G. Burdette

Isabel sat for several minutes, reading and rereading the letter, unable to absorb the full import of its contents.

Recall seemed impossible, considering all that she had accomplished. In Training School there had been whispers about "failed missionaries" recalled from the field. Never had she ever thought it might happen to her.

She refolded the letter, so emotionally devastated she could confide in no one—not even Lucius.

Taking only the letter, she walked away from the house and across the pasture to the foot of the mountain. She climbed until she felt a cooling breeze.

Perched on a boulder, she reread the puzzling message several times, concentrating on every word. Only gradually did she begin to see her situation in the perspective of the Mission Board.

Safe in their comfortable homes, with food forever as close as the corner grocery and with servants to cook and serve it, the gentle ladies had no inkling of conditions in the field. For them, starvation was an abstraction.

Isabel often had described the wearing, daily anguish of

treating sick and emaciated children. She had tried to convey
the soul-gnawing pain of constantly burying the dead.

But her "stories"—born in human agony and deprivation—
were to them merely proof that a missionary had many roles
to play. In their eyes she had failed in her assignment.

Somehow she had neglected to convey her conviction that
Christianity was not a game of numbers. She long had felt
that Brother Clouse was so concerned with "winning souls to
Christ" that he often neglected to prepare his converts
adequately.

Preparation was the key to a lasting and meaningful religious life. Her father had taught her that, if nothing else.

But surely survival came first.

Was she so woefully in error in teaching the Indians to care
for themselves physically as well as spiritually?

Perhaps she was, from the viewpoint of the Board.

And she was forced to concede one point: She *had* been
doing government work. But there had been no one else to
do it, and it had to be done.

The ladies in Chicago had no way of comprehending all
that she had accomplished. Life on the reservation was hopelessly beyond all their experiences.

Somehow she must bridge those two worlds.

Kneeling in the grass at the foot of the mountain, she
prayed.

"Dearest Lord, please grant me the strength and the wisdom to serve as the lightning rod to send understanding
across this vast chasm. I believe I have prepared the Indians,
as you have given me the talent and dedication to do so. I
have always asked You to use me as You will. Sometimes I do
not understand why I must suffer so, but I will do it gladly.
Lord, I know I am different, but it You who have made me
so. I believe it is for a reason. Now I am convinced it is time
for testing. I plan to push the Indians to the limit this
evening, for I know of nothing else to do. If I am wrong,
please guide me right. If it would serve best for me to return
to Chicago, give me courage, for I will need it."

Isabel knelt on the fresh green grass beside the running
stream and bathed her face, washing away her tears. She had
come straight down from the mountain, not bothering to go
by the house for a change of clothes. The sun was setting,
sending red hues into the clouds above the mountain. Soon

the Indians would be arriving for her first Jesus talk at her refurbished arbor.

During the past few weeks she had grown increasingly concerned over the constant disruption her mission caused in the Aitsan household. Indians were underfoot throughout the day, attending her cooking classes, fishing in the missionary barrels, seeking her advice on their crops and gardens, bringing her cuts, scorpion and centipede bites, and illnesses to heal.

In the evenings her Jesus talks always brought even more Indians to the Aitsan household. Lucius and Mabel were never given a minute alone with their children, or with each other. Now Mabel was pregnant again and should be accorded at least a measure of privacy.

When Isabel had proposed restoring her old arbor, Lucius had not demurred. He and other men of the community had spent an afternoon cutting and trimming brush.

Now her first Jesus talk in it might also be her last.

She crossed the creek on the boulders Lucius had so carefully arranged, and examined her old campsite. Lush grass had returned to the meadow, covering the scars of her campfires. She could not find the spot where she had pitched her tent only a year ago.

So much had happened since then.

And now it all seemed to be coming to an end.

Isabel sank to the grass, pulled the letter from her pocket, and read it once again in the fading light of day.

Across the creek, the Indians strolled toward the arbor in the gathering dusk. Lucius moved about the arbor, lighting the lanterns.

Isabel lingered in the gloom, reluctant to face them.

The Indians took their places. Still Isabel waited. A buzz of curiosity spread over the arbor as the Indians noticed her absence and began to wonder why she was not there to greet them as usual.

Slowly Isabel rose, recrossed the creek, and walked out of the darkness and into the lanternlight. The Indians fell silent, watching her every move, alert to the fact that something was different.

Isabel walked to her wooden-box pulpit. Lucius came to stand beside her, his eyes sharp with concern.

Without even an opening prayer, Isabel went straight into her talk.

"When I first came to Saddle Mountain, you said you wanted to hear about Jesus. Now I have been here one full year and I have told you about Jesus until I am blue in the face. We talk and talk and get nowhere. You got mad at Hamlet because he talked and talked and did nothing. Now I must tell you here tonight you Kiowas are worse than Hamlet. I am ashamed for you. All of you agree that the Jesus road is good. I have heard every one of you say that it is. But not one of you will take the first step on it. What am I to do? We can't go on this way."

As Lucius translated her words, the Indians sat motionless, their faces frozen in shock.

Isabel could not hold back her tears. She waved the letter in the air.

"Now my council has told me that if I cannot get you started on the Jesus road, I must go home. If I don't send them some names, they will close down the mission here at Saddle Mountain. No more money. No more clothing. No more chuck. I don't know what to do. I love all of you. I don't want to leave you. But that is what will happen if you don't get on the Jesus road quick."

Every head went down. No one would meet her gaze. For a time there was only the sign of the soft night breeze through the trees, the faint hiss of the lanterns.

Not one Indian responded.

Humiliated, unable to go on, Isabel stepped away from the pulpit.

Lucius came and put his arms around her. He guided her to a log. Once seated, Isabel gave way completely to her tears. She gave Lucius the letter and gestured for him to read it to the congregation.

After the translation, Ananthy rose. "I do not understand the letter. They say you have not been helping us with good spirits." She made the sign, spread forefinger and middle finger spiraling down from above. "Do they not know about all your Jesus talks? Do they not know that we Indians have been listening, and thinking hard?"

"They are saying that the Jesus talks have done nothing," Isabel explained. "And they are right. I have not put anyone on the Jesus road. The only Christians at Saddle Mountain are the few who were here when I came—Big Tree, Ah-to-mah, Sape-mah, Mah-yan, Lucius. All were baptized at Rainy

Mountain, Elk Creek, or Anadarko before I came to the reservation. I have done nothing."

"We will have Lucius write them for us," said Pope-bah. "We will tell them all you have been doing here. We will tell them you have taught us to cook white-man food, to plant food so we will not go hungry."

"They did not send me here to teach cooking and farming," Isabel said. "They sent me here to put the Indians on the Jesus road. And in that I have failed."

"What about our church?" asked Domot. "Will we not have a church here for our children?"

"There will be other missionaries," she said, fighting tears. "Someday they will build a church here, for it is plainly needed. I'm only sorry that I will not be the one to do it."

"We will have Lucius write the woman council and tell them we want you to stay," Domot said. "We do not want Jesus men here. We want you here."

"The woman council has spoken," Isabel said. "They have told me to go home. I am shamed in their eyes. There is nothing else I can do."

The resulting uproar did not need translation. Isabel knew the word for "no"—*hawnay*. She heard it often as the entire congregation shouted in protest.

Lucius walked across the podium to the pulpit, raised his hands, and the congregation quieted. He began to speak, first a sentence in Kiowa, then the translation in English.

"When the Jesus woman asked me to be her translator, I told her I would speak for her but not for myself. Now that is all changed. Tonight I speak my own words, my own thoughts."

He paused and studied the congregation for a moment before going on. Even in her misery Isabel was impressed by his authoritative manner. Dr. Burdette could not have taken more complete control of the congregation. Lucius stood tall and handsome in his dark suit. He seemed totally at home behind the makeshift pulpit.

"Tonight I have listened to the Jesus woman. I have read the letter from the woman council, and my heart hurts. The Jesus woman says she has failed. I do not believe that. I believe it is the Indians who have failed. The Jesus woman is right. You have listened to her Jesus talks for a year and done nothing. When you went away from her talks you did not think hard about her words."

Several Indians raised their voices and tried to respond. Lucius cut them off with a gesture.

"This is what I think. We Indians lived in darkness for many years, but the Great Father was kind to us and sent us light. That light is the Jesus woman. Tonight when you were coming over here you were in darkness till you saw the lanterns, and then you turned and followed them until you got under this arbor. We have hunted the Jesus road in the same way. At first we saw just a little light, but we hunted and hunted and now we are in the light the Jesus woman has brought to us. She is angry with us because we have seen that light and done nothing. Her angry words are true. I am ashamed for us. But I am not ashamed to stand here before your faces and tell you I have kept all the words of the Jesus woman in my heart. She told us that the Great Father sent the only son He ever had to die for us. I believe this is true. She said He did not come only for white people or black people or Indians. He did not come for skins. He came for hearts. The Jesus woman told us that the Jesus road is for Indians just as much as for white people. I believe this is true. I believe the Jesus woman is the only good thing that has happened to us since this whole white-man business started."

A murmur of agreement came from the congregation. Lucius continued as if he had not noticed.

"When the ice, snow, cold, sickness, and hunger came last winter, the Jesus woman walked and rode all over the reservation. She gave medicine to the sick. She carried food to the hungry. The wolves chased her but she threw rocks at them and did not stop. When the government rations did not come she sent hot words to the chiefs in Washington on the talking wire. You all saw what happened. Food came. No Indian has done more for the Kiowas than the Jesus woman."

A stronger response came from the congregation. Isabel felt quick tears start again despite her every effort.

Lucius raised his hands to quiet the congregation, then went on.

"All Indians here know I have been reading the Bible and thinking hard about it ever since I came back from the white-man school. Five years ago a Jesus man at Anadarko put water on my head and said I was a Christian. But I did not feel like one. Now I have listened to the talks of the Jesus woman for a year, and I feel like one. I am ready to walk the

Jesus road. I want the Jesus woman to tell the woman council that there is one Indian she has put on the Jesus road: Lucius Ben Aitsan."

Almost blinded by her tears, Isabel crossed to the pulpit, reached for Lucius's hands, brought them up, and kissed them. She put her arms around him, and they stood embraced for a long moment.

Battling to regain control of her emotions, wiping away her tears, Isabel then stepped away and signed to him and to the congregation.

"You made a good talk. I am sure Jesus heard you. But I do not want you or anyone to walk the Jesus road for me. I want all of you to walk the Jesus road for yourselves."

"I will walk it for myself and for the Kiowas," Lucius signed back.

Odlepaugh stood and shouted for attention. His deep voice rang out in lilting Kiowa, and his long arms conveyed his words to Isabel even before Lucius translated.

I have listened to the words of my brother with a happy heart. You all know he is very smart. I think his words are true. When the white man drove us onto this reservation I was all-the-time mad because the Kiowas did not fight and die in the Palo Duro Canyon on the day the soldiers killed all our horses. All Indians know I have listened hard to the words of the Jesus woman and spent much time thinking Jesus. Now I am not mad all-the-time. I am not sure Jesus will want me. But I am ready to walk the Jesus road with my brother."

Isabel went into the congregation and embraced him.

Queototi rose. "I am an old man," he said. "When I was young I received a great vision. It lived in my heart for many years. I walked the Sun Dance road, and I was happy. Now that the old ways have gone under, I have looked at the cactus button road and the Ghost Dance road. I do not think they are right for the Kiowas. I am now ready to walk the Jesus road. I think I will stay on it for the rest of my days in this world."

An ancient woman rose at the back and began speaking in a high, piercing voice. She was small, stooped, and so wrinkled that her features were almost obscured. Isabel had not seen her before, but clearly she had been rummaging in the missionary barrel. She wore a dress that perhaps once had belonged to a white child about ten years of age. Her scrawny arms were poked through the sleeves, and the dress was so ill-fitting that it was partially drawn up on her shoulders. The hem of the skirt failed by a handspan to reach the knees, and her legs were covered with one white and one black stocking.

Never had Isabel seen anything so ridiculous.

Not one Indian so much as smiled.

In translating, Lucius gave her the respect he would have granted a dignitary in gorgeous apparel.

"I am the oldest woman here, and I will make a talk. Two moons ago I went to hear the Jesus man at Rainy Mountain. I had never heard anything like what he said. I cannot tell you today whether I believe it or not.

"I have lived many winters. I have seen much trouble. You would not believe me if I told you how much. My husband has gone over into that other world. My daughters who are living have many children. My work is to carry the children on my back every day when they are sick and when they are well. I am all-the-time tired and hungry for rest.

"When the Jesus man at Rainy Mountain told me about the Beautiful Home and the Kind Chief who wanted to divide up with everybody, I thought that is the kind of place that would suit me. I did not get up at that meeting. I wanted to think about it some more. I did not go back to Rainy Mountain, for it is a long way. When I heard that the Jesus woman would talk tonight, I came to Saddle Mountain.

"I hear that if we pick up this new road we must dress like white people. I have put on this dress to let everybody know that if I can have Jesus as my friend and go to live with Him after I get through with this life, I am willing to go around like this the few winters that are left to me, even if all my people think I am crazy. I think it is a good road. I have spoken."

One by one other Kiowas spoke. Isabel stood marveling, making no attempt to hold back her tears of joy.

Kokom, Pope-bah, Tonemoh, Long Horn, Gahbein, Heen-key, Ananthy, Spotted Horse, Hattie, Dawtobi, and Ah-to-mah made eloquent professions of faith.

By the end of the service, sixteen Indians had made commitments to baptism.

Isabel sensed that others were wavering.

She recovered sufficiently to close the evening with a prayer.

After the lanterns were extinguished, she climbed into the Aitsan wagon for the short trip home. Soon the children were asleep on the floor of the wagon. Mabel gathered quilts and lay down beside them. Isabel rode on the spring seat beside Lucius. A three-quarter moon bathed mesquite and sage in silver, the mountain in patterns of light and dark shadow.

"I want to send a letter to the Mission Board as soon as possible," she said. "I don't know if it will change their minds, but it might."

Lucius guided the wagon around some treacherous boulders and across a dry gully. "Mo-keen and Domot are driving to Fort Sill tomorrow. They will take the letter for you."

"Then I will write it tonight to tell them we have sixteen souls ready to receive Jesus."

"You can tell them there will be more soon."

"We're still no closer to a church than the day I arrived."

"A church will not be easy," Lucius said. "When the Ghost Dance people hear what happened tonight, they will kick harder."

"The converts will pose a new problem for the Mission Board," Isabel said. "We have a congregation but no church or pastor."

"The Kiowas don't care about a pastor. You are better with your Jesus talks than any Jesus man."

"A Jesus man has his uses," Isabel pointed out. "I'm not authorized to baptize the converts. We must find an ordained minister for that."

"Big Tree told me the new Jesus man at Rainy Mountain is good. We could go there."

"I haven't had time to think. But do you suppose the Indians would go with me to Elk Creek? I know it's a sin, but I'm so *proud* of all of you. I would like to show you off. And Brother Clouse is such an inspiration. He may be able to advise us on how to solve our problems."

"They will go," Lucius predicted. "They will be happy for the chance to travel off the reservation, even if only for a day or two, if we can get permission."

"Then we will do it. Somehow I'll get word to Brother Clouse that we're coming."

"Maybe you'd better get word to Jesus. He may not be ready for sixteen Kiowas."

Isabel laughed, "I'm sure he has seen stranger sights."

BOOK TWO

God's Light on the Mountain

It seems a startling asser-
tion, but it is, I think,
true, that there are no
people who pray more
than Indians. The God or
force to which they ap-
peal is in their regard as
omnipotent as all the
forces of nature; as invis-
ible as music; as indef-
inite and intangible as all
space.

U.S. ARMY CAPTAIN WILLIAM
PHILO CLARK,
*The Indian Sign
Language, 1884*

Chapter Ten

Isabel and forty-six Kiowas set out well before dawn for the Elk Creek Mission. They rode in six wagons, men, women, and children piled high atop eight tipis and a small mountain of bedding and cooking gear. Isabel sat beside Lucius and Mabel in the lead wagon. All morning they moved northward toward the Washita. Despite the rough terrain, Lucius kept the horses at a fast walk.

In late afternoon, well beyond the boundaries of the reservation, they turned onto a well-traveled wagon track through newly settled farm country. Dugouts, half dugouts, and sod shanties defined each spot where some frontier family had chosen "to prove out a claim." The white settlers often stood silent and stared at the strange sight passing along their road.

Indians and whites exchanged waves.

That night the caravan camped in a heavily wooded grove beside the Washita. With hardly a word spoken or an order given, the Indians raised their tipis and built a bonfire with an ease and speed that left Isabel amazed.

After supper, Isabel sat beside the fire and brought her journal up to date, recording for future correspondence the sights and sounds of her "gospel caravan." Around her the Indians were singing, laughing, and telling stories. Isabel understood little of what was said, but their high spirits were infectious.

Lucius came to sit a while beside Isabel. "Everyone is happy," he said. "This is a little like the long-ago days. The evenings around the fire are what we remember most."

When Isabel at last retired to her cot, most of the Indians were still up. She was worried that the caravan would get a late start the next morning.

But at dawn the Indians stirred, breakfast was cooked and

eaten, camp was quickly "unpitched," and soon the wagons again were on their way.

The trip was surprisingly brief compared with Isabel's memory of her journey to the reservation eighteen months before. Late in the afternoon the Elk Creek Mission came into view.

Isabel was unprepared for the emotional impact of her return to the unpainted buildings, the steepled chapel. As the caravan moved through the lower meadow and up the slope toward the compound, Sister Everts came running from the little cottage where Isabel had spent three years of her life.

Lucius helped Isabel down from the wagon. Sister Everts seized her in a bear hug.

"You look so different!" she said with a squeal.

For the first time in months, Isabel was fully aware of her sun-bronzed and wind-dried skin, her unkempt hair.

She had not even thought to use her comb.

She felt momentarily embarrassed and confused. "I know. Don't say it. I've aged twenty years."

Sister Everts held her at arm's length. "No! You look younger! Just so different! You're so thin!"

"It was a hard winter," Isabel said.

Brother Clouse and his wife came from the rectory. Clouse took Isabel's hands, looked down upon her, and gave her his best smile. "Sister Crawford! It's good to have you back. Colonel Baldwin has written, telling me what a courageous battle you waged for the Indians last winter. He said you deserve a medal. He is certain you saved many lives."

As ever, Isabel could not hold her tongue. "And the government probably cost us many more. The Indians were so starved they couldn't fight off disease. We lost fifty-six."

Clouse glanced uneasily at Lucius, Domot, Heenkey, and the Indians who had left the wagons and now stood behind Isabel. "Well, it's all over now. Colonel Baldwin has been very outspoken in complaints to his superiors. I understand there is talk in Washington he may be replaced."

Isabel also had heard the reports, by way of Chicago. She was furious that everyone was blaming Baldwin. He was a fine man with a brilliant military record, the holder of the Medal of Honor, and now his long career was in jeopardy. He was being used as a scapegoat.

"It wasn't his fault," Isabel said heatedly. "The deficiency lies in Washington. Distribution of rations is conducted catch-as-catch-can. The Indians are expected to subsist on the white man's diet when they've never seen some of the food before. Their stomachs won't tolerate some of it. And no one seems to care!"

Crouse frowned and again glanced at the Indians.

His meaning was clear: he was reminding her that such matters were not discussed before the inferior races.

Isabel had lost the habit.

"I'm sure the authorities are doing all they can," Clouse said. "Perhaps we will see some results soon. Your work is a big step forward. We've prayed for you every day. And I'm deeply honored that you've brought your first converts to me."

Isabel instantly regretted her outburst and wondered why her anger had flared so fiercely. She had always felt deep affection for Clouse despite their many disagreements. "I wouldn't think of taking them anywhere else," she said.

The Kiowas set up their tipis in the meadow above the mission. In the early evening, as their cooking fires were lit, Isabel was tempted to demonstrate her loyalty and camp with them. But Sister Everts's invitation to enjoy the luxury of the cottage and her old feather bed was irresistible.

After supper, they left the dirty dishes and went into the parlor. Isabel sat in "her" rocking chair, holding the cat Othello in her lap. He seemed to remember her and their long evenings together and purred his contentment. Soft lamplight cast familiar shadows over the room where she had read through so many nights with the cat in her lap.

"I can't get over how different you look," said Sister Everts. "You're so . . ."

Words seemed to fail her. She appeared about to abandon the thought.

"Mannish?" Isabel suggested.

"Oh, no! Why, if anything, you're *more* womanish!" Sister Everts blushed. "I only meant to say you're so much more *direct*. So self-possessed. The way you tied into Brother Clouse about the rations! You would never have done that before."

Isabel nodded. "I know I've changed, and maybe not all for the best. But there is always so much to do, and I have no time to worry about nuances. I know I boss the Indians unmercifully. I lecture them when I don't intend to. You remember how I was going to teach them in a womanly way?

'Be a woman and you can be anything you want to be.' But I
soon found that if the Indians are to survive, they must learn
a whole new way of life quick. It's hard to teach them many,
many things every day with a woman's gentleness. You try to
feed them with a spoon and you wind up pounding it into
them with a stick."

Sister Everts laughed and shook her head.

"And I stay so angry over conditions on the reservation,"
Isabel went on. "Those miserable people we ministered to in
the Black Hole in Chicago could blame only themselves for
their low station in life. Liquor. Laziness. Ignorance. You
may remember I found it difficult sometimes even to feel
sorry for most of them. But *we the people* have done this to
the Indians. When we came upon them, they had their own
way of life. I now believe it was much better than we suspect.
Then we went to war with them, murdered most, penned up
the rest, starved them, destroyed their spirit, and now we
have the audacity to call them worthless and shiftless!"

"But something had to be done," Sister Everts protested.
They committed so many depredations!"

"Nothing like the depredations *we've* committed. After
living with them, I see things differently. I'm thoroughly
convinced that as a professed Christian nation, we have dishonored our God before the heathen nations in our constant
breaking of faith with the Indians."

Sister Everts did not answer. They sat for a time in silence.
The cat had gone to sleep.

"In eighteen months I buried sixty-eight Indian babies,"
Isabel told her. "Part of me dies with every one. My nerves
are wearing out. I don't know how much longer I can go on."

Sister Everts studied her for a moment. "Maybe the Mission Board can assign someone to help you."

"I don't see how. I'm living in a two-room shanty with five
Indians—three children and two adults. Another is on the
way. They don't have room for me, but they were Christians
in their hearts before they ever heard of Jesus or saw a Bible.
Our part of the reservation is ruled by the Ghost Dance cult,
which won't allow houses to be built even though the children are freezing in canvas tipis. There is no place for another sister at the moment, and I don't know when there will
be."

"What did the babies die of?"

"Grippe. Consumption. Starvation. Cold and exposure. I

estimate about one in three Kiowa babies survives the first three years of life. The rest die, and no one seems to care except the Indians. The Kiowas possess a greater capacity for grief than any mortal ought to be required to endure. I used to cry for days every time I buried a baby. Now I've reached the point where I no longer can shed tears over them. Instead, I cry inside—all the time. I've even asked God why He allows it to happen. Lucius thinks the Kiowas are being tested like Job. Maybe he's right. I don't know."

Sister Everts spoke hesitantly. "Do you ever question your commitment? I do."

It was delicate ground. Not even in Training School had the subject of personal dedication been mentioned among the students. Isabel found she had no qualms about discussing it.

"Sister, I don't think I ever told you this. After Training School, I told the Lord on my knees that I would go wherever He sent me. But when Miss Burdette wrote that I had been assigned to the Indians in Oklahoma Territory, my first words were, 'I won't go!' I wanted China! Or India! Oh, I was mad! I cried my eyes out because I didn't want to go to those 'dirty' Indians. Two weeks passed before I remembered my promise to go wherever God sent me. So I wrote Miss Burdette that I would go. There's justice in it. Now I'm crying my eyes right back in again."

"And you've never doubted?"

"Never! I remember a story my father used to tell about the English minister Charles Haddon Spurgeon. When he became a Baptist his parents said, 'Well, Charles, we did pray that you would become a Christian, but we never prayed that you would become a Baptist.' And Spurgeon said, 'That is the way with the Lord. He always gives us more than we ask.' Sister, I think that is our situation. We've received far more than we ever asked."

The next morning, Brother Clouse delivered his regular Sunday service. Taking his text from the Book of John, he opened, "Then Jesus spake again unto them, saying, 'I am the light of the world. . . .'"

Lucius interpreted for the Kiowas. A young Cheyenne man signed for the other Indians. For the first time in years, Isabel relaxed and enjoyed a stirring sermon.

After a hymn and closing prayer, the congregation walked

the half mile to a bend in the creek, where the currents had carved a placid pool slightly more than waist deep.

Lucius was to be first. He stood on the bank of the stream while Clouse prepared the converts.

Isabel tied small stones into the hem of her Mother Hubbard so the billowy skirt would not balloon up in the water. When all was in readiness, she went to stand with Lucius.

When it was time Isabel waded into the stream and stood beside him to lend both physical and spiritual support. Brother Clouse prayed, spoke the ritual words, and firmly pushed Lucius under water to cleanse his immortal soul.

Twenty-one more Kiowas followed. Isabel stood beside each.

Not one resisted total immersion.

As she walked out of the water the final time, her tiny gold necklace broke and her ear trumpet tumbled into the water.

Kokom ducked under water and felt along the bottom with both hands until he found it.

He handed it to Isabel. "Now your ear bugle is baptized, too," he signed.

Mrs. Clouse had invited Isabel and Sister Everts to Sunday dinner. Isabel felt awkward in accepting, for the Clouses clearly assumed that the whites and Indians would eat separately, and she badly wanted to be with the Indians through one of the most important days of their lives.

But she could not invite even Lucius to the Clouse family table—not when she herself was a guest. And she could not very well refuse the Clouses, who had been so kind and supportive.

"We'll dine on fried chicken," Brother Clouse said. "It's traditional, you know. Every Sunday, all over America, thousands upon thousands of chickens enter the ministry."

It was an old, old joke, and Brother Clouse's favorite. Isabel laughed dutifully.

More than the chicken and the other food, Isabel appreciated the white linen tablecloth, napkins, English silverware, and china.

It was all so *civilized*—her first non-Indian meal in more than a year.

Afterward, while Mrs. Clouse and Sister Everts cleared the table, Isabel and Brother Clouse went into his small study to discuss her problems on the reservation.

"I suppose I just wasn't looking ahead," she began. "Now that I have converts, I don't know what I'll do with them. There's no hope we will have a church anytime soon. We might make a jaunt to Rainy Mountian once or twice a month, but now that the Indians are working in their fields, it would place a considerable burden on them."

"You've done fine work in introducing them to the basics of Christianity," Clouse said. "I talked some with Lucius Ben Aitsan today. He seems unusually intelligent for an Indian."

Isabel opened her mouth in rebuke and just as promptly closed it.

A year ago she might have said the same thing.

"Lucius is one of the most brilliant men I've ever encountered, white or Indian," she said. "If he had received the advantages of a white education beyond his four years at Carlisle, no telling what he might have accomplished. Now he's just another Indian, stuck away on a reservation and forgotten. Out of sight, out of mind. A terrible waste."

Clouse smiled at her. "That may be. But at least he apparently has achieved the goals of his education at Carlisle. He seems to be leading his people into the white world."

Isabel hesitated. How could she explain to Brother Clouse that she now sometimes doubted the *wisdom* of bringing the Indians into the white man's world? He would never understand.

"The Kiowas are a very spiritual people," she said. "They have always lived close to the Great Spirit or—as I understand the translation of *Dom-oye-alm-daw-k'hee*—the Great Mystery. I've found them far more religious-minded by nature than most whites. Now I wonder if I lived for three years here among the Cheyennes and Arapaho without ever truly knowing them."

Clouse studied her for a long moment. "I've long been aware that the Indians have their own primitive forms of worship and beliefs, some surprisingly sophisticated. But a heathen religion is a heathen religion. We must bring them forward. You've done wonders. You've made them see the light. I don't understand why you're chastising yourself. What *more* can you do?"

Again Isabel hesitated. The problem was difficult to put into words. "The Kiowas I brought here today deserve to be more than an orphan herd of converts. You say we must move forward. I agree. But we must do it in some tangible way. We need something that will start us toward a proper church—something to make the Indians feel that they are truly progressing."

Clouse thought for a moment. "You might formalize a Bible study group. A sort of Sunday school in conjunction with the church here, or at Rainy Mountain. That would be a start."

Isabel shook her head. "We've more or less had exactly that, operating entirely on our own. It seems to me that we now deserve funds for a church, or at least the hope of a visiting pastor. The Indians say they don't want a white pastor, but I'm hoping that in time they will relent."

Clouse frowned. "The possibility of a circuit rider for the district to the west of Cache Creek was discussed at our last convention. The proposal was turned down. With all the settlers coming into the territory from every direction, preachers are in extremely short supply at the moment. And, of course, the whites receive preference."

"Of *course*," Isabel said, perhaps sharper than she intended.

Clouse seemed not to notice. "And I see no hope at all for an allocation of building funds," he went on. "With all the new white communities springing up, the convention is strapped." He paused while he considered possibilities. "I could bring the matter before the Board at the next convention, but I wouldn't anticipate success. I regret to say this. But I think you must throttle your ambitions for a church for a while."

Isabel started to protest, then decided not to bother.

Brother Clouse was only a pastor.

Although she would need his support, the real battle would be fought elsewhere.

That evening Brother Clouse offered a brief sermon. The mission sanctuary was filled with Kiowas, Cheyennes, Arapaho, a few Comanches, and a sprinkling of white settlers.

After his sermon, Brother Clouse asked for testimonials from the new converts to illustrate how Christianity already had altered their lives.

Pawtwadle—Poor Buffalo—spoke first. Lucius stood beside Clouse and translated for the whites present.

"When me and Jesus were plowing the other day, the devil got mad and put a piece of barbed wire in the way. The horses got tangled up in it. I pulled the wire off the hooves of the horses and cut my hand and the blood came." Pawtawdle raised a bandaged hand for all to see. "But I did not get mad. I sat right down and told the Great Father about it. Then I tore a piece off my shirt and tied my hand. Me and Jesus went right back to work and finished plowing."

Doybi rose and spoke next. "The devil has beaten me awful bad. I told him I was going to come here and tell on him. I have tried hard since I started hearing the talks by the Jesus woman. After the last grass money payment, other Indians came into my tipi and began to gamble. I laid down with a blanket over my head and asked Jesus to help me not to get up and gamble. That time I beat the devil. Next day I said to my wife, let's go home. I want to get away. She said the Bible says we are to obey our parents, and they say we are going to stay here some more. If you want to go back to Saddle Mountain, you can go by yourself. This made me awful mad. I took hold of my wife and shook her and knocked her down. I stood there for a while and began to think of Jesus, and how sorry I was, because I love my wife very much. I asked Jesus to forgive me and help me not to do such a thing again. The devil is mean. If he can't catch you on one road, he will catch you on another. I was watching the gamble road, and he caught me another way. I've got the devil down now and I am sitting on his head and I won't let him up."

Pope-bah rose, so nervous that she was trembling. But she spoke loud and clear. "I have tried hard to follow Jesus Christ. I am trying to walk straight. I believe I am leading all my children behind me. Now I am a different woman. When I am hungry inside, Jesus fills up my soul. Many of my friends dance the Ghost Dance and belong to the devil. I try to go easy with them, for I want them to come and hear the Jesus woman. I believe that after a while they will travel with us on the Jesus road."

The congregation stirred. Brother Clouse's eyes widened, and he seemed to start from his chair, then think better of it. Isabel turned to see the source of the disturbance.

Loki Mo-keen stood in the shadows at the back of the church. He had not traveled with the caravan but had ridden forty miles alone on horseback to see his son baptized.

He raised both arms, palms outward. His booming voice filled the chapel, and his son interpreted.

"Now hear me, Loki Mo-keen. I am here today to see my son Lucius Ben Aitsan take up the Jesus road. My son talks to me all the time with tears in his heart, telling me I should walk the Jesus road with him. I have walked other roads so long I cannot change. When I was a young man, I asked the Great Father for a vision. He sent me a vision, and I have lived my life by it. My son's vision of the other world with no-hungry and no-crying is a good vision. My vision is good also. I have thought long and hard about our different roads, and this question has given me much trouble. This is what I now think: My vision and my son's vision both were sent by the Great Father. I think He knows what He is doing. That is why I will stay on the long-ago road. And that is why my heart now sings to know that my son is on the Jesus road. I, Loki Mo-keen, have spoken."

Then Domot rose and spoke.

"I am one of the lost sheep all the Jesus men talk about. I have two wives, and I love both. I do not want to throw either one away. It is hard for me, but I cannot help it. I try the best I can. I lived in the long-ago time when Indians went on the warpath. For a long time I was crazy in my heart and was mad at all white people. Then I came here to this place and looked a long time upon the Jesus woman. I saw that her heart was good and that she never gave us lies. After a long think I asked her to come to the reservation and teach us about Jesus. I was surprised when she came, for she was all alone. She is like a long-ago Indian, for she is never scared. Now she tells us about Jesus, and I listen to each word. Every day she is getting bigger and bigger in our hearts. I am happy I asked her to come to the reservation and that she has helped some Indians find the Jesus road, because I think it is the right one."

Isabel was more than a trifle embarrassed, yet thrilled and elated.

"I believe Mr. Domot's testimonial calls for a response," said Brother Clouse, smiling at her.

Isabel rose and faced the congregation.

"This comes from my heart," she said, making the sign. "I went to the reservation to teach, but I have been learning every day. I know now that when the Great Father made the Indian, He created one of His noblest creatures. Now the Indian has many troubles. I believe that if anyone can survive them, it is the Indian. And if I am growing bigger in the hearts of the Indians, I will not worry about finding enough room, for I know that the Indian heart is as big as all outdoors."

* * *

On the long ride back to Saddle Mountain, the idea was born. At first it seemed bold and farfetched. Isabel tried to put it out of her mind. But it would not go away.

As soon as she arrived home, she sat down and wrote a long letter to Miss Burdette, explaining the idea and requesting a quick answer to an essential question.

For three weeks she waited anxiously, not even confiding her plan to Lucius.

Heenkey brought the reply from Anadarko. Hardly able to contain her apprehension, Isabel went into a corner and opened the envelope. She skipped to the pertinent lines:

> While the possibility of the Women's American Baptist Home Mission Society ever accepting a circle composed of men as well as women has never before been considered, we immediately recognized your special situation, as explained, and were sympathetic. We also acknowledged that the history of your mission has been highly unorthodox from the beginning. None other has brought in so many converts in one fell swoop!
>
> The question you raised was brought before the Board yesterday, and after much discussion, the ladies decided that there was no reason in the world why men as well as women might not belong to the circles, *especially if they paid their dues.*

Isabel kept the information to herself until the members of her congregation had gathered under the arbor on Saddle Mountain Creek for the evening Jesus talk. After the invocation, she announced through Lucius that she had something important to discuss with them.

"Most of you are now Christians," she said. "That is a good thing. A wonderful thing. But you cannot just sit around and enjoy it. Christians must be hard workers, because they work for the Lord. Before Jesus went away, He said to all the apostles, 'Go into all the world and preach the Gospel to every creature, and I will be with you.' They went out and did what He told them to do. In the days after Jesus rose from the dead, little churches were formed all over that part of the world. The devil did not like this. Many of the early Christians were killed only because they were Christians. They had to meet on the sly to hear Jesus talks. Men went out two by two to carry the news that Jesus rose from the dead. They walked every day until they were tired, and then they walked some more. The women did what they could, and everyone prayed and prayed. Now almost nineteen hundred winters have passed, and still the work is not done. Today all Christians must carry on this same work, spreading the Word of Jesus."

Her congregation sat silent and wary. Isabel could see their expressions plainly in the light of the lanterns.

Queototi raised his hand to speak. "Who does not yet know about Jesus? I thought the Kiowas were way-behind."

"In some ways, the Kiowas are far-ahead," Isabel told him. "There are many people in the world who have not yet received the message. Right now there is a young woman among the Hopis. Her name is Miss McLean. She and I were in Training School together. She is one of my closest friends. Someday I will read you letters from her. She and the Hopis are having a difficult time. All over the world there are missionaries like her, spreading the Word of Jesus everywhere. Now that you are Christians, you must help them by sending money, clothing, and your prayers."

A disturbed ripple swept through the congregation. Ananthy voiced the general concern. "How can we help them? We are poor Indians. We do not have enough food or clothing for ourselves. Only what the government gives us. We have a little grass money, but it is not enough. And soon it will be gone, too."

"You must work," Isabel explained. "When Jesus said, 'Go into all the world and preach the Gospel' he did not say, 'One, two, three, go.' He just said 'Go!' He wants us to hurry. That means we are to start right off as soon as we become Christians. But he did not mean that we must take food out of the mouths of our babies to send to the Hopis. No! He meant that after we have worked and provided for our families, we should work a little extra each day for the Lord."

Queototi stirred. "After we plow all day, we are all wore out!"

"Good! You can be thankful. When you are all tired out and still do a little more work for Jesus, He will know that you do it out of love."

"How can we work for money?" Ananthy asked. "Not all of

us have big wagons to haul for the Army, like Domot and Mo-keen."

"There is not a woman among you who cannot sew a little on a quilt each day," she said. "The white settlers moving into the territory admire the colors and designs on Indian blankets and quilts. They will buy them. Just as the women in Chicago worked a little each day to send me here, we can work and send money to help Miss McLean and the Hopis. That is the Jesus road we must walk."

"I cannot sew," Queototi said. "That is the road for a woman."

"You men can do your part. I am told that Kiowa men are great hunters. Yet your dogs are fat and lazy, and wolves sing around us all night long. The wolves eat your chickens, and you do nothing. We can thank the Great Father that the wolves have not eaten some of your children. The government pays a bounty for the ears of wolves. And you can sell the pelts."

A general discussion erupted. With everyone talking at once, Lucius did not try to translate. Isabel allowed the uproar to continue for several minutes, then clapped her hands for attention.

"I have told you all this because I have wonderful news. The Woman's American Baptist Home Mission Society in Chicago has granted us permission to establish our *own* missionary circle here at Saddle Mountain. We will be the same as circles in cities and towns all over the country! The Kiowas will no longer be way-behind on the missionary road. The Kiowas will be way-ahead. You will be the first Indians anywhere to help other Indians find their way onto the Jesus road. I will be very proud of you. The women in Chicago who sent me here will be very proud of you."

Slight signs of encouragement gave Isabel enough confidence to broach the second part of her plan.

"We will make two money roads. Half of the Jesus money we make with our work will go to help other Indians. Half will be set aside toward building our own church here at Saddle Mountain!"

Cries of dismay swept through the congregation.

Ananthy spoke. "Miss Crawford, the Ghost Dance people will kick hard. They do not want a Jesus house here."

The entire congregation nodded in agreement. Again a loud discussion erupted.

Isabel held up her hands to quiet them. She had come to the delicate part. She chose her words with care, hoping Lucius could find a way to translate them accurately. "This is not money for a church tomorrow. Not even the day after tomorrow. This is for a some-day church. You all know how quick everything is changing around us. If the Jerome Agreement is approved by the next big council in Washington, it will be like a great shaking-of-the-ground. White people will move onto most of this reservation quick. What little land is left will be divided among you. All the world will be upside-down for a while. Maybe by then no one will kick because we want to build a church. Maybe by then even the Ghost Dance people will be glad to see it. We must have the money ready when that time comes."

Ah-to-mah gestured frantically to be heard. "When the white men brought lumber to Sugar Creek to build a government school, my husband and some other men got on their horses with guns and drove them back. The school later was built at Rainy Mountain. My husband does not like the Jesus road. He does not want me to be here tonight. He walks the Ghost Dance road. He told me that if lumber for a church is brought in here, he will get up in the night and throw it in a ditch."

"We Christians are not many," Ananthy said. "We must listen to what other Kiowas on this reservation say."

Isabel was hesitant to reveal the final part of her plan.

But the die was cast.

"When my mother died, she left me three hundred dollars. My mother said the money was to be used for my own comfort, and that if I used it for anything else, it would be against her last wish. I have thought and thought. Now I see a way to use the money for the some-day church, yet not go against my mother's last wish."

Isabel paused. The congregation was hanging on her every word. Belatedly she wished she had discussed the matter with Lucius.

"I forever will be grateful that Lucius and Mabel took me into their own home. It was a Christian thing to do. I know I have been much trouble to them. The Ghost Dance people have abused Lucius hard. My work brings Indians to their house all through the day and night, and they have not had much peace. I would like to use the three hundred dollars to build a den. Not really a house. Just one room. I could live in it, and it would be the council house for our mission circle."

The congregation again erupted in a general uproar, louder than ever. For a time nothing could be heard but the babble. At last Lucius raised his hands and silenced the uproar.

Odlepaugh was on his feet. Lucius gestured that he could speak first.

"All of the Indians here tonight agreed that no white person can own land or build a house on the reservation," Odlepaugh said. "Our words went into the council fire. We cannot call them back."

"The den would not belong to me," Isabel said. "It would be built on skids and kept on land now used by Lucius. If the some-day church is ever built, the den would become a part of it, one little room in a corner. I will give it to the church now. If the church is never built, the den will belong to Lucius. He can use it or tear it down, whatever he wants to do after I am gone."

Domot signaled for silence. "We must council on this and not stumble," he said. "If the Jesus woman builds her house, there will be much kicking and many hot words."

Isabel sat excluded while the Kiowas discussed the proposal. After the better part of an hour, Lucius rose and ended the debate. He spoke in Kiowa, and translated for Isabel a sentence at a time.

"I now speak my own words, not those of the Jesus woman. All of you remember that when I took the Jesus woman into my home, there was much kicking. I did not pay much attention, and after a while it all went away like smoke on the wind. The Jesus woman's mother wanted her to live in comfort. She is not living in comfort now. She has only a corner to sleep in and my children crawling over her like fleas. I think we should help her build the den. The other Kiowas can kick as much as they want. When a big storm comes up, our horses bunch together between the mountains and stand with their heads down, trying to keep each other safe and warm. I think that is what we Christians must do. We will not build the den on the sly. We will tell the Ghost Dance people about it and let them speak in council. We will keep our heads down and let the storm blow over us until it is gone. That is the Kiowa road. I, Lucius Ben Aitsan, have spoken."

Chapter Eleven

With the start of harvest in late summer, the hardest work began. Pooling their money, the Indians purchased two large pressure cookers in Anadarko. Set up over special grates in the Aitsan yard, they operated from early morning until midnight, every day except Sunday.

Each family used their grass money to buy heavy Mason jars with glass tops secured by heavy wire straps. Isabel showed the women how to prepare their food for the pressure cookers, and how to affix the rubber rings to seal the jars.

The women helped each other as they preserved basket after basket of garden vegetables. No time could be wasted when tomatoes, squash, beets, or greens were ripe and waiting. The Aitsan household became a sweatshop. Water had to be brought from the creek, the vegetables washed, sliced, and cooked. The women divided the work. The older children snapped beans, shelled corn and peas, hulled dried pintos and butter beans, harvested carrots, cucumbers, okra, cabbages, and melons.

Isabel taught the women different ways to prepare vegetables. She turned corn into roasting ears, grits, hominy, cornbread, pancakes, and boiled dishes of varied seasonings.

The men went from home to home, digging root cellars. As potatoes and yams were harvested, Isabel demonstrated the way to store them in darkness below the freeze line.

Lucius bought a scythe, and the men went from one patch of wheat and oats to the next, cutting and stacking grain into shocks. As soon as it seasoned, Isabel taught them the way to flail the grain on wagon sheets, then bounce it into the air before a brisk wind. It was hard, dirty work, and the men did not like it. Those downwind caught the chaff right in their faces. With both hands occupied, there was nothing they could do but squint, keep their mouths closed, and try not to breathe.

On a day in late August, with every Indian at work, a detachment of cavalry arrived in the Aitsan yard unexpectedly, escorting two sturdy Army ambulances.

Isabel was inside the house, showing Pope-bah, Ananthy, and Hattie the hominy road for corn. Isabel was rinsing the corn in cold water to remove the husks and lye when she glanced out the door and saw a phalanx of officers alighting from the ambulances. She smoothed her hair the best she could, doffed her apron, and hurried into the yard.

Aside from Lieutenant Ryan, the men were strangers.

"Mornin', ma'am," Ryan said, touching his hat brim. "I would like to introduce Commissioner of Indian Affairs William A. Jones, and the new agent for the reservation, Colonel James F. Randlett."

It was almost too much to absorb. Commissioner Jones was supposed to be in Washington, not riding around in carriages on Indian reservations. And "new agent" meant that Colonel Frank Baldwin had indeed been dismissed for his outspoken criticism.

Isabel curtsied before the commissioner and offered her hand. "This is a surprise, Mr. Jones," she said. "If we had known you were coming, we could have arranged a better reception. You may not recall, but we have corresponded. Months ago you granted me permission to come onto the reservation."

Jones was a large man, with a full head of dark hair and luxuriant sideburns. His complexion was florid, and his thick eyebrows lent him a serious demeanor. "Certainly I remember, Miss Crawford. As a matter of fact, I reviewed your file before I left Washington, especially your reports of conditions on the reservation last winter."

Isabel felt her cheeks burn. Her telegrams and letters had been filled with hot words.

"If anything, I understated the case," she said. "When the rations came, they were a full two months late. I can show you the graves of the victims. But I do not hold Colonel Baldwin in the least responsible. I believe he did the best he could."

Jones seemed uncomfortable. "The shortage of rations was an unfortunate circumstance, compounded by the weather.

Colonel Randlett already has initiated plans to store more supplies on the reservation. Perhaps that will prevent a repetition."

Randlett was small and rotund, with wide shoulders and a full girth. His face was round, adorned with a lush moustache and a sprig of whiskers on his chin like those of a billygoat. His voice was firm and all business.

"We've heard reports at the agency of your bootstrap effort with the Indians here. I thought the commissioner should see it firsthand."

"We've tried for years to turn the Plains Indians into farmers, without the slightest success," Commissioner Jones said. "Perhaps we should study your methods."

"Farming is not in their nature, Commissioner," Isabel said. "If we've succeeded, it is because last winter helped to convince them of the necessity."

Jones glanced at the pressure cookers at work over fires in the yard, rows of preserved vegetables cooling under the arbor. "We would be most appreciative if you could give us a tour."

Isabel escorted the delegation into the house and explained the community effort to store the garden harvest of each family. The group examined the Aitsan garden, the root cellar with its potatoes, yams, and preserved vegetables.

"At the moment, the men are harvesting Mr. Domot's wheat," Isabel said. "Perhaps you would like to inspect the fields."

She rode with Jones and Randlett in the stout-springed ambulance. En route to the Domot place, Jones praised each patch of grain and stubble.

Lucius, Domot, Kokom, Heenkey, and Odlepaugh were thrashing grain on a wagon sheet when the delegation arrived. Quickly they rolled down their sleeves, straightened their shirts, and brushed away chaff, "shamed" that the obviously important visitors had caught them not dressed in their best.

After introductions, Isabel tried to put them at ease.

"Commissioner Jones has come to see you at work. Please show him some of the grain you have thrashed."

Jones and Randlett examined the wheat, taking a few grains into their mouths to sample. They walked through the Domot garden and peered into the cellar.

On learning that Lucius was adept with English, they

questioned him at length on the varieties of grain, the growing seasons, the results achieved with each type of soil.

The men talked more than an hour, discussing the crops and the farm implements used.

Afterward, as they drove Isabel back to the Aitsan home, both Jones and Randlett expressed surprise about Lucius's knowledge of farming.

"He is a natural scholar," Isabel replied. "When we adopted the plan, he bought two books on farming and has absorbed them thoroughly. He has taught the other Indians."

"From what I've seen today," Jones said, "I believe past government programs came to naught because they failed to follow through. The Indians were told what to do, then left to their own devices. I think maybe you have found the proper method. If it works here, perhaps it will work on other parts of the reservation."

"I can't see why not," Isabel said, never dreaming what those five words would cost her.

Isabel wrapped the plums carefully in cloth, then plunged them into boiling water. Her cooking class burst into laughter. "The plum road is heaped-up crazy," Pope-bah signed.

Isabel joined in the merriment. The plum pudding recipe did seem daft until one tasted the results. But the women had doubted her bread-medicine until they saw loaves rise as if by magic. Since then, they had accepted other recipes on faith. She was sure the class would adopt her approach to plum pudding. Late-summer plums were ripening in thickets along the rivers and creeks. Most of the Indian men loved sweets.

The day was hot and sultry, with not a breath of air stirring. Isabel felt rivulets of sweat on her skin beneath her loose Mother Hubbard. While the plums stewed, several members of the class went into the yard to escape the heat of the kitchen.

In a moment Ah-to-mah returned with a glint of fear in her eyes. "Cut off cooking," she signed. "Many Ghost Dance people come here."

Isabel had been expecting them.

All week a debate had raged in the Kiowa council over her proposed den. The Saddle Mountain Kiowas seemed evenly divided on the issue. She glanced out the door.

The space beneath the arbor was jammed with Kiowa men.

More were arriving. Lucius had come in from the field and was hurrying toward the house.

He entered, his face taut with worry. Isabel knew he had been abused terribly over her request. She regretted putting him in that position. But the den would not be just for her. Ultimately all the Kiowas would benefit.

"The Kiowa chiefs have come to council with you about the den," he said. "They want to ask questions."

Isabel gave Mabel hurried instructions on how to finish the pudding. Then Isabel went into the bedroom, changed her dress, and combed her hair. When she emerged, Lucius was still waiting.

"Many different stories have been told about the den," he said. "The Ghost Dance people are saying the den may be another mistake, like the Jerome Agreement."

"We must convince them otherwise," Isabel said.

She followed Lucius out of the house. The entire yard was now covered with seated Kiowas. Behind them, others stood. Some were perched like blackbirds on the railings of the corral.

As Isabel and Lucius walked toward the arbor, the crowd parted to let them through.

Isabel did not see a single friendly face.

The chiefs and elders were seated in a circle. Little Robe, Komalty, Red Eagle, Mo-keen, Amon, Ahm-ot-ah-ah, Apeahe, and other Ghost Dance followers were much in evidence.

As Lucius squatted to take his place on a blanket, Isabel knelt and prepared to sit beside him. Domot gave her the "no" sign. He pointed to an old stump, sawed off at both ends, that Lucius used as a butcher's block for quartering beeves. "You sit in middle," he signed. "You not to make funny. This is a serious talk."

Isabel sank onto the hard makeshift stool, facing Domot and Lucius.

Amon began to speak. Isabel knew him only as a leader in the Ghost Dance movement, perhaps even more powerful than Little Robe or Loki Mo-keen. Lucius gave her snatches of translation during the old man's long pauses.

"This thing with the Jesus woman is not good. She says the Great Father first sent her to Elk Creek. Why did she not stay there? Why did she come to Saddle Mountain? She is all-the-time getting ahead, getting ahead, getting ahead. Now she wants to build a house here for herself. This is the white man's road, to push ahead all of the time, to make everyone move over. If we tell her she can do this, soon a Jesus man will come, put up a fence, and the Indians will be cut off. I have seen this happen other places. We must tell her to go back to Elk Creek and sit down in the house that was built for her there."

Isabel glanced at Lucius. His face showed nothing. Her other allies on the front row of the council—Odlepaugh, Tonemoh, Heenkey, Long Horn, Gahbein, Domot—all stared straight ahead, their faces devoid of expression.

She wondered if anyone would dare speak for her.

Ahm-ot-ah-ah began to speak. "Three or four winters ago we told Mo-keen's son Aitsan he could build a little house for his family. You see what has happened. Now he wants to make another white man's house here. If we keep on this road, soon there will be only white man's houses on the reservation and nothing Indian anywhere. This road is dangerous. It is like coming against rocks."

Shouts came from far back in the crowd. Other voices rose, and for a time all was chaos. Domot stood, raised both hands, and restored order. He gestured for Lucius to translate and spoke to Isabel.

"Different things have been said about what you want to do. Maybe we do not have the true words. Tell us what you want."

With the future of her mission resting on her reply, Isabel lowered her head and prayed briefly for guidance. She then spoke straight to the elders who had talked against her.

"Four winters ago I came to this country to tell the Indians about Jesus. First I went to Elk Creek. After three winters, all the Indians there had heard Jesus talks. The Great Father told me to go out and hunt more Indians. Domot, the oldest man in this council, came to Elk Creek and asked me to come to Saddle Mountain. I came, and you all know how I have lived among you just like a Kiowa woman, never asking for anything but your protection. I lived in a tent until Lucius asked me into his home."

Isabel paused, allowing Lucius time to catch up, and wondered what to say next. From what little she had heard of the argument, tribal control of the land seemed to be a principal issue.

"You all know, for I have told you, that I will never ask anything for myself. And I am not asking land for Jesus. What you do with your land is your business, not mine. A Jesus house will not be built until the way-ahead time. When it is built, it will be Kiowas who will build it, not white men. What I want is to build a small house on land now used by Lucius, to be moved off when the far-ahead church is up. I do not have a place of my own to sleep. My head is tired all the time. At night I jump and turn like a fish when it is pulled out of the water onto the bank. I must write many letters each month if the Christians all over the country are to keep sending us clothing and food. If I do not thank them they will stop sending things. And I have no place to write my letters, only a corner with Indians coming and going all the time. If the Jesus house is never built, the little house will belong to Lucius. He can do whatever he wants to do with it. My father and mother are both dead. Jesus has given me to you, and I now ask you to make a wise road for me."

One of the elders signaled to Lucius to cut off the translation and the debate continued. Isabel sat listening to the tone of the voices, searching for clues as to what was being said.

She watched Loki Mo-keen. He sat without speaking, or giving any indication of his thoughts. Isabel assumed that since his son was involved, he had disqualified himself from participation in the decision.

Not since her earliest days on the reservation had she felt so alienated from the tribe. Even Lucius, now solemn and silent, seemed strange and distant. At times such as this, all of his Indian qualities came to the fore and all signs of his experience in the white world seemed to vanish.

Phrases oft repeated in letters from home filled her mind: "Are you truly safe?" "Don't you think you had better come home?" "You are a dear brave girl not to be afraid." And, invariably, "Can't you find enough Christian work among people of your own kind?"

What was she doing here among people who thought differently, spoke a different language? Why did she so keep driving herself, working every day until she dropped into her cot exhausted?

Were the meager results worth the price?

Around her, the argument flared anew. The chiefs shouted at each other. They shook their fists, pounded the earth in lengthy orations.

At last some order was restored. Each of the chiefs made a speech. Eventually an agreement seemed to emerge. Isabel heard some grumbling, but most of the chiefs appeared satisfied.

Domot signaled for Lucius to translate his words. He spoke to Isabel so solemnly that she braced herself for the worst.

"I am the oldest man here. I will make my talk to you first. The Indians who are not walking the Jesus road are very mad, but I am not afraid of them. I have spoken for you. I am not a Christian, but I have been thinking wisely. You left Elk Creek and came here and you have been kind to us and our children. You have helped us, and your white friends have helped us, sending dresses, patchwork, coats, and pants. Some of us are old, and after a while we will all die. We want you to teach our children this good road and keep them on it. The Ghost Dance people who are making all the trouble do not help anybody. They are trying to pull us all back. This is true, and everybody here knows it."

He waited for the stir of agreement and disagreement to subside.

"Now we have counciled hard, and this is what we think. You may build your little house. We think something else also. The Jerome Agreement has now gone into the white council fires, and we cannot pull it back. After a while, white men will come in here and cut up the land. We must hurry and look for land for Jesus and put His brand on it so that when He comes back to burn everything, He will know that we did not forget Him."

Isabel sat stunned. She had never dared dream that the Kiowas would grant land for a church until she had won many, many more converts and the Christians were in a position to wield much more influence in the tribe.

Now the Indians were giving the land of their own accord!

Kokom rose. Isabel understood the custom. Her case had been carried all the way to the Kiowa Supreme Court. Domot had just handed down the decision.

Now she would hear the concurring and dissenting opinions.

"I am the oldest Christian man here and I will make my talk next," Kokom said. "We have made a wise road for you. If we do not look for land for Jesus, white men will take it all and you will have no place to go. We have opened our hearts to Jesus and today we open our land."

An-pay-kau-te, son of the dead chief Satank, was next. He had attended many Jesus talks but never had come forward. Brother of the prayed-to-death Joshua Given, An-pay-kau-te was known as Frank Given by the whites. He seemed to be a very troubled Indian. Lucius had confided that Given's eldest brother had been killed by whites, and Frank Given himself had taken part in many raids in Kansas, Colorado, and Texas. The men he had killed weighed heavily on his conscience. He was the son of a great Kiowa chief and had inherited his father's George Washington Medal. But gambling and liquor had made him weak.

"I have been very wicked," An-pay-kau-te said. "I have been going back, back, back ever since the soldiers pushed us onto this reservation. I have listened to some of the Jesus talks and I think they are all that have kept me from going under. But I cannot settle on any one road of thinking. Now I am like a snake. I get a new skin every year. I want the Jesus woman to have her land, and I want to come and hear more Jesus talks until I get stronger."

Paudlekeah rose and began to speak. He had attended several Jesus talks, but he was not yet a Christian. He spoke in friendly tones. "Before you came, there were not many Christians at Saddle Mountain and we did not want a church here. Now we think we are ready and we want a church for our children who are growing up. It is good for you to have a home to write in so you can tell our friends to help us and to send our children dresses and toys."

Odlepaugh spoke. "There is just one thing that gives us trouble. The Ghost Dance people are kicking and abusing my brother because he is willing to put the house on his land. This is what I think: We will let their talk hit us like the wind. We don't fight the wind. We don't look at it. The wind hits us and passes over, and soon it is gone and we are not hurt. That is what we must do. I, Odlepaugh, have spoken."

Queototi was next. "I am a very quiet old man and I don't talk much. But when I do talk, people better listen, because I get hot quick. Not much of my life is left. Before I go into the other world, I want to help the Kiowas all I can. I think the Jesus road is good. From the day we were pushed onto this reservation we have been whirled around every way until we are dizzy. We don't know what will happen next. The Jesus house is the only thing I see coming that I do not fear."

Dawtobi raised a hand for attention. "I have seen the white people walking around with their pistols and rifles. They get drunk on whiskey and act crazy and shoot off their pistols. I think when the white man moves onto the reservation we must have a Jesus house and walk the Jesus road every day. If anybody points a pistol at your head, you must shut your eyes and pray for him like I did for Poor Buffalo that time when he came at me. If the white man sees that we are Jesus Indians, he will walk softly around us."

Lucius performed his feat of speaking in two languages, a sentence at a time. "I think it is a good road for you to build a small house on my land. You can sit down in it until you die. Our children and grandchildren and great-grandchildren will be growing up and we want you to teach them the good road so that we can see them again in the next world. We want to build a church for them and keep a place for their graves."

Heenkey rose next. "When I was a young man I never heard a word about Jesus or the Bible. Then the Jesus woman came and our ears were opened. We planted our farms and built fences. Many of the Kiowas here today spoke against Jesus. One day when I went for my horses a man said, 'Don't work today, Heenkey! Just cry to the Lord!' He was against Christians and this was funny talk. This man stands today high on the Jesus road. He used to be strong for the devil but now he is strong for Jesus. I will call out his name: Kokom! About the same time there was a cactus-button eat near Saddle Mountain and I was there. After I left the cactus road and became a Christian I went again to talk to the young men about Jesus. One of them said to me: 'We do not want your talk and we do not want you to come here anymore. We eat mescal and gamble and dance and we do not want your Jesus words. Our hearts are our own and we can do as we please.' Not a long-time after that I saw the same man at a Jesus talk and he said: 'I used to walk on all the bad roads but I have given them all up.' I will call out his name: Dangerous Bear! I used to be the same as the men I am talking about. I tried to stay away from Jesus but I could not do it. He brought me in. Jesus is stronger than the devil. I now walk two roads—the Jesus road and the farm road. I love it. Some day the Kiowas speaking now against Jesus will say the same, so I do not think long or hard on what they say today."

Amon spoke. As a leader in the Ghost Dance religion, he had raised his voice many times during the debate. Isabel knew that his would be the principal dissenting opinion. He shouted his message in the Indian oratory style. Lucius translated his words more softly.

"In my life I have seen many things. When I was a boy,

white people went in wagons like ants toward where the sun sets and they did not bother us. Sometimes we traded meat and skins to them for gunpowder and bullets. Then the Texans cut off the road to the south and we fought with them some but we lived the same. After the war between the whites, the soldiers began pushing and pushing until today we are penned up in this little place. The white man is always pushing. This Jesus house is more pushing. I do not like it. The time is coming when the Kiowas must push back. The Jesus woman should not be here to get hurt."

Spotted Horse replied in angry tones, "I do not like to hear this bad talk about the Jesus woman. You all know she has a good heart. She knows that many Kiowas dance the Ghost Dance and have taken the feather. She has not told the white soldiers anything. The Ghost Dance people say all dead Kiowas will someday come back from the other world in a great spirit army and push the whites back. If this is true, I will ask the spirits not to harm the Jesus woman. I will tell them she is the same as a Kiowa."

After several more opinions were voiced, Domot again addressed Isabel. "We do not want to be tricked again like with the Jerome Agreement. White men are sly. Maybe after all we old men are gone, they will come in here and drive our children out of the Jesus house and worship the Great Father in it themselves. We want you to make a talking paper right now that will make this an Indian Jesus house forever."

She went into the house and returned with paper, pen, and ink. Kneeling at the butcher's block, she drafted the document, using every high-flying legal phrase that came to mind. When she was finished, she read the text to Lucius for translation into Kiowa.

Apparently everyone was satisfied. With great ceremony, Isabel and the Indians signed the paper.

Not until after the visitors had departed did Isabel find time to reflect on her new situation.

She had won twenty-two converts who in the strictest sense could not be termed a congregation, for she had no church. She had a fledgling women's missionary circle like no other in the country; half of its members were men.

Now she had received the promise of some-day land for a some-day church, and there was not enough money in the tribe even to lay the cornerstone.

Moreover, most of the community was dead set against the church, yet they had approved it solely on principle.

It was a heaped-up crazy road.

"Tonight we must elect officers," Isabel said, opening the first meeting of the Saddle Mountain Baptist Home Mission Circle. "Tomorrow I will send our application for a charter to the Board in Chicago. I must include the names of our officers. We have just enough money to pay our dues. We must get to work right away, raising money for other Indians and for our Jesus house."

"How much will the Jesus house cost?" Ananthy asked.

"About a thousand dollars," Isabel told them. "Maybe a little more, maybe a little less. That should be enough money to build a mission house also."

Her congregation groaned in dismay.

Even white men seldom earned more than thirty dollars a month.

"We can start immediately," she said. "We have plenty of colorful cloth in the missionary barrels. I will send for more. You men can organize your hunts. And on the way over here tonight, Lucius offered another moneymaking idea: You men can cut trees along the creeks and saw the wood into stove lengths. The white men who live in the towns around the reservation do not have time to cut their own wood. They will be happy to buy some. You can use my wagon and team if you need them."

Odlepaugh raised a hand. "I think the killing of wolves is not a good thing."

Isabel sighed. Who would believe that this man once lifted scalps?

"The mountains are overrun with them," she pointed out. "They ate your pigs. Almost everyone here has had calves killed by them. Last winter you scolded me because I walked across the reservation at night alone, with the wolves following me. You said the wolves would get me next time. What about your children? The wolves will be killed anyway. The white men will kill them the first thing when they move onto the reservation."

Odlepaugh did not look happy, but he did not argue further.

"Now you must elect officers," Isabel said. "Since Domot is the oldest man here, I think he should conduct the election."

Domot walked to the front of the arbor and immediately

assumed the mantle of authority. "This is a Jesus thing," he warned them. "We must not name anyone who has gambled or walked the least bit crooked. Most of the men here must scratch off their names quick."

Lucius sat beside Isabel and kept her informed as the election progressed. She listened with amazement as the candidates were selected not for leadership abilities but for their depth of spirituality.

And never would she have dreamed that such a male-dominated society would elect a woman.

Pope-bah was named president by acclamation. Big Red was elected vice president; Ananthy, treasurer; and Lucius, secretary.

"Only one thing more is needed for our charter application," Isabel told them. "We must now name our circle. What shall we call it? I think it should be something beautiful, for some day our Jesus house will have the same name."

Domot again faced the circle as Lucius translated for him. "I have sat in many councils everywhere, and I have heard many wise talks. I think the wisest talk that ever fell on my ears was made to us by Lucius Ben Aitsan when he told us how we came out of the darkness and found the light of the Jesus lanterns. I think you should call this society . . ."

Lucius hesitated over the translation of the proposed name.

He repeated it in Kiowa, as if testing it on his tongue: "*Daw-kee-boom-gee-k'oop.*"

The mission group voiced enthusiastic approval.

"How does that translate?" Isabel asked.

Lucius thought for a moment.

"God's Light on the Mountain."

The vote was unanimous.

Chapter Twelve

In mid-September, Lucius hauled lumber from the nearest railroad siding, eighty miles to the east, and began construction of Isabel's den. Mo-keen, Domot, Smokey, Kokom, Odlepaugh, and several other Indians came to help, and the work went quickly. On the last day of the month, Isabel moved into her new home.

Unpainted, unadorned, embellished only by a single door and window, the clapboard shack rested on bridge-timber skids beside the shallow, unnamed creek less than a hundred yards from the Aitsan home. Only thirteen feet square, the interior seemed as spacious as a barn after her two-year residence in a cot-sized alcove. Isabel made blue-and-yellow chintz curtains for the window.

The good people of Pueblo, Colorado, recently had sent donations of clothing in a large wooden crate. "It's either a coffin for Goliath or a bed for a missionary," Isabel told Lucius as it was unloaded.

She placed it under her window, lined it with cloth matching the curtains, and turned it into a daybed. Compared with her cot—now relegated to storage—its feather-stuffed mattress was heavenly.

Once everything was in order, she sat down and wrote Miss Burdette a long letter, describing the new house in detail:

"It is very efficient. The walls are lined with pegs. When company comes I can hang up everything but myself. A lean-to shed behind the house provides sufficient storage space for the missionary barrels, supplies, etc.

"I now have plenty of room for a companion if the board should find a way to grant one. And I promise she will find enough to do! There are Indians on the place from dawn till

midnight, and all want something. Last week I buried six
Kiowas—two old ones and four babies. At present I have
three Indians 'down' with illnesses, and although I am not
qualified, I must do what I can for them. Hardly a day goes
by that I do not make at least one 'visitation' somewhere on
this portion of the reservation, tending to the sick or praying
over the dying. These duties inevitably interrupt our regular
schedule, for often I must travel a distance and be away
overnight. English classes, cooking classes, Jesus talks, etc.,
must be postponed, causing considerable disruption. Several
of the Indians are progressing well in their English lessons,
and I regret every setback. If there were two missionaries
here, one could keep the 'regular' schedule humming while
the other tended to the supplemental duties. I do hope the
Board can find funds and a willing candidate."

Miss Burdette answered almost by return mail. She said
the Board was taking the request for a companion "under
advisement" but that at the moment no additional funds were
available.

From the day the roof went on, the den became a full-
fledged mission. Now that Isabel no longer lived with the
Aitsans, the Indians seemed to feel less constraint in visiting.
Kiowas, Comanches, and Apaches she had never seen before
dropped by to explore selections in the missionary barrels.
Members of God's Light on the Mountain missionary circle
considered the den their headquarters. At least four or five
quilts were constantly in progress in the yard, the frames
resting on sawhorses Lucius made of surplus lumber. Arriving throughout the day, the Indian women spent the long
afternoons and early evenings quilting, chatting, and joking
in their singsong Kiowa as they worked.

At first Isabel introduced traditional quilt patterns—Texas
Star, Pennsylvania Spider's Web, Log Cabin, Golden Stairs,
Irish Chain. But with no prompting on her part the Indians
soon were sewing their own highly stylized designs, inter-
mingling tipis, buffalo, lightning bolts, war shields, drums,
deer, bears, horses, owls, moons, flowers.

Recognizing their artistry, Isabel did not interfere.

The quilts were startling in their originality.

Lucius took the first three dozen to Anadarko and sold
them for $63.15.

The men and their dogs roamed the mountains on a series

of wolf hunts. Bounties and pelts added another $56.15 to the circle's funds.

In early November, two men arrived from the government school at Rainy Mountain, searching for truant children. They asked Lucius why Amos and Jessie were not enrolled. Lucius told them he was teaching his children himself, that they did not need to go to school. The explanation was not accepted. The men said attendance had been made mandatory.

Lucius came to Isabel greatly upset. "I cannot give them up. I think I will take my family and leave the reservation."

"Please don't do anything foolish," Isabel said. "They would only find you and bring you back."

"The teachers at the school whip the children."

The Indians were sensitive on this subject, and rumors abounded. Isabel had tried not to interfere.

"I'm sure those stories are exaggerated," she told him. "Children tend to turn a simple spanking into a life-or-death matter. Amos and Jessie are good children. They won't need disciplining."

"They will run away from school and freeze. They will die of sickness."

It was a fear of every Kiowa parent with children at the school. Seven winters before, three Kiowa boys ran away from the government school at Anadarko after a whipping. A blizzard struck while they were walking the thirty miles to the nearest Kiowa home, and they froze to death. Several Kiowa men armed themselves and went to the school to kill the teacher, a man named Wherrit.

Fortunately, he had fled the territory.

Even more tragic was the stupidity of the teachers during an outbreak of measles the summer before Isabel arrived at the Elk Creek Mission. Lacking facilities to care for the sick, the teachers sent them home.

The Indians had little resistance to the disease. Two hundred twenty-one Kiowas died that summer of measles—out of a total population of sixteen hundred. Every family had been affected.

Isabel attempted to console him. "Amos and Jessie won't be far away. You will be able to visit them every week or two. Think what it must have been for Loki Mo-keen when you went away to Carlisle."

Lucius nodded. "I did not know then what was in his heart. Now I know."

After several days agonizing over the matter, Lucius surrendered and drove Amos and Jessie to Rainy Mountain for enrollment.

In the following weeks, he wandered the creeks and mountains as if lost.

One afternoon Mabel brought her new baby Leslie to the den and resumed work on the quilts. "I cried when I lost two of my children to the school," she signed. "Now I think I have lost a husband."

Kokom awoke Isabel well before daylight, knocking hard at her door. Slipping a dress over her head, she peeked out the window, then let him in.

He was carrying a rifle. He leaned it against the wall.

"Come quick," he signed. "All the Kiowas have picked up their guns. There will be a big fight quick."

He was so distraught that Isabel could not fathom the elaborate story he was trying to tell. She gathered only that it had something to do with dead people, Indians, and fighting.

She made the "cut it off" sign.

"Let's go wake Lucius," she signed.

They walked up the slope to the Aitsan house, Kokom leading his horse and carrying his rifle.

After a brief knock, Lucius opened the door.

Kokom talked excitedly in Kiowa for several minutes, frequently pointing to the mountain and making the "dead people" and "fight" signs.

Isabel waited, frantic to obtain the complete story.

"It is bad," Lucius said. "Yesterday at sunset Beathomah went to pray at the grave of her grandfather. Someone has dug up all the dead people there and robbed them. Odlepaugh, Mo-keen, and some others are getting ready to go track the men who did it. If they find them they will kill them."

Horrified by the crime, Isabel was even more concerned over what might yet happen. She asked the first question that came to mind: "Why would anyone do such a thing?"

Lucius looked at her a moment before answering, his face devoid of expression. "Everyone knows that valuable things are buried with dead Indians."

Sickened, Isabel forced herself to think of the consequences. If the Indians tracked and killed the grave robbers, the Indians probably would be tried in a white man's court and hanged.

Lucius had the same fear. "If I thought it would help, I would go kill those white men myself," he said. "But those men are not worth the life of a single Indian."

He went into the bedroom to get his rifle. Opening a box of ammunition, he began stuffing cartridges into the magazine.

"How do you know they are white men?" Isabel asked.

Again Lucius looked at her. "No Indian would do this. A black man would not do this. It must be white men."

Lucius went out to saddle a horse. Isabel called after him, "Catch Jeremiah. I will go with you."

Isabel borrowed Mabel's fleece-lined coat and hurried out to the sheds. As soon as the horses were saddled, Lucius and Kokom set out at a fast lope. For a time Isabel feared she would be left way-behind. But after the men reached the hogback that provided a view of Sugar Creek, they slowed to a steady trot. Both rode with heads erect, alert.

With a prickling along her scalp, Isabel realized that she was riding with two former Army scouts who were searching for tracks, or any sign or sighting of the grave robbers.

She remained safely behind them throughout the five-mile ride to the cemetery.

Twenty or more Kiowa men were waiting. Some sat on the ground. Others stood motionless, cradling their rifles.

Not one seemed to be doing anything.

Lucius signaled for her to dismount. He tied the reins of the horses to a mesquite bush. They approached the cemetery on foot.

Only then did she see the desecration of the graves.

More than a dozen bodies lay scattered around like fallen logs. In various stages of mummification, they posed unspeakable horrors. Empty eye sockets gazed into the sky, into the dirt, and at Isabel. Mouths grinned without lips. Hair clung to skulls in scant patches. One body was missing an arm, another a leg. Bones littered the ground. The plundered graves gaped without form or neatness. It was as if some deranged animal had been pawing the earth.

For a moment Isabel could not breathe. Her legs seemed to turn to water. But she was determined not to flinch in front of the men. She looked toward the distant mountain peaks and let the cold, crisp north wind hit her face.

Mo-keen was sitting on a mound of dirt, his gun across his lap. He spoke to Lucius in sharp tones. Father and son had a brief, heated exchange. Mo-keen kept looking at Isabel, and apparently Lucius felt an explanation was in order.

"My father, Loki Mo-keen, asked me why I brought you here. I told him I wanted you to see what white people have done. I told him I want you to tell the women in Chicago. He said this is not for a woman's eyes to see. He is very hot. I told him that Beathomah saw it first, when she came here alone to pray over her grandfather. If I did wrong, I am sorry."

"You did right. I came because I wanted to see it, and for the same reasons. But why are they waiting? Isn't anything being done? At least they could rebury the bodies."

"Last night Domot went to get Colonel Randlett. They want him to see this. He will come with soldiers. Hunting Horse and Red Eagle began tracking the white men this morning. They are leaving a plain trail for the soldiers to follow quick. All the Indians are hot. But Mo-keen has told them that they must hand the men over to the white man's law."

Isabel walked to a grassy spot away from the cemetery and sat down to wait. Lucius circled the cemetery, kneeling occasionally to study the ground.

Colonel Randlett arrived before the sun was two hours high, riding at the front of a cavalry patrol from Fort Sill. Randlett dismounted, tipped his hat to Isabel, and shook hands with the Indians. Then he and the officer in charge of the troops walked through the cemetery, pausing occasionally to look at the graves, the corpses. The troopers sat on their horses, staring in silence at the ransacked cemetery.

"Terrible. Absolutely terrible," Randlett said to Isabel. "I'm tempted to let the Indians have their way with those men."

"I've been trying to imagine. Who would do such a thing?"

"No telling. Could be drunk cowboys, hunting a little fun, daring each other. Might be emigrants on their way to California or Oregon, curious as to what the West has to offer. The Washita bottom for a hundred miles in each direction is full of bandits, murderers, white trash of every description. Sometimes they elect to rob the dead instead of the living. There's less risk."

"It has happened before?"

Randlett nodded. "Indian curiosities bring good money in saloons all over the West."

"There were three of them," Lucius said. "They were riding three horses and leading another. They left here about noon yesterday."

Randlett glanced at Lucius. "I learned a long time ago not to ask Indians how they know such things. We'll get right on their trail. Maybe we can catch up with them."

Lucius, Mo-keen, Odlepaugh, Red Eagle, and Domot rode west with Randlett and the cavalry patrol. Men and horses soon disappeared to the west at a steady lope.

Heenkey, Long Horn, Smokey, and Papedone brought shovels from their horses and began scooping out the graves preparatory to reburying the bodies.

"I will ride home with you now," Kokom signed to Isabel.

She made the "no" sign. "I will wait and pray over the dead," she explained.

"They have been prayed over until they are all worn out," Kokom answered. "They will be prayed over as long as Kiowas walk the earth. What we do here today does not matter to them."

Isabel did not protest. She had little heart for spending the entire day in the cemetery.

They rode back to the Aitsan place. Kokom stripped Isabel's saddle from Jeremiah's back, slipped off the halter, and released him into the pasture.

"For a long time after we were driven onto the reservation, I was ashamed to be an Indian," Kokom signed. "Today I am not ashamed to be an Indian."

Throughout the remainder of the day a pall seemed to hang over the Saddle Mountain community. No women came to work on quilts. Isabel spent the afternoon alone, reading, writing letters, cleaning the floors.

Despite her efforts, she could not erase the terrible images of the cemetery from her mind. Her heart cried for vengeance. She wanted justice done.

That evening she attempted to read, but not even Dickens's *Oliver Twist* could divert her mind. Afterward, her sleep was troubled by recurring nightmares. Even awake she kept seeing images of half-rotted corpses, detached limbs, and open graves.

At last she lit a lamp and sat up through the remainder of the night.

She spent the morning in the Aitsan garden, removing

plants already killed by frost. Lucius returned early in the afternoon, his face lined with exhaustion and disappointment.

"We rode hard but we did not catch them," he said. "The tracks were plain until after we crossed the North Fork. Then we lost them in the tracks of many cattle. We could not find where the men rode out again. Colonel Randlett said they are probably into Texas by now."

After saying he was too tired to eat, Lucius went into the bedroom to sleep.

Isabel walked back to the den. Too emotionally disturbed to concentrate, she put her books aside, went into the storage shed, and began a chore she dreaded: making an inventory of a new shipment of donated goods.

But the harder she worked, the more furious she became.

She felt everyone in the world should know what had been done to the Indians. And she felt driven to tell them.

The conservative editors of *The Saturday Evening Post* would never print such controversial material. And *The Woman's Companion* was aimed at home and hearth.

But *The Baptist Standard* of Chicago might not shy away from it. The editors often published fiery articles.

Isabel gathered every recent issue of the newspaper she could find and studied them. Then she began writing.

Heading her article "Saddle Mountain, Oklahoma Territory," she described in detail what had occurred, the scene of horror that had greeted her at the cemetery. She stressed the civilized reaction of the Kiowas in summoning the proper authorities. As she wrote, her anger mounted.

"We have fought the Indians, we have scalped them, we have pounded their brains out with mallets, we have cut them open, we have exterminated whole tribes, we have wiped out whole villages, we have swindled them out of their land, we have villainously lied to them, we have drowned them, we have burned them, we have lassoed them and dragged them till dead. Now we cannot even allow the poor corpses to rest in peace.

"And after all this we stand up and sing, our hearts bursting with patriotism, *My country, 'tis of thee, sweet land of liberty*!

"Is there no law in our land to defend the helpless? Must the missionaries stay here and see their Indians demoralized and trampled under foot by the so-called march of civilization?

"America once galled under the paw of the English lion, but how does that tyranny compare with our own?

"We laud the name of George Washington and justly so, because he dared to stand out for liberty. Yet when a Red Jacket, a Sitting Bull, a Big Tree, or a Lone Wolf strikes in his weak way for the same liberty, we brand him a 'red devil' and a 'wild Indian' and shower buckshot on his whole tribe!

"These Indians on this reservation are promised protection. They have not the protection of your cat.

"When twenty-two Kiowa Indians wished to travel forty miles from their homes to receive Jesus Christ in baptism, they were required to obtain permission from the U.S. government to leave the reservation, even for a day.

"The shackles of slavery have yet to be removed in this our nation.

"The Christian commonwealth of Massachusetts at one time offered a large bounty for every Indian scalp, be it man, woman, or child. The governor of Pennsylvania offered bounties for Indians captured, scalped, or dead. South Carolina appropriated at one time $17,500 for Cherokee scalps. North Carolina offered $50 for every Indian killed. Virginia in 1775 enacted a law giving $50 for every male Indian above the age of twelve taken prisoner, killed, or destroyed within the boundaries of the colony.

"We all know this sad history. I need not go on and on.

"We have made nine hundred treaties with the Indians and driven them from one end of this broad land to the other. And now we dig up the graves of their grandfathers in hopes of finding yet more plunder.

"When my Indians tell me, 'White men are liars,' how am I to answer?

"When they say, 'White men are sly, they cannot be trusted,' how may I tell them any different?

"When they say, 'White men are dangerous,' where in God's name is my argument?

"An Indian once ordered me out of his tipi with a knife and told me that he did not wish to hear anything a white person had to say. I told him I did not blame him, that if I were in his moccasins I would say the same.

"Today that man is a Christian.

"Yes, a good *Baptist* Christian!

"When the Ponca chief Standing Bear left his reservation near this place in 1879 to return his dead son to Kansas for burial, he was arrested. During his trial in Federal District Court in Omaha, a great debate arose over his exact status vis-à-vis the Constitution. Our great U.S. government argued that Indians were 'wards of the state' and therefore not 'persons' within the meaning of the Constitution! In what is surely a landmark decision, the learned judge in his exemplary wisdom held that the American Indian is indeed a 'human being' and therefore entitled to the same protection under the law as a white man.

"The Indians here at Saddle Mountain are still waiting."

Carefully, Isabel reread what she had written. Although she suspected editors of *The Baptist Standard* might take exception on a point or two, there was not a single line she would amend or retract. She signed the article, placed it in an envelope, and addressed it.

Two days later Tonemoh came by on his way to the agency.

Isabel sent the letter with him to be mailed, giving little thought to the consequences.

Chapter Thirteen

Despite the threat posed by the Jerome Agreement, the reservation had seemed a placid island during Isabel's first two years at Saddle Mountain, relatively safe from wave after wave of white settlers claiming the land around it. But with the arrival of 1898, uncertainty began to gnaw at the foundations of the community.

Reports persisted that at last the Jerome Agreement was close to approval in the U.S. Senate. Every item in the newspapers concerning the stalled legislation was discussed at length by whites and Indians both on and off the reservation.

The Kiowas could not understand the political intricacies involved in the long delay—nor, for that matter, could Isabel. The senators apparently did not care a whit that thousands of people residing in the southwestern portion of Oklahoma Territory were left in limbo while they dallied.

In heightened anticipation of Senate confirmation, railroads suddenly were in fierce competition to enter the region. Awarded a franchise, the Rock Island Railroad already had crossed the Kansas line to the north and was rapidly laying track southward toward the reservation.

Slowly the attitudes of the Indians toward their situation began to change.

They remained reluctant to throw away their tipis, symbols of their lost freedom.

Yet they hungered for *anything* permanent.

On the southern portion of the reservation, some of the Comanche chiefs had allowed the government to build houses for them. Although proud of the structures, they disdained to live in them. Instead, they continued to sleep, cook, and eat in their tipis, and they quartered their livestock in the white-man houses.

Gradually some of the Kiowas began to regard the government houses in a different light. The Jerome Agreement at least guaranteed each Indian a hundred sixty acres. Although little respect remained among the Indians for contractual wording, they began to see that a house might pose a solid stamp of ownership difficult to refute.

Odlepaugh, Kokom, Heenkey, Smokey, Tonemoh, Long Horn, and Domot petitioned the agency for houses, assuming that when selection of allocations started, they would be able to choose the land on which the house sat.

The Ghost Dancers kicked hard, but the house movement spread.

As the petitions came in, Colonel Randlett sent word to the Indians that white contractors would be hired in the spring to begin work on the houses.

From Miss Burdette came a surprising offer. She explained that the mission society had acquired a large tent, donated by creditors after the bankruptcy of a traveling carnival. If God's Light on the Mountain Missionary Circle would forward the fifty dollars required to pay a storage bill, the Atchison, Topeka, and Santa Fe Railway had offered to ship the tent free to charge to the nearest siding, eighty miles east of the reservation.

Isabel summoned her mission circle into an emergency
meeting in the den. Twenty-six Indians came through a pouring rainstorm, tracking mud and dripping water onto the
floor. They crowded into the single room, some sitting cross-
legged, some squatting, and some standing. Isabel stood on a
box so all could see her.

"I know this may seem a step backward," she told them
through Lucius. "We do not have money to spend foolishly.
But our church is still in the far-ahead time. This large tent is
now. It is big. Three hundred of us can sit down in it. If we
get it, we can have our Jesus talks when it is raining or
snowing. The sides can be raised to let the wind blow through,
and it will be a cool place to meet in summer. I think we
should pay this money and get it. But this is your decision.
The church money belongs to you, not to me, or to the ladies
in Chicago."

"Can we have the Jesus eat in the tent?" Kokom asked.

Isabel thought carefully before replying. The Indians placed
high value on Holy Communion and were eager to receive it
in their own church. She did not want to place the possibility
completely out of reach. Yet she knew she must stress the
sanctity of Holy Communion, so that when that day arrived
they would understand its full significance.

"No, we cannot have the Jesus eat in the tent," she said.
"We are only a missionary circle. The Jesus eat is for a
church. But I have a plan that might help us build our church
much faster."

The idea had occurred to her on first reading Miss Burdette's letter. She explained.

"Sometimes when a church or little group of Christians
needs money quick, they have what is called a *revival*. They
invite powerful Jesus men to come and make strong Jesus
talks. Then they ask all their friends to come from all over—
people from other churches, everyone who wants to hear the
big Jesus men. It is much like a big eat, except that there are
many Jesus talks. After the people have heard the strong
talks, they are asked to give money to help pay the Jesus
men, and the group who has gone to all the trouble to offer
the revival. This is a road to make money quick and it is a
good one."

"How will we get the Jesus men here?" Pope-bah asked.
"Why would big Jesus men want to come here to talk to poor
Indians?"

"For most of them, it would be something different, so they would like to do it. The brother of Miss Burdette is a big Jesus man who gives very strong talks. His name is Robert Burdette, and he is known in churches all over this country. I am sure he will come if we ask him. I will think of others who might come. I am sure we can get the Jesus men here."

Awed by the enormity of the plan, the Indians remained silent for a time, thinking hard.

"How will all the people sleep here at Saddle Mountain?" Pope-bah asked. "What will they eat? How will they get here?"

"Those are things we must work out. It will take much time, much planning. Certainly we cannot have the revival next week, or even next summer. Maybe the summer after that. The railroad is building here quick. Our visitors should be able to ride almost to our front door, maybe no more than twenty or thirty miles away. If that happens, Miss Burdette and the women from Chicago may come, too. But these are all busy people. They keep calendars for the time-ahead to remind them what they have agreed to do. We must speak now to get a place on their time-ahead calendar."

The Indians were familiar with calendars recording the past. Several Kiowas kept them, recording the history of the tribe from year to year. But the notion of drawing calendars for the future was new to them. Isabel could see them grappling with the concept.

She offered another point in favor of acquiring the tent. "The ladies in Chicago are thinking hard about sending another Jesus woman here to help us. If one comes, she will live with me in the den. As you can see, there is little room in it now. If another Jesus woman puts her bed here, there will be even less. The big tent will be a good place for our missionary circle to meet."

The proposal was discussed at length in Kiowa. Odlepaugh and Heenkey spoke hard against parting with the money, but eventually they also were persuaded.

The circle also approved a resolution to make plans toward a revival in the new tent during the summer of 1900.

As the meeting ended, the rain slackened to a mere sprinkle. The Indians departed quick, hurrying to reach home before the next deluge.

Isabel was deciding whether to try to push the mud outside before going to bed, or whether to wait until morning, when she saw that Domot had lingered behind. More and more frequently, he had been dropping by to share his worries and troubles.

He sat quietly until the other Indians were gone. Isabel asked him if he would like for her to warm a cup of cold coffee. He made the "no" sign and continued to sit.

"I think the new houses will be good," he signed after a while. "More of the Kiowas are thinking hard about Jesus. Soon there will be many more Christians here."

Isabel was intrigued. "Who is thinking hardest?"

Domot answered obliquely, which was his habit. "Only eleven Kiowas are left here who still think the way of our grandfathers. I will call their names: Mo-keen. Taboodle. Poor Buffalo. Gush-at. Komalty. Gaw-aggie. Geepaw. Frank Given. Ahpeatre. Buffalo Tom."

Isabel counted ten. She assumed that Domot was the eleventh.

"All the other Indians here at Saddle Mountain are walking the cactus road, the Ghost Dance Road, or the Jesus road," he added.

"I thought Mo-keen walked the Ghost Dance road," she said.

Domot seemed to realize he had conveyed privileged information. His face did not alter expression, but he thought long about his answer.

"Mo-keen is the keeper of the Tai-may," he signed. "The old chiefs honored him by making that road for him. If someone told him of a Sun Dance tomorrow in the hot place the Jesus men talk about, he would be there. He is hungry for the old roads. He has looked hard at the Ghost Dance road. Now he does not look much at it. His son Aitsan has pushed and pushed and turned him from it. Now he is listening hard to the Jesus talks. I think maybe some-day he will walk the Jesus road. I do not know this to be true. But it is what I think."

The revelation lifted Isabel's spirits until they soared.

Brother Clouse had called Mo-keen one of the meanest men alive.

And now there was hope she might win him for Christ!

After Domot left, she decided to wait until morning to clean the floors.

Instead, she knelt in the mud and prayed for guidance in bringing Mo-keen into the fold.

*   *   *

Weeks went by and Isabel heard nothing from the editors of *The Baptist Standard*. Eventually she assumed that her article had been rejected as too controversial or too opinionated. She almost forgot about venting her wrath on paper.

Then in late January the bombshell burst. Her first inkling came from a woman in Cedar Falls, Iowa. The letter, brought from the agency by Heenkey, was written in a feeble hand. Isabel spent several minutes puzzling over it before realizing that the woman was referring to her article in *The Baptist Standard*.

"Perhaps you are too young to remember the Minnesota Uprising of 1862," the woman wrote. "I am not. Two of my sisters, a brother, and my parents were murdered by your 'red devils.' I hid out in a plum thicket, or I would have been killed, too. At least five hundred white settlers died in that uprising. We will never know how many. All the Indians should have been wiped from the face of the earth in 1862. It was your missionaries who saved them to kill again."

Isabel was disturbed by the letter. She felt she should set the record straight. She promptly sat down and wrote the woman, opening with an expression of sympathy for the deaths in her family. She then went on to point out that the Minnesota uprising came after the Sioux were starved by a government agent who had ample food stored in his warehouses. She reminded the woman that sixty-two white persons were rescued from the hostiles by *Christian* Indians, who hid them and escorted them on a dangerous three-day journey to safety. She also added that Episcopal Bishop Henry Whipple's direct appeal to President Lincoln for the lives of 306 Indians condemned to die was based on fundamental rules of justice. She cited later evidence proving that many of the thirty-eight Indians eventually hanged were innocent— some having served as peacemakers throughout the uprising.

Three days later, seven more letters arrived. One was from a retired Army major. Three were from ministers.

All attacked Isabel's article.

"I served among Indians more than thirty years," the major wrote. "In that time I saw no more than a half dozen who were 'worth your house cat.' I cannot find it in me to be concerned over a few violated graves on your reservation. I lost many fine comrades on the frontier. Some were tortured and died in agony. Some never knew graves. The present government program for Indians may be the best attempted. As the older Indians die off, the young may absorb some semblance of civilization. But as a people they are an inferior race and they will always remain a burden."

Isabel finished the major's letter in blinding fury. She would have answered it immediately if she had not stopped to read the rest.

A minister in Springfield, Illinois, wrote that like birds and animals of the field, Indians did not possess souls and therefore were beyond salvation. "They may learn to parrot biblical phrases and sing simple hymns, but to coat them with a thin varnish of ceremony and call them Christians is a sham," he went on. "You would do best to perform your work among your own kind, where it is needed."

He was merely the most eloquent of the three ministers. The other two offered essentially the same argument.

The three remaining letters—two from men, one from a woman—claimed vast experience with Indians and offered the view that the "red devils" would never be civilized.

Not one letter expressed the slightest regret over the plundered graves.

Shaken, Isabel put the letters aside and pondered what to do about them.

Two days later, Tonemoh returned from the agency with a bundle containing sixty-seven letters. Isabel spent most of the night reading through them, growing more heartsick by the hour.

She never dreamed that such hatred existed. And in people who claimed to be Christians!

After a time the letters became intermingled. Only phrases lingered in the memory: "My taxes are going to feed those worthless savages. They should have been eradicated long ago." "I've never known one not to lie and cheat and steal." "General Sheridan was right when he said the only good Indian he ever saw was a dead Indian." "The only answer is to move them to some other country, like Africa, where they can rob and kill to hearts' content." "If more of the colonies had posted bounties earlier, a more realistic Indian policy would have prevailed, and we would not be faced with the problem of Indians today." "Colonel Chivington was right; nits make lice. If we took the same precautions with Indians as we take with farm animals, the problem would soon vanish."

One man wrote in favor of opening Indian graves. He said

he once found a .50-caliber Sharps rifle in an Indian grave.
The name of a white man was inscribed on the stock. He said
he later met the man's brother and learned that the owner
had been killed and scalped eleven years before. "Other
murderers could be found if more Indian graves were opened,"
he concluded.

"You are a dear, brave girl," said a woman in Minneapolis.
"I find few of my friends agree with me, but I have always
felt we have done the Indians a terrible injustice. If we had
allocated a vast portion of this huge continent to them in the
first place, most of the bloodshed over the past hundred years
could have been avoided."

Isabel treasured that letter. It was the only one sharing her
views without qualification.

In the days that followed, a bundle of letters arrived with
each Indian returning from the agency.

And not one word came from the Mission Board in Chicago.

The silence of Miss Burdette and the Board soon became
Isabel's greatest concern. With the number of letters she had
received, she easily could imagine the amount of correspondence and complaint arriving at 4026 Grand Boulevard in
Chicago.

Isabel forced herself to stop reading the letters. Just glancing at them could keep her disturbed for the remainder of the
day. Their existence seemed to serve no purpose. Most contained only hatred. Few offered any reasoned argument.

They were so biased that she felt she should not share
them with the Indians—not even Lucius.

She bore the burden alone.

Her original intention of answering every letter became a
physical impossibility. She counted two hundred ninety-
three.

At last a note arrived from Miss Burdette, written on
personal stationery. Enclosed was a clipping from *The Baptist
Standard* article—the first copy Isabel had seen.

It was the most intimate letter she had ever received from
Miss Burdette.

Dearest Belle,

I hardly know where to begin. You have kicked up a
storm that has fallen on our poor heads without mercy for
the better part of three weeks. Nothing like this has ever

happened before. I do not know whether to laugh, cry, or pray.

Officially I will be required to chastise you for such an intemperate expression of independent views involving the Woman's American Baptist Home Mission Society.

The Society has taken great care to avoid political involvement throughout its long history. It is not the Society's intention to make or to amend government policy toward the Indian, or even to comment thereon. Our concern is solely for the spiritual and physical well-being of those in our charge. Our commission comes from God and not from Washington. We must govern ourselves accordingly. I'm sure you know this. However, in your indignation over the insult to the Indians, you plainly shoved such basic considerations aside.

The good ladies of the Mission Board have been most understanding, and I daresay some are in full sympathy with you. But we cannot condone such outspokenness. The Baptists in Chicago have talked of little else for weeks, and the lay newspapers have devoted attention to it. We have received notes from almost every Baptist leader, and from those in several other denominations, urging us to admonish you. This I do.

Having said that, I feel moved to add that it was a most wonderful article. Your righteous stand and deep knowledge of the subject came through. If it were not for the Society's delicate situation, so dependent on public support, I would have no quarrel with it. Jesus overturned the tables of the moneychangers. I believe He demonstrated for us that there is a time and place for righteous anger.

Therefore, I have been slow to act in this matter. We shall not recall you, as some have urged us to do. Our sympathies are with you. But we ask that *your* sympathies be with *us*! When you feel moved to speak out, please consider the consequences.

Yours in Christ,
Mary G. Burdette

The winter remained unusually mild until early February, when a week of frigid temperatures, freezing sleet, and cold rain kept the Indians at home. None came to work on the quilts or to attend English classes.

For months Isabel had reveled in the comparative privacy of the den. After the Indians departed each night she usually had the place to herself until dawn. She could read, write, wash her hair, or devote herself to any personal pursuit with no one the wiser.

But eventually she began to find the isolation wearing. In the quiet days and long nights of winter, she again felt the onslaught of loneliness.

One evening the solitude became unbearable. She thought back fondly to the long winter evenings she had spent with Lucius, the rare intimacy of their shared silences, the exhilaration of their lively discussions.

Throughout the year she had been lending him books. She remembered she had promised to lend him James M. Barrie's *The Little Minister* but had not yet done so.

Pulling a yellow rain slicker around her, she picked up the book and walked in the rain across the meadow to the Aitsan house.

As she expected, Lucius was sitting alone in the front room, bent over a book beside the lamp. He answered her soft knock and held the door open for her. She shook the raincoat at the door and hung it on a peg.

"I brought the book I promised," she said.

Lucius gestured toward a chair by the lamp. *In His Steps* by Charles M. Sheldon lay open on the table, next to the dictionary and a tablet page filled with notes.

"How far are you into that one?" she asked.

"I have finished it. Now I am going back through it, looking again at all the words I did not know."

"Did you like the story?"

Lucius frowned and sat for a moment, thinking.

In lending him Sheldon's novel, Isabel had believed he would be intrigued by the challenge the hero minister posed to his congregation, to ask before every decision, "What would Jesus do?" and to act accordingly.

"I do not understand it," Lucius said. "Why doesn't every Christian try to do what Jesus would do?"

"That is the point of the book," Isabel explained. "The thought is beautiful, but the author demonstrates that the goal of perfection is not only difficult but almost impossible in everyday life."

"Some of the people in the book did it."

"And most paid dearly. Remember the man who told the authorities that his company was cheating the public? He lost his job, and his family suffered."

"Do you think he did the right thing?"

Isabel sensed that the question was not objective. She now knew Lucius as well as any member of her own family. Something was troubling him. She answered cautiously. "Perhaps. I'm not sure."

"How do we know what Jesus would do?"

Isabel studied him, certain now that a deeper question lay behind the one he was asking. He was watching her, his eyes begging for an answer.

"Lucius, none of us is wise enough to do the right thing always."

He rose and walked to the stove. Adding a few small pieces of wood, he looked at the fire for a moment before closing the lid.

Isabel waited. She did not push.

"The agent has asked me to be a government farmer," he said, not meeting her eyes. "They will pay me fifty dollars a month to show the Indians at Rainy Mountain how we planted the crops here last summer. I do not know what to do."

Isabel felt her heart skip a beat.

She did not think she could bear to lose Lucius. If he went to Rainy Mountain to farm, he would not be able to travel back and forth to serve as interpreter. She would have no means of communication with the Indians except through the limitations of sign language.

Yet she could understand his quandary. Few white men made fifty dollars a month. He would be near Amos and Jessie at the Rainy Mountain school. He would be able to buy luxuries to make his family's life much easier. And now there was another son to consider.

"There's no question, Lucius," she said. "You must accept."

He looked at her with tears welling in his eyes. "I do not want to go."

"It won't be forever," she said, trying to console herself with the thought. "If you cannot teach them in a year, they cannot be taught. And it is money that will not be there forever."

"What will you do about the Jesus talks? The missionary circle?"

"I can manage."

Lucius sat down again, facing her. "I will come back every Sunday."

"No. I can't ask you to do that. You will be tired after six days of work in the fields."

"What about the revival?"

"That's a long time away. I won't need you for the preparations. If the government wants you for a second year, we'll manage some way."

Lucius stared at the floor. "I do not want to quit the Jesus talks. My head tells me to do it, but my heart does not think it is the right thing to do."

Isabel reached for his hand. "Lucius, your first responsibility is to your family. You cannot deny them the comfort this money will bring. And you will be doing the Lord's work, showing the Rainy Mountain Kiowas how to plant and harvest. Our only reasons in not wanting you to go are selfish."

Lucius looked totally miserable. "Mabel and Sarah and Leslie will go with me," he said. "You can live in the house while we are gone."

"I'll look after the house for you, but I will live in the den. We fought so hard to get it. I should live in it."

Isabel thought ahead to the empty house, the long months ahead. She did not know if she could endure the loneliness.

She rose, walked to the door, and tented the raincoat over her head. "The rain has stopped. I'd best go before it starts again."

She fled into the night. She feared that if Lucius knew the full effect of his impending departure on her, he might not go.

Chapter Fourteen

Aside from a few magazines sent to Isabel by her sisters, news from outside the reservation seldom reached the Saddle Mountain community. But when the U.S. battleship *Maine* exploded and sank in Havana Harbor on February 15, 1898, every Indian on the reservation soon knew of it. Great excitement among the whites convinced them that something extraordinary had occurred.

They understood that once again the whites were taking up the war road.

On the last day of February, Isabel received her second telegram since coming to the reservation. This one was from Miss Burdette:

BOARD SUGGESTS YOU ASSESS SITUATION CAREFULLY STOP IF DEEMED ADVISABLE COMMA COME HOME STOP

At first the message made no sense. But as letters followed from her sisters, her brother, and mission circles across the country, the concern for her safety became clear.

Newspapers throughout the nation were inciting the fear that once troops were removed from forts throughout the West, the Indians would go on a bloody rampage.

The situation became even more ridiculous on the morning Lucius and his family left for Rainy Mountain. With the wagon loaded, and cow and seven horses tied behind, Lucius walked down to the den.

He handed Isabel a huge pistol. "I think you should keep this."

Isabel almost dropped the heavy, man-sized weapon. "Lucius, I don't need this," she protested, trying to hand it back. "I hardly know which end to point."

He refused to take it."You will be all alone here. Strange white men have been seen on the reservation. Some of the Comanche houses have been robbed while the Indians were away drawing rations. If anything happens here, you can shoot into the air. Odlepaugh or Kokom will hear it and come quick."

The precaution seemed wise. Both Odlepaugh and Kokom lived less than two miles away. If the wind was right, they might hear gunfire. She accepted the pistol. Lucius showed her how to load and unload it and how to cock the hammer to make it fire.

Then he stood for a time silent, ill-at-ease, clearly upset. How much of his disturbance stemmed from the move itself, and how much from concern for her safety, she could not tell.

"I will come and interpret your Jesus talk every Sunday, no matter how tired I am," he said.

"Lucius, I would love to have you come, but that would be a thirty-five-mile ride here and back. You can't do that."

"I want to do it. And I will not take money for it. You can give the money to the some-day church."

"If you really want to make the trip, I'll not speak against it. But I don't want you to feel obligated."

She walked up the slope with him and said good-bye to Mabel, Sarah, and Leslie. Then she stood waving as the Aitsans drove away toward Rainy Mountain under a pale blue wintry sky.

In the weeks that followed, Isabel grew intimately acquainted with every aspect of loneliness.

A few months before, she had only a cot-sized space to call her own. Now she had two houses and a tent on the way that could seat three hundred people. And she had never felt more alone.

Heenkey, Mo-keen, and Domot hauled the tent from the railroad. The men of the missionary circle spent three days setting it up in the pasture below the den. It was grimy, patched in many places, and as big as a barn.

Isabel moved her coffee-box pulpit, mission stores, and the quilting frames under its soaring canvas. It quickly became headquarters for the entire community. Mo-keen put a huge stove in its center and vented the smoke through the top. Even on cooler days a big fire in the grate removed the chill from the air. Indians spent the entire day under it, quilting, chatting, laughing, exchanging gossip.

Only Isabel was excluded, due to the language barrier. In the mornings she conducted her English lessons. At night she gave her Jesus talks in sign language. Throughout the remainder of every day, she saw not one person who could utter more than the simplest phrases in English.

True to his word, Lucius rode from Rainy Mountain each Sunday morning to translate her Jesus talk. But he did not linger. Usually he saddled his horse and started his long trip back even before the congregation dispersed.

As the months went by he lost so much weight that Isabel grew increasingly concerned. He labored ten or twelve hours each day, six days a week, breaking land for the demonstration farm. The long ride on Sundays gave him no rest.

"Lucius, we are endangering your health," she told him one Sunday. "If you become ill I will never forgive myself."

Tired and drawn, Lucius did not argue. "Maybe I will come every other week for a while," he said.

At night Isabel had two houses, the huge tent, and several square miles of prairie to herself. She had never been frightened of darkness. But through her ear trumpet she could hear the flapping tent, howling wolves, and other nocturnal noises. She felt especially vulnerable because she knew there were other sounds she could *not* hear.

The huge pistol under her pillow became a comforting presence.

In late April, after Spain declared war on the United States, most of the Army garrison left Fort Sill to take part in the coming invasion of Cuba.

Contrary to the fears expressed in newspapers across the country, the Indians did not seize the opportunity to lift scalps.

Instead, white trash of every description felt sufficiently emboldened to trespass on the reservation.

One morning Heenkey arrived and signed that the tipis of An-pay-kau-te—the Indian the whites called Frank Given—had been robbed.

Isabel saddled Jeremiah and rode with Heenkey to the Given place to see if she could help.

When she arrived, Given was seated on the ground beside a fallen brush arbor. The tipis had been wrecked beyond repair, the canvas slit, the lodgepoles shattered. Apparently the brush arbor had been pulled down with ropes.

"They took everything," Given signed. "Blankets, clothes, silver and beads, dishes, everything. They took the war shield and lance that belonged to my father, Satank. They took his gun and his bow and arrow. They did not take this medal only because I had it hidden where they could not find it."

He held in his hand the George Washington Medal awarded to his father.

"We can replace the blankets and the dishes," Isabel signed. "We will find clothes for you. I am ashamed that this has happened to you."

"I am ashamed I did not catch them," Given signed. "If I had been here, I would have killed them."

Heenkey brought his wagon and moved Frank Given and his wife into the Gospel tent until their tipis could be repaired.

That night, when the congregation arrived for her Jesus talk, every male Indian carried a rifle.

On the following day Isabel rode with Heenkey and Given to the agency to help Given file claim for his loss.

Afterward she insisted on a private moment with Colonel Randlett.

"The Indians are scared and angry," she told him. "They are going armed. If an Indian kills one of these worthless whites, we both know who will suffer most."

"It is a bad situation," Randlett agreed. "But I don't know what I can do. Civilian authorities have no jurisdiction on the reservation. U.S. marshals assigned to the territory have their hands full with the lawlessness in all the new towns. I can't establish and arm an Indian police force without sanction from Washington. I will explain conditions here and ask for permission."

"That will take months," Isabel said.

"Probably. I'll rush matters as much as I can. I've been told that ten years ago, when rations were months late and the Indians were starving, the Kiowas decided that the only way to gain attention in Washington was to kill the agent, a man named White. Komalta, Polant, and Little Robe were elected to do the job. Fortunately, Texas drovers arrived with a herd of beef just before the plan was put into effect." Randlett smiled, but his eyes were serious. "I hope Little Robe doesn't settle on that solution this time."

* * *

In May government contractors came onto the reservation and set to work building houses for the Indians. Isabel helped the women plan curtains, cabinets, and other furnishings.

She quickly recognized that the construction workers were not of the highest social order. They stared at her and the Indian women in ways that could not be mistaken.

Isabel did not feel safe with the white men sleeping on the reservation. Each night before going to sleep she made sure the door was locked, and she kept the big pistol tucked under her pillow.

In late afternoon on a day in early June, she happened to glance through the door of the Gospel tent and saw movement near the Aitsan house. She walked outside in time to see a white man approaching the tent. He was riding a pale sorrel mare and leading a spotted packhorse.

Pope-bah, Ananthy, Hattie, and Sapemah were working at a quilting frame. When they saw the man they stopped work and awaited Isabel's cue.

As far as she knew, there was not an Indian man on the place.

The rider sat loose-limbed in the saddle, as if he had traveled from a vast distance. He stopped before the tent, glanced at the Indian women, and turned to Isabel. He carried a big pistol at his waist. The stock of a rifle protruded from beneath his left leg. Isabel put the conversation tube to her ear and waited.

"Afternoon, ma'am," the man said. "Last thing I expected to see here was a white woman. You speak English, don't you."

Isabel wondered for a moment if she could indeed pass for an Indian. She concluded with regret that she could not. No Indian had such light hair.

"I speak English," she said.

The man pointed. "Right pretty quilts." He glanced toward the mountain, the Aitsan house. "My name's Will Irwin. Got a little place up in Missouri that's about cropped out. Missed the run for the unassigned lands in '89, and the big one in '93. I figure this may be the last call. Not much left now. I hear this reservation's going to be opened soon. Good land around here. I'm out looking it over and to see if it's worth making the run. I may try my luck."

A Boomer.

Isabel realized she should have been expecting them. They explored ahead of the official runs in order to gain an advantage.

She wondered how much of her distrust of the man came from the attitudes she had absorbed from the Indians. At the moment, he seemed to embody all the white prejudices and insensitivity she had ever witnessed.

She was struck by a harsh fact: She felt much closer to the Indians around her than to any white man she had seen in months—even Colonel Randlett.

"This is an Indian reservation," she said. "You're not supposed to be here."

Irwin laughed. "Begging your pardon, ma'am. You look white to me. And you're here."

Kokom, Smokey, and Little Robe stepped quietly out of the trees. Each carried a rifle.

"I'm a missionary," Isabel said. "I have papers from Washington. I have permission from the tribal council. But this reservation is still closed to white people who have no business here."

Irwin eyed the rifles. "Well, I mean no harm. I've been in the saddle most of three days. My horses are tired."

Isabel looked at the horses. Standing with heads lowered, hindquarters hip-shot to ease the burden on at least one hoof, they did indeed seem near exhaustion. Reluctantly, she relented.

It was a sad state to abuse animals just because a man had the wrong shade of skin.

"You're welcome to water your horses in the creek," she said. "We're Christians here. We'll have supper in a bit. I'm afraid it's only coffee, beef, and beans. You're welcome to share. But I feel I must warn you. If the soldiers catch you, they will put you in jail at Fort Sill."

Irwin smiled. "I'll take my chances. And I appreciate the invitation."

He swung down from the saddle. Once on the ground, he seemed harmless enough. Small and bandy-legged, he wore a ragged, flaring moustache and carried his pistol high at his waist, on the left side, the butt facing forward.

Kokom, Smokey, and Little Robe walked close to the gospel tent and sat on the grass, their rifles resting across their laps. Even with their protection Isabel did not feel completely at ease. The Wichita valley to the north, the Arbuckle and Kiamichi mountains to the east still were infested with outlaws.

Irwin walked his horses to the creek, loosened the girths, stripped off the halters, and put them on a long lariat tether to graze.

He returned to the Gospel tent. Isabel offered him a camp stool in the shade. Pope-bah and Ananthy built a fire in the open and began warming the food. Kokom, Smokey, and Little Robe sat quietly, never looking directly at the man.

"Any of these Indians speak English?" Irwin asked.

"Only a few words. None of them can converse."

"How long have you been here?"

"Going on three years. I spent three years with the Cheyennes and Arapaho before that."

Irwin glanced at the Indians, the den, the Aitsan house. "I don't see how you stand it," he said.

Isabel did not need to be reminded that she had worn the same Mother Hubbard for days. "I can stand it as well as the Indians," she snapped.

Odlepaugh, Hunting Horse, and Spotted Horse seemed to materialize out of nowhere. They also were carrying rifles. Irwin seemed not to notice.

Isabel served him a cup of coffee. As dusk deepened, she lit the lanterns.

Heenkey, Dawtobi, Gahbein, Long Horn, other Indians, and their wives arrived. Irwin began to eye them nervously.

"After we eat, we have a Bible talk," Isabel explained. "You're welcome to stay and participate."

Irwin gave an uneasy laugh. "I'm not much on religion, ma'am. I've read the Bible. I only believe about half of it."

Isabel could not keep her mouth closed. "Which half? There's enough in half of it to save you."

The rebuke sobered him some. "I don't know. I've never given it much thought."

Isabel checked her tongue. After all, she and the Indians were hosts. She knew she should show common Christian courtesy.

When the meal was served, Irwin attacked a plate of ribs with gusto. He accepted a second plate of beans and Sapemah's cornbread. The Indians ate quietly.

Afterward, with a full stomach, Irwin grew talkative. "There's some awfully good land right through here. I think I'll try my luck."

"The Indians will be given first choice," Isabel said. "As I understand it, every Indian man, woman, and child will be allotted a hundred sixty acres. Most of the land on this side of the mountains probably will go to them."

Irwin frowned. Apparently this was news to him. "That's a shame. Some of the best soil in this part of the state lies between here and the Washita."

"Why is it a shame?" Isabel asked quietly.

Irwin paused while Ananthy refilled his graniteware cup with coffee. He seemed completely oblivious of his situation. "Well, the Indians certainly don't know how to farm it. I saw some of their places today. The ground's barely scratched. A few kernels of corn here, a scattering of maize there. You can see they don't know the first thing about farming."

Isabel glanced at the Indians. She doubted any understood Irwin's remarks, but they were ever alert to tone and inflection.

"How would *you* farm this land?" she asked.

Irwin gestured with his coffee cup. "First, I'd take out all timber and brush. Put *all* the land to use. Second, the soil must be plowed deep to bring up the moisture, trap rain when it falls. Third, I'd take out the native grasses, try some new varieties. Finally, I'd plant cotton, other cash crops. That's the only way to make this land pay."

"What if you didn't have the equipment to plow deep?" Isabel asked. "What if you wanted to keep the beauty of the trees and open fields?"

Irwin smiled. "Ma'am, there's beauty enough for me in a good stand of cotton. And as for plowing deep, that's the problem. It's a waste of good land to give it to these Indians. They don't know how to farm, and they're lazy and shiftless to boot. You can just look at them to see that."

For a moment Isabel lost all reason.

"It seems to me you could show some appreciation for the Indians, seeing that you're filling your face with their hard-earned food."

Irwin jumped as if he had been stabbed in the brisket. He glanced at the Indians as if seeing them for the first time. "Miss Crawford, I certainly didn't mean that the way it sounded. There's probably a lot of good in them. It's just that I've seen enough of their work in the last few days to see that they're not farmers by trade."

"Nor will they ever be, with men like you to teach them. You said you've 'cropped out' one farm. Now you want to come here and ruin another good patch of ground. If I had my way, you wouldn't get a square foot of it!"

Isabel turned her back on him and went into the gospel tent. "Go get the man's horses," she signed to Kokom. "I do not want him here."

She worked off some of her anger by lighting the remainder of the lanterns in preparation for her Jesus talk.

By the time she returned to the yard, Kokom was leading Irwin's horses from the creek.

"I think it best that you not sleep here." Isabel told him. "A few of the Indians in this part of the reservation are Christians, but most are not. None is happy about the land agreement. You might not be safe here." She pointed to the north. "If you ride in that direction, you will be off the reservation quick."

"I can't ride across this country in the dark," Irwin protested. "Maybe it will be all right with everyone if I just camp down the creek a ways."

"You will have a quarter moon in about an hour," Isabel told him. "It will give you enough light to get off the reservation."

Irwin mounted his horse. "Well, I thank you for supper. I hope you don't think hard of me for what I said. Could be that we'll be neighbors."

He rode off into darkness, leading his packhorse.

Isabel was still trembling with anger. The Indians asked no questions, but she felt some explanation was required.

She waited until they were seated for her Jesus talk.

"A long time ago I told you it is not always easy to be a Christian," she signed. "Tonight I am ashamed. I pushed that man with hot words and told him to leave because he is not smart enough to see things he should see. I will have to ask Jesus to forgive me."

The next day word came that a house on the other side of the mountain had been robbed while the Indians were away drawing rations. Odlepaugh and Heenkey wanted to track Irwin. But Kokom and Little Robe said they had watched him a long time from the mountain and did not think he had robbed the house.

Isabel hunted in the sheds beside the Aitsan corral until she found a length of old harness strap. Working with an awl, she fashioned a wide belt for her pistol and holster.

Through the remainder of that summer and fall, she kept the gun with her when none of the Kiowa men was present.

She did not inform Miss Burdette or even her sisters of the new situation.

She did not wish to alarm them, but she could not ignore the irony.

Two years ago she came to the reservation to live "all alone among wild Indians," armed only with her Bible.

Now she felt required to keep a pistol handy for protection from the whites.

The months passed slowly. Through summer and fall Isabel kept her mind occupied with work. She tended and harvested the Aitsan garden and traveled about the reservation, helping each family. The pressure cookers were set up in the Gospel tent, and again everyone worked long hours preparing for winter. For a time, sewing ceased on the quilts.

Then, at the end of a brief Sunday visit, Lucius revealed that he had been asked to serve a second year as government farmer.

He made the announcement as Isabel walked with him toward his horse.

She was devastated.

For eight months she had consoled herself with the thought that at the end of the growing season he would return.

She opened her mouth to protest, then closed it. He had just told her that Mabel was expecting another baby. She had no right to ask him to reject the opportunity for more money. He felt bad enough about leaving his job as translator. She could not burden his conscience further.

"I thought it was only for a year," she said lamely.

"Many Ghost Dancers live near the mouth of Elk Creek," he explained. "The government wants to teach them to farm."

The mouth of Elk Creek was ten or twelve miles beyond Rainy Mountain. He would not be able to return to Saddle Mountain at all on Sundays.

"Lucius, it's a terrible disappointment," she said. "I won't try to deny that. But we've made do for almost a year. I suppose we can struggle through another."

Lucius glanced at the Indians, the gospel tent. "I want to come back here quick. But I can do much with the money. And I tell myself that I am also helping the Kiowas as a government farmer."

"You are," Isabel said. "We mustn't forget that."

She stood and watched as he rode away toward Rainy Mountain, and she wondered how she possibly could endure another year without an interpreter, without Lucius.

Somehow she managed to keep her composure through the evening service. But in her lonely den that night she cried until she could cry no more.

In the days that followed she thought seriously of resigning her commission, packing up, and going home.

It was her worst time since coming to the territory.

She felt she could not continue to live in such complete isolation. Even her books—for so long a means of temporary escape—no longer penetrated her loneliness.

All accomplishments seemed to be behind her. She had won to Christ every Kiowa in the community not dedicated to the old ways, the cactus button, or the Ghost Dance. The some-day church still loomed hopelessly distant.

Despite all the work, less than two hundred dollars had been raised toward the thousand-dollar goal.

And without Lucius, her elaborate plans for a revival seemed hopeless.

She had sent out scores of letters proposing the revival for the week of July 4, 1900. Thus far the replies had been lukewarm. How could she lure the big Jesus men to Saddle Mountain when she had no one to translate their words?

She became convinced that she must abandon the mission, at least for a time.

Yet she dallied, praying and hoping that some new event or inspiration would come to the rescue.

When it did, it came from a most unexpected direction.

Late one afternoon Kokom came by the den for his periodic "chat." He arranged himself in the chair by the door and began to sign.

"Frank Given's wife will soon give birth to a baby."

That was hardly news. She was as big as a house. Isabel signed that she knew.

"Six babies of Frank Given have died. Not one has lived."

"I did not know it was so many."

"He says that if the baby dies this time, he will kill himself."

After a moment of reflection, Isabel took the threat seriously. Frank Given was a very troubled Indian. He sat around and moped constantly, mourning the loss of the old roads. He could not take up the new.

"I have promised to fix Papedone's house tomorrow," Isabel signed. "When I am through there, I will go talk with him."

"I have talked to him until my tongue is all worn out," Kokom signed. "He has closed his ears. My words hit him like pebbles bouncing off a stone."

The next morning Isabel was teaching Sapemah and Papedone how to scrub their floors, when Heenkey arrived on a well-lathered horse. "The new little son of Frank Given came into this world dead," he signed.

Isabel handed her bucket and cloth to Sapemah. "I must go to the Given tipi quick. We will cut off work here."

She had left Jeremiah and her sidesaddle at home, so she walked the two miles to the Given place. She found Frank sitting in front of his patched and battered tipi, his head in his hands. He looked up as she approached.

"I have heard," Isabel signed. "My heart cries for you and your family."

Frank raised his right hand and began making the "question" sign repeatedly. Isabel believed he was asking "Why?" But she was not sure. She waited until he stopped making it and completed the sentence.

"Why does Death follow me like a dog, sniffing at my moccasins? All of my life Death has been there, right behind me. I kick and kick and kick and he will not go away. Why has he taken everyone in my life?"

No blanket was proffered, so Isabel sank onto the dirt in front of the tipi.

From inside came quiet sounds of women weeping.

"My father was a Jesus man all his life and very wise," Isabel told him. "People asked him that question all the time. This is what he told them: There are things on this earth that are beyond the thoughts of a human being. We cannot know those things. Only the Great Father knows. We must walk with Him and trust in Him."

Given sat and studied Isabel. He had dark, contemplative eyes deeply set under heavy lids. His face was broad and weathered, with lines and creases forming patterns around a firm mouth.

Of all the Kiowas, he appeared to be the most beaten, the most whipped. His gray hair was pulled straight back into braids. He seemed to be considering Isabel's words. He began to sign.

"In the long-ago time when I was a young warrior, we went to a white man's fort far to the north of here. We camped near the fort and there was much fun. All the Kiowas were there, eating and dancing and having a good time. My father, Satank, and another Kiowa chief walked to the fort to council with the colonel there, as they had done many times before. No one thought of trouble. This time a soldier stood there at the gate with a gun. He had been told to shoot anyone who crossed a line. No one told the Indians why he was standing there. When my father, Satank, and the other chief crossed the line, the soldier raised his gun to shoot. My father, Satank, and the other chief put several arrows through him before he could pull the trigger. Everyone at the fort began yelling, and someone blew a bugle. We were surprised and not ready to fight. We ran away quick. We did not want the soldiers to chase us, so we took all their horses with us. Other soldiers came and chased us hard. For two winters we stayed on the warpath. We fought many battles. In one I saw my older brother killed. All of this happened because my father, Satank, did not know why the soldier was standing there. Why did they not tell him? What was the matter?"

Isabel felt her pulse race as she realized she was hearing a firsthand account of the big fight at Fort Larned, Kansas, in 1864. It had set off a general uprising of Plains Indians that had persisted for years.

She signed carefully. "I have found that most trouble between the white man and the Indian has come because each did not know the thoughts of the other. It is sad."

Given nodded. "About twenty winters ago I killed and scalped a Texan who cheated me. The soldiers came and abused me hard. I tried to tell them what the man had done to me, but they would not listen. Today the soldiers still say I am a bad Indian."

Isabel did not answer. Given had been accused of murdering a cowboy near Fort Sill in 1872, scalping him, and taking an ear. That was only one of many violent acts attributed to him.

He continued. "My little brother Joshua made a mistake and was thrown away by the tribe. My heart is still hot for what the tribe did. For a long time I did not want to live."

Again Isabel remained silent. The death of Joshua Given

seemed to linger on everyone's conscience and was still a source of much ill-feeling. But it was "a Kiowa thing." She had not interfered.

"Now we are penned up in this little place, and my seven little ones have died," Given went on. "If we had buffalo to eat, the mother would be strong, the babies would be strong. We have nothing but white-man food, and it is weak."

As far as Isabel knew, what he said was true. The current horrendous mortality of infants had been unknown while the Indians lived on the Plains.

"I do not want to live in this world anymore," Given signed, stressing his movements. "I think I will go over to the next one quick."

Isabel made the "no" sign. "It is the Great Father who tells us when to go," she signed. "We must not quit the road He has made for us."

"He has not made a road for me. If He has made it, I cannot find it."

Isabel pointed. "Look at that old mountain. Think hard about how long it has been there. Our life is like one rock in that mountain. Maybe it is only one little rock, but it is needed. If it is not there, the mountain will not be the same. Our life is one little rock in the Great Father's heaped-up plan for this world, maybe other worlds we know nothing about. The Great Father has a use for us. We must not question the road He has made for us in this world. Maybe we cannot see it. But it is there."

Given remained silent for several minutes. Isabel waited, allowing him time to consider what she had said.

"I tried one time to take up the Jesus road, but it is not for me," Given signed. "I am a full-blood Indian and a full-blood sinner. I drink whiskey and gamble away my money. Jesus does not want me. He threw me away."

Isabel had heard all about that. Given had joined the church at Rainy Mountain several years before, along with Big Tree and several others. After much drunkenness and gambling, he had been dropped from the rolls as a backslider.

She took a deep breath and began to sign.

"Jesus did not throw you away. The church threw you away. Sometimes men do not do the wise thing—not even Jesus men. But Jesus is always wise. Jesus does not throw *anyone* away. If we ask Him and work hard, we can put you back on the Jesus road."

Given was silent for a time.

"You have made a wise talk for me," he signed finally. "I will think hard about it."

Isabel went into the tipi. She comforted the women and washed and prepared the tiny body for burial.

As she worked, Indians began gathering in the yard for the nightlong vigil.

"We must have a coffin," she signed to the women. "I will go make one. Heenkey will help me bring it here. We will bury the little one when the sun rises tomorrow."

On her way home, crossing a boulder-studded ravine, the thought struck her that her father's "wise talk" was as applicable to herself as to Frank Given.

She looked up at the mountain rising above her.

The words of the 121st Psalm flooded into her mind: "I will lift up mine eyes unto the hills, whence cometh my help."

Before her, the stark, rugged beauty of the Wichitas stretched away to the horizon—Mount Scott, Mount Sheridan, Baker Peak, Saddle Mountain. The pink granite of the foreground faded with distance into burnt umber, mauve, and delicate shadings too wondrous to label—all under God's blue sky.

It was enough to make one shove aside earthly concerns and think about heaven.

Who was *she* to turn aside from God's purpose, any more than Frank Given?

Kneeling on the hard stones, she prayed.

"Lord, like these Indians, sometimes I am weak. I ask you to let me be a teacher. Yet I keep learning the same lessons over and over. Please grant me the strength to carry on even when—like Frank Given—I do not understand."

After the Given baby was buried, Isabel wrote an impassioned plea to Miss Burdette:

"It is not giving the gospel that wears me out. It is the mopping and cooking, the walking and riding, the suffering and dying, the birthing and burying, the wind and loneliness, the dust and mud, the fleas and lice, the delicate handling required by the uncivilized side of human nature, both white and red. Scorpions, centipedes, and rattlesnakes I take in stride. Last night I killed a snake with a pair of scissors as easily as tying off a quilt. I have learned the Indian road of taunting a rattlesnake into striking, then to brain him with a rock before he can again get to his "feet." I am as dark as a Kiowa and as agile as a cowboy and still I can say, 'I am first of all a woman.' I live alone in this wild land and yet I am not afraid. It is my *soul* that is wearing out! Thoughts rattle around in my head day and night and they have no place to go. Miss Burdette, I no longer can endure a life without *sharing*. Please, please send me a companion!"

Sitting up night after night, she wrote to every missionary circle in the nation that had been kind to her and the Indians. She explained her loss of the translator and how her work had suffered as a result.

Although she had lectured the Indians constantly that they must stop begging, she did not hesitate to take up the practice.

"I must raise fifty dollars a month to hire Lucius Ben Aitsan back from the government," she wrote. "The Mission Board in Chicago sends twelve dollars and fifty cents. They cannot send more. If you can see your way to pledging five dollars, ten dollars, any amount, I promise I will make your generosity known in every corner of heaven."

Miss Burdette again wrote that the Board was taking under advisement her request for a companion.

Slowly, responses came from the far-flung mission circles.

Her father's former congregation in North Dakota pledged ten dollars a month. Youngstown, Ohio, added five. Pueblo, Colorado, promised seven and a half.

Isabel waited.

Other circles answered that they would continue with support as in the past but that all cash donations were allocated for the present.

Then, just before Christmas, a letter arrived from Miss Burdette:

My Dear Sister,

We have long known that you are overworked, and we have done our best to find you relief. I am most happy to say that we have succeeded!

After due consideration of our budget, we have assigned to you a companion missionary, Miss Katherine E. Bare of Traverse City, Michigan. She has just completed training and is presently at home on leave awaiting assignment. The instructors speak highly of her, and all have found her dedication to service an inspiration. She will proceed to Saddle Mountain as soon as transportation is arranged.

In the first week of the new century, Isabel rode Jeremiah to Rainy Mountain to see Mabel and the new baby—a healthy boy named Richard.

Lucius was preparing his family for the move to the mouth of Elk Creek and his second year as a government farmer.

As soon as possible, Isabel took him aside. She did not dare hope for success, but she felt she should make the attempt.

"Lucius, I can offer you thirty-five dollars a month to come back to Saddle Mountain as interpreter—and as assistant missionary. That's the best I can do. I can't offer you more. But you will be free to freight for the government when you are not needed."

Lucius did not hesitate. His face broke into a broad smile.

"We have made a covenant," he said. "I will come back to Saddle Mountain. From now on I will be a farmer for Jesus."

Chapter Fifteen

From the moment Katherine Eunice Bare hopped off the stage like a little robin, Isabel knew many of her difficulties were solved.

A small woman with a solemn face, Miss Bare wore her dark brown hair pulled back into a severe bun. Her somber navy blue cotton dress was unadorned, the choke collar tightly fastened. Clearly there was no nonsense about her. She gazed upon the world through thick, silver-framed lenses that enlarged her unwavering, button-black eyes.

The train station at the new railhead was loaded with Indians bound for Washington and yet another conference on the Jerome Agreement. Miss Bare stood studying them with unbridled curiosity. Isabel pushed her way through the crowd and introduced herself.

"I hope you had a pleasant journey," she said.

Miss Bare answered in a voice surprisingly gruff and abrupt. "*Unusual* would be the word. I had expected heathen conditions. But I must say I was hardly prepared. In one town I came through they had just killed an outlaw. They had strapped his body to a board and it was on public display, right on the main street, blood and all. The passengers were allowed off the train so they could stand and gawk."

"That was Red Buck," Isabel explained. "A train robber and murderer. He has been hiding in the Washita bottom a long time. We heard they finally caught him. I'm sorry you were subjected to such a spectacle. It must have been most gruesome."

"It certainly was." Miss Bare raised a small box camera by its leather strap. "I shot him with my new Kodak. I do hope I can get the picture developed properly. It will make a wonderful souvenir of my journey."

Heenkey and Kokom placed her trunk in the back of the wagon. Soon they had cleared the confusion of the railroad town and were on the way to Saddle Mountain.

The men wore their Sunday best—dark suits, wide-brimmed black hats, and brogans. They rode up front and tended to the driving, talking little. Isabel and Miss Bare occupied the second spring seat of Heenkey's wagon.

Although the road to Saddle Mountain still traversed open prairie, constant use had smoothed the surface, and the many crossings had been graded until one no longer risked life and limb fording each stream. The improvements had shortened the journey by hours. Overnight camp was no longer necessary. Heenkey kept his team moving at a fast, mile-consuming trot. They arrived at Saddle Mountain before sunset.

Miss Bare did not seem in the least dismayed upon introduction to the spartan den.

"I'm sure we can make do," she said. She walked to the door and studied the distant mountain peaks while Heenkey and Kokom unloaded her trunk. "What an absolutely beautiful view!"

"I haven't grown tired of it, not after all this time," Isabel said. "The colors change constantly with the light. It never looks the same twice."

Isabel could not help casting covert glances at the woman,

taking her measure. She seemed too perfect to be true. Isabel kept hunting for a flaw. There seemed to be none.

Miss Bare was mesmerized by the view. "I want to climb that mountain first thing. Have you climbed it?"

Isabel laughed. "A few days after I came here. I went right up it, never once thinking of snakes. It's a wonder I wasn't bitten."

"Rattlesnakes? Are there many?"

"They're all over, but you seldom see them unless you turn over rocks and brush. The Indians say they won't strike unless surprised or forced to defend themselves. I suppose that's true. No one has been bitten in the three years I've been here, and we've killed dozens of them. Black widow spiders are numerous now. You want to be careful going into dugouts and cellars. But the most troublesome are scorpions and centipedes. Their bites are very painful, and it seems every time you turn around, you encounter one. You learn to shake out every article of dress, *always*, before you put it on. Shoes, blankets, everything. It soon becomes a habit."

Miss Bare shuddered. "Have you been bitten?"

"More times than I can count. I fear centipedes the most. The sting of a scorpion fades after a few hours. But you remember a centipede for days."

Heenkey and Kokom finished unloading and drove away. Isabel lit the lamp, built a fire, and warmed supper while Miss Bare unpacked. They dined on cornbread, beans, and beef stew.

"Our customary food seems heavy at first," Isabel said. "But in time you find you burn it away in work. When I first moved from Toronto to farm country in the Canadian West, I couldn't understand how the men could eat such huge meals and remain as thin as rails. Now I know."

Miss Bare approved of the food. "It's far better than I expected," she said. "In the novels I've read, people in the West always eat beef jerky and hardtack."

"We're hardly that primitive. In fact, Kiowa cooking is quite tasty. The Indians wanted to have a 'big eat' for you tonight, but I convinced them that you would be tired from your journey. Since tomorrow is the Sabbath, they agreed to wait until the day after. I'm sure they will give you a most gracious welcome. Everyone will be in costume. There will be dances and singing. It is truly something to see."

As the night progressed, Isabel found that she could not

keep her mouth closed. It seemed to work of its own accord, chattering inanely.

At last she apologized. "I'm afraid you'll find me perfectly capable of talking off an arm and a leg, at least for the first few days. You see, there's been no one here who speaks English since our interpreter left almost a year ago. I'm starved for conversation."

"Perhaps that's fortunate. I'm sure I have much to learn," said Miss Bare. "And I've been intending to ask. Miss Burdette mentioned that you're hard of hearing. How bad is it? How can I help?"

In that moment Isabel wanted to hug her. She felt her eyes fill. So few people bothered to ask.

"It is serious enough that I'm sure it will be a burden for you at times. I hear, but all sounds come to me as if from deep in a well, echoing and reechoing on the way up until all definition is lost. The trick is to gain my attention before you speak. Throw something at me, say my name, stomp the floor, anything. If you just start speaking without preamble, I miss the first few words by the time I turn my attention to you. Volume isn't the problem. It helps if you raise your voice a little, but shouting only increases the confusion. I read lips, but that art is highly overrated. Often I miss a phrase and try a dozen similar-sounding words to fill in the gap. When you say something to me and I look blank for a time before I answer, that's what I'm doing, substituting words, hunting one that fits. On occasion the words I find aren't the right ones. I may answer a question you never asked. Living with me will be exasperating, but I hardly think you'll find it uneventful."

Isabel washed the dishes while Miss Bare prepared her cot. They changed into nightgowns, but Isabel was far from sleep.

"I've formed the habit of reading until the wee hours," she confessed. "Would the light bother you if I turn the lamp low?"

"I'm a night owl, too," Miss Bare said. "And today has been so exciting. I didn't sleep much on the train, but now I find I'm still wide awake. If you're not ready for bed, there's so much I want to know."

"Then we'll sit up a while and talk."

Miss Bare arranged herself in a sitting position on her cot, her back against the wall, her feet tucked beneath her nightgown. "At school we mostly wondered how it would be in the field, if we could measure up to the challenges. We didn't know what to expect. I still don't."

"It's certainly different from the impression we were given in Training School," Isabel said. "When I was there, all concentration was upon teaching the Gospel. I've found that the easiest part. The Kiowas absorb Bible teachings like the desert soaking up rain. I've written Miss Burdette and the Mission Board time and again, telling them that the Indians are far more spiritual than white people. I doubt they believe me. But you will quickly find that it is true. The Board keeps reminding me that our primary goal is to bring the heathen races to Christ. I can't make the good ladies see that the problem here is not spiritual but practical. The Kiowas are attempting to move from the stone age to the twentieth century in one great leap. No one in Training School ever mentioned such a thing. But that is exactly what I have been doing here for almost four years—helping them to make that leap."

"Mr. Heenkey and Mr. Kokom seem to have made it," Miss Bare said. "I was surprised that they are so civilized."

"In many ways, they *have* succeeded," Isabel admitted. "They are learning to grow crops. Slowly they are moving away from total dependence on government rations. For years they would not give up their tipis. Now they are building white man's houses. But they have no concept of a permanent floor—to them it is the same as the ground. When they're done with something, they just toss it wherever it falls. Chickens, dogs, pigs wander through the house, doing whatever they want. Lucius, my interpreter, says that in the long-ago time, the Indians kept a piece of wood in the tipi to scrape away the top layer of dirt every day or two, and that put them back on clean soil. They were nomads. Every time they packed up and moved, they left the dirt behind. Now they're stuck in a white man's house, and they keep coming to me, asking me to 'fix' it. What they mean is to clean it. That is what we will be doing, probably for the next year— teaching Indians how to live in a white man's house."

Miss Bare gave her low laugh. "That's hardly what I expected. But it doesn't sound difficult."

"It isn't, if you don't mind hard work. In time I think the Indians will succeed. It is the general situation here—the unfeeling attitude of *white people*—that taxes the spirit. I've never questioned my vocation. But I've often wondered if I can see it through."

Miss Bare waited, studying Isabel through her owlish glasses. Isabel attempted to explain further.

"There is such *sadness* on this reservation. One week I buried twenty-six Indians. Hardly a week goes by I don't bury at least one. When someone lies dying, they gather like blackbirds and wait. At the moment of death they start such a clamor of anguish you think your heart will break. It goes on for hours, sometimes all night. There is something so *fundamental* about it that it strikes right to the core of your being. I remember when Spotted Horse and Hattie lost their last baby. We had a simple service. Then Spotted Horse went up one side of the canyon behind the graveyard, and Hattie stumbled up the other, both wailing with every step. The sound echoed back and forth from the mountain, and if their cries weren't heard in heaven that day there is no hope for the world." Isabel wiped her eyes. "You will learn to love them," she said.

"I'm sure I shall," said Miss Bare. "But we were told at Training School to keep our emotional distance."

"I managed to do that at Elk Creek, at least to some extent," Isabel said. "Here it has been impossible."

"I read *Ramona* and wept buckets," said Miss Bare. "Helen Hunt Jackson made Indian life seem so idyllic. Do they talk about the way they used to live?"

"They talk about little else. At times they've had *me* crying because I wasn't an Indian living on the Plains thirty years ago. They have such a soul hunger for the long-ago time it fair breaks your heart. Their tribal life must have been like growing up with all of your favorite uncles and aunts around you. As a child you played with your cousins and they became like brothers and sisters. Small bands went off to hunt, and when they came together again there were new stories to tell. You lived close to nature. It was your religion, part and parcel of your soul. You fought for your family, your tribe, and you loved them so much you would gladly die for them. It must have been a very satisfying way of life. From all I've heard, Mrs. Jackson wasn't far off the mark."

"Some critics say she over-romanticized."

"If they think she over-romanticized, they should hear the Indians. The Kiowas swear that no white man's house is as comfortable as a buffalo tipi. I've been told how to make one so many times I believe I could do it if I had the buffalo—ten for an ordinary tipi, seventeen to twenty-two for a big lodge. The slaughter of the buffalo is still difficult for them to comprehend. If we could convince the older Indians that the buffalo is truly gone forever, we would stamp out the Ghost Dance in one fell swoop. But they will never believe it. They know it, but they don't believe it. They will not face reality. That is what we must make them do."

Miss Bare spoke hesitantly. "Somehow that doesn't seem right. Maybe they should be left with some of their dreams."

"Much of what we must do here doesn't seem right. But we have to remember that the world around them has changed, and they are forced to live in it. Their children will see even more changes and must be ready to deal with them."

"Will we be teaching the children?"

"No. The government takes them away to boarding school. At first I disagreed with that policy. Now I think it has its good and bad points. But it's difficult for the Indians. They love their children far more than most white families I have known. They dote on them, live for them. Then the government takes all children away when they are five to seven years old. At the government school each child has his hair cut in the white man's fashion. His clothing is sent home, and he is dressed in a little blue uniform. He is given a white name that usually means nothing to him, and he is punished if he speaks his native language. From the first day he must speak English. The policy is harsh, but perhaps it is justified. They will be living all their lives in the white man's world, speaking English. But it is sad to see the suffering of both parents and children. Kiowa mothers are accustomed to giving their children anything they want. They don't even wean them until the children are shamed into it by taunts from playmates. I was told of one mother who camped at the school, demanding to feed her seven-year-old boy. I suspect that ending this practice has doubled or tripled pregnancies on the reservation. And since half of the infants die in the first year, the suffering here has been compounded."

Miss Bare asked, "Have you learned to speak Kiowa?"

"Only a few words. It is an impossible language."

"Until the interpreter returns, how will I make myself known?"

"You will catch on quick with the Plains sign language. It is quite elaborate, easy to learn, and everyone uses it. I will lend you some books. They will have everything except a few words I suppose could be termed local dialect. For instance, a few years ago there was an Indian agent named Darlington. One afternoon he absentmindedly took his false teeth out of his mouth, and the Indians who were with him almost fainted. Afterward he pulled the trick on every unsuspecting Indian he could find, and to this day the sign for 'agent' is the one-hand gesture of taking false teeth out of your mouth!" Isabel fluffed the pillows on her bed. "And so saying," she went on, "I suppose I'd best take out my own and get some sleep."

Miss Bare's head shot up from the pillow, her eyes wide.

Chuckling at her joke, Isabel blew out the lamp.

The Indians promptly named the new missionary "the Bear Woman." Isabel laughed aloud when she first heard the nickname.

It was so apt.

When busy, Miss Bare was easily irritated. She spoke in deep, clipped phrases reminiscent of the growl of a bear. Her high choke collars and multilayered skirts gave her a short, lumbering stride.

If anything, Miss Burdette had grossly understated her worth. She attacked work as if fighting a fire. Within a few weeks she learned enough sign language to converse in limited fashion among the Indians.

When summoned to "fix" an Indian house, she did not flinch at what she found. She did not shy from the sick, or from corpses. When not otherwise occupied, she could always be found at the quilting frames, laboring to earn money for the some-day church.

Isabel sent Miss Burdette a one-line letter: "She is a treasure!"

In early March, Lucius completed his year with the government and returned to Saddle Mountain. Once again his warm presence was felt, not only by Isabel but also by everyone in the community. Again the Aitsan home became part of the mission headquarters.

With his earnings as a government farmer, Lucius bought Mabel a sewing machine. It was kept humming day and night as the Indian women learned its mysteries. Soon every scrap of cloth vanished from the missionary barrels, and Isabel was writing for more to feed the sudden interest in handmade clothing.

Lucius hired a contractor from Anadarko who successfully drilled a well a few paces from the house. With only four or five vigorous movements of the pump handle, cool, sweet water came forth in an abundant stream. The Indians agreed that the water from the Aitsan well was the best to be found anywhere on the reservation. Its benefits could be appreciated by anyone who had carried hundreds of buckets from the creek, or hauled big barrels over the rocky terrain from Odlepaugh Springs.

For a hundred thirty-five dollars, Lucius acquired an ornate, covered hack. He drove Isabel wherever she wished to go. He resumed his mission work, translating for both Isabel and Miss Bare.

Isabel renewed her campaign to attract visitors to the revival. Her early plans for a "big name" revival seemed dashed. Several territorial churches and ministers had expressed interest, but Miss Burdette had written that she feared the trip would be "too arduous" for herself or the Mission Board. Thus far, Isabel's "names" were "big" only in the territorial sense. Brother Wicks, an Episcopalian, and Brother Methvin, a Methodist, had promised to come, bringing members of their Anadarko congregations. The Dutch Reformed Church near Medicine Bluff wrote that they would participate. Isabel's biggest "catch" was Brother Murrow, a widely respected minister who had spent the better part of two decades among the Creeks and Choctaws in the Indian Nations.

Then in late March a letter arrived from Miss Burdette that changed everything:

Dear Sister,

As you may know, the husband of one of our Board members, Mrs. Parker, is Captain Parker, Vice-President of Rock Island Railroad. When he learned recently of your plans for a revival at Saddle Mountain, and its close proximity to his new trunk and branch lines, he promptly took charge.

He has offered to run *special excursion cars* to your revival! He promises to entertain us in his private car all the way!

Mrs. Parker, Mrs. Bonnell, the entire Board will come if you can find accommodations for us all!

As soon as these plans were made, I promptly wired my brother Robert and his wife. He now informs me that he believes he will be able to come. *He offers his services if his invitation is still open!*

In addition, I have secured the services of *Dr. E. E. Chivers of New York City!* He will be making a tour of western churches, and he has fitted the revival into his busy schedule. He and his wife have promised to attend. I believe you heard Dr. Chivers speak while you were here in Chicago. You may remember that he delivers the most soul-stirring sermons and is an inspiration to all.

Also, William Justin Harsha, a writer of Indian stories from New York City, is most desirous to camp among the Kiowas. He has asked to travel with us if you can accommodate him.

In addition, I have written to Sister McLean in the Arizona Territory, urging her to attend. She may bring representatives from her tribe. Other tribes from that region also may attend. Captain Parker has promised transportation to any and everyone!

As you see, our plans are still "abuilding"!

We are writing *everyone* about your plans. We are aware of what you have accomplished at Saddle Mountain, and we hope to witness it firsthand. Your mission has become a model we hope others will emulate.

I will write further when our plans are more complete.

> Yours in Christ,
> Mary G. Burdette

Appalled by her own success, Isabel collapsed into a chair, the letter in her lap.

She looked at her bed, perhaps the most comfortable on the reservation. It was created from a packing crate and stuffed with grass and feathers. She doubted if any of the Chicago ladies would allow such a rustic invention inside the door of her home. Miss Bare's canvas cot, two spindle chairs, and a rickety folding table completed the furnishings of the den.

Faced with this reality, Isabel wondered what had been in her mind while dreaming up the revival.

How could she possibly feed, house, and entertain such important people, accustomed to every modern convenience?

She summoned the Daw-kee-boom-gee-k'oop missionary circle into an emergency meeting in the Gospel tent. As she read the letter, Lucius and the other Board members received the news in awed silence.

Only Miss Bare seemed undismayed. "I think it's wonderful. Robert Burdette, Reuben Torrey, and Dr. Chivers are probably the most famous evangelists alive today, now that Dwight Moody has passed on. And we will have two of the three right here!"

Lucius was quick to pick up Isabel's worry. "How will we feed so many people?"

"I don't know," Isabel admitted. "But we only have three months to prepare. We must start thinking about it now. How about bringing some white churches into it as cosponsors?"

Lucius had not completed the translation before Pope-bah, Kokom, and Odlepaugh all made the "cut it off" sign.

"This is an Indian thing," Odlepaugh said. "We do not want white churches here, telling us what to do."

Isabel retreated a bit. "We can ask them for support. I think they will give it."

The Indians discussed the proposal at length and found no objection to accepting money from the white churches.

"Fortunately, we have the Gospel tent for the meetings," Isabel went on. "It should be large enough. If the crowd is too large to get into it, we can raise the sides, and some can sit around it on the grass. The biggest problem will be sleeping arrangements, especially for our honored guests."

"Maybe we could put them up in tipis," Miss Bare suggested. "I should think it would be a lark for them."

Her idea was quickly adopted. Many Indians had built houses. Spare tipis were available.

One by one, all problems seemed to be resolved.

But the elaborate plans made at that first meeting quickly proved inadequate. Acceptances began pouring in from every part of the nation.

An enthusiastic letter arrived from Sister McLean, saying she would be bringing a delegation of Hopi. Missionaries among the Cheyennes, Arapaho, Comanches, Osage, Choctaws, Chickasaws, Cherokees, and Creeks wrote, saying they would attend with representatives from their tribes.

White churches from throughout the territory pledged support and representation.

A letter from Brother Clouse brought more news: He had been called to the pastorship at Rainy Mountain. He and his wife certainly would attend the revival, along with many Rainy Mountain Christians.

Isabel totaled the number of acceptances with a sinking heart.

More than six hundred people had pledged to come to the revival.

She summoned her mission circle into another meeting.

"I see only one way to sleep so many people," she told them. "We can use the Gospel tent as a kitchen and dining hall by day, and a men's dormitory by night. The women and honored guests can sleep in tipis. And even that will take all we have. We must ask the territorial Indians to bring their own tipis."

Pope-bah raised a hand. "If we use the Gospel tent for cooking and sleeping, where will we have the revival?"

"We must build a great arbor. At least twenty times the size of the first one I built on Saddle Mountain Creek. It must be so large that at least six hundred people can sit in its shade."

The mission circle remained silent, contemplating such a giant edifice.

"The men can build the arbor," Isabel went on. "The women will prepare the food and bedding. We now have a little more than two months to do the work. Most of you men have your seed in the ground. You will not be needed all the time in the fields. If we work hard together, I believe we can do it."

The new plan was put into effect. Since timber was limited near Saddle Mountain, the men hauled poles and brush from the banks of the Washita, twenty and more miles to the north. All the children still young enough to live at home were sent onto the surrounding prairies to gather grass, horse apples, and cow chips.

Miss Bare organized work in the Gospel tent. Old quilt tops, linings, worn-out tarpaulins, threadbare dresses, every scrap of cloth that could be found were sewed into mattresses and stuffed with dried grass. Biscuit boxes were converted into washstands, flour sacks into pillowcases, bottles into makeshift candlesticks.

Lucius set up tipis and decorated them for Dr. and Mrs. Burdette, Dr. and Mrs. Murrow, Dr. and Mrs. Chivers, Miss Burdette and her party, and the writer of Indian stories, Dr. Harsha.

Isabel extended her mission budget to the limit, borrowed more, and at last dipped into the church building fund to lay in supplies. Merchants and churches in Anadarko were cajoled into contributing goods. Colonel Randlett sent a wagonload of "surplus stores" from the agency.

As May ended, Isabel began to hope that all their preparations could be completed in time.

But on June 6, after all the long delays, word came that the Jerome Agreement had been ratified by the U.S. Senate.

Panic swept across the reservation like a prairie fire.

Now only a presidential proclamation was needed before the land would be thrown open to white settlement. Gloom settled over the Saddle Mountain community like a fog.

The reservation had not been the best of all possible worlds for the Kiowas, but every Indian realized the protection it had offered from the final encroachment of the whites.

Now the reservation had entered its last days.

No one knew what was to come—or when.

The first thoughts of the Indians were for the bones of their ancestors.

Work on the huge brush arbor stopped.

Guided by the oldest memories, each Kiowa family fanned out over the prairies to hunt for ancient graves.

"I haven't the heart to say a word," Isabel told Miss Bare. "As the Indians say, this is 'a Kiowa thing.' I can sympathize with them. I wouldn't want the bones of *my* ancestors in some farmer's field."

The Indians stayed away for days, and then weeks.

In the glade below Odlepaugh Springs, the huge brush arbor stood half finished. The Gospel tent still needed to be moved from Aitsan's pasture to the glade. Folding chairs and benches, offered by the Anadarko churches, waited to be hauled. Dishes, beds, cooking gear were not yet in place. Menus, programs, all last-minute details of planning remained to be done.

One by one, the families returned with wagonloads of

sorrow. All told dreadful stories. Sometimes they had found only shattered skulls, a few flakes of bone. More often they had unearthed mummified corpses that renewed ancient griefs.

Isabel and Miss Bare conducted services as each bundle of relics was reinterred in Saddle Mountain Cemetery.

Domot came to Isabel after the reburial of two of his sons. "Dead or alive, the Indian must keep moving over to make room for the white man," he signed. "Where will it end?"

She could give him no answer, only her sympathy.

Slowly work toward the revival resumed. The gospel tent was moved and erected. More brush was hauled from the banks of the Washita. Domot and Heenkey harnessed heavy freight wagons to bring the folding chairs and benches from Anadarko. Miss Bare became a human dynamo, directing the Indians as they raced against the calendar.

June ended with much yet to be done.

On the afternoon before she was scheduled to leave for the railroad station to meet the first guests, Isabel received a telegram from Miss Burdette, confirming the time of arrival.

Miss Burdette added a personal note:

ALL EAGER TO SEE YOU STOP DOCTOR CHIVERS IS
CONFIDENT THIS WILL BE THE GREATEST CONGREGATION
OF CHRISTIANS EVER ASSEMBLED IN THE NEW
TERRITORIES EXCLAMATION POINT WE ANTICIPATE A
MARVELOUS SPIRITUAL EXPERIENCE STOP

Isabel looked up from the telegram to her ragtag, worn-out little band of converts, the tattered gospel tent, the uncompleted brush arbor—all as primitive as anything in biblical times.

She wondered how anyone would find inspiration in such a setting.

Chapter Sixteen

A hawk circled lazily against the clear blue sky over the Washita. The heated, still air offered no relief from the late-afternoon sun. Isabel braced herself as Lucius guided the horses cautiously across a rugged gully, one of the few rough places yet remaining on the road to Saddle Mountain. Beside her, Mrs. Murrow and Miss Burdette grasped the frame of the hack and held on for dear life. Dr. Burdette sat on the front seat beside Lucius. He seemed preoccupied, studying the distant mountains.

Behind them, in wagons, rode Dr. and Mrs. Chivers, Captain and Mrs. Parker, Dr. and Mrs. Bonnell, William Justin Harsha, the ladies of the Board and their husbands and friends.

Isabel had managed to keep the conversation going for two hours. Now she had exhausted her repertoire of small talk.

She could not put out of her mind the drab scene that awaited them at Saddle Mountain. And she had not recovered from the shock of meeting the Chicago and New York group at the railhead.

All of the women were attired in the latest fashions, heavily corseted, with tiered, grand gowns that swept the ground, and imposing, ornate hats. The men wore tailored, well-fitting suits, spats, and carried gold-headed canes. They came from another world, far removed from frontier conditions. Isabel felt like an impoverished relative. How had she ever dreamed that they would welcome "roughing it" under canvas?

"What do the Indians think about the Jerome Agreement?" Burdette asked Lucius. "Are they fully prepared for the change in their situation?"

Lucius did not answer immediately. Isabel wished fervently that she had kept members of the Board better informed about the growing unrest on the reservation. But she had not wanted to alarm them concerning her safety.

"They are not feeling good about it," Lucius said. "Many of them do not care for anything now."

Dr. Burdette sat contemplating the answer. He was a tall, slender man, with deep-set, thoughtful, dark eyes. "Surely they know that the agreement will make them property owners, comparatively wealthy even by white men's standards."

Lucius did not reply.

Isabel felt moved to speak in his defense. "Dr. Burdette, when Lucius was a child, the Indians in a sense owned all of this, as far as the eye can see. They really don't think they are gaining a thing with the Jerome Agreement."

Dr. Burdette remained silent while he absorbed this new thought. "I suppose you're right. Still, they must see that the agreement is the best solution for them. No matter what, they will have to adapt. History cannot go backward."

"It is more than the land," Lucius said. "The Indians are afraid of everything that is coming. Especially the old ones. All of their lives, they have fought and feared the white man. Now they are being forced to lie down beside him."

"But Lucius, the Indian wars are over!" Miss Burdette protested. "The Indians have nothing to fear *now* from the whites!"

Cicadas sang as Lucius guided the wagon through a clump of mesquite. Isabel waited until she was certain Lucius would not reply. "Miss Burdette, there isn't an Indian family on the reservation who has not lost loved ones in those wars. And every family has known deaths from disease and starvation, mostly through sheer neglect. When the Army brought them to the reservation, the Indians were put into a stone corral— men, women, and children—and raw meat was thrown to them as if they were wild animals. We really can't blame them if they have hard feelings toward the white man."

"It is a problem for both sides," Lucius said. "I do not have to read far in books and newspapers to learn that the white man does not think much of the Indian."

"I regret to say that's true," Dr. Burdette said. "But I'm optimistic that matters will improve. And we must make the Indians understand that the white people who will be taking up land on the reservation will be vastly different from the soldiers and adventurers they have known. These new people will be homesteaders, most with families of their own. They will be too busy to make trouble for the Indians. And the vast majority of them will be Christians."

Lucius nodded. "Miss Crawford has told the Kiowas many times that Christianity is the only thing we share with the white man. Many of us believe this. We are working hard to build the church."

Dr. Burdette seemed relieved to change the subject. He turned in his seat to glance back at Isabel. "How are plans for the church progressing?"

"We have five hundred sixty-two dollars and forty-eight cents," Isabel said. "Our goal is a thousand, for we also plan to construct a combination mission house and pastorage."

"Then you are well on your way. In another year or so, you should be there."

"I'm afraid we don't have that much time left to us," Isabel informed him. "You see, we must build the church *before* the reservation is opened to settlement."

"But I thought the Indian tribal council had agreed!" Miss Burdette said.

"Our difficulty doesn't lie with the Kiowa council now," Isabel explained. "Final allocation of land will be made by the Bureau of Indian Affairs. They have warned me that unless we have a church in existence, they can't grant land for it."

"How much time do you have?" asked Dr. Burdette.

"I don't know. I'm now told that the Indian allocations probably will be made early next spring. The openings will follow during the summer months. So we have no more than a year at best."

As they topped a hill, the foot of Saddle Mountain came into view, less than two hours away.

"You have been making sizable contributions to the mission work of others," Miss Burdette said. "Perhaps you should put all of your revenue into the church fund until it is built."

Lucius spoke from the front seat. "The Indians have talked about this and agreed, Miss Burdette. We must do all we can for the other missions so the other Indians will hear about Jesus. If we wait until the church is built, it will be too late for the old ones."

Dr. Burdette, his face a study in surprise, glanced at Lucius. He then turned to Isabel. Their gazes met.

She smiled, for she understood exactly what was in his mind.

The learned doctor of theology had just made a total reassessment of the "savage Indian" seated beside him.

Isabel was not surprised.

She only wished that everyone, everywhere in the United States could experience the same revelation.

The sun was sinking behind Saddle Mountain as they drove down the hill and into the glade where Isabel fought Odlepaugh's pigs so long ago.

Isabel gazed at the scene in astonishment.

During the brief twelve hours she had been away, the dreary encampment had been transformed into an enchanted wonderland.

Every Indian now wore a colorful costume.

All the Saddle Mountain Kiowas had gathered to greet the guests. Many wagonloads of their friends had arrived from Rainy Mountain. The glade was filled with costumed Indians—Kiowas, Cheyennes, Arapaho, Comanches, Chickasaws, Kiowa-Apaches, Creeks, Choctaws.

Painted faces bore every hue of the rainbow. Bright, elaborate designs lent new life to the tired old tipis. Fresh cedar wreathed the poles of the brush arbor, hiding the ugly ax scars. Even the grass seemed greener, the trees more animate. A towering fire burned in the center of the meadow to light the evening festivities. Under a glorious sunset, Saddle Mountain itself provided an awe-inspiring backdrop.

As the hack and wagons entered the meadow, the thunder drum began sounding a rhythmic beat.

The guests from Chicago and New York alighted from the wagons and stood in the light of the brilliant sunset, thoroughly enthralled.

"I have never seen anything more beautiful in my entire life!" said Miss Burdette.

Pope-bah, Ananthy, and Hattie came forward to greet the honored guests. All wore beaded buckskin. Behind them, the Christian Kiowas formed a receiving line.

The contrast was startling—the white women in tiers of filmy pastels, the Indians in bold primary colors, against a sky tinged with deep hues by the setting sun. Isabel fervently wished she had sufficient time and talent to capture the scene on canvas.

She introduced the guests and Indians. Lucius translated the words of welcome.

Odlepaugh served as spokesman for the welcoming committee. He stood in front of the group and shouted in full oratorical style. Lucius interpreted his words.

"We are all poor Indians here, and we don't know much. Our hearts jump because you have come here to give us wise talks. Many things have happened to us since we came onto this reservation. Most of them were bad. The one good thing has been the Jesus women. We thank you that you have sent them here. They have taught us the Jesus road. For a long time the Kiowas were far-behind. Now we are not so far-behind. Our ears are open to hear the wise words you bring us. We will think hard about them and carry them in our hearts forever."

Robert Burdette spoke in reply. "I only hope we preachers are half as eloquent as Mr. Odlepaugh. God in His wisdom has brought us together here at Saddle Mountain."

"I'm sure you travelers would like to freshen up before supper," Isabel said. "Your guides will show you to your tipis."

Ananthy, Pope-bah, Hattie, and Sister Bare escorted the group toward the camping area. Lucius strolled away with Dr. William Justin Harsha, New York City writer of Indian stories. The man was full of questions, and Lucius was doing his best to answer them.

Isabel walked Miss Burdette toward the tipis.

"Everyone is absolutely stunned with this reception," Miss Burdette said. "It's all so gorgeous!"

"The color and strangeness first draw your attention," Isabel agreed. "But after a time you see that it is the Indian himself who is truly beautiful."

On the following day Navajos, Hopis, Pimas, and Papagoes arrived from the western territories. Heenkey, Mo-keen, Domot, Kokom, and Odlepaugh hauled them in wagons from the railroad. All the new arrivals were also resplendent in tribal costumes.

Most of the western Indians were traveling by rail for the first time, and even the stoic elders found it difficult to restrain their high spirits.

Isabel managed to greet Sister McLean and her Hopis, but there was time only for a quick hug before a clamor arose in the middle of the meadow.

Isabel hurried across the creek. Dr. Murrow and his wife

had arrived from Atoka in the Choctaw Nation and immediately were surrounded by hundreds of shouting Indians. Before Isabel could interfere, Dr. Murrow stood, quieted the Indians with raised arms, and blessed them in flowing sign language.

He was tall and imposing, with a riveting gaze and a wild, full beard that rippled in the breeze. After twenty years of preaching among the five civilized tribes, his reputation was well known, even among the Plains Indians.

Brother Clouse and his wife arrived a short while later, bringing with them most of the older students from the Indian school. The children joined the confusion about the grounds, engrossed in their own private world. Isabel noticed that Amos roamed constantly in the company of Minnie Goombi, daughter of the captive white woman, Say-haye-do-hole Goombi. Watching them, Isabel saw that clearly Amos and Minnie were deep in the throes of puppy love; she wondered if Lucius and Mabel were aware of it.

Amos was developing into a handsome young man. Already almost as tall as his father, he had adapted quickly to the white mold expected of him at the school. His black hair was cut short, and he wore dark trousers and a white shirt barren of Indian adornments.

Jessie apparently had been less successful in making the transition. Her hair was long and loose, and she seemed more "Indian" than ever. She trailed along behind Amos and Minnie as if confused over the first serious competition for her brother's attention.

Throughout the afternoon difficulties rose like weeds. The Papagoes did not have enough tents. A Cheyenne woman was very sick. She had broken out in a rash. For a time it was feared she had smallpox. Then Sister Bare discovered weevils in the flour. A hurried search revealed that most of the last load from town was infested. Heenkey was dispatched for more. Two Indians—a Comanche and an Arapaho—encountered each other for the first time in decades and promptly revived an ancient dispute over a horse long dead. Lucius was sent to restore peace. Dr. Harsha came to Isabel in a state of great agitation, explaining that he had soaked an injured foot the previous evening in a pail of water diluted with a patent medicine. He had just discovered that the other gentlemen in his tipi had used the water for their morning wash. Isabel carefully watched the gentlemen for a time.

Apparently they suffered no ill effects. She suggested to Dr. Harsha that they keep the secret between them. A delegation from a white church in Anadarko objected to the camping space allocated to them. They did not wish to sleep in such close proximity to Indians. Isabel assured them that their neighbors were Christian Indians, not thieves, and were not hosts to infestations of fleas and lice.

By the time the Indians lined up at the Gospel tent that evening for supper, Isabel was exhausted. She wondered how she could possibly survive the week.

"Oh, Belle, I've thought so often of the good times we had in Training School. You were always such fun," said Sister McLean.

"Empty-headed would be more descriptive," Isabel said.

"We were *all* empty-headed. Remember our parody of the Women's Congress?"

Isabel laughed. She and her friends had staged a production that lampooned the world women's movement unmercifully.

It was now past midnight and the camp had grown quiet. They were seated in Sister McLean's tent with the lamp turned low. Isabel studied her longtime friend. Gone was the soft, flighty schoolgirl. In her place sat a lean, older woman, mature beyond her years. Her skin was brown, with gatherings of crow's feet at eyes and mouth.

"Thank the Lord we didn't take the movement too seriously," Sister McLean said. "Women far older than we were swept up in it."

"I think we were helped by our work in the Black Hole," Isabel said. "We learned there were issues more serious in the world."

"But we didn't know how serious. No one at Training School ever told me I would carry water two miles for a bath! Or pack stovewood down from the mesas like a burro. Sister Burdette left out all the juicy parts."

"Some practical advice would have helped," Isabel agreed. "Yet, looking back, I believe we were taught that there *is* a place for women, not by emulating men, but by developing our own potential."

Sister McLean gave her a measuring look. "Any regrets?"

Isabel was uncertain how to answer. "What do you mean?"

"You know perfectly well what I mean. Giving up your life.

For this." A sweep of her hand encompassed the Indians, the revival meeting, the reservation.

"Only in my weaker moments," Isabel confessed. "Most of the time I know I could not possibly have found a more useful purpose for my life."

"I'm not always so certain we *are* serving a purpose," Sister McLean said. "Sometimes I think the Indians won't be any better off a century from now."

"Then it is our failure. I'm convinced that only we women can better their condition."

Sister McLean made a face. "That sounds like our parody of the Women's Congress. Women, unite and save the world!"

Isabel hastened to explain. "I'm not talking about winning the vote or gaining recognition in the professions. If the Indian ever finds peace with the white man, it will be because *we* led the way. The Indians have a long-standing hatred and distrust of the white man. But we women have taught them trust. My Indians say they never want a Jesus man here. They only want a Jesus woman."

"Then what will you do when you build your church? Surely you will have to ask for a pastor."

"I really don't know. Perhaps I can change their minds by then."

"I saw Brother Clouse among them today. He seems to work well with them."

"They are polite. But they are distrustful of *all* Jesus men. Especially Brother Clouse."

"Why?"

"They won't tell me. When I ask, they only make the 'crooked' sign."

"Your church will never be accepted into the association, and allowed to function, without at least a part-time pastor."

"I know that," Isabel said. "Somehow I must change their minds by the time the church is built."

On the edge of the Tonkawa encampment Lucius balked and refused to go a step farther. "They are cannibals," he said. "No other tribe will sit with them. There will be trouble."

In his buckskins, with face painted, Lucius seemed unfamiliar, a different person than the man she knew. He now reverted to his Indian ways so seldom that Isabel was caught off guard.

She had little patience with him. Since daylight they had been visiting the camps of new arrivals, welcoming them.

The small Tonkawa group was the last. Already Isabel was due back at the Gospel tent for a meeting with the revival preachers.

"Lucius, the Tonkawas also want to hear about Jesus. Surely no one will deny them that!"

Lucius shook his head. "The Tonkawas have killed and eaten the brothers and sisters of many Indians here. There will be much trouble. I do not know what will happen."

Isabel took his arm. "I know exactly what will happen. When we go back to the Gospel tent, we will put out the word that the Tonkawas are to be treated as God's children and that we expect every Indian to behave. Now come with me. We will make these Indians feel welcome."

Reluctantly, Lucius followed Isabel into the camp. The Tonkawas stood waiting uncertainly.

They were a miserable-looking bunch of Indians. Once lords of a large portion of southern Texas, they had been decimated by other Indian tribes for their flesh-eating practices, real or imagined. Now few were left.

Only ten were in the group. They appeared to be taller and darker than most of the Plains Indians.

Isabel conveyed to them by sign language that she was happy that they had come. She told them that old battles were in the long-ago time, that everyone would meet under the cross as brothers. Pointing to the arbor, she told them that the ringing of an anvil would signal each morning that services were starting. She told them she would expect to see them at the arbor.

Returning to the gospel tent, she summoned the elders of the Kiowas, Cheyennes, Arapaho, and Comanches. While the preachers waited, Isabel faced the Indians and explained in sign language that two families of Tonkawas had arrived to attend the revival.

The reaction was loud, heated, and sustained. Several minutes passed before Isabel could restore order.

"The Great Father is very smart," she signed. "He has given you a road here today to show that Jesus is in your hearts. You all remember that Jesus said we must love our enemies."

"Jesus did not know the Tonkawas," Odlepaugh signed.

"Jesus and the men who were with him had many enemies," Isabel told them. "One of the worst was the Apostle Paul. He fought the long-ago Christians. But Jesus came to him in a vision and made him a friend for life. The Tonkawas have come here in peace and with only good thoughts. We must show them we do not fear them. We must walk tall in our own camp."

Grumbling, the elders thrashed out the matter in their own languages. Eventually they agreed that no trouble should arise during the revival. They promised to talk to their tribes and to tell them that the Tonkawas were to be received in peace.

Isabel hurried on to her meeting with the preachers to iron out the exact schedule of the revival. Afterward she hardly had time for a sigh of relief before Pope-bah arrived with news that the food supply was disappearing at an alarming rate.

"Tonight we have food," she signed. "In morning we have food. Tomorrow noon, maybe. Tomorrow night, no food."

And the revival would continue for five more days.

"We can't allow our guests to go hungry," Isabel told Lucius. "I'm not sure the merchants in Anadarko will have enough. We can send wagons there, and also to the suttler's post at Fort Sill."

"What will we use for money?"

Isabel answered with a sinking heart. "The only money we have: the building fund."

Lucius looked at her in silent concern.

"It's my fault," Isabel admitted. "I had no idea the revival would draw Indians from all over the country. But we're doing God's work. The Bible tells us to cast our bread on the waters. Perhaps it will be returned in the collection plate."

Lucius studied the surrounding tipis. "I don't think so. These Indians are as poor as Kiowas. They have brought nothing but their chuck bags."

Chapter Seventeen

The revival quickly fell into a routine. At first light each morning the entire encampment began to stir. The pace quickened as everyone dressed and hurried to the huge brush arbor, where Robert Burdette conducted sunrise services.

Isabel and Lucius took turns translating the preacher's words into sign language.

Upon conclusion of worship, the Indians rushed to the Gospel tent and formed lines for breakfast.

At midmorning, Dr. Murrow spoke on the life of Christ. His lectures were more informal. Occasional interruptions came as finer points were resolved in the various tribal tongues. But for the most part the Indians listened in attentive silence.

As Isabel conveyed Brother Murrow's sermons to the Indians, she understood for the first time the poverty of her own Jesus talks. His grasp of his subject was so complete. Brother Murrow stressed that the life of Jesus had been recorded in the long-ago time on different talking papers written by inspired individuals. He brought Sts. Mark, Matthew, Luke, and eventually John to life in vivid verbal portraits, dwelling on their personalities, their steadfast faith, and their devotion.

His lectures were especially effective, for he himself resembled a tribal patriarch sprung from the Old Testament. As he paced the platform in the July heat, he peeled off his coat and worked in shirt sleeves, his long gray beard rippling in the wind. To illustrate the harmony of the gospels, he moved to a different portion of the stage to quote from each. At one spot he was Matthew speaking, at others Mark, Luke, and John.

After the morning lectures the Indians would sit in the shade of the trees along the creek and discuss what they had heard. The drone of many languages turned the glade into a veritable, extraordinary Babel.

Following dinner at high noon, Dr. Chivers lectured on the message Christ brought to earth. His talks were calm, well reasoned, and filled with the words and parables of Jesus. He carefully defined the duties of a Christian in relationship to his church and to God. He described in clear terms the more mystical aspects of Christian belief—the concept of the Holy Trinity, the sanctity of Holy Communion, the doctrine of baptism.

Although many of Dr. Chivers's points were difficult for Isabel to convey, the Indians made an honest effort to understand. They sat quietly through the talks, their faces taut with concentration. Afterward, the discussions under the tress were loud and animated.

Before sunset the Indians formed lines for supper at the Gospel tent. Children, women, and men ate separately at plank tables set up under the trees.

As darkness deepened, lanterns were lit throughout the brush arbor. Indians and the white guests gathered, filling not only the arbor but also the surrounding glade.

After a brief invocation by Brother Clouse, Dr. Burdette spoke on the Christian experience, couching faith and service in wondrously personal terms.

Robert Burdette was blessed with a rich, melodious voice that brought conviction to every syllable. He was an exciting speaker, yet not sensational.

As she translated, Isabel saw rapt attention on every face.

She ended each evening exhausted but thrilled.

Never before had her life seemed to hold so much meaning.

On Wednesday, the Fourth of July, the routine changed.

A few minutes after the sunrise service, Colonel Randlett arrived with a small detachment of soldiers, escorting Bureau of Indian Affairs Commissioner William A. Jones.

"The commissioner is making his annual tour of the western reservations," Randlett told Isabel. "We don't wish to intrude on your revival. But I felt the commissioner should witness what your Indians have accomplished."

"I can only stay a few hours," the commissioner said. "I'm due to entrain tonight for Flagstaff."

While Randlett and the commissioner attended Dr. Murrow's morning lecture, Isabel and Sister Bare made hasty preparations for a special dinner at noon in the commissioner's honor.

Partitioning a portion of the Gospel tent with sheets, they created an impromptu dining hall. With sheets for table-cloths, and blankets for upholstery, the facilities were exotic but comfortable enough.

Yet as Isabel sat down to dinner she found herself strangely ill-at-ease. She had not dined exclusively with white people for more than three years—not since the baptismal visit with Brother Clouse and his family at Elk Creek.

Most of the guests—especially the ladies from Chicago—were reveling in the fact that they were "roughing it."

Isabel was seated at the most civilized meal she had seen since coming onto the resevation.

She held her conversation tube to her ear and concentrated on the talk at the far end of the table. Dr. Burdette was explaining the plan of the week-long revival to Commissioner Jones and Colonel Randlett.

"With most congregations, one can begin converting on the first night and build momentum through the course of a revival. But I've learned that in speaking to Indians and those not well versed in Christianity, teaching is the essential ingredient. We have divided the work—Dr. Murrow speaking on the life of Christ, on the gospels. Dr. Chivers defines the Christian experience. I speak on the inspirational aspects of Christianity. Not until Friday night will we call for converts. At this point there is no way of measuring our success."

"Christianity is complex enough without the language barrier," Commissioner Jones said. "Do they truly understand?"

Dr. Burdette frowned. "They have been most attentive. I believe they do. Sister Crawford, you know them best. What do you think?"

Isabel recognized a golden opportunity to state her case before the commissioner. She did not hesitate.

"I'm sure they do, Dr. Burdette. In fact, I've often thought that perhaps the Indian is in a better position than we to understand the Christ story."

Immediately all eyes were upon her.

"In what way?" asked Dr. Burdette.

"Lucius Ben Aitsan believes the situation of the Kiowas today is much the same as that of the Jews in the time of Christ," she explained. "We whites are the Romans, who have occupied their land, imposed our laws, our government upon them. The Christ story is as new to their ears as it was to the Jews in the time of Jesus. The Kiowas even have their own Sanhedrin—the tribal council—battling to preserve tradition, resistant to every change. Some Kiowas on the reservation seek to preserve their ancient religion, just as many Jews refused to acknowledge Christ and maintained their traditional religion even after destruction of Jerusalem and the Temple. The time of Christ is very real to the Kiowas, because in a real sense they are now living it."

A murmur of comment swept the table. Miss Burdette and the Chicago women seemed disturbed. They cast warning glances.

Apparently they had not forgotten her tirade in *The Baptist Standard*.

"An interesting parallel," said Dr. Burdette. "You say this is Lucius Aitsan's observation?"

Isabel nodded. "He is a very thoughtful man, and he has read his Bible most thoroughly."

"I'm intrigued by what his illustration might make me," Commissioner Jones said. "Would I be Pontius Pilate?"

Everyone laughed. Isabel felt the heat of embarrassment rush to her face.

"I've never thought of myself as a Roman centurion," said Colonel Randlett. "But I must admit I rather like the idea."

Isabel rushed on. "There are other parallels Lucius has drawn. Until the Kiowas were brought onto the reservation, they lived much in the manner of people during the time of Christ. They were nomadic. The Indians see nothing unusual in the wanderings of the Jewish tribes, or in Christ's migratory preaching. The constant change of names in the Bible is alien to our ears—Abram who became Abraham, Simon who became Peter, Saul who became Paul, Jacob who became Israel. For years I could never keep them straight. But the Indians do not find this unusual. Almost every Indian changed his name two or three times during his lifetime. He had one name as a child, another as a warrior, perhaps another left to him as an honor by a great chief or revered relative. Now most also have white names." She paused to catch her breath, and then went on.

"I think white Christians often encounter difficulty with the biblical dependence on visions and prophecies. Mostly we accept those accounts on faith. But the Indians—especially the old ones—have sought and experienced religious visions.

They have lived their lives by them. I find that they accept without question that Jesus appeared to the Apostles time and again after the Resurrection. If they have not experienced something similar, they know of someone who has. Most of the older Indians are convinced that they have talked with the Great Spirit at some time in their lives. The younger Indians have grown up in this tradition. They have no trouble believing. Their faith is fundamental."

In the silence that followed, Isabel felt she might have gone too far. But she could not retreat.

Dr. Burdette smiled at her. "I gather you are saying that while we teach the Indian, we also could learn from *him*."

"Sir, that lesson has been driven home to me almost every day for the past four years."

"I've found a great variance in morality among tribes," Commissioner Jones said. "Some are honest to a fault. Others can't be trusted to hold a horse."

"I think it's more a matter of *different* moralities, Commissioner," Isabel said. "The same Indian who would never tell a falsehood may have no qualms about stealing a horse. To his way of thinking, horse stealing may be a matter of keen competition, something to be admired, much in the same way certain segments of our society esteem a sharp horse trader. In both instances, it's a way of showing superiority over the other man."

"And of acquiring a good string of horseflesh," Dr. Murrow said.

Commissioner Jones waited until the laughter died away. "Liquor is such a problem with some tribes," he went on. "Apparently that is one temptation of civilization the Kiowas have been able to resist. I wonder why."

"There are notable exceptions," Isabel said. "And I understand that a few years ago liquor was more of a problem. But now most Kiowas see drunkenness as a sign of weakness. They won't subject themselves to a loss of dignity."

"Gambling is the big problem among the Kiowas," Brother Clouse said. "Many times I've seen them lose their grass payments in a single afternoon."

"There are white gamblers who flock onto the reservation to take the money after grass payments," Colonel Randlett said. "We try to drive them away, but it's difficult to prevent, especially when they enjoy the full cooperation of the Kiowas."

"If civilization doesn't ruin the Indian in one way, it seems to in another," observed Miss Burdette.

"We can't blame white society for the gambling," Isabel told her. "Gambling among them dates from the long-ago times. It is now thoroughly ingrained. They have all sorts of games and sports that depend on it. Not long ago my mission circle solemnly urged me to bet our building fund on a horse during the races at grass payment. I had a great deal of trouble convincing them that Jesus wouldn't approve."

Dr. Burdette smiled. "Did the horse win?"

Sheepishly, Isabel nodded yes.

Again the canvas dining hall was filled with laughter.

Isabel felt a prickling of conscience; she had vowed she would never again speak condescendingly of the Indians. Now she was participating in such a discussion.

She hoped Lucius was not eavesdropping.

"How is the building fund progressing?" Dr. Murrow asked.

Isabel tactfully avoided the fact that the building fund was being depleted by every bite taken at the table. "As of last Friday, we had in hand five hundred sixty-two dollars and forty-eight cents."

"Remarkable!" Dr. Burdette turned to Commissioner Jones. "The Kiowas raised that money through their own efforts." He glanced at Isabel. "Isn't that correct?"

"We received some small donations from two or three white churches in the territory and from some Chinese Christians in Oakland and San Francisco. But most of the fund was obtained through the Indians' own hard work."

She described the quilting, the hunts conducted by the men.

"I'm afraid that in the end it won't be enough," she added.

"But you're so close!" said Miss Burdette. "Only a few hundred dollars!"

"We're running out of time," Isabel explained. "With the Jerome Agreement approved in the Senate, we're now only months away from the opening. We must have a church erected before the land is allotted."

"That's true," said Commissioner Jones. "After the Indians are given a few weeks to select acreage they will receive under headright, then only existing schools and missions will be allocated land."

"Perhaps the Baptist Convention could help," said Sister

Burdette. She turned to her brother. "What do you think? Only a few hundred dollars . . ."

Before Burdette could answer, Dr. Murrow shook his head. "I wouldn't count on it. The whole territory is covered with new white communities, all organizing churches. Very little money is available."

Isabel battled to prevent her guests from seeing her total dejection.

Commissioner Jones and Dr. Murrow had just confirmed the worst. She could expect no loopholes in the land allocation. And there would be no money from the Baptist Convention.

Her own foolish expenditures for such an elaborate revival may have cost the Indians whatever chance they ever had for a church.

Each time Robert Burdette dipped a convert beneath the surface of the pool, loud laughter erupted from the hillside where hundreds of whites stood gawking.

Isabel could not contain her fury.

"Lucius, I've half a mind to go home and get my pistol. I wouldn't shoot to hit. But I would sure aim close enough to scare them."

Lucius glanced up at the mountain. "White people always make funny with Indians. We are used to it."

One hundred four Indians were being baptized in the pool below Odlepaugh Springs. Seventy-eight had responded to Brother Burdette's first call on Friday. Twenty-six more had made their way to the mourners' bench on Saturday.

The white spectators had begun to gather early Sunday. Dr. Burdette's morning service had been interrupted twice by rebel yells from beyond the trees.

After the services, the congregation had walked upstream to the pool. The white onlookers had moved with them and now stood in a semicircle along the base of the mountain and along projecting ridges. Many were clad in their Sunday best, obviously out for a frolic. Others wore soiled work clothing.

Some were of the lowest sort. Isabel had seen the glint of bottles. Sister Bare had whispered that she had heard shouted profanity.

Isabel wished she had asked Colonel Randlett to leave a few troops to protect the revival. She was sure he would have done so. Now the troops were several hours away, even by fast horse.

"I would attempt to speak to them, but I doubt they are capable of shame," said Dr. Murrow. "Perhaps, under the circumstances, it is best to ignore them."

The Indians seemed to be succeeding in doing so. Not one so much as glanced at the mountainside. But the whites from the territorial churches seemed embarrassed.

Miss Burdette and the ladies from Chicago obviously did not know what to do. They kept looking up at the mountain, casting glances at Isabel, and whispering among themselves. Mrs. Parker was most upset. Captain Parker stood with one arm around her, offering comfort.

Dr. Burdette and Dr. Chivers were in waist-deep water, baptizing the converts one by one.

A large Comanche woman was next. Dr. Burdette consulted with her through the Comanche interpreter, placed a hand on her forehead, and intoned a brief, quiet prayer. He then pushed her beneath the water to wash her sins away.

She emerged from the water like a breaching whale. Losing her footing, she fell backward and sank again. Dr. Burdette could not hold her. Dr. Chivers and the Comanche interpreter rushed to help. The woman fought to her feet, strangling, fighting for breath.

Laughter came in waves from the mountainside.

"I've had enough," Isabel said. "I'll put a stop to this."

She picked up her Bible and started toward the nearest group of whites.

"I'll go with you," Lucius said.

"No, you stay here. You will be needed for translation. Besides, there are some young toughs among those people. They might fight you."

"Then you should not go alone."

"They wouldn't dare try me."

Sisters Bare and McLean materialized from the crowd around the pool. "We will go with you," said Sister Bare.

Isabel hugged them. "You both must remember one thing drilled into us in Chicago: Not even the worst element will harm a woman alone armed with a Bible. I think we should go separately. Sister Bare, you take that ridge. Sister McLean, that one. I'll go up the mountain itself."

They left the pool and began climbing. Isabel did not look back.

Six young men were perched on boulders not far above the springs. Isabel had been watching them. They were among the loudest. Each wore soiled work trousers, a plain shirt, boots, and a wide-brimmed hat.

The group eyed her warily as she approached. Isabel gave them a warm smile.

"Why don't you gentlemen come down and join us?" she asked. "You're certainly welcome to do so."

Several of the youths glanced at each other. An empty whiskey bottle lay on the ground near their feet.

"No, thank you, ma'am," one said. "We'll just watch from up here."

Isabel did not lose her smile. "You've been laughing at the sacred rite of baptism. What do you think your mothers would say about your performance here today?"

Again the youths glanced at each other uneasily.

One shrugged. "Well, you have to admit some of those Indians are funny when they come up out of the water."

"Not nearly as amusing as spending eternity in hell for blaspheming the work of the Lord," Isabel said. "Have you thought of that?"

The young men stared at the ground in silence. Now they would not look at each other.

"This is a free country," Isabel said. "I suppose everyone can go to hell in his own way. Or he can save his immortal soul through Jesus. I would be happy to take you down to those springs and introduce you to a man who probably has saved more souls than anyone living today. He would be glad to show you the way to salvation. Do you want to go with me?"

Again the group remained silent.

"What you have been doing here is beyond human decency. Moreover, you stand in violation of the law. This reservation is not yet opened. Unless you have permits, or have been invited by the Indians, you are trespassing on government land, a federal offense. Interference with religious services is a serious crime in any community. I'm sure there are statutes that apply here."

One of the youths stepped down from his perch on a boulder. "Well, it's probably about over anyway," he said.

"To the contrary, there are about seventy or eighty more baptisms to go," Isabel said. "Dr. Burdette may not be done till sundown. But I'm sure he could make room for six more."

The group began moving away. Their horses were tied on lower ground several hundred yards distant.

"Thank you, ma'am," said one youth. "But we'll be getting on."

Isabel waited until she was certain they were leaving. She then started up the mountain to the next group.

Two couples and eight children stood on a level area that provided a view of the springs. All were well dressed. They appeared to be two families on a Sunday outing. Picnic baskets and light blankets lay on the ground behind them.

The adults seemed sheepish, defensive. Isabel spoke first.

"Hello. I'm Isabel Crawford. I've come up to invite you down to the services."

One of the men smiled. "Well, thank you. But we're just out on a holiday, looking over the country."

Isabel returned his smile. The children were standing still, listening to the conversation. They ranged in age from toddlers to adolescents.

"You've been laughing quite a bit," Isabel said. "My parents must have reared me wrong. I've never been able to see anything amusing about the most sacred moment in a person's life, Indian or white. Is this an example you've chosen to set for your children?"

The smile vanished from the man's face. "Lady, I'll raise my children in the way I see fit."

"I'm sure you will," Isabel said. "And perhaps they will thank you in later years for the fine qualities you're teaching them."

The man opened his mouth for a quick retort. The woman beside him grabbed his arm.

"Henry!" she said.

The other man stirred. He was older, more refined in appearance. "Wait a minute, Henry," he said. "I think we *have* been out of line. Miss, I apologize. We meant no harm."

"Perhaps not," Isabel said. "But people are sensitive to slights on their day of baptism. The Indians are especially so. You people new in the territory?"

"We're building at Mountain View, a new railroad town," the older man said. "We'll be opening stores there as soon as the track's laid."

Isabel pointed. "Captain Parker, the vice-president and one of the principal owners of that railroad, is down there helping to baptize those Indians. He's a fine, upstanding, God-fearing man. What do you think he'd say about this?"

Neither man answered.

"You've moved to Indian country," Isabel said. "If you're opening stores, those Indians down there could be your customers. You might do best to study them, not laugh at them."

"Henry, I think we'd better go," one of the women said.

"You're welcome to come down and join us," Isabel said again.

"Thank you, but my woman's right," the man said. "We'd better go."

As the group picked up their baskets, Isabel walked on up the slope. But the other spectators also had begun to move away, apparently assuming that Isabel was armed with sufficient authority to clear the mountainside.

Below, onlookers were leaving the ridges. Sisters Bare and McLean already were returning to the pool.

Isabel walked back down the mountain.

Captain Parker and Miss Burdette came to meet her. Sisters Bare and McLean arrived from different directions.

"What in the world did you say to those young ruffians?" Captain Parker asked Isabel. "They sure cleared out in a hurry."

"I just appealed to their better natures."

"I'd like to put you sisters in charge of laying track. I haven't found anyone capable of handling rough men so efficiently. Three of my section bosses were badly beaten last week. What's your trick?"

"Miss Burdette taught us the tremendous power of the Word. She proved to us that a woman can go anywhere without trouble if she carries a Bible. She believes everyone possesses a hard core of decency, that even the most degenerate won't raise a hand against God."

"I suppose I might try giving my section bosses Bibles to carry, but I doubt that'd work," Captain Parker said. "I strongly suspect it's the character of the person carrying it that accounts for the success."

Miss Burdette laughed. "Now you *have* hit upon my secret."

Chapter Eighteen

On Monday morning, with an entire day of leisure before train time, Dr. Burdette surprised everyone by expressing a desire to climb Saddle Mountain. A holiday mood swept over the encampment. Challenges and counterchallenges were voiced. Guests returned to their tipis and changed into practical shoes and clothing. Within an hour, all were ready.

Isabel led the way, following the route she had discovered by trial and error on that spring day four years before.

Soon a few climbers turned back because of the sun and heat. But most persisted. A party of more than forty reached the top.

While the climbers regained their breath, Isabel stood on a boulder and identified the distant peaks. She pointed out the land to the west taken away from Texas and given to Oklahoma Territory, the area in all directions soon to be given away in the coming land rush.

"A magnificent, awesome view," said Dr. Burdette. "And a fitting end to a wondrously inspirational week. I propose that we now raise a cairn in commemoration of our winning one hundred four souls for Christ."

The climbers worked for the better part of an hour, gathering weathered granite rocks and piling them at the peak. Dr. Murrow contributed a tobacco tin. Dr. Burdette found a sheet of notepaper in his pocket and wrote a suitable inscription. Every climber signed it.

The tobacco tin and inscription were placed in the cairn and covered with a cap of stones.

Dr. Burdette knelt by the cairn. "And now let us pray."

As Dr. Burdette appealed for the success of God's Light on the Mountain, Isabel found herself curiously unmoved.

The long week, the depletion of the building fund had drained her of all emotion.

She thanked Dr. Burdette for his prayer and followed the party back down the mountain.

The conversation on the way to the railhead depressed her even further. She was talking with Dr. Burdette when she happened to overhear a phrase from the conversation among the Chicago ladies. Intrigued, she asked Miss Burdette to repeat.

"Mrs. Parker and I were telling about this horrible store in Flagstaff, where they have the skeletons of two Indian babies in the window."

Isabel felt her gorge rise. "What on earth for?" she asked.

"I talked to the man who owns the place," said Miss Burdette. "He calls them curiosities. He claims that people who come by on the train want to see them."

"It's where you leave the main line to go up to the Grand Canyon," Mrs. Parker explained. "There's a wait while they make up the excursion cars. You can spend your time on the train if you wish, but most go into the stores to buy souvenirs."

"The prices are outrageously high," said Miss Burdette. "I suppose they think they must entertain the travelers in some way. The man said I was the only person who had ever objected to the display in his window."

"I can't believe that," said Mrs. Parker. "I was revolted by it. I heard considerable talk about it on the train."

Isabel was acutely aware that Lucius was listening, although he continued to devote his attention to the horses and gave no indication he had heard.

"What is that man's name?" she asked. "I would love to write him a letter."

Miss Burdette and Mrs. Parker did not know. Nor could they remember the name of the store.

"It's unfortunate, but I suppose there will always be people like that," said Dr. Burdette. "Sometimes I feel like apologizing to God for half of the human race."

He seemed to be addressing his remark to Lucius.

"It would be hard to tell the difference between an Indian baby and a white baby from the skeleton," Lucius said. "The man may have white babies in his window."

Dr. Burdette turned and shared his grim amusement with the women. "An excellent observation. The next time I am through there, I will go in and tell that to the man."

An hour later Isabel stood on the train platform and said her tearful good-byes.

"I'm so sorry there was no more time for us to talk," she told Sister McLean.

"I knew you would be busy," Sister McLean said. "We had more time than I expected. Promise you'll write."

Isabel promised, knowing even as she spoke that letters to the home office and to mission circles would take precedence. But their friendship would continue, defined by hastily scribbled notes and past affection.

Miss Burdette lingered as the others boarded. "Lucius Ben Aitsan told me about your first winter with the Kiowas. You said nothing in your reports about being chased by wolves, or the miles you walked through blizzards to carry food to the starving. Why not?"

Isabel phrased her answer carefully. "If you remember, there was such concern at the time for my safety. I didn't want to chance that the danger would be exaggerated."

"From what Lucius told me, I doubt that it could have been. I urged all of you to keep journals of your experiences. Have you done so?"

Isabel nodded yes.

"Could you send me the journals you kept that winter? I believe they could be used to further our work."

Isabel did not want to say yes, but she could not in good conscience say no.

She had not reread those entries since they were written. They probably contained personal thoughts she would not want to share. Yet she felt her eyewitness account should be told for the sake of the Indians, if not for the missionary society.

She compromised. "I can copy those entries and send them to you. What will you do with them?"

The whistle tooted. As the conductor called for final boarders, Isabel and Miss Burdette walked toward the train.

"Perhaps I can use them to demonstrate the fine work of our missions," she said as she stepped onto the train.

Isabel stood and waved good-bye, wondering about Miss Burdette's answer.

Miss Burdette was seldom vague without purpose.

Once again Sister Bear added and subtracted. But she obtained the same result. "I make it two hundred fifty-six dollars and eighty-nine cents. That's all that's left."

It could have been worse. The preachers had donated their services for the week. Captain Parker had contributed fifty dollars in the name of the Rock Island Railroad. Colonel Randlett had added twenty-five, Commissioner Jones twenty, and Mr. and Mrs. Bonnell twenty-five.

Isabel faced her mission circle Board. "It's my fault," she told them. "I should have realized what would happen. The Indians who came had no money to give. The white Christians who helped us are busy building their own churches. They have no money to spare. These are things I should have foreseen."

Lucius spoke her words in Kiowa. A murmur of protest rose from the circle Board.

"We have done Jesus work," Pope-bah signed. "We have made Jesus happy."

Odlepaugh disagreed. His long arms moved in his elaborate, sweeping gestures. "We have thrown away the money for the Jesus house. Jesus will not like that."

"It puts our thousand-dollar goal far beyond reach," Isabel conceded.

"We can make the money again," Lucius said.

"There isn't time," said Sister Bare. "The land will be given away before we can possibly build a church."

"We will work hard," Pope-bah insisted. "Everybody will work hard."

"I will sew quilts," Odlepaugh signed. "Indian men can walk the quilt road. We will make heaped-up many quilts."

"Twice as many," Pope-bah agreed. "Twice as quick."

Domot spoke and Lucius translated. "One time the Jesus woman told us that men do big things and when they are done they sit down. She said that women do little things and their work is never done. Those words come from the heart. But men also can sit down and do little things. I will make quilts because I think we need a Jesus house here at Saddle Mountain."

The other men nodded and voiced their agreement.

Isabel could not bring herself to discourage their enthusiasm. She doubted if the men could make quilts that would sell. But they wanted to help, and game had become scarce. Bounty hunting no longer brought in much money.

The odds against success seemed insurmountable. She did not want to see the Indians make further sacrifices and then be disappointed.

Lucius raised a hand and began to speak, a sentence at a time in English, followed by translation.

"I do not talk much in the mission circle about my own thoughts. But I will tell them to you now. The Ghost Dancers say the Jesus women want only to steal our money. Every time I hear this talk I get mad. The Jesus women could have stayed home with their families and lived an easy life. But they came here to help us. When we were hungry, they were hungry. When we were cold, they were cold. When we worked, they worked harder. We have done much work since Miss Crawford came to us. All of it was good work, and I do not want to see it thrown away. If I could make money for Jesus and put it in His hand, I would do it every day. Our mission circle work is the same thing. We are working for Jesus. Every time I look at all the Kiowas who have not taken up the Jesus road, it is like a stone on my heart. We need to build the Jesus house so the other Kiowas will come into it with us. The money road is hard for Indians to walk. We better cut off talking and get on it quick."

A chorus of approval filled the crowded den.

Isabel glanced up at Sister Bare. Their gazes met.

By unspoken agreement, they remained silent.

On the following day Lucius and Domot constructed more quilting frames and sawhorses. The men set to work.

Isabel was surprised to learn that many of the men could sew a fine stitch. A few were even more adept with needle and thread than the women.

"All their lives the men have made arrows, bows, horsehair ropes, halters for the horses," Lucius said. "They have made beaded necklaces and moccasins. They may not like to plow, but they can work with their hands."

Soon the men introduced their own designs, even bolder and more colorful than those of the women. Isabel's favorite was a stylized thunderbird created by Odlepaugh. The others were hardly less talented. Tipis, horses, deer, elk, and stick-figure folk creatures came to life on the quilting frames as if by magic.

When weather threatened, the frames were moved into the Gospel tent and the Indians continued their work. Seldom a day passed that six or eight quilts were not tied off.

Isabel sent quilts to Chicago by the bale to be sold by Home Mission volunteers.

At last Miss Burdette begged her to cease and desist.

"Half of Chicago will sleep under Kiowa quilts this winter," she wrote. "They are priceless works of art, but I fear the market here is saturated at the moment."

Isabel sat up night after night writing letters, seeking new outlets for the quilts through churches in the newly settled portions of Oklahoma and Indian Territories. In various ways, most of the replies gently pointed out that the mission at Saddle Mountain was not unique in its poverty.

Typical was the pastor who wrote:

Dear Sister Crawford,

My parsonage is a half-dugout, half-sod shanty. Each night my wife, my four children, and I bed down in its single room with four hundred fleas, sixteen centipedes, and whatever varmints happen to wander in. The sod roof leaks. The dirt floor crawls until you step on it.

Yet compared to most members of my congregation, I live in the lap of luxury.

I sincerely believe that in time this will be God's country, but at the moment it's a tossup. Even if we had the wherewithal, I would not recommend the introduction of your quilt finery into our present squalor.

Yet sufficient orders trickled in to keep the quilting frames busy through the winter months.

Meanwhile, the bureaucratic mills in Washington ground slowly. Nothing was heard all winter concerning the imminent opening of the reservation.

Then in late February Mo-keen returned from the Indian Agency with a government handbill that outlined a complex schedule for the opening.

Isabel summoned the Saddle Mountain Kiowas into the Gospel tent and explained the rules.

"Government surveyors will measure the land and mark it in portions of a hundred sixty acres each," she told them through Lucius. "They say that will require sixty to ninety days. As soon as the surveyors finish work, every Indian head-of-household must select a hundred sixty acres for himself and for every Indian in his household, including his children."

Lucius stopped in his translation. "Chief-of-tipi is the only way I know to say it."

"That is what they mean," Isabel agreed.

The time element remained difficult to explain, for every month had to be translated into the appropriate Kiowa moon.

"The surveyors have been at work since December," she said. "They should finish work soon. Each Indian will have sixty days to select his land. Then you must go to the Old Agency at Fort Sill and tell them what piece of ground you want. They will write your name on their map, and that will be that. No one can scratch out your name. The land will be yours forever. After the Indians have made their choices, the white man will put the white names into a pot and a certain number of them will be drawn out. This drawing-of-names will take place in June."

"I have two wives," Domot signed. "Do they both get land?"

Isabel made the "yes" sign. "Every Indian gets one hundred sixty acres. Every wife. Every baby. That is the rule."

Isabel waited until everyone understood.

"The lucky white men—those whose names are drawn—also will get a hundred sixty acres. Only white chiefs-of-tipi. No white wives, no white babies will get land. This is one time the Indians are way-ahead. The lucky white men will have sixty days to pick the land they want. On August sixth, they will be permitted to run to the land they have chosen. If some lucky white man beats them to it, they must pick another place quick."

Odlepaugh raised his hand. "What if two white men want the same place? Will they fight?"

"Probably. But they will have sixty days to sort it out. Then the unlucky white men—those whose names were not drawn—will be turned loose on the reservation to pick what *they* want. That run is set for October. Afterward, the public will be allowed to come in and settle on any land that is left."

"What about the Jesus land?" Pope-bah asked.

Isabel did not see any reason to minimize the risk. "The white chiefs in Washington will decide if Jesus is to get land at Saddle Mountain. We can put Jesus's name on it. The Kiowa council and Colonel Randlett can ask that His name be left on it. But the white chiefs in Washington can scratch His name away quick if they want. That is the rule."

"Will the white chiefs scratch His name off?" Domot asked.

"I don't know. If we had a church standing here instead of a Gospel tent, they could not do it. But we do not have half the money we need. I see no way we can build a church before June. And the white chiefs can do anything they want."

Lucius seemed deeply disturbed. He paced the platform, his head lowered. Then he turned to face the Saddle Mountain Kiowas.

"I will now speak my own words," he said in English, then in Kiowa. "When a man shoots into a bunch of quail, some are killed and some fly off to hide in the long grass. When the man is gone, the live quail call to each other and soon they get together in a bunch again. We are the same. When the white chiefs sugar-talked us into the Jerome Agreement it was like a gunshot into the Kiowas. We all scattered. We were lost, alone, and scared. Then Miss Crawford came with her Jesus talks and called us together again. Now we are coming out of the long grass. I did not want to be interpreter. But when I gave my heart to Jesus I told Him to use me any way He wanted. Now I believe He wants me to tell you what I think. The white chiefs in Washington are wise. They know that if they keep us scattered into the long grass we will stay weak and scared. We need the Jesus house to call us together so we will be strong and unafraid. We must keep trying, trying, trying. We must make the white chiefs in Washington see that they cannot keep us in the long grass forever."

Isabel opened her mouth to voice agreement but found she could not speak.

Lucius was forever a constant, precious surprise.

She turned aside to regain control of herself. When she recovered, she smiled at Lucius and raised her hands to the Indians in the "worship" sign.

"Let us now pray to God, each in his own way, and ask Him to keep us always out of the long grass."

In early April, Lucius saddled a horse and rode off to select the allotments for his family. With a family of seven, he qualified for eleven hundred twenty acres.

After three days of search he seemed satisfied.

"I knelt and asked Jesus to choose the land for me so I would not make any mistakes. I have marked the land. Tomorrow I will go to the Old Agency and tell Colonel Randlett to put the names of my family on his map."

One by one the heads of families made their decisions.

Isabel was impressed that the selections were completed with so little animosity.

At last only the land for the church remained in doubt.

Without interference from Isabel or Sister Bare, the members of the mission circle Board decided that the church allotment must have certain requisites. First, it should be central to the congregation so that no member would have far to travel. Second, it must be near a pool of water to serve as a baptistery. And last, it must encompass the cemetery.

The Board members pored long over a copy of Colonel Randlett's map.

No single remaining tract contained the requisites.

At last Lucius pointed out that two eighty-acre parcels a half mile apart might serve better than a single tract.

Isabel and the Board climbed into a wagon and toured the sites.

The first parcel was nestled into the base of Saddle Mountain. It included the glade where Isabel first camped on coming to the reservation, and the pool upstream that had served as a baptistery.

Despite its beauty, this eighty-acre tract contained little tillable soil.

The second block of land contained the cemetery and considerable ground suitable for cultivation.

The Board made a tentative decision and sought Isabel's approval.

"As far as I'm concerned, it's perfect," she told them. "But the decision is yours to make. You and your children must live with it."

The selection was presented to the Kiowa Council. Although Isabel attended, she did not speak, allowing the Kiowa Christians to make their own case.

Lucius outlined the history of the mission circle and explained the role the church would play in winning respect of the whites.

Domot spoke for the unconverted Kiowas. He told members of the council that he walked the two-wife road and could not become a Christian, but he wanted his children and his children's children to follow Jesus.

The council had heard all the arguments before. The oratory merely formalized the selection and satisfied the Indian custom of elaborate ceremony.

Allocation of the Jesus land was approved, and two members of the council rode with Lucius to present application to Colonel Randlett at the Old Agency near Fort Sill.

Another month passed before a letter arrived from Colonel Randlett:

Dear Miss Burdette,

A week ago I forwarded to Washington a complete listing of all Indian headrights for distribution of land under the Jerome Agreement. Included in this list was my personal recommendation for approval of allocation for your mission and future church.

My recommendation will be either approved or disapproved by the Commissioner and, ultimately, by the Secretary of the Interior.

Although the matter is now out of my hands, I thought you would like to see a copy of my recommendation, and perhaps forward same to your Mission Board in Chicago for their edification.

James F. Randlett
U.S. Indian Agent

Randlett had included pages from a lengthy report. Under a large bold heading, the text was written in firm Spencerian script:

MISSIONS

All have done well, but the mission conducted by Miss Isabel Crawford under the patronage of the Woman's American Baptist Home Mission Society of Chicago deserves special mention.

Miss Crawford has spent eight years at her isolated station (including three years at Elk Creek), surrounded by no other inhabitants than these Indians and (only recently) a single young lady associate in her work for companionship. The theme she instructs upon is that the Master worked and that those who would follow Him must work also, and that able-bodied Indians should be producers of the necessities of life, thereby attaining self-support and ability to help those who cannot help themselves.

Early in the commencement of her mission work she announced that her worship of God while with them would be in open air or tents until the time should come when from their own contributions and labors a house could be built for that purpose. Her following now has about $400 deposited to the bank for that purpose, her Indians following well her example and precepts. Her efforts are appreciated and praised by all who have known her.

Isabel duly forwarded a copy of the letter to Chicago and awaited word from Washington. As she went about her daily routine, she found herself unable to concentrate.

The days passed in a tedious blur.

On a day in late April Lucius returned from the agency on a well-lathered horse. Over his head he waved a large rolled-up parchment. His beaming face told Isabel the whole story:

The application for church land had been approved!

But when Isabel sat down to read the document, her elation quickly vanished.

"This is not right," she told Lucius. "It says 'The American Baptist Home Mission Society.' It should read 'Woman's American Baptist Home Mission Society.' They have made a mistake."

"Will it matter?" Lucius asked.

"They have given the land to the Rainy Mountain church," Isabel explained. "That is a totally different group. They are affiliated with the church. We are members of an independent group, organized and administered solely by women. The people in Washington are confused. I must go see Colonel Randlett the first thing in the morning."

At daylight, Lucius harnessed his fastest horses to the hack. They made the trip in record time. Colonel Randlett received them in his office.

"I don't understand it," he said. "I remember writing 'Woman's' in the application. I certainly know the difference. We will have this straightened out immediately."

He drafted a telegram to Commissioner Jones and handed it to Isabel for approval. The wire stated that two tracts should be designated "Woman's American Baptist Home Mission Society."

Randlett gave the telegram to an aide for dispatch. After

thanking the Colonel profusely for the inconvenience, Isabel and Lucius returned home.

The next afternoon, Mo-keen came by the den and signed that Colonel Randlett wanted to see Isabel quick.

Lucius again harnessed his horses and they made another dash to the agency.

Colonel Randlett was not in a good humor. He handed Isabel a telegram. "What do you suppose this means?"

The wire was brief and to the point:

Colonel James F. Randlett
Agent, Anadarko, Oklahoma Territory

WOMENS AMERICAN BAPTIST HOME MISSION SOCIETY NOT ON NESLER SCHEDULE STOP WIRE CORRECT NAME AND DESCRIPTION OF LAND STOP

William A. Jones
Commissioner, Indian Affairs

"To begin with, it's 'Woman's,' not 'Women's,' " Isabel pointed out. "And we sent the correct legal description day before yesterday."

"There's something afoot," Randlett said. "Why should Brother Nesler's Rainy Mountain schedule enter into it?"

"It shouldn't," Isabel said.

Randlett gave her a long stare. "I think you'd better tell me the full of it. What is happening here?"

Isabel was reluctant to speak ill of anyone, especially fellow Christians. But she could see no other course.

"I can only tell you this. Ever since we began our work at Saddle Mountain, an effort has been made to place us under the auspices of the Rainy Mountain Baptist Church. Our Saddle Mountain Christians are enrolled at Rainy Mountain only because they must be church members *somewhere,* and we have no church. I can only assume that Commissioner Jones has conflicting applications in his possession."

Randlett's eyes flashed in anger. "In other words, there are some good Baptists trying to gobble you up."

"It would appear so, sir. They may gobble me up. But they'll have trouble gobbling me down."

"I'll blister their britches. I'll put it in plain English so Commissioner Jones will understand the true situation. We will keep after it until we get it straightened out."

"I'll be eternally grateful," Isabel said. "I only hope Lucius's poor horses can hold out."

Two weeks later a revised document arrived bearing the correct designation.

Isabel's subsequent discovery that the allocation was marked "tentative approval" failed to lessen her exhilaration. The document was accompanied by a personal letter from Commissioner Jones:

My Dear Miss Crawford:

I want to congratulate you heartily on the outcome of the assignment of land at Saddle Mountain, but it was a close call. Colonel Randlett is right in his assessment that there are some good Baptists trying to gobble you up.

If it had not been for the fact that I had visited you and knew personally the conditions surrounding the mission the matter would have failed. But knowing as I did the good work that you have been doing among the Indians, the secretary finally consented to approve the allotment.

I would be derelict if I did not warn you that final allocation hinges on your continued efforts. We must be able to show the secretary and all concerned substantial progress within a reasonable period, or the situation could be reversed.

W. A. Jones
Commissioner

That evening Isabel read the letter to her mission circle Board, omitting only the accusation against the Rainy Mountain Church.

The Indians were confused. "What does it mean?" Lucius asked.

"It means that God is with us. It means we are moving ahead even when we make mistakes. If we hadn't had the revival, Commissioner Jones wouldn't have visited us. If he hadn't seen with his own eyes what the Kiowas have accomplished here, he wouldn't have been able to convince the bigger chiefs to approve the land."

"What is this word 'tentative'?" Lucius asked.

"It means they have given the land to us with the understanding that if we fail to prove ourselves worthy, they can take it back quick."

"What must we do?" Pope-bah asked.

"Work," Isabel said. "Work until we can work no more."

In early July, the Kiowas, Comanches, and the few Apaches on the reservation joined in a final effort to stop the inevitable.

A lawyer by the name of Springer convinced the Indians that he was a great chief in the white courts and had the power to block the Jerome Agreement. He filed in the territorial courts for a temporary injunction to stop the land opening.

When the writ was issued—a routine step toward a formal hearing—the Indians were convinced that Springer had won a big battle for them. Excitement ran high among the Indians.

Isabel fully understood that the temporary injunction was meaningless. She knew Springer was only holding out more false hope.

"The tribes are wasting their money," she told Lucius. "The land giveaway has prevailed in this country for a hundred years without being stopped once. It won't be now."

When the hearing for a permanent injunction came before the court, the poverty of the lawyer's case was plain even to Indians who did not possess a word of English. They saw immediately that the man on the bench held the power. He spoke hot words to their lawyer, who skulked from the courtroom.

A spirit of rebellion swept over the reservation. Council fires were lit night after night. The Indians debated long and hard on what to do.

Every adult Indian male began carrying his rifle wherever he went.

"There's nothing on earth quite as mad as a mad Indian," Isabel told Sister Bare. "I just hope we can get through the land opening without a killing."

Chapter Nineteen

Heenkey came late to the mission meeting. He did not take his seat, for he was too excited. "Jesus is coming quick," he signed to Isabel. "This world is going under."

Isabel turned to Lucius. "What is he talking about?"

Lucius spoke with Heenkey for several minutes in Kiowa, then answered reluctantly. "Heenkey says Amon has received a new vision. The Great Father told Amon that Jesus will come here to Saddle Mountain July fifteenth at twelve o'clock noon."

Isabel studied the members of her mission circle. Obviously they already had heard the news. Their faces were animated, and they were following the conversation between Isabel and Lucius closely, even though they could not understand the words.

"Does Amon mean the real Jesus, or the Paiute Jesus with dirty feet?" Isabel asked.

Lucius looked at her. "This is a serious thing, Miss Crawford. Do not make funny with it."

"I'm *not* making funny. To me the Ghost Dance Jesus is a Paiute with dirty feet. I cannot think of him in any other way."

Lucius spoke hesitantly. "The Bible says Jesus will come again."

"It also says there will be many false prophets. Do all the Indians believe what Amon says?"

"They do not know what to think."

"Do *you* believe it?"

Lucius spoke slowly. "I believe Amon received a vision. He would not lie. I do not know where his vision came from."

Isabel sighed. The Kiowas had reason enough to think

Armageddon was near. She signaled for Lucius to resume translation.

"Listen to me," she told the group. "We must not speak against the Ghost Dance people. They will be sad enough when Jesus does not come, without our telling them 'We told you so.' We must ignore what is happening."

"You do not believe Jesus is coming?" asked Ananthy.

"If Jesus were coming again, there would be signs. The last time Jesus came, stars moved in the heavens and everyone knew something wonderful was about to happen. The last I looked, all the stars were still in their places. I would like to believe that the Second Coming is near. But in truth I do not think the news would be given *only* to an Indian sitting in a tipi on a reservation at the edge of Oklahoma Territory. If I'm wrong, I'll be the happiest person alive."

Their faces conveyed the general disappointment.

Isabel attempted to describe her new plan for selling quilts to homesteaders, but the Indians seemed unable to concentrate. Their minds were still on the Second Coming.

Afterward, Isabel took Lucius aside. "How serious is this? How many Indians believe what Amon says?"

Lucius did not want to talk about it. He shook his head. "I don't know. Some think maybe it will happen."

"What are the Ghost Dance people doing?"

Lucius glanced at the departing Indians before answering. "They are dancing all night. Many more Indians have taken the feather and joined them."

Isabel could see frightening possibilities ahead. The Indians had been pushed to their last ditch. Any slight incident could unleash their wrath.

With the confusion attendant to the land opening, the Army also was edgy and anticipating the worst.

"Lucius, we must do something. If word gets back to Fort Sill about this commotion, the Army will send troops out here and there could be trouble."

"This is Kiowa thing. You said we should not speak against them."

"Lucius, I want to speak *for* them. You remember what happened at Wounded Knee. This is *exactly* the same situation. It could happen here."

Lucius was silent for a time. "If the Army comes to stop the Ghost Dance, the Indians will fight."

"Then we must do what we can. And I don't want to go

behind their backs. Would Loki Mo-keen talk with me about it?"

"My father, Loki Mo-keen, no longer walks the Ghost Dance road."

"I know that. But he is the keeper of the Tai-may, one of the most respected men in the tribe. The Ghost Dancers will listen to him."

Lucius considered the matter at length before making his decision. "I will go talk to him. Maybe he will come."

Lucius and Loki Mo-keen arrived late the next afternoon. The day was warm, so Isabel spread blankets in the shade of the Gospel tent. Lucius sat between Isabel and Mo-keen to interpret.

"I have heard what is happening among the Ghost Dance people," Isabel told Mo-keen. "I see bloodshed coming if something is not done. I also see a way to stop it. But I do not want to wear two faces. I must get the permission of the Ghost Dance people to do it."

Mo-keen studied her through eyes drawn to mere slits. "This is not your road to walk," he said. "You have your Jesus road. The Ghost Dancers have their road."

"If I do nothing and the Army comes out here and kills Kiowas, it is my road," Isabel told him. "Some of our Christians have quit coming to my Jesus talks. I have wondered why they stayed away. Now I think they have left the Jesus road and taken the Ghost Dance feather. They are my friends, and I love them. I do not want to see them killed."

Mo-keen studied her. "What do you want to do?"

"I will write a letter to Colonel Randlett and tell him exactly what is happening so he will get the truth and not the bad stories. I will tell him that the Indians are excited over Amon's vision but that there is no reason for the Army to intervene. Jesus either will or will not come on July fifteenth at twelve o'clock noon. If He doesn't, the excitement will die down. If He does, then we can all rejoice and carry His banner. Colonel Randlett is a Christian and a good man. He will listen to me."

"Randlett is not chief of the soldiers."

"No. But the soldiers listen to him. They do what he asks."

Mo-keen frowned in deep thought. "I cannot speak for the Ghost Dance people. This is Amon's vision."

"But you can take me to them."

After several minutes of silence, Mo-keen began a formal oration. Lucius translated:

"There are things you should know. The Kiowa Ghost Dance did not begin with the Paiute called Wovoka. The Kiowa dance started right here. Fifteen years ago, a Kiowa named Pa-tepte received a vision. He was told that the buffalo would come back from under the ground and that all dead Kiowas would return in a great spirit army and drive the whites away. Pa-tepte's vision came a long time before the Paiute's vision. But Pa-tepte died not long after. Two years later, a Kiowa named Poingya also received a vision. He was told that Pa-tepte's power had been given to him and that a great whirlwind would blow away all whites and all the Indians walking the white man's road. A great prairie fire would clean the land. The buffalo would return. The Kiowas would go back to living like in the long-ago time. Poingya said the Kiowas must form a new religion of their own and not let the white people know about it. Many Kiowas believed him. But later his baby son died, and Poingya said he would dance him back from the other world. When Poingya could not dance his son back, the Kiowas turned away from him. He died quick. When news of Paiute's vision first came to us, we remembered Poingya and Pa-tepte. About that time Afraid-of-Bears also had a vision. In it he saw what the whites now call the Kiowa Ghost Dance. We call it Awh-mai-goon-gah, the Feather Dance. It is not the same as the dance of the Sioux. Afraid-of-Bears is now chief of the Kiowa Ghost Dance people. So you see, Wovoka's vision is not a new thing. It is a longtime Kiowa thing."

In all her five years among the Kiowas, no one had taken her so deeply into tribal secrets. Isabel was fully aware of the trust placed in her.

"Will Amon and Afraid-of-Bears talk with me?"

Mo-keen and Lucius conversed in Kiowa for several minutes before Lucius conveyed the answer.

"My father said to tell you the Ghost Dance people are at Sugar Creek. He will take you there. He will tell them what you want and listen to their answer."

"Will you go with us?"

Lucius shook his head. "The Kiowas remember that I came with the Army to stop the Sun Dance. There is much *guan a'dalk-i* at the Ghost Dance." He paused while he searched for the correct word. "I do not know how to say that in

English. *Dance craziness*, maybe. If they saw me, there might be trouble."

"But I need you to translate."

"Mo-keen knows what you want to do. He thinks it is good. He will speak to Amon and Afraid-of-Bears for you."

"Will they listen?"

"Mo-keen says he does not know. But he agrees that we must try. He said if the Army tries to stop the Ghost Dance, many Kiowas and soldiers will be killed."

Tonemoh, Odlepaugh, and Spotted Horse agreed to accompany Isabel and Mo-keen to the Ghost Dance camp. The next morning they climbed into Mo-keen's wagon and set out across the open prairie.

Long before they reached Sugar Creek, Isabel heard the reverberations of the thunder drum.

A large medicine lodge was set up in a meadow beside the creek. A circular frame of poles supported a conical roof, lending the structure the appearance of a walled tent, perfectly round.

As Mo-keen drove his wagon into the fringes of the camp, scores of Kiowas were cavorting around a cedar pole, their hands linked to form a circle. The dancers were chanting in the rhythm of the thunder drum. The repetition was hypnotic. Each dancer moved with a peculiar gait, dragging one foot along the ground. Every Indian wore a single feather pointing straight up. Faces and bodies were painted in a bewildering variety of patterns. Every Indian wore his elaborately painted Ghost Dance shirt.

Mo-keen stopped outside the compound and stepped down from the wagon. "Sit," he signed to Isabel.

Odlepaugh remained with her in the wagon while Tonemoh, Spotted Horse, and Mo-keen went to talk with the dance leaders.

The beat of the thunder drum, the chants, and the merciless sun were enough to make anyone giddy.

Isabel felt that if she sat there long enough, she also might begin to see visions.

She held up a hand to shade her eyes. Out in the middle of the circle, a shaman pointed a feather at a dancer, who dropped out of the group. The shaman then held the feather between the dancer and the sun. Staring into the sun, the dancer crouched low to the ground and began whirling rapidly. Around and around he went, until he fell to earth and lay stone still.

In a moment, the shaman selected another. The vision-seeking dance was repeated.

Several minutes later, Mo-keen returned alone.

"Amon and Afraid-of-Bears are praying," he signed. "They will talk with us when they cut it off."

Mo-keen helped her from the wagon. She and Odlepaugh followed him into the camp. As they walked through the throng, Mo-keen motioned Indians aside, paying no more attention to them than if they had been a swarm of gnats. Isabel kept her gaze lowered, hoping to avoid any challenge of her right to be there.

Tonemoh and Spotted Horse were waiting at the entrance of the medicine lodge. A doorkeeper said something to Mo-keen and motioned them forward. Isabel followed Mo-keen into the lodge.

Amon, Little Robe, and Afraid-of-Bears sat in painted glory at the center of a medicine circle. The walls of the lodge were ablaze with colorful symbols. Shafts of bright sunlight slanted down from openings in the roof, lending the interior of the lodge an eerie, timeless aura. Dust motes drifted lazily in the shafts of sunlight.

One by one, Odlepaugh, Tonemoh, and Spotted Horse delivered brief speeches. Each talk drew a short response from Afraid-of-Bears.

Then Mo-keen spoke at length, gesturing occasionally toward Isabel.

She stood facing the Ghost Dance chiefs with absolutely no idea of what was transpiring.

Afraid-of-Bears answered Mo-keen with an impassioned oration.

A lengthy exchange followed.

Then Afraid-of-Bears motioned for Isabel to come closer.

"I have sunshine in my heart because you have come here," he signed. "I cannot ask you to stay. Some of the people here would not like it. This dance is a Kiowa thing. Mo-keen has told me you think there will be trouble if the soldiers come here. You have true thoughts. If the soldiers come, we will fight. We have counciled on what you have said, and this is what I think: You can write the letter. Colonel Randlett is a good man. We do not want him to hear bad stories about us. If he knows the truth, maybe he will not want to fight."

"I also have sunshine in my heart that we have talked," Isabel replied. "I will write the letter."

Isabel followed Mo-keen, Odlepaugh, Tonemoh, and Spotted Horse back to the wagon, remaining way-behind as the Indians would expect her to do.

On the ride back to Saddle Mountain she drafted her proposed letter in her mind.

Her apprehension grew.

The plan for the letter contained within it a calculated risk.

Colonel Randlett was only the Indian agent.

He could make recommendations, but he did not command the troops.

If an Army officer of the ilk of George Armstrong Custer or John Chivington had arrived at Fort Sill, her letter might spark a disaster even greater than that at Wounded Knee.

Through late June and early July a paralyzing sense of anticipation settled over the reservation. Men no longer went into the fields to work. The women cut off the cooking classes. Only a loyal handful arrived each night for Isabel's Jesus talks.

For a time even Isabel wondered if the world truly was entering the last days. Calamities came in appalling succession.

First Domot appeared one evening at the Aitsan home with lips quivering, wailing that his "way-behind little one" was dying.

Through two days and nights Isabel and Sister Bare took turns tending to the child. Domot crouched over the bed constantly, stooping to kiss the little hands as they were flung from place to place in fitful restlessness. The mother—wife number two—lay with head pressed close to the child's heart.

On the second night the short, quick breathing grew softer. Time after time Isabel thought the spirit had flown, but she found that the tiny heart continued to beat. The struggle continued well past midnight. At last, with a slight shudder, the infant died.

Isabel took the death as a personal defeat. For reasons she could not fathom, the baby had failed to shake her winter illness. Isabel had tried every remedy she knew.

Remembering how Domot had comforted her when the

news came of her mother's death, she went into the yard and embraced him. They cried for a time together.

"Jesus has carried her up," Domot signed. "I have lost many children and I have always been afraid when they died. This time I am not afraid. You have told me the true road. I know now that my little ones are with Jesus. He knows what is best. I am not afraid but my heart cries."

Isabel constructed a coffin while Sister Bare prepared the body. The entire community came. The lamentations were long and loud. Domot was almost helpless in his grief, for the baby had been the child of his old age—probably his last.

The coffin was placed in a wagon and driven to the graveyard. There it was found that the grave had not been made large enough. The mourners waited while the hole was lengthened.

Isabel delivered a brief sermon, and Sister Bare said the prayer. The tiny body was lowered and covered. Everything that belonged to the child was buried with her, and even her bed was placed upon the grave.

Two days later, Saing-poh's tiny baby boy took a turn for the worse. He had been born prematurely, and Isabel had doubted from the first that he would live. But she became absorbed in doing all she could. Her battle over the precious little bundle had offered a few brief moments of hope. When the end came, the sorrow was almost more than she could bear.

Isabel and Sister Bare again prepared the body and conducted the funeral.

Then word came from Cache Creek that Old Soldate lay dying and wished to see "the deaf woman" before departing this world.

Soldate had been a wife of the old Chief Lone Wolf—the old chief, not the new one with the same name. Lone Wolf had been one of the greatest of the war chiefs. He led the Lost Valley raid, and he was in the second battle at Adobe Walls. The Army considered him dangerous enough that they sent him to prison in Florida. There he contracted the malaria that later killed him. Before his death, he gave his name to a younger Kiowa, Mamay-day-te.

Soldate's life dated back to times when few Indians had seen a white man. Despite her great age, she had attended almost every Jesus talk.

Lucius drove Isabel to the woman's house in his hack and translated a final, feeble exchange.

"If the Great Father takes us both into the other world, we will see each other there with no trouble," Soldate said. "I will be waiting there for you. When you come over I will find you quick."

Isabel took her hand. "I will look for you there," she said. "Our hearts may cry now, but it is written that the Great Father will wipe away all tears from our eyes, and in His presence shall be fullness of joy."

After Lucius translated, Soldate nodded her understanding, smiled, and closed her eyes. She did not speak again.

Isabel sat and held her hand until the old woman died just before sunrise.

Indians came from all over the reservation to attend the burial.

Soldate's body was large, and no suitable coffin could be found. Lucius attempted to make one from the bed slats, but they proved too fragile. From expediency, in consideration of the summer heat, the body was rolled in quilts and bound with ropes. When the men came to carry her to the wagon, the bundle bent in the middle and they were forced to lower it to the ground several times to find better holds.

When all of Soldate's possessions were placed in the grave, it was almost filled. Stones were stacked upon it to thwart wolves.

Everyone had loved Soldate. She was even older than the storyteller Taboodle and also had preserved early tribal memories. The entire tribe went into mourning.

Then, for more than two weeks, Isabel and Sister Bare took food to Gah-yi-day as he lay dying. He was not a Christian, for he had two wives, but he had attended the Jesus talks and contributed some of his grass money toward the some-day church. He had said that Jesus was in his heart.

Isabel was in his tipi when the end came with both wives beside him on the bed. As he breathed his last, the women tried to outdo each other in their wailing. Afterward they argued over who had loved him more. The competition continued throughout the funeral service and left Isabel completely undone.

She felt as if she had been living in the graveyard. Her days were hounded by dark thoughts, and her nights were made vivid by troubled dreams.

Still the tragedies did not cease.

While Isabel and Sister Bare were seated at breakfast one morning, Aycompto rode up on a horse and signed that Smokey, the jovial chief of the cactus religion, was dead.

Not until Lucius arrived a few minutes later was the full story told.

During a nightlong session in the cactus tipi, Smokey chewed four peyote buttons and fell over in a trance.

The vision quest ceremony continued uninterrupted. Not until an attempt was made to rouse Smokey at daybreak was it discovered that he was dead.

Mo-keen brought the body to the den and laid it on the floor. Still painted in bright, ceremonial colors, Smokey's face was relaxed in a slight smile, as if he perhaps had indeed glimpsed a good vision at the instant of death. His wife arrived, and after a suitable period of mourning a decision was made to bury him in the beautiful ceremonial blankets in which he died.

Lucius and Mo-keen pulled up a portion of the flooring from the platform in the Gospel tent to make the coffin.

Smokey's burial posed a quandary, for he was a Christian of a different sort. Somehow the followers of the cactus vision quest had managed to combine the Jewish traditions of the Old Testament, the teachings of Jesus Christ, and elements of the long-ago Kiowa religion into a unified hodgepodge.

In his eyes, Smokey had been a Christian.

Yet few white men would have accepted him as such.

Isabel ignored caution. She announced that she would give Smokey a Christian burial.

Sister Bare objected. "Surely you don't think he was saved."

Isabel did not feel like arguing the matter. "I'll leave that to God. Smokey attended my Jesus talks. He was a good man, respected by everyone who knew him. He told me he believed in Jesus Christ, but he thought there should be an Indian road for worship, not just a white man's road. I will bury him as a Christian. As far as I know, that cactus tipi over on Sugar Creek qualifies under Christ's promise that 'where two or three are gathered together in my name, there am I in the midst of them.' "

Sister Bare threw up her hands in a gesture of helplessness. "I just hope the women in Chicago don't learn of it."

"I've shocked them before," Isabel said. "I'm sure I will again."

Kokom and Papedone dug the grave. Lucius and Mo-keen put the body into the coffin. When all was in readiness, the mourners followed the wagon to the graveyard at the foot of the mountain.

Isabel spoke from the Twenty-fifth Chapter of the Book of Matthew: "Watch therefore, for ye know neither the day nor the hour . . ."

In her diary she had recorded Smokey's last testimonial at her Jesus talks. She read it beside the grave, and Lucius translated:

"Some of you think I have quit the Jesus road but I have not. When I walked the white man's Jesus road, Mr. Clouse pointed at me one day and said I was a great sinner. I was not ashamed. I grew up with Kiowa Indians and I know we are all sinners. We all have some kind of medicine. The Great Father made the cactus button, and it is great medicine. Nobody made it with their hands. The Great Father put it on this earth to grow. It has brought me visions of the other world. If Jesus tells anything in the Book against the cactus button I do not know of it. In the cactus tipi we do not put the buttons ahead of Jesus, for He is ahead of everything."

After Sister Bare offered a prayer, Isabel concluded the service.

"Smokey was never baptized," she told the mourners. "I do not know if his soul is saved. It is an awful lesson. But maybe we can learn from it."

She closed her Bible and lowered her head.

"Dear Lord, we grieve the loss of our fine friend. Our lips refuse to say his soul was lost, for he may have given his heart to Jesus. Our friend Smokey sleepeth. We pray that someday we may see him again in Your holy kingdom. Amen."

Kokom brought word that six missionary barrels had arrived at the train depot. Lucius said he would go get them. Depressed by weeks of illnesses and death, Isabel welcomed the opportunity to get away from the reservation, if only for a few hours. She decided to turn the trip into an outing.

She urged Mabel and the children to go with them. "Maybe we can sell some quilts. New people are coming here all the time—people who have not yet seen our quilts."

Isabel, Lucius, Mabel, Leslie, and Richard set out early to take advantage of the relative coolness of morning. Mabel sat in the middle and held the baby. Isabel kept close watch on Leslie to see that he did not fall out.

Even before they reached the Cache Creek crossing they began to see changes. The margins of the road were amply decorated with empty whiskey bottles. Once past the boundaries of the reservation, travelers were always in sight. Hacks, buckboards, buggies, wagons, every type of horse-drawn contraption imaginable dashed across the landscape. Every creek bottom was filled with the tents of whites awaiting the opening. Each time Lucius met conveyances coming from the opposite direction on the narrow road, he put the right wheels of his wagon onto the prairie to give them room.

The whites stared in passing but seldom spoke.

Lucius had just driven across a deep ravine when a buckboard stopped in the road ahead. The three men in it were drunk, floundering around in their vehicle and shouting.

Lucius reached behind him for his Winchester and put it at his feet. Isabel pulled little Leslie closer to her.

One of the men began to yell at Lucius. "Hello, John! Hello, John! Wantum whiskey?"

"Whiskey peddlers," Isabel said. "Don't stop."

Lucius put the right side of the wagon onto the prairie and drove toward them.

The man raised a bottle. "We gotum whiskey, John. We gotum cards. Wantum gamble? Playum monte?"

Lucius's rich baritone voice rose in answer. "We are all Christians here. We do not drink. We do not gamble."

The men stared in open-mouthed amazement.

Apparently they had mistaken Isabel for an Indian. She thought she should add to their confusion.

"It's a federal offense to sell liquor to an Indian anywhere in this territory. If you can't abide by the law, you'd best go back wherever you came from."

The men continued to stare. Lucius trotted the horses past without looking at them.

Once safely down the road, Isabel began to laugh.

"With that kind of trash flying in here from all directions, I really wonder what kind of state this will become someday."

A tall plume of dark smoke rose in the distance. As they drove closer, Isabel saw flames at its base.

"It's Oakdale," she said. "Some buildings are burning."

The new town had been built in anticipation of a branch

line westward from the trunk railroad. It consisted of saloons, a few stores, and makeshift shanties.

Lucius turned at the crossroads and drove into town. The best business block was burning, the flames soaring high into the air. A large crowd stood in the street, watching. The heat on the July air was oppressive.

Two men stood fighting in front of a saloon. The one getting the worst of it picked up a carpenter's square and struck the other over the head with it. Blood spurted. Isabel stood and prepared to step down from the wagon.

"They are drunk and dangerous," Lucius said. "We should go."

"We can't let that man bleed to death," Isabel said. "I don't think anyone else here has sense enough to help him."

She climbed down from the wagon and went to the man. He sat on the ground, holding his head. Blood streamed over his hands and down his arms. A group of men stood around him, apparently deciding that the sight of a man bleeding to death was more interesting than the fire.

"Is there a doctor in this town?" Isabel asked.

A tall, gray-haired man shook his head. "There's one in Anadarko," he said.

"I know that," Isabel said. "It isn't what I asked. This man won't live to see Anadarko. That bleeding must be stopped. If you don't have a doctor here, I can do it. But I must have needle and thread."

The man pointed. "I think my woman has needle and thread at home."

A boy was sent to fetch it. During the wait, Isabel ordered the man moved into the shade of an awning and arranged on a nail keg. He seemed drunk enough to be feeling little pain.

"Who is he?" she asked.

"His name's Bradford," said the gray-haired man. "I don't know his given name. He's a carpenter. You one of them woman doctors?"

"I'm not a doctor," Isabel said. "I'm not even a nurse. But I sew a fine stitch."

One of the buildings across the street collapsed with a roar, falling into the flames.

"Well, there she goes," said the gray-haired man. "That was all the money I have in the world."

"Your store?" Isabel asked.

"Was. Now you're looking at a sod-buster, I guess. I'll have to put my name in the pot and make the run."

The boy returned with the needle and thread. Isabel propped Bradford against the front of a building and began sewing his wound closed. She found two arteries spurting blood and tied them off, not certain what the effect would be. Bradford winced a few times but did not protest.

"What you doing with them Indians?" asked the gray-haired man.

"I'm a missionary," Isabel said. "I live on the reservation."

"You might be right handy to have around. Doctor and preacher all rolled into one."

Isabel finished the sewing. A bucket of water and a bottle of whiskey was brought from the saloon. Isabel cleaned the wound with the alcohol and then washed her hands in the water. She bandaged Bradford's head as well as she could. He was laid out full length in front of the building.

"I've done all I can," Isabel announced. "He either will live or he won't. Would anyone here like to buy a quilt?"

The fire had dwindled to charred embers. Isabel led the crowd to the Aitsan wagon. She climbed into the back and held up the quilts, calling out the prices.

"I'm always in the market for quilts in July," said the gray-haired man. "Almost froze last night. I'll take that one with the big tipis on it."

Isabel sold six. Soon she and the Aitsans again were on their way to Anadarko.

Lucius drove several miles in silence. "Will that man live?" he asked.

"I think so," Isabel said. "But I don't know. The wound could fester."

"And not one of his friends seemed to care. If that had been a Kiowa that was hurt, Indians would have gathered around him and prayed all night long."

Isabel did not answer. Lucius had spoken the truth. She had been the only one to help, and even she could have shown more compassion.

"The more I see of the white man, the less I understand him," Lucius said.

Isabel was tying off a quilt when Heenkey galloped his horse across the meadow toward the Aitsan house. Isabel watched as he dismounted and Lucius walked toward him. After they talked briefly, Lucius went into his house.

He returned carrying his Winchester.

Heenkey also was carrying a rifle.

Isabel left the women sewing in front of the den and ran across the meadow as Lucius and Heenkey started walking toward the mountain. From their purposeful strides, she knew they were not hunting wolves.

"Lucius, stop!" she called. "Wait!"

He turned to face her and stood until she reached him.

"What is it?" she asked. "What are you about to do?"

For a moment she thought he would not tell her. But perhaps he saw the concern on her face.

"There are four or five white men hiding in the mountains. No one knows what they are doing. We will find out."

"They're probably Boomers. Let them go! If a white man or an Indian is shot now, the Army will come. There's no telling where the killing would stop."

Lucius gave her an abrupt nod. "That is why we must find them first. The Ghost Dance people are hunting them now. They think maybe the men have been spying on the feather dance. If the Ghost Dancers find them, they will kill them."

He and Gahbein walked on toward the mountains.

Isabel did not know what to do. She did not want Lucius to take the risk. Yet he spoke the truth. Little Robe, Amon, Afraid-of-Bears, or any of the Ghost Dancers probably would kill to protect their sacred ceremony.

"Lucius, be careful!" she called after him.

Lucius raised his gun to show that he had heard.

Isabel returned to the Aitsan house and sat with Mabel through the long afternoon. She tried to sew, but she could not concentrate. She expected to hear gunshots from the mountains any instant.

Lucius and Heenkey did not return until after sundown.

Lucius entered the house and placed his Winchester on the pegs over the door. "There were five of them," he said. "They were hunting for gold. Odlepaugh was with us. He has gone to tell the Ghost Dance people the men were not spies from the Army."

Isabel found relief from tension in her fury over the foolishness of the prospectors. "The complete idiots!"

Lucius smiled and sat down. "I told them they have no business here. I promised them that if they did not get off the reservation, I would have the Army come and get them. They left quick."

Mabel lit the lamp. Heenkey used the light to tell Isabel his own version of their adventure.

"Lucius made them jump with his white talk," he signed. "They were heaped-up scared white men. We will not see them again."

"They may not have believed me," Lucius said. "One of them asked about a mine with an iron door. He said he had heard that the Indians knew all about it."

Rumors of gold in the Wichitas had persisted for years. The story of the mine with the iron door—supposedly abandoned by ancient Spaniards and hidden by the Indians—had been told and retold.

Isabel first heard the story at Elk Creek, long before coming to the reservation. She had always assumed that there was not a grain of truth in it. But it was the kind of story that would make men do foolish things.

"What did you tell him?"

Lucius grinned. "I asked him if he thought the Indians here would be poor and hungry if they knew where to find gold."

"The white men ran like scared rabbits," Heenkey signed, still savoring the moment. "They will not be back."

"I hope Heenkey is right," Isabel told Lucius. "But no doubt there are other idiots we should worry about."

July 15 dawned hot and sultry. Not a breath of air stirred. By midmorning the heat had built until not even deep shade offered relief.

It was not an auspicious day for the Second Coming.

Not a single Indian arrived to work on quilts. Apparently all remained at home, waiting.

Isabel, Sister Bare, and the Aitsans spent the morning under the arbor, shelling peas, watching the shadows of a stick Lucius had driven vertically into the yard. The shadow shrunk shorter and shorter until it was no more.

"It is noon," Lucius said.

Isabel put her peas into the pan and looked toward the mountains. "Well, I see no celestial fireworks. I feel sorry for the Ghost Dance people."

"I feel sorry for all of us," said Sister Bare. "They had me half believing it."

Lucius sat watching the mountains. After a while he grew restless. He rose to his feet.

"The beans in the garden are dying from the heat," he said. "I will haul some water from the creek for them."

Mabel watched him walk away to harness his team. "Lucius is sad," she signed. "Amon and Afraid-of-Bears will die quick."

"Why do you say that?" Isabel asked.

"Medicine men always die quick after they make a mistake."

Isabel did not bother to contradict her. She had found that most of the Indian superstitions were based on acquired experience. Therefore they were incontestable as far as the Indians were concerned.

That evening, despite the lingering heat, Indians assembled, almost filling the gospel tent to hear Isabel's Jesus talk.

At first Isabel was inclined to ignore what had happened. But after giving the matter much consideration, she decided to meet the Ghost Dance issue head-on.

Under the hissing lanterns, with Lucius interpreting her every word, she spoke of Christ's revelations concerning the Last Days.

She quoted from the Book of Luke:

"And there shall be signs in the sun, and in the moon, and in the stars; and upon the earth distress of nations, with perplexity; the sea and the waves roaring; men's hearts failing them for fear, and for looking after those things which are coming on the earth: for the powers of heaven shall be shaken.

"And then shall they see the Son of man coming in a cloud with power and great glory."

She paused, then switched to the Book of Matthew, preferring his phraseology of the next part:

"Of that day and hour knoweth no man, no, not the Angels of heaven, but my Father only. . . . Watch ye therefore, and pray always, that ye may be accounted worthy to escape all these things that shall come to pass, and to stand before the Son of man."

She put aside her Bible to show that she now was speaking straight from her own heart:

"We have all wasted too much time worrying about the Ghost Dance people and what they have seen in their visions. We are Christians. We must get back on the Christian road and build our Jesus house quick. There are many things to be done and there is little time to do them. We can't sit back and look proud and say 'I am a Christian.' That is not the Jesus road. We do not even have a Jesus house. We cannot rest a minute.

"Don't blame the Ghost Dance people," she went on. "They have made a mistake, but we all know their hearts are good. Tomorrow I must go see Amon and Afraid-of-Bears and tell them that we are sorry Amon's vision did not come to pass."

Lucius broke off his translation. He spoke to Isabel in English. "Amon and Afraid-of-Bears will not want to see anyone. They are very shamed."

"That's why I must go to them. Now is when they need friends most."

Lucius completed the translation. A stir of discussion grew among the congregation.

"What are they saying?" Isabel asked.

"They think this is a new road for living with the Ghost Dance people. Most of them say we should walk it."

The next morning Isabel and Lucius drove to the Ghost Dance encampment at Sugar Creek.

They found Amon and Afraid-of-Bears alone in the big medicine lodge. Both had removed their paint and ceremonial costumes. They were seated upon faded government blankets.

"I'm sorry your vision did not prove true yesterday," Isabel told Amon through Lucius. "We have come here to tell you that the Christians all know you spoke only what was in your heart."

"My vision was very good," Amon replied. "I do not know what happened."

"I also think your vision was very good," Isabel said. "I know in my heart that Jesus is coming again. I think maybe you misunderstood only about the day. I do not believe Jesus will come again until the far-ahead time."

"Many of the dancers had good visions, too," said Amon. "Some of them saw their children and their grandfathers who have gone over to the other world. Some saw the buffalo and the long-ago time. Three of them saw and talked with Jesus in Kiowa."

"The Kiowas need Jesus to come back right now," said Afraid-of-Bears. "My heart cries that he did not."

"Jesus came to us once in the long-ago time," Isabel pointed out. "Maybe that is why He does not come again now. While He was here on earth He told us that wherever He was needed, He would be there in spirit if we called Him. That is the Jesus road. We all pray to the same Great Father. I would be happy to pray with you now."

With no thought as to what her Mission Board in Chicago, the U.S. Army, or every last Baptist church in the country might think, Isabel knelt with Lucius on the dirt floor of the Ghost Dance medicine lodge and prayed for the souls of *all* Kiowas.

BOOK THREE
The Opening

If I were an Indian,
hounded as they are and
cheated and insulted by
low down whites, I would
resent every proffered
kindness and expire of
sheer desperation *if I
could not fight.*

ISABEL CRAWFORD, Diary
entry, December 10, 1898

Chapter Twenty

The spectacle took Isabel's breath. On the once-empty prairie where she had traveled many times now stood tents as far as the eye could see. Thousands of people were milling about, frantically pursuing their dreams amid unbelievable confusion and excitement. Overnight a city had flowered. Four hundred places of business vied for attention, yet not a single permanent structure was in place anywhere. The first edition of a daily newspaper was being hawked by vendors, streets had been named, and handpainted signs were going up everywhere.

Lawton, Oklahoma Territory, born a city, not a town, was only hours old.

Around it, the country had been opened to the fifteen thousand holders of "lucky numbers."

Another hundred fifty thousand "unlucky numbers" still waited, hoping for an eventual piece of the pie.

Apparently many if not most of the unlucky multitude had come to see the birth of the city of Lawton.

Isabel sat marveling at the constant uproar as Lucius drove his wagon and team through the swarm of horses, wagons, buckboards, drays, buggies, and hacks. Long trains of ox-drawn freight wagons wound through the throng, accompanied by barking dogs and shouting bullwhackers. Lucius adroitly dodged Indians, beggars, bootblacks, fruit peddlers, adventurers of every description. Mabel, Richard, and little Leslie rode on the spring seat beside Lucius. Isabel and Sister Bare sat on cane-bottom chairs on the flat bed of the wagon, every jolt of the heavily rutted street traveling the length of their spines. The wagon box behind them was filled with bales of folded quilts.

Thrilled by the drama, Isabel was aware of its significance.

Not only a city, but also a state was being born before her eyes. Already talk of admission to the Union was in the air. The only question remaining to be resolved was the form this new state would take. Some believed Oklahoma Territory should go it alone, that the eastern portion—Indian Territory—was not yet ready. Others felt the "twin territories" should be merged into a single state stretching from Arkansas on the east to Texas on the the west. Much of the region was as unfinished as this overnight tent city. The new citizens were as varied as the headgear she now saw on the streets of Lawton—from English bowlers to Indian feathers.

Isabel felt gooseflesh rise with the thought that what she was seeing would never be seen again.

"Look!" said Leslie, pointing.

A circus wagon blocked the intersection ahead. High-stepping black men in scarlet uniforms waved large, colorfully illustrated banners depicting circus acts. A five-piece brass band seated at the tailgate of the wagon burst into a blaring rendition of "Camptown Races."

Wagon, band, and high steppers quickly organized into a small parade. At their approach Lucius turned his wagon aside to give them room. Two women attired in black tights and frilly red skirts carried a banner bearing the likeness of a female trapeze artist. Across the top was the legend: *A FLYING WOMAN!*

"As if that's anything new," said Sister Bare.

Isabel doubted that the circus could possibly offer attractions more exotic than the humanity moving along the tent-lined streets. She recognized representatives from most of the Indian nations—the darker Choctaws and Creeks; pudgy, round-faced Osages; swarthy Apaches; tall, handsome Cherokees; and the lean, lighter-skinned Plains tribes. The white tribes were hardly less intriguing, or varied: soldiers, booted cowboys, grim-faced farmers, black-suited lawyers and gamblers, snowy-bearded old men, tender-faced youths, pith-helmeted surveyors, teamsters carrying their telltale black-snakes, lawmen burdened with pistols and rifles, black-bearded backpack peddlers, white-sleeved merchants. Women were among them, too: mothers with babies in arms, wives following in the wakes of their husbands, Indian women, and some Isabel dared not speculate upon.

Edging back into the traffic, Lucius drove past a tent-saloon bearing a sign: *WELCOME ALL NATIONS BUT CARRY*.

"The newspaper said seventeen railcar loads of liquor were brought in for the opening," said Sister Bare. "Obviously there wasn't room for razors and soap."

Lucius rose to his feet in the wagon, shaded his eyes with his broad-brimmed black hat, and peered ahead. "I do not see a place for us."

"It won't have a sign on it," Isabel told him. "Keep driving. We'll know it when we see it."

Sister Bare's hand flew to her face in astonishment. "Oh, look!"

A broad-shouldered man fought his way across the street, his passage through the crowd made difficult by the fact that he had no legs. His hands and stumps were encased in black leather. He moved along close to the ground with a peculiar crab motion, his muscular arms churning. He disappeared into the throng.

"Probably a railroader," Sister Bare said. "They fall under the engines and lose their legs."

A gap appeared in the row of tents ahead. Isabel tapped Lucius on the shoulder and pointed. "There's a vacant lot. Right beside that big tent."

"That's a gambling hall!" Sister Bare protested.

Isabel sighed. Most of the new business establishments seemed to be either saloons or gambling dens. "We can't be choosers," she said. "This is as good a location as we'll find. Lucius, park the wagon sidelong to the street. I think there's room."

Lucius drove wagon and team into the empty lot, maneuvered into position, and set the brake. He jumped to the ground and helped Mabel, Isabel, and Sister Bare from the wagon. The children were handed down. As Lucius unhitched the trace chains, a red-faced white man stormed out of the gambling hall. He wore a frock coat, high collar, string tie, and spats, and carried a pool cue. He pointed the butt end at Lucius.

"Hey, Indian! You can't park that wagon there!"

Isabel moved between them. "Why not?"

"Because this lot's taken."

Passersby slowed. Isabel ignored them. "I don't see anyone occupying this space. The rules are that you must occupy and improve a claim to hold it."

The man's beefy face turned a shade redder. "Lady, *I'm* occupying it. And my brother's busy improving it. He's gone for lumber. Next week a two-story hotel is going up right where you're standing. You're trespassing on private property. Get that wagon moving or I'll call the law."

"Belle, we can't afford trouble," Sister Bare said. She took Isabel's arm. "Let's go."

Isabel kept her gaze on the angry man. "Mister, we only want it for today. Would you consider leasing it to us until midnight?"

The man's gaze flicked from Isabel to the wagon, to Sister Bare, to Lucius and Mabel, to the boys, and back to Isabel. "What is this, a sideshow?"

Sister Bare gasped and readied a quick retort. Isabel raised a hand to stop her. They were in no position to take offense. "We're Baptist missionaries. We only want to sell quilts."

"Blankets?"

"*Quilts.* One hundred thirty-two of them, to be exact." She lifted one with Odlepaugh's thunderbird design from the wagon. Lucius helped her spread it. "They sell from one and a half to two dollars each. We're raising money to build a church."

The man traced the design with stubby, well-manicured fingers. "I might consider renting the lot. How much you willing to pay?"

"How much you asking?"

The man studied the wagon, Lucius and Mabel, the quilt. "For the rest of the day, ten dollars."

"Why, that's the equivalent of three hundred dollars a month! I could buy a farm with three hundred dollars."

"So you could. This is prime location, right on Main Street. None better. Ten dollars. Take it or leave it."

Isabel knew it was out-and-out robbery. But this was one day when everyone in this part of the territory was out to make a fortune. She knew she would find no one in the mood for charity. "We'll take it on one condition. We want to tie a line to the top of your front tent pole."

"Why?"

"To hang our quilts."

The man looked at the tent pole, then nodded. "Done."

Isabel wrote a simple, one-paragraph contract, asked the man to sign it, and learned that his name was Benjamin Maxey. She paid him the ten dollars.

Maxey returned to his gambling hall. Lucius tied two lariats together, roped the top of the pole, and stretched a line from the big tent to the tailgate of the wagon. Isabel, Sister Bare, and Mabel draped it with quilts. Lucius then raised the wagon tongue and arranged another line to the front, extending the display.

For good measure, Isabel and Sister Bare also covered the side of the wagon with quilts.

As Isabel expected, the abundance of color quickly drew a crowd. Women came to admire the designs, the fine stitching. Their compliments were not wasted. Overhearing, men who had traveled to the territory alone were moved to buy quilts to send back home to wives and families. For them, the quilts were the perfect gift— practical, yet proof they truly had arrived in Indian country.

The quilts sold so fast that Isabel raised the prices.

Sister Bare was shocked. "Two dollars fifty cents for a quilt?"

"You'll find nothing cheap in this town today," Isabel said. "I just wish we'd done it sooner."

By nightfall the last quilt was sold. Around them, the celebration began to grow rowdy. Whoops and yells split the air, along with an occasional gunshot. Every man in town seemed to be drunk. Isabel put the money into an empty cheesebox and hid it under the wagon seat.

"How much is it?" asked Sister Bare.

"I don't know. Let's not risk counting it here. We'd best be on our way back home."

"In the dark? Someone will follow and take the money."

"The open prairie will be safer than here. Lucius brought his rifles."

Lucius harnessed the team and they set out. Lanterns lit their way through the streets. As they drove past the last tents and onto the open prairie, a thin sliver of moon offered just enough light for Lucius to keep on the wagon tracks. As they drove westward, the children bedded down on pallets in the back of the wagon and soon were asleep.

An hour or more west of Lawton, Lucius turned in his seat and handed Isabel a rifle. "Maybe you should hold this."

Isabel did not want to take it. "Lucius, I've fired a gun only four or five times in my life. I couldn't hit anything."

"You could scare them."

"It might be another opportunity to become a heroine," said Sister Bare.

Isabel ignored the teasing. The pamphlet was an embarrassment she would never be allowed to forget. A first copy had arrived two weeks ago, and others were now distributed among every mission circle and Baptist church in the country. The seventy-eight-page book was entitled *The Heroine of Saddle Mountain*. The cover depicted a woman running through snow and surrounded by huge, snapping wolves. It reminded Isabel of Eliza's flight across the ice floes in *Uncle Tom's Cabin*. Inside the book, the words were her own, judiciously selected by Miss Burdette, but they seemed so different in bold print.

"You take the gun," Isabel said to Sister Bare. "Then we both can be heroines."

"No, thank you," said Sister Bare. "I'm content to be a mere missionary."

Isabel considered the possibility that some robber might have watched them leave town, and followed to take the church money. If the circumstances warranted, she *would* shoot.

There could be no harm in scaring a robber away.

The rifle felt cold and deadly in her hands. She put the wooden stock across her lap and held the barrel in the crook of her elbow, as she had seen men do.

Occasionally she looked back.

She could see nothing on the road behind them but darkness.

They drove for hours, traveling through the large tract set aside by the federal government for the Fort Sill Military Reservation and the Wichita Mountain Forest Reserve. It was devoid of any signs of human habitation.

Gradually the moonlight grew bolder. Near Mount Scott, Lucius guided the wagon into deep shadows beneath a stand of trees. He set the brake, wrapped the reins around the handle, picked up his other rifle, and disappeared into the nearby brush.

"Is he leaving us here alone?" asked Sister Bare.

"Be quiet," Isabel whispered. "He's looking to see if we've been followed."

Isabel, Mabel, and Sister Bare sat in the shadows and waited. After long minutes Lucius returned.

"I saw three men on horseback," he said. "They turned off a half mile back and rode toward the south."

"Night riders," said Sister Bare. "They're up to no good, that's for sure."

"They were singing and talking, making a lot of noise. I think maybe they are not after us."

Lucius drove on, keeping the horses at a steady trot, pausing only occasionally to let them blow. Mount Scott, Mount Sheridan, and Cut Throat Gap moved by eerily in the pale moonlight.

The eastern sky was beginning to lighten as they arrived at the Aitsan home.

Isabel and Mabel carried the boys into the house and put them to bed.

Then, while Lucius unharnessed the team and Mabel cooked breakfast, Isabel and Sister Bare counted the money.

"Three hundred nineteen dollars and seventy-six cents," Isabel said.

Another count produced the same total.

Sister Bare recorded the amount in her journal and added it to her earlier figures. "That gives us seven hundred eighty-eight dollars and ninety-two cents. We have enough to build a little church right now!"

"We will not settle for a smaller church," Isabel said. "From the beginning we planned a church to serve all the Kiowas here at Saddle Mountain. I won't accept less."

"But we still lack two hundred dollars. That may take months!"

Isabel was tempted, especially in light of the risk that Washington might rescind the allocation for the church if construction were not started soon.

But she had held the vision of the church and mission house in her mind for six long years. She could not bring herself to abandon that dream. She spoke her hopes aloud.

"If we hurry and move the den onto the church land, we will satisfy the inspectors that we have made an 'improvement' on the claim. With the people in Washington, another few months probably won't matter. Besides, we now have white families to think about. We will need the larger church."

Sister Bare made a face. "It doesn't seem right, allowing whites to worship in a church the Indians have worked so hard to build."

"I can't think of anything more right," Isabel told her. "The Indians may oppose me. But I've long dreamed of Indians and whites worshiping together in the same church. Truly, that would be something to see."

"There's only one way to do it," said the mover. "We've got to jack up the whole thing and put wheels under it. A couple of bridge timbers, and the axles and wheels from two wagons. That ought to do it."

"I thought we could just skid it, using poles as rollers," Isabel said. "I've heard of that being done."

The mover frowned. His name was Jack Russell, and he had settled on a "lucky number" claim a few miles to the west of Cache Creek. He shook his head. "Ground's too rough for rollers. No, we've got to get it up on wheels."

Russell, Isabel, Lucius, and Sister Bare circled the den, studying the situation.

Somehow they had to move the den more than a mile and onto church land to qualify under the clause of "occupying and improving" the claim.

"Won't the den be too heavy for wheels?" Isabel asked.

"I've moved houses a sight bigger than this one on wagon wheels," Russell said. "There's a knack to it."

"How much would you ask to do the job?"

Russell shook his head. "Nothing. No charge. Me and my lady are pleased to find a church under way so near. Both of us was raised Methodist. But I've never been one to worry about how many angels can dance on the head of a pin. I'm not keen on those churches where they shout and roll on the floor. But any other will suit us fine."

"We don't roll on the floor," Isabel told him. "But sometimes we speak in unknown tongues."

Russell looked at her blankly until it hit him. He roared with laughter. "You mean the Indian talk?"

"I've spent six years here, and it's still unknown to me."

"I'd like to ask you something: It seems to me the government may be rushing these Indians too fast into taking up our ways. You know them. Do you think they're ready?"

"No. But trying to hold back the white settlers would be like when King Canute ordered the ocean waves to stand still. The whites are coming, and nothing will stop them. I think the Indians are better prepared to live with the whites than the whites are to live with the Indians."

Russell laughed again. "That's probably right. I know several settlers *plenty* worried about taking up a claim in the middle of Indians." He thumped the side of the den with an open palm. "Looks solid enough. I don't think we'll have any trouble. If everyone agrees, we'll hitch onto this house to-morrow and take it across country in high style."

Early the next morning, Russell and Lucius brought their wagons and strongest teams to the den. While the wagons were disassembled, Isabel, Mabel, Sister Bare, and Mrs. Russell packed the housewares and missionary goods into boxes for moving.

Mrs. Russell was at least a decade younger than her husband. Tall and thin, she possessed a pleasant but serious manner. She seemed ill equipped to be a pioneer in a new land.

"I can't get used to the wind here," she confided to Isabel. "I've never lived anywhere that didn't have a lot of trees. Here there's nothing to stop it. Does it always blow like this?"

"No. Most of the time it blows harder," Isabel said. "You *do* get used to it."

"And I never thought I'd live in a dugout. How in the world do you keep a *dirt* floor clean? Yesterday I killed a scorpion just before he got me. Do their bites hurt?"

"Like fire," said Sister Bare, already a veteran. "Keep a bottle of bluing handy and daub some on the sting. It doesn't really help. But it gives you something to do."

Throughout the morning, Indian children too young for the government school gathered, excited by the thought of a white man's house rolling across the prairie. Soon it became apparent that every child and dog from miles around had come to see that strange sight. Fearing they might be hurt, Isabel banished them to a safe distance.

Lucius and Russell placed stout bois d'arc poles on stone fulcrums and raised each corner of the den a fraction of an inch at a time. With each tiny gain, more wedges and blocks were inserted.

The den rose slowly. By early afternoon the floor of the house was barely a yard off the ground.

"That's high enough," Russell said. "Those blocks are risky. If it topples, we've got nothing but a pretty mess of kindling."

The eight- by ten-inch bridge timbers were dragged into position by a team of horses and placed beneath the house.

Clearly the timbers would be far too low to rest on the wagon wheels. Isabel voiced her disappointment.

"There's a trick to it," Russell said. He went to his wagon box, now resting on the ground, and returned with pick and shovel.

Working steadily, Lucius and Russell dug deep trenches to accommodate each set of wagon wheels. The completed trenches gradually sloped up to ground level.

With much toing and froing, the wagon wheels were maneuvered into place. The bridge timbers were positioned across the axles and securely chained. Slowly the house was lowered until its full weight rested on the wheels.

Eight horses, harnessed into two spans, pulled the den up the inclined plane to level ground.

Then, accompanied by excited Indian children, barking dogs, and worried women on foot, the den began its slow trip across country.

Lucius drove one span of horses, Russell the other.

"Easy does it," Russell called to Lucius. "Remember, Miss Crawford forgot to put brakes on her house."

The procession moved along smoothly until arrival at the first of three creeks to be crossed. Russell halted the den and walked down to the water to assess the situation.

When he returned, he leaned against a wagon wheel, wiped the sweat from his hatband, and gestured toward the creek. "If we take a run down that bank, we ought to get up enough speed to make it halfway up the other side."

"Won't the house tip over?" Isabel asked.

"Not likely. The ground's solid and level."

Isabel, Sister Bare, Mrs. Russell, and Mabel were positioned on the opposite bank with short posts. When the house stopped moving forward, they were to block the rear wheels to prevent it from rolling backward into the creek.

That was the plan.

"Everybody ready?" Russell called. "Here goes!"

He lashed the horses. The house began to move, and picked up speed rapidly. Within moments the horses were running for their lives as the traces slackened and the house nipped at their heels.

The race continued down the long slope and into the creek.

There Russell's plan collapsed as the ends of the heavy bridge timbers dug solidly into the opposite bank.

The den bounced high, teetered, then came down hard on the bridge timbers.

Seized in their harness, the eight horses turned somersaults backward and went down in a tangle.

Poised to dash forward to her assigned wheel, Isabel instead found herself backpedaling frantically to escape tumbling horses and flying hooves. She sailed into the creek and sat down in shallow water with a tooth-rattling thump.

The big bois d'arc post she was carrying grazed her forehead as it fell beside her.

Lucius and Russell hurried to prevent the thrashing horses from injuring themselves in the tangle of trace chains and harness leather. As the men worked to free the teams, Isabel struggled to her feet in the middle of the creek.

A few yards away, Sister Bare knelt beside Mrs. Russell, who lay full length near the bank.

Isabel hurried through the water toward them. "Anyone hurt?"

"Mrs. Russell is pinned by her skirt," said Sister Bare. "The beam just missed her."

Isabel and Sister Bare could not free her.

Mrs. Russell looked up at the den, poised precariously over them. "Tear the dress," she said. "If the chains break, the house will slide back on us."

Isabel ripped the dress free and they moved out of danger.

Mabel came from the opposite side of the den, walking unsteadily, rubbing the back of her head. Isabel asked if she were hurt. Mabel signed that she was only scratched and bruised.

Isabel at last had time to examine herself. Her backside was covered with mud. Her palms and knees were skinned from the harsh contact with gravel. The falling pole had left a bruise on her forehead. Her shoes were full of water. She waded to the bank and tried to wring out her skirts. She looked at the other women. They also were soaked to the skin and covered with mud.

Across the stream, Lucius and Russell had untangled the frightened horses and were quieting them with gentle strokes and soothing words.

The Indian children stood at a distance, staring at the scene with complete solemnity.

Isabel and the other women exchanged glances.

As sometimes happens inexplicably, the same thought struck them simultaneously.

They burst into laughter.

Before they could control their mirth, Lucius and Russell came to ask if they were hurt.

The question set them off again.

It was a joke that transcended language or racial barriers. In the moment of crisis, the men first had looked to the safety of the horses. Only after rescuing the horses had they concerned themselves with the women.

With the teams straining mightily and the women pushing, the den was pulled out of the creek. The second and third crossings were made more cautiously and without incident. By dusk the den stood safe on the mission claim, in the meadow beside Saddle Mountain Creek where Isabel had spent her first nights on the reservation so long ago.

As the night deepened and stars appeared, Russell aimed a stick at Polaris and drove it into the ground, maintaining the angle. He explained that on the following day it would serve as a guide in squaring the den with the rest of the universe.

Lucius built a fire. After their clothing dried, Isabel and Mabel cooked supper Indian style.

They ate under the stars. Time after time they laughed over the mishap in the creek. As the Russells prepared to depart for home, they solemnly shook hands with the Aitsans, Sister Bare, and Isabel.

"We thank you for your help," Isabel told them. "We could not have done without you."

"Our pleasure," Russell said. "I'd like to think we've contributed in a small way toward building our future church."

The den was placed on permanent foundations the following day. Carrying water from the creek, Isabel and Sister Bare scrubbed the house from top to bottom.

While Isabel made a new shelf for her books, Sister Bare created a clever china cupboard from a biscuit box, a piece of white oilcloth, and a dark green silk throw. Isabel then made a cover for the extension table under the front window. She converted spare boards into shelves for the lean-to behind the den. There she stored the missionary supplies, food, and medical stores.

In the days that followed, Isabel and Sister Bare continued to concentrate on making the den more livable. Russell helped

Isabel sink a barrel into the spring for a well to keep eggs and other perishables relatively cool. She placed a biscuit box beside it for a larder.

The Indian women came to marvel and to ask that their houses be "fixed" in similar fashion. Isabel showed them how to do the work themselves.

Lucius erected the quilting frames in the yard, but through the next few weeks production steadily declined as the Indians prepared for winter. Isabel and Sister Bare took turns with the ax as they added to their own rick of stovewood.

Around their familiar little world at Saddle Mountain, all was changing. The unseen presence of the "lucky number" settlers on their surrounding claims hung heavily in everyone's mind. The wild, open country that Isabel had crossed with Jeremiah and Jonah six years before was now covered with people. The new settlers were building dugout homes, digging wells, and plowing senseless furrows across the prairie to "qualify" their claims before the government inspectors arrived.

Isabel felt fenced in, confined.

The effect of the first wave of settlers upon the Indians was even more pronounced. They were quiet, uncommunicative, and strangely subdued as they came to the den and Gospel tent for the Jesus talks, the English lessons, and clothing from the missionary barrel.

In early November Lucius joined Mo-keen and Domot in a contract to haul freight for the Army.

With Lucius away, Mabel was at loose ends. She often walked across the prairie to the den to while away the day with Isabel and Sister Bare.

"I do not know what is coming," Mabel signed one afternoon. "But I wish it would get here."

Isabel could not have said it better.

Chapter Twenty-one

With the first cold norther that fall, Domot stopped at the den and signed that a white child lay critically ill in a tent on Saddle Mountain Creek seven miles below the mission. He said he had tried to help, but when he made signs he only scared the woman there. Lucius was still away from home. Isabel and Sister Bare harnessed Jonah and Jeremiah to Isabel's battered old wagon and drove downstream to the campsite.

An emaciated woman and five bawling children—two boys and three girls—hovered over a pitiful open fire. One glance told Isabel that the children were well on the way to starvation. The body of a little girl about six years of age lay on a board placed across two logs. Soiled bedding, pots, pans, rags, and filth littered the camp.

Isabel had never seen even the poorest Indians living in such squalor.

She stepped from the wagon and introduced herself. The woman held back her lifeless hair with a long, rail-thin arm and stared at Isabel. The woman wore no coat. Her dress was hardly more than a rag.

"We're here to help you," Isabel said.

The woman turned to look at the body of the child. "I think Rebecca died."

Isabel and Sister Barer exchanged glances. The woman seemed half out of her head.

"Where are your menfolks?" Isabel asked.

The woman waved a hand listlessly. "Out hunting land."

"Your husband? This is your husband we're talking about?"

The woman nodded.

"What's his name?"

"Dunn. Roger Dunn."

"Mrs. Dunn, when did Rebecca die?"

Again the woman looked at the body. "This morning, I think. I don't know exactly when."

"You understand, she should be buried. It's a matter of health. We must think of the other children."

Mrs. Dunn shook her head. "Not until Roger gets back. He'll know what to do."

Again Isabel and Sister Bare exchanged glances; Roger had not known how to prevent his family from freezing and starving.

"Don't the children have more clothes?" Isabel asked.

The woman shook her head no.

"Mrs. Dunn, we must think first of the living. Let's take the children to my house, feed them, and find warm clothing. We can leave a note here at the tent, telling your husband where you've gone."

"He can't read."

"Then we can leave him a map."

"I can't leave Becky."

"We'll take the body with us. Gather whatever you need. We must hurry."

The body was cold and stiff. Isabel and Sister Bare rolled it in an old Army blanket long used as a lap robe. They placed the bundle at the tailgate of the wagon.

Isabel took a piece of charcoal from the fire and drew a crude map on a scrap of bedsheet, using the creek and Saddle Mountain as points of reference. She assumed anything else might confuse the man. At the appropriate place she made a box to represent the den, and with artistic license placed a small cross upon it. Beside the den she drew stick figures of a woman and six children.

For a moment she considered depicting one of the children supine but decided against it.

The man would hear the bad news soon enough.

Isabel and Sister Bare helped Mrs. Dunn and the children into the wagon, and Isabel drove the seven miles back to the den.

She built a big fire in the stove, went into the lean-to, and rummaged in the missionary barrels for suitable clothing. The children were so weary they seemed to be sleepwalking. Isabel had to help some of them into warmer clothing. Mrs. Dunn sat silently in a chair before the fire, listlessly fingering the dress Isabel handed her.

"We will find you some nice coats," Isabel told the children. "But first we will eat."

She fried eggs and bacon and warmed scraps of leftover biscuits and cornbread.

Sister Bare carried the body out to the shed. When she returned and found the children in their new finery, she pulled Isabel into the lean-to. "Belle, this food and clothing was donated to the Indians. What will the Chicago Board think?"

"I don't care," Isabel said. "As far as I'm concerned, a cold, hungry child is a cold, hungry child. I doubt God notices the difference. Right now I'm more worried about getting that body into the ground."

"That husband may not come back at all," Sister Bare said. "Maybe he has abandoned them. I've heard that happens out here."

"We can't worry about it. We must convince her to bury the child. If you'll finish cooking, I'll go prepare the body."

"I'll do it," said Sister Bare. "At the moment I couldn't stand to look at food."

The children fell upon the makeshift meal like famished pups.

Assuming that their little stomachs were shrunken, Isabel limited each to a single plate.

Mrs. Dunn left her food untouched and could not be coaxed into eating. Isabel divided her portion among the children.

A few minutes later Sister Bare returned breathless, her face pale. Again she pulled Isabel into the lean-to pantry.

"It's smallpox!" she said. "That child died of smallpox!"

Isabel's heart seemed to freeze in her chest.

She remembered an epidemic of smallpox in Canada during her childhood. Scores had died. Whole communities were devastated.

And the Indians seemed to have no resistance whatsoever to the diseases of the white man. Nine years before, an outbreak of measles had killed two hundred twenty-one Kiowas. What would be the toll from an epidemic of smallpox, a far more deadly disease?

"Are you sure it isn't chicken pox?"

"Think I don't know the difference?" Sister Bare snapped. "It's smallpox! The pustules are deep, as hard as birdshot, and all in a single eruption."

Isabel's faint hope vanished.

She thought of the hundreds of Indian children crowded together in the government boarding schools. She thought of the new tent-cities without the beginnings of sanitation, the hundreds of new homesteaders without adequate shelter.

The whole countryside was ripe for an epidemic.

"We must get word out," she said. "I'll send Odlepaugh to Colonel Randlett with a note. These children here have been exposed. I suppose we're infected, too. We must keep the Indians away from the den."

"Do you think we'll have to go into a pesthouse somewhere?"

"Probably not unless we show signs of the disease. The first thing for you to do is to wash your hands thoroughly. With disinfectant."

"I already have. I almost took a bath in it. What about the body?"

Isabel understood the question. The Army surgeon would want to confirm Sister Bare's diagnosis.

"Let's soak the blanket with disinfectant and hope for the best. Perhaps this cold weather will hold until help arrives."

Isabel hurriedly wrote a letter describing the Dunn family's plight, the child's death, and Sister Bare's discovery of the postmortem signs of smallpox. She added that she would keep the Indians away from the den, and board the Dunn family until some other arrangements could be made.

Not bothering with the saddle, Isabel hiked her skirts, mounted Jeremiah bareback, and rode up the creek to Odlepaugh's new house. Dismounting a stone's throw away, she called to Odlepaugh. After a moment he and Ananthy emerged from the house and came toward her making signs of greeting. Isabel stopped them with a gesture.

"Maybe I have bad sickness," she signed. "Do not walk close to me. I do not want you to pick it up."

"What sickness?" Odlepaugh asked.

Isabel remembered the Cheyenne sign for smallpox. She did not know if the Kiowa sign was the same, but she used it. With right hand curved, she tapped her face and chest as if touching the marks of the disease. She then added the signs for "smell" and "bad" and looked at Odlepaugh questioningly.

Apparently the Kiowas' sign was the same. Odlepaugh signed that he understood.

He added the "throw it away" sign. "Come into my house, away from the cold wind. Smallpox does not scare me."

"It is time to be scared," Isabel answered. "Many Indians and whites will die if they pick up this sickness. I have made a talking paper. I want you to take it to Colonel Randlett quick."

Odlepaugh nodded. "I will go," he signed.

"Tell all the Indians here at Saddle Mountain: Do not go near the Jesus woman house until all the sickness is gone."

Odlepaugh made the "no" gesture. "Kiowas are not afraid of smallpox."

"Do not make funny with this," Isabel signed rapidly, showing her anger. "The Kiowas say that in the long-ago time the Caddos all died quick. Maybe this same sickness killed them. This I know to be true: In the long-ago time smallpox killed heaped-up many Indians far up big rivers. Smallpox is bad for whites. Smallpox is heaped-up bad for Indians. You remember when measles killed many Kiowas. This sickness is worse."

"It is not good that the Jesus woman is scared," Odlepaugh insisted.

"The Great Father gave us brains to use," Isabel shot back. "If the Kiowas are smart, they will be heaped-up scared. I want smart Kiowas, not dead Kiowas."

Ananthy interrupted. "I remember the little bugs so small you cannot see them. I will go tell all the Indians."

Isabel placed the letter under a stone and backed away.

By the time she returned to the den, the youngest Dunn boy was running a fever. Sister Bare had put him to bed.

"It could be a fever from exposure," she said. "But it looks like smallpox to me. He's a very sick boy. I'm not hopeful."

That evening the boy was wracked by chills and vomiting.

Isabel examined him. She could find no evidence of smallpox, but the telltale "shotty" pustules normally would not appear for two or three days. If they did, then she and Sister Bare would know for certain they also had been exposed. The little girl's body might not have been virulent. But if the boy had smallpox, he was infectious.

"How long before we come down with it?" Sister Bare asked.

"Ten to fourteen days, if I remember right," Isabel said. "These children probably were infected by the same carrier."

Isabel and Sister Bare surrendered their beds to the guests and sat up through the night, tending to the child.

Colonel Randlett arrived before noon the following day,

accompanied by an Army surgeon, two ambulances, and six soldiers.

The doctor went into the shed and returned a few minutes later. "You're right," he told Isabel. "There's no doubt. I'm placing this house under quarantine."

"I've already done so," Isabel told him. "What about this family?"

"We'll take them with us. A pesthouse will be established at the post. The dead child should be buried as soon as possible."

Isabel pointed. "The graveyard is over that way about a half mile. You will find tools in the shed."

"Won't the Indians object to a white child being buried in their cemetery?" the doctor asked.

"I doubt it," Isabel told him. "I've never known a Kiowa to say no to a child, Indian or white, living or dead."

Two soldiers went out to dig the grave. Isabel and Sister Bare found coats for Mrs. Dunn and the children. When the grave was ready, the body was carried to the cemetery and lowered with ropes. Isabel attempted a ceremony, but she was so tired she knew she did not do an adequate job of it.

After the grave was filled, Mrs. Dunn and the children were loaded into the ambulances and driven away.

Isabel and Sister Bare were left alone.

The doctor had said they were to remain in quarantine fourteen days.

"I've felt feverish from the moment I first saw that poor child's spots," said Sister Bare. "I'm sure I'll die from the suspense, if nothing else."

"We must keep busy and take our minds off of it," Isabel said. "We can spend the time quilting. If we die, at least we'll leave behind something nice to be buried in."

Three days later Roger Dunn rode into the yard on a gaunt horse. Sister Bare had gone to the creek for water. Isabel saw the man ride up and dismount.

She opened the door and shouted a warning for him to stay away from the door. She explained about the quarantine. "I apologize, but I can't invite you in. Your family is at Fort Sill. You are to go straight there and report to the post hospital. I'm sorry to be the one to tell you, but your little girl Rebecca was the first stricken. She is buried in that graveyard a half mile east of here."

Dunn glanced in the direction of the cemetery. He seemed not to comprehend.

"Little Jimmy was sick, but he's receiving good care," Isabel went on. "The other children are being fed. At least they won't starve."

Dunn did not answer. He stood in the yard and stared at her without showing any sign he understood.

Suddenly Isabel could contain her anger no longer.

"What on earth possessed you to go off and leave your family without food, without shelter?" she shouted.

Dunn's eyes narrowed. "I was providing for them. I was out hunting them a home!"

"A hundred sixty acres of raw prairie is a long way from being a home," Isabel informed him. "Winter's here. You have no house. Just because you're land-crazy, why make your poor children suffer?"

Dunn flushed beet red. "Woman, all that's none of your goddamned business!"

Isabel took an involuntary step out the door. "Mister, any time I see a cold and hungry child, it's my business. The government's not doing you any favor by giving you a claim. Handing a hundred sixty acres of unbroken land to most of you homesteaders is like handing a drowning man a stone."

"Not me," Dunn said. "All I need is a chance."

"A chance? I saw your camp. Where are your plows? What'll you use for seed? How will you feed your family through a year or more until you clear the land and raise your first crop? Where will your family live until you build a dugout or a sod house? In that threadbare tent? The government advertises free land, and men like you swarm out here without a thought in your heads. It's the women, children, and horses who suffer."

Sister Bare returned from the spring. She circled cautiously behind Isabel and went into the house.

Dunn's eyes were blazing. "It's the only way a man can get ahead in this country. It's always been so."

Isabel's anger left her as quickly as it came. Suddenly she felt dizzy. She leaned against the doorframe for support.

"Yes, Mr. Dunn, you're right," she said. "It has always been so. The men do, and the women and children suffer. Go with God. Tell Mrs. Dunn she has our prayers."

Isabel stepped back into the den. She glanced out the

window in time to see Dunn climb onto his horse and ride away toward the east.

"What was *that* all about?" asked Sister Bare.

The full import of what she had done hit Isabel. She could not hold back tears. "I just told that man his child was dead and in the same breath berated him for it. It was a blessed poor time to lay the blame on him."

"Maybe not," said Sister Bare. "He deserved every lick you gave him. What do you want to eat tonight?"

Through the next few days they spent every spare moment quilting. But they lacked the flair for the bold Indian designs. The traditional patterns Isabel had always loved now seemed hopelessly drab. The weather turned cold and wet, and the roof began to leak. It was with a sense of relief that they put away the quilting to prevent water stains on the cloth.

As time wore on, the close confinement made them irritable. Isabel tended to stay awake until all hours and sleep late each morning. Sister Bare preferred to go to bed early and awake at dawn.

One evening, unable to sleep, Isabel lit the lamp and spread her writing material. Isabel turned the wick low to keep from awakening Sister Bare.

Engrossed, Isabel lost track of time. Late in the night, as she reached for an envelope, she was surprised to see Sister Bare not only awake but also fully dressed and furiously gathering her bedding.

"Scratch! Scratch! Scratch!" Sister Bare shouted. "I'm going out to sleep in the shed!"

Isabel's own temper flared. "Sneaky mean! No wonder the Indians call you 'the Bear Woman.' *I'll* go out there to sleep. *You* won't be disturbed!"

She yanked up her mattress and plunged out the door and into inky blackness.

Struggling against the cold wind, she bumped into the woodpile, barking her shins. Better oriented, she managed to find the shed. She groped in darkness until she found two planks. She placed them atop two barrels, spread her mattress, and stretched out on the hard surface. Icy wind whistled unhampered through cracks over her head.

Sleep would not come. For more than an hour Isabel lay daydreaming in darkness. She created an elaborate fantasy of her own death by freezing. She took delicious pleasure in imagining how contrite and sorry Sister Bare would be the next morning when she came out and found only a cold corpse.

Caught up in her exhaustion, the worry over her exposure to smallpox, and more than a good measure of self-pity, Isabel began to cry.

Minutes later, the door swung open and a match flared.

"Do you want me to go home?"

Isabel choked back a sob. "No, of course I don't."

"Then you get up right this minute and come back into the house!"

"I won't. I can't sleep any more in that stuffy house! I was just going to bed when you—"

The door slammed.

Isabel lay for a time, listening to the lonely wind. She scooted deeper into her blankets. As her feet and legs slowly turned to ice, her anger cooled.

She gathered her bedding and returned to the house. Sister Bare lay motionless, her form barely visible in the faint glow from the stove. Isabel spread her mattress and crawled into her box.

Almost instantly she was asleep.

For days thereafter Isabel and sister Bare remained distantly polite with each other. Instead of an occasional "Belle" or "Kate" or "Sister," it was now "Miss Crawford" and "Miss Bare." They no longer discussed personal matters or voiced idle thoughts, speaking only when absolutely necessary.

At last the fourteenth day was marked off the calendar.

"I believe we're safe," said Sister Bare. "We should have seen symptoms by now, if ever."

Tension in the den eased as the threat faded.

Lucius was the first to break the quarantine. He brought news from Fort Sill: A deadly smallpox epidemic had erupted among homesteaders and the new railroad towns across the North Fork of the Red River to the west. But the Army now believed the outbreak had been contained.

The Dunn boy was recovering. The father already had been released from quarantine to make the "unlucky number" land rush.

But Lucius also brought sad, more personal news: "Montahahty is dying."

Isabel groaned.

Death always seemed to take the best. Kokom's daughter

Montahahty had worked hard for God's Light on the Mountain. She was still in her twenties and had five young children.

"Lucius, I must go to her at once. Surely Mabel will want to go, too."

Lucius nodded. "She is waiting for us at my house."

Isabel, Lucius, and Mabel drove around the mountain in the Aitsan surrey and arrived at Montahahty's bedside early in the afternoon.

Isabel's quick examination determined that she was ill from double pneumonia, probably complicated by advanced tuberculosis. With nothing to be done for her physically, Isabel turned to the spiritual. Hour after hour she held Montahahty's hand and prayed. The poor woman bit her own arms and hands in pain and frustration and thrashed continually from side to side. Isabel could find nothing to give her comfort.

Late in the evening Lucius came to stand beside Isabel. "I think we should go now. I must tend to the livestock. We can come back tomorrow."

"Can we drive home in the dark?"

"The moon will rise before midnight."

Isabel, Lucius, and Mabel set out in starlight. They rode in silence until they reached the high ground west of Saddle Mountain.

Suddenly Mabel pointed into the distance and said something to Lucius in Kiowa. Lucius stopped the team.

"What is it?" Isabel asked.

"She said it looks like a firefly, but it is too far away."

A pinpoint of light flared in the distance and slowly faded. Then came another and another, each in a different place.

Suddenly Isabel understood.

The "unlucky number" land rush was scheduled to start at midnight.

"It's Sooners," she said. "They're hiding along the creeks and ravines, waiting. They're striking matches to look at their watches so they will know when to come out of hiding."

The midnight opening was the government's answer to much criticism over the danger posed by the land rushes. Men had been hurt, even killed, in the pell-mell races for Oklahoma land. Congress had attempted to impose order through lottery, limiting the participants. That, too, had failed. Now the white chiefs in Washington, in their infinite wisdom, had decreed that the "unlucky number" opening would begin at midnight. They assumed that by throwing open the land in the middle of the night a dangerous, headlong race would be prevented.

No one had taken into account the desperation of the homesteaders—or of man's propensity for foolishness.

The race was being run in the dark.

A distant cannon boomed, its echoes resounding along the peaks of the Wichitas.

Within minutes specks of light—distant lanterns—appeared on the horizon to the south and moved almost imperceptibly along the prairie.

The sky slowly lightened with the rising of the moon behind the mountains to the east. Isabel, Mabel, and Lucius sat in the wagon as the drama unfolded on the prairie below.

More lights materialized in the creeks and dry washes as the Sooners lit lanterns and left their hiding places to begin the dash for their chosen claims.

They were far ahead of the wave of lights advancing from Owl Creek, the designated starting point.

A rider passed on a flat, open space less than a half mile away. He was holding a lantern high and plunging recklessly over scattered boulders.

"That man should blow out his lantern," Lucius said. "His horse could see better by moonlight."

The row of distant lights drew closer and spread steadily over the prairie. Soon Isabel could distinguish men on horseback, wagons, and buckboards racing across the rugged landscape.

A small red glow appeared in the distance and rapidly grew in size.

Another blossomed a mile or more away.

"What is that?" Isabel asked.

For a time Isabel, Lucius, and Mabel were mystified. Then Lucius offered the answer.

"They are burning the grass to find the cornerstones."

Isabel could not believe anyone capable of such foolishness. In this region, prairie fires were a constant danger. "Good thing we've had rain. Otherwise they'd burn up the whole country," she said.

Soon more fires were growing across the landscape. The southwest wind grew heavy with smoke, dust, and cinders.

Isabel, Lucius, and Mabel sat in the wagon and watched the strange display.

Lucius swept a hand from horizon to horizon. "Now all the

squares on the maps are filled. The whole country is gone. Where did all these white men come from?"

"From all over," Isabel said. "Probably every state and territory in the Union."

"Now they will turn all the grass upside down. They will plant and plow and plow. Who will eat all the food they make?"

Isabel thought of the thousands of new farmers all over Oklahoma Territory, building homes, planting crops, rearing families.

"I don't know, Lucius," she said. "It's all beyond me."

At last Lucius slapped the reins against the rumps of the horses and they resumed the journey home.

The next morning, Domot brought word that Montahahty had died during the night.

Isabel washed her best dress and made preparations to conduct another burial.

Three weeks before Christmas, Mo-keen stopped at the den and told Isabel that at least eighteen wagonloads of missionary barrels were waiting at the Anadarko depot.

Lucius and Isabel drove to Anadarko in his wagon.

Mo-keen had not exaggerated.

"If there's anyplace on God's green earth that hasn't sent you a barrel, I want to know it," said the station agent.

The bills of lading told the tale; every tribe and individual who had enjoyed a week of hospitality at the summer revival was now making certain the Saddle Mountain Kiowas would have a good Christmas.

Several barrels had arrived C.O.D. Sixteen dollars and forty cents was due.

"I don't understand this bill," Isabel told the station agent. "Captain A. H. Parker, a vice-president of this railroad, has told me you ship all church and missionary supplies gratis. He said it was railroad policy."

The station agent frowned. "Well, I don't know anything about that. The bills came with the freight."

Reluctantly Isabel parted with money from the church building fund, reasoning that if the clothing were not needed, it would serve as a bottomless supply of quilting material.

The next day she and Lucius recruited eight wagons and drivers. Two trips were required to haul all of the barrels and boxes to Saddle Mountain. For want of space, the donations were stacked high in the old Gospel tent.

Isabel, Sister Bare, and occasional Indian volunteers spent every spare moment for the next two weeks sizing and ticketing the donations. They were completing the task one afternoon when Lucius returned from Anadarko with the mail.

Isabel first opened the three letters from Miss Burdette. Although they offered the usual wealth of cheer and hope, none contained a single cent.

Next she read a brief note from Captain Parker. He had been informed of the mistaken billing by the Anadarko freight agent. He said he had ordered immediate restitution.

Isabel breathed a sigh of relief. The letter was a week old. The money no doubt was waiting at the Anadarko depot. If so, the church fund was back to eight hundred dollars and a few odd cents.

She then came to a letter from Colonel Randlett:

My Dear Miss Crawford:

I am just writing to tell you a pretty little story about a ride I took yesterday with the president and directors of the Rock Island Railway Company.

The vice-president, Mr. Parker, wired me that the train would pass here at 12:30 and invited me to join them on a trip to Lawton. I closed my desk and went with them—was just away three hours. On the way up from Lawton Mr. Parker kindly inquired about you and the prospects of your mission. I told him you were prospering in your labors, under trials and tribulations that were enormous, but that you were not disheartened. Those of the gentlemen who listened to Mr. Parker's praises of you and your young lady associate became much interested when he remarked that you ought to be helped with funds to enable you to commence the construction of your little church building.

This resulted in one of the party taking out a twenty-dollar bill and saying: "Here is a starter. Let us raise the two hundred dollars she needs."

One of the young gentlemen went out into the other car and in a few minutes returned with the cash in his hands and handed it to me to deliver to you. When he

counted it into my hand it was found to amount to $240.
A Mr. Cabel then pulled out a ten-dollar bill and made
it $250. By this time I began to feel my pig nature aroused
and said to myself: "I wish I could have told them she
needed $400 instead of $200, for I know those kind-hearted
fellows would have handed it out cheerfully."

As I was leaving the car Mr. Parker said: "Now tell
Miss Crawford that we raised the two hundred dollars to
go toward the completion of the church building but the
fifty dollars in excess she must keep and devote to com-
forts for herself and her assistant."

Now my happy story ends. What say to the Doxology?

With congratulations, I remain,

> James F. Randlett
> U.S. Indian Agent

For a moment Isabel could not speak. She waved the
letter in the air. Lucius, Sister Bare, and the Indians gathered around her.

"We have the money!" she managed to say. "Now we can
build the church!"

Lucius interpreted the news to the Indians. For a time all
was chaos. The Indians hugged each other, wept, danced,
prayed, and filled the old Gospel tent with their shouts.

When the excitement at last began to quiet down, Isabel
stepped onto the Gospel tent platform and spoke to them.
Lucius translated.

"This is bread upon the waters," she said. "You remember
that the revival seemed to be a total disaster for the church
fund. But if we had not invited everyone here, Commissioner
Jones would not have known about our church work and he
would not have spoken for us and saved our application for
church land. If Captain Parker hadn't visited us, this two
hundred fifty dollars wouldn't have been raised. God truly
works in mysterious ways."

That evening she summoned the mission circle Board to the
Gospel tent. Lucius built a council fire and they gathered
around it.

"We must plan carefully," she told them. "Always remember, this is *your* church. It is an Indian church. It belongs to
no one else. In time, I must go elsewhere. But you will live

here and worship in your church for the rest of your lives.. Your children and maybe your children's children will use it. You must decide *exactly* what kind of church you want. Will it be of brick, stone, or wood? Do you want to make it into an Indian church, with Indian symbols and decorations, or do you want a white man's church, full of white-man things? You must think hard about these questions."

"What do *you* want us to do?" Pope-bah asked.

Isabel shook her head. "You must make up your own minds."

"Something else must be decided," Isabel went on. "I had not intended to talk about it for a while. But all this has happened so fast. You now have many white neighbors. You have all met Mr. Russell, a very nice man. Your new church will be the only one near to serve dozens of white families. Not all will want to come to your church, but some will. You must think about inviting them into your church."

A chorus of dismay followed the translation.

"White people are dangerous," Heenkey signed. "They will come with rifles and pistols and act crazy."

"They will laugh at us," Pope-bah said. "All-the-time at Anadarko and Fort Sill the white people laugh at Indians. Remember how they came to the revival and laughed."

"We do not want white people here," said Kokom. "All we want is to have our own little place to talk to Jesus."

Isabel waited until Lucius translated all the protests.

"I'm not telling you what to do," she said again. "I only want you to think about this: You are Christians. You remember what Jesus said about loving your neighbor as yourself. The white people coming in here have their own difficulties. In many instances they will need help. It is your place as Christians to help them. Also, you remember that every Christian has an obligation to spread the Gospel. You must consider all of this very carefully."

The Indians seemed deeply disturbed over the prospect of an integrated church. Their voices rose in heated debate. The discussion lasted far into the night.

They could find no way around their Christian duty.

"Jesus said he will come back sometime to separate the sheep from the goats," Heenkey signed to Isabel. "Maybe we can start the work before he gets here."

Chapter Twenty-two

Isabel took her theme from the story of Saul who became Paul. She told how he had been a mighty warrior for Rome. She described his unrelenting ferocity in his persecution of early Christians and the way mere mention of his name struck fear among them. Then she read the biblical account of his blinding vision of Jesus on the road to Damascus, his instant conversion, and his subsequent life as an apostle.

Bright lanterns made the Gospel tent a comfortable island in the darkness of the night. The forty or more white homesteaders listened politely, waiting patiently through her pauses as Lucius translated into Kiowa. Occasionally the whites cast uneasy glances at the Indians, seated on the left side of the Gospel tent. The Indians remained quiet, subdued, their downcast gazes the only clue to their apprehension over the presence of the whites.

"Paul's experience has special meaning for us all," Isabel concluded. "Even after nineteen hundred years, his conversion is still one of the most dramatic in all Christendom. Before his vision on the road to Damascus, he was an unrelenting foe of Christ. But from that moment on, his faith never wavered. He became the voice of the early church, perhaps second only to Peter in influence. Paul probably was the most eloquent spokesman Jesus has ever had on this earth. As we tell and retell the story of Paul, how can we ever doubt the power of conversion?"

Isabel paused and spoke directly to the visiting whites. "Here at Saddle Mountain, we have conducted Bible studies for six years. For you who have just arrived, the Indians have graciously consented to offer testimony tonight. First our interpreter, Lucius Ben Aitsan, will speak in English. He then will introduce each Indian and translate their testimonies from Kiowa into English."

Isabel stepped off the platform. Lucius glanced at her uncertainly. His face was set and his breathing was short. But he retained his aura of calmness and dignity. Only anyone who knew him well would suspect that he felt ill-at-ease speaking his own words before whites.

After a few nervous movements of his mouth, he spoke:

"We Indians lived in darkness for many years. But the Great Father was kind and sent us the light. Tonight when you were coming here you were in the darkness till you saw the lanterns. Then you turned and followed until you got under this tent. We were the same way. We saw just a little light at first but we hunted and hunted and now we are in the light. That is why we call this church God's Light on the Mountain."

Isabel could not repress a smile.

Lucius was not the first preacher to fall back on his most successful sermon.

"We are all weak yet," he went on. "The devil beats us many times. But we try all we can to follow Jesus. I am not ashamed to stand before your faces to tell you that I am saved. You white people know much more than the Indians. You can read the Bible for yourselves. But some of you are in the darkness yet. I do not understand why."

Again he hesitated and glanced at Isabel. She gave him a slight nod of encouragement.

"I talk now to those who still stand in darkness. The Great Father sent the only son He ever had to die for you. Why don't you love Him and give Him your hearts? Jesus came to this world to seek poor sinners. He did not come for only Indians or only black men or white people. He did not come to look for skins. He came to look for your hearts and mine and everybody's. We will pray for you that the Holy Spirit may show you the way."

Isabel turned in her seat to gauge the reaction. Most of the whites were staring at Lucius. More than one jaw was slack.

Next Kokom rose and faced the congregation. He spoke in a rich baritone, his voice rising and falling in singsong Kiowa. He paused with each sentence to wait for translation.

"I am a Christian Indian but I don't know much. When this country was opened for settlement a lot of white people came in here. Some whites are Christians and some are very bad people. We don't know yet which are the good and which are the bad. We hope to know soon and then the Christian Indians and Christian white people must stand together and try very hard to find the poor sinners and bring them to Jesus to be saved.

"If you make fun of me tonight I am not ashamed. The Holy Spirit has told me to stand before your faces and make this talk. If you laugh I can't help it. But I will pray for you and ask Jesus to forgive you and give you new hearts."

The new convert Botallee followed. "I live on the other side of the mountain, a long ride from here. But before I was converted I came here many times to hear the Jesus talks. I heard something very new. Before I came here I never hunted for Jesus anywhere. Now I believe Jesus has changed my heart and the Holy Spirit has made me come here. I still walk many bad roads. One bad thing I like is gambling. Now I follow Jesus and I never go near where they have cards or dice. I believe Jesus will help me to cut off this bad road."

Long Horn rose and spoke. "I am an old man and I know all the old Indian religions. There is no power left in any of them anymore. The Jesus road has the power. It goes all the way through. Your souls are saved now and when you finish this life your body will drop off and be put into the grave. But your souls will go up to Jesus. He will put new flesh and new skins on them and then you will never die. Why the Great Spirit wants to do it this way I do not know. But I know it is so."

Other brief testimonies followed. Although the white visitors were complimentary afterward, Isabel was not certain of the full impact upon them until the following day.

Joseph Beatty, a Tennessean who had settled on a claim near the Washita, rode five miles out of his way to give Isabel and Sister Bare his reaction.

"I always thought all Indians were very ignorant. Last night I got my eyes opened. That talk by Lucius Ben Aitsan really surprised me. That fellow knows what he's talking about. The white people hereabouts don't understand that the Indians know a lot more than people think. And I'll tell you one thing: No white man is going to throw off on Indians while I'm around."

"I talked to a stonemason in Anadarko," Isabel informed the building committee. "He said that if we will take rock from the mountain, we can build a beautiful stone house for Jesus."

Queototi sprang to his feet and made angry signs. "You Jesus women have been walking the stone road on the sly. Now you want the Kiowas to walk on it. I will not walk on it with you."

"The stone road is only one of many in front of you now," Isabel signed back. "This will be your Jesus house. I will not tell you what road to walk."

Lucius intervened. "Why are you pushing for a stone Jesus house now? You never talked about it before."

"I'm not pushing *anything*," Isabel insisted. "It only occurred to me the other day to wonder. So I asked. Wood is not the only road. You could build the Jesus house of brick, except you have no brick. To build a wooden Jesus house, the lumber must be milled elsewhere and hauled here by the railroad. But stone—good, solid granite rock—is already here for the taking. I'm only asking that the committee look at the stone road and see if it is the right one. Maybe the Great Father put mountains of stone here for a purpose."

The committee burst into a flurry of talk.

Pope-bah put their misgivings into words. "For six years we think all-the-time of a white-man Jesus house made of wood. We see it in our sleep. Now you tell us to think of a stone Jesus house. We cannot do it."

"A stone Jesus house would last much longer," Sister Bare told them. "It would wear forever and never have to be painted."

"How much would it cost?" Lucius asked.

"Slightly less than for a wooden one," Isabel said. "The biggest expense would be for the stonemasons. Each stone must be chiseled to size. Construction would take longer. The only other major expense would be for the windows, doors, and flooring."

Pope-bah still could not visualize the finished product. "How will it look? Like a tipi?"

"I have brought some pictures," Isabel said. "The stonemason lent them to me."

Isabel passed the various magazines, books, and photographs among the Indians.

Some pictures were of large churches, others of small. "This is about what I had in mind," she said, holding up a photograph of a modest-size New England church.

The committee studied the picture at length.

"It is heaped-up pretty," Pope-bah agreed.

"Why the Jesus women walk the hide-road?" Queototi insisted. "Why we never see all this before?"

"I told you. I just thought of the possibility," Isabel told him through Lucius. "It is one more thing for you to think hard about before you decide."

The question was debated through most of the afternoon. At last a vote was taken.

Stone construction carried, eight to six.

Two days later Lucius came into the den long-faced. "Queototi, Heenkey, and some of the others are kicking," he said. "They do not want stone."

"The committee voted," Isabel said. "The minority will have to go along with the majority. That is the democratic way."

"That is not the Indian road. Those who lost will not help now. They will stand to one side and kick. That is the Indian road."

"Oh, for heaven's sake, Lucius, we can't have the Kiowas fighting and fussing among themselves like this. They should be pulling together."

"You pushed stone," Lucius pointed out. "The committee would not have voted for stone if you had not said it was best."

"Lucius, I told them it was *their* church. I left it for *them* to decide."

"How will the builders get the stone from the mountain."

"The man I talked with said they would dynamite the rock loose, cut it to size, and sled it down here with mules or oxen."

"Will the dynamite make a big hole in the mountain?"

"A little hole, I think."

Lucius stood for several minutes in silence. When he spoke, his lips were trembling with emotion. "Miss Crawford, I have never spoken against you since the day you came to the reservation. Now I do. I do not think we should build with stone."

"You're changing your vote?"

"I voted for stone only because you wanted it."

Isabel sighed in exasperation. "Lucius, you haven't been listening to me! None of you has. Call another meeting of the building committee. We'll thrash this out."

Again the Indians assembled in the Gospel tent. Isabel waited until all were seated.

"I am told that some of you voted for stone because you thought the missionaries wanted it. You let me and Sister Bare push you, and that is wrong. Jesus wants no bosses in his church. Lucius tells me he does not want to hurt the mountain by taking stone from it. The stonemasons would set off dynamite and make a scar on the face of the mountain for all time and for everyone to see. If we use wood, the trees cut down will grow back after a time. Maybe Lucius is right. Maybe that is the best road."

Queototi frantically made signs. "What? What? You push wood now? This is a new road."

"I only want you to do what I asked you to do from the first," Isabel signed back. "I have told you this over and over but clearly I cannot make you believe it: I will not be here among you forever. You are building the Jesus house. Look long at every road. Take up the right one."

One by one, the committee members said they liked the stone church, but they did not want to hurt the mountain.

Another vote was taken.

The vote for wood was unanimous.

Along with her books and magazines, Isabel had collected pictures and drawings of churches she admired. The Indians pored over the various possibilities for hours at a time. Isabel made sketches combining features they admired. Gradually a concept of the almost-here church took shape.

It would consist of two boxlike wings brought together at right angles. A small, square entry at the middle would be topped by a steeple and bell tower. Arched windows would contain depictions of biblical scenes in stained glass. A small cross would rise at the peak of the steeple.

Inside, pews in each wing would face the altar upon a raised platform at the center. The communion rail would be constructed among the edges of the platform. The design would place the entry and door not far from the altar, and close-by seating to the left and right. Sturdy chimneys in each wing would serve large stoves to make the building snug and warm in winter. Plenty of windows would provide more than adequate cross-ventilation during the hot summer months.

The completed sketch was approved by the building committee.

Then the search for a contractor began.

"It is the white road to ask around and find who is considered the best," Isabel explained to the Indians. "But everyone is new to this country. No one knows anyone. It would be easy for us to get fleeced. We must look for a good Christian builder and hope for the best."

It was Colonel Randlett who first suggested Charles C. Cooper. Isabel had asked the colonel for recommendations, and he promptly replied.

"A young widower, Mr. Cooper came to this country from Michigan in hopes of finding a fresh start. He was not lucky in the lottery. Since then he has turned to building. He put up a large store in Anadarko, and I have heard praises of his work. He has attended church services here regularly, and I have been impressed with his character. I do not believe you could do better."

On Isabel's invitation, Cooper came to Saddle Mountain and met with the building committee. He was a small man, light and agile, with dark hair and a profuse, curly moustache. His eyes were soft and thoughtful.

He studied Isabel's drawings at length. After making preliminary estimates on a small tablet carried in his shirt pocket, he nodded.

"Your design is good. It should make a sturdy structure. If I can locate two or three carpenters, I can do the work. My only difficulty would be in bringing the materials here from the lumberyard. I would have to hire that done."

"All of the Indians have wagons," Isabel said. "We can haul the lumber."

"Then we're in business. I can give you a list of the materials that will be required. I'm contracted for a building in Mountain View. By the time I'm done, you should be ready. I believe it will work out fine."

He spent the afternoon talking with the building committee, asking questions through Lucius. He was courteous with the Indians but not condescending.

As the afternoon progressed, Isabel noticed that his gaze followed Sister Bare everywhere she went. Isabel assumed that Sister Bare observed that fact. Her cheeks were tinged a high shade of pink.

"I believe we could have talked Mr. Cooper into doing the

work cheaper," Isabel said later to Sister Bare. "I gathered he liked the scenery around here. And I'm not talking about the mountains."

Sister Bare blushed crimson. "I don't know what you're talking about," she snapped.

Once the list of materials arrived, Lucius and Isabel drove through a steady downpour to the new town of Apache, twenty-five miles to the east. There they submitted a copy of the list to the lumberyard, asking that the bid be returned by mail.

But the Indians balked when Isabel proposed visiting other towns to request more bids.

"This is a heaped-up crazy road," Heenkey signed. "The other lumber chiefs will be mad at us. They will be mad at the lumber chief who sells us the lumber. It will be our fault when they are all mad."

"This is the white man's road," Isabel explained. "The different lumbermen will tell you what they will charge. Then you choose the one who sells you lumber the cheapest and best."

Pope-bah sided with Heenkey. "We would not be Christians if we make these men fight. This is a sly road."

"White men *expect* to sell lumber this way," Isabel insisted. "They will think *you* are crazy if you do it any other way."

Seven bids were received.

A lumberyard at Gotebo—the new railroad town named for a famous Kiowa war chief—was the winner.

Two weeks later, word came that the lumber had arrived.

Tonemoh was named hauling chief. Odlepaugh was appointed wake-'em-up-in-the-morning chief. He said he would be awake first because his heart was hitting so hard he could not sleep and he just kept turning over and over all night long.

Each day for a week the wagons set out before dawn on the fifty-mile round trip to Gotebo and returned late at night. The lumber was unloaded and stacked by lanternlight.

Men, women, and children worked together. The Ghost Dancers and the cactus people also came to help.

A steady rain, mud, and deep water at every crossing failed to halt the hauling.

"The devil is trying to beat us," Heenkey signed. "He cannot do it."

Seventy-nine wagonloads were required. Sister Bare calculated that the wagons traveled a total of four thousand miles in transporting the lumber.

The Indians finished the job exhausted but jubilant.

"My back is all busted," Kokom signed after making his last trip.

"I am all busted." said Heenkey.

Akometo and Doymah were delayed on their last trip by the birth of a baby girl.

"She is very smart," said the father. "She got here in time to help with the hauling."

Lucius said her cries sounded like a church bell.

So the new addition to the tribe was named Church Bell Akometo.

In early November Cooper arrived with two helpers to start work on the foundation of the church.

On the following Sunday, the congregation assembled for the laying of the cornerstone. The piles of lumber served as bleachers. Indians were perched everywhere.

Isabel opened the ceremony with a prayer.

Resplendent in a new dark suit, Lucius unfolded his carefully prepared history of the church and began to read:

"On April 12, 1896, Miss Isabel Crawford came to the reservation and her mission work began on this spot. She built the first arbor here for Jesus.

"On November 16, 1897, the Gospel tent was set up.

"On May 10, 1898, Daw-kee-boom-gee-k'oop was organized as a missionary circle.

"On July 19, 1898, the first money was given to Jesus, $17.20 toward sending the Gospel to another tribe, and $17.34 toward the church building fund.

"On October 4, 1898, one hundred sixty acres of land were promised to Jesus by the Kiowa Council.

"For five days beginning June 28, 1900, the first revival was conducted at Saddle Mountain.

"On May 12, 1901, the land for Jesus was selected.

"On August 6, 1901, the reservation was opened for settlement.

"Today, November 9, 1902, the cornerstone of the church building will be laid."

Lucius stepped aside as the Indians formed a line to drop mementos into a tin box. Mabel put in a small Bible. Lucius dropped in a list of everyone who had contributed to the church. Heenkey added a Sunday school card depicting small children giving money to Jesus. Beads, coins, blocks of patchwork, photographs, and other treasures were included.

The box was closed and placed in the recess prepared for it. With trowel and mortar the contractor completed the cornerstone.

The Kiowas knelt on grass and lumber. Lucius raised his voice in prayer:

"We thank you today, Jesus, because you have been kind and helped us get started on this, our church. We want You to forgive the mistakes we have made, pass them back behind You, and help us to get stronger so all of us will see the light of our church get brighter and brighter. Keep Your eye on our names so the devil will not scratch any of them out. I have spoken. Amen."

The church rose with amazing speed. Each day a crowd of Indians gathered to watch. First the carpenters raised the frame, high as the tallest trees. They then shingled the roof and completed the siding.

The steeple soared above the open bell tower. Carefully, the stained-glass windows were put into place. Made by a firm in Illinois, they dramatized stories from the Bible. Above the doorway, an arched stained-glass window depicted Christ on the cross. Colored glass spelled out the words:

HE DIED FOR US.

Two coatings of white paint completed the exterior. Inside, the carpenters installed rich mahogany paneling. Cooper himself built a handsome pulpit.

"I would feel more comfortable if we had waited until we convinced the Indians and obtained a pastor before erecting the pulpit," Isabel confided to Sister Bare. "But Mr. Cooper was so enthusiastic about it, I could not very well refuse."

Cooper also spent an evening at his makeshift forge, hammering a wrought-iron cross. The result was quite artistic. It was raised into place at the top of the steeple.

Isabel closely watched every step of the construction. Sister Bare kept the men supplied with cool water, refreshments, and a parade of delicacies from the stove.

Captain Parker sent a brass locomotive bell for the belfry. The Chicago Home Mission sent a clock.

At last the work was completed. Firmly planted on high

ground at the foot of Saddle Mountain, the white church was visible for miles.

Isabel doubted that a church more beautiful stood anywhere in the entire territory.

"We must have a grand dedication," said Sister Bare.

"No. We've imposed on others enough," Isabel said. "Let's wait until everything is ready. Then we'll have a nice, quiet ceremony."

Work began on the mission house on the day the contractors completed the church.

A two-story framework was erected over the den, destined to become the new dining room and kitchen. In keeping with Isabel's design, the house blossomed into a large, saltbox clapboard lent elegance by a modified mansard roof, a full-length first-floor gallery, and a widow's walk fronting the second floor. A dormier at the end of the upstairs hall granted access to the widow's walk.

As the mission house approached completion, the roof of the den was removed, and Isabel and Sister Bare could look straight up into a second-floor bedroom where Mr. Cooper and his carpenters were at work.

When time came, they found it easier to hand their furniture and personal effects up through the hole and into the new house.

"If anyone ever moved in a crazier way, I've never heard of it," said Sister Bare. "I don't think I've seen anything done in normal fashion since I came here."

Isabel and Sister Bare were arranging furniture in the new house one afternoon when the front door burst open and in came Captain and Mrs. Parker, Miss Burdette, and Dr. and Mrs. Murrow.

"Surprise! Surprise!" said Miss Burdette. "We've come for the dedication!"

It was a surprise indeed.

Isabel had nothing to serve them, and nowhere to put them.

Captain Parker was amused by her consternation. "We were informed that the house is not yet completed," he said. "So we brought tents with us."

As if in a dream, Isabel escorted her guests through the newly completed church.

Compliments and praise fell like spring rain.

The men examined the exquisite carpentry of the interior

paneling and expressed their amazement that the church had
been built for anything less than twenty-five hundred dollars.

As news of the visitors circulated throughout the Saddle
Mountain community, the Indians hurried to the mission
house to welcome them.

The Chicago women hugged Pope-bah, Ananthy, Hattie,
and Mabel as if greeting long-lost friends.

Lucius could not have been more graciously received by
the men if he had been the president of a railroad.

"On Sunday we will dedicate the church," Isabel told the
Kiowas through Lucius. "Dr. Murrow has consented to serve
as presiding officer."

It was Pope-bah who best expressed the mood of the day.

"I am crazy with happy," she signed.

The church was packed. Indians and whites came from throughout the former reservation. Unfortunately, the pews had not
yet arrived. Planks were arranged across nail kegs for the
honored guests. Scores of Indians sat on the floor. Others
stood along the walls, in the entryway, outside the open
windows.

The ceremony began as Brother Clouse presented formal
papers dismissing the sixty-four Saddle Mountain members
from his own church so that they could form the new
congregation.

Lucius accepted the membership roll in the name of God's
Light on the Mountain.

Next the mission circle was dissolved so that the new
church organization could rise from the ashes.

President Pope-bah wept openly as she rapped her gavel
and declared all mission circle business ended.

At last Dr. Murrow rose to conduct the ordination of the
church.

As church secretary, Lucius had been thoroughly drilled
on the procedure. He in turn had coached the Indians.

"Is it your desire to give this house to God?" asked Dr.
Murrow.

"Yes, sir," Lucius answered, with stress upon the "sir."

"Is there any debt on this building?"

"No, sir!"

Brother Clouse read the Articles of Faith. Miss Burdette
offered a dedicatory prayer.

Lucius then read the names of those nominated for church

office. Sister Bare had been chosen as clerk and treasurer, and Lucius as secretary. Candidates for the Board of Deacons were Lucius, Gahbein, Akometo, Tonemoh, and Spotted Horse.

"I trust you have prayed earnestly and selected men full of love for Jesus," said Dr. Murrow. "Are you ready to vote?"

Kokom solemnly rose and spoke. He bobbled his English words only slightly. "I am first motion."

"I am second motion," said Mon-cha-cha.

"All in favor say aye."

The response was almost deafening.

"All opposed, nay."

Dr. Murrow smiled in the silence.

"Then I declare God's Light on the Mountain Baptist Church open for worship."

Dr. Murrow quoted from the Book of Matthew concerning the dialogue between Jesus and the apostle Simon Peter.

" 'Whom say ye that I am?'

" 'Thou art the Christ, the Son of the Living God.'

" 'And I say also unto thee, That thou art Peter, and upon this rock I will build my church; and the gates of hell shall not prevail against it.' "

"Today we have sanctified this building as a portion of Christ's earthly church," Dr. Murrow solemnly warned the Indians. "You must keep it holy. Christ told us, Where two or three are gathered together in my name, there am I in the midst of them."

Never in her entire, churchgoing life had Isabel seen a congregation more attentive. Lucius frowned in concentration as he battled to convey Dr. Murrow's every word accurately.

"You must always remember that Christ is here with you in this church," Dr. Murrow continued. "Although it was built by men and women with great effort, these beams, these girders, these walls contain far more than our pitiful contributions. They contain the spirit and blessings of Christ. It is forever a holy place. That we must never forget."

After a brief prayer, Dr. Murrow conducted the first "Jesus eat" at God's Light on the Mountain.

Isabel fought in vain to hold back tears as the Indians filed to the rail to receive Holy Communion.

Almost from the first day she came to the reservation they had asked, "When can we have the Jesus eat?"

Almost seven years of hard work had gone into the moment. Just before the benediction, Dr. Murrow offered his own surprise. "I am pleased to announce that Brother Hamilton, the circuit rider from Lawton, has offered to visit God's Light on the Mountain once each month to conduct services. He can continue in this capacity until a permanent pastor can be found for this church."

The translation was followed by an intake of breath, a murmur of astonishment from the congregation.

Lucius stared at Isabel like a man stricken.

Isabel felt a moment of self-chastisement.

She had known, in the back of her mind, that this day would arrive. Yet she had kept shoving the obstacle aside, hoping that in time a solution could be found.

Now she could not escape the truth: She should have prepared the Indians for the fact that the Baptist Convention would expect them to accept a white pastor.

"Why is a Jesus man coming here to talk in our Jesus house?" Pope-bah asked in signs. "You are our Jesus house chief. Why is a man coming here?"

Isabel studied the earnest faces gathered around her. The Chicago guests had walked on ahead to the dinner tables set up in the Gospel tent. They were glancing back, curious about the cause of the commotion.

Isabel sought a simple explanation. She motioned for Lucius to translate her words.

"All of you know that I cannot do the work of a Jesus man. This is nothing new. I have told you this over and over."

Lucius suddenly seemed to find both languages difficult. The Indians were not satisfied with his translation. Kiowa words flew back and forth. Lucius held up his hands for silence.

He spoke to Isabel in English. "We thought you would keep on with your Jesus talks in the church. That was why we built it. You promised us this would be an Indian church forever."

"I promised no white man would be sent here as pastor until the Indians asked for him. I still stand by that. Every Baptist church in the world *calls* its pastor into the pulpit. The Baptist Convention can't force you to take anyone you don't want. But you yourself have said that Jesus pays no attention to skins. And I've never wavered in my belief that whites and Indians should work together. Now the church is built. The time has come for the Indians to think hard about seeking a white pastor."

Lucius spoke in a voice heavy with emotion. "We want *you*. We are not ready for all this."

"Lucius, you *are* ready. You and the other Kiowas are landholders, citizens, franchised to vote. The reservation is gone like long-time-ago snows. Saddle Mountain is now a *community* made up of whites and Indians. Soon we will have our own post office. The Jesus talks have been the most precious part of my life. But now we must all go on to these other things."

Lucius shook his head stubbornly. "We will call you as our pastor."

"Lucius, I've told you over and over. A Jesus woman *can't* be a pastor. It must be a *man*—an ordained minister."

Lines of anger creased Lucius's forehead. "But *you* built this church! If you had not come to us, we would have nothing here!"

"You mustn't think that. Not ever! You Indians did the work. I was only God's instrument."

Lucius glanced toward the visitors. "The Indians will not vote for a white pastor. This I know. They want you to keep on with your Jesus talks."

Isabel followed his gaze to the dinner tables, the waiting guests. "Lucius, nothing will be done immediately. We'll have plenty of time to talk about it. Right now we have guests. We mustn't ignore them."

She walked up the slope to the tables. Behind her, Lucius attempted to translate what had been said.

"What's wrong?" asked Miss Burdette, watching the Indians.

The other guests also were politely awaiting an explanation. Isabel could think of no recourse other than the truth.

"I'm afraid it has just dawned on all of us that with the completion of the church, we will need a pastor. Somehow the Indians thought I would just go on forever with my Jesus talks."

Dr. Murrow tugged at his beard. "It's my fault. I shouldn't have made the announcement about Brother Hamilton. I should have left it for you to do later."

"No, the fault is mine," Isabel said. "I should have prepared them for what is coming."

"Why do they object so to a white pastor?" asked Miss Burdette. "They would still have Lucius for translation."

Again Isabel could think of no alternative to the truth. "The Indians have a deep animosity toward all white men, and with considerable justification, I might add. They have been lied to, cheated, harassed for decades. Many white pastors have developed the habit of shouting when they preach. This upsets the Indians, for they think the pastors are angry at them, or even angry at God. Most white pastors tend to lecture them, to call them great sinners. The Indians are very sensitive to personal remarks. They resent them deeply."

"I once made those same mistakes," Dr. Murrow admitted.

Isabel nodded. "Dr. Murrow is one of the very, very few white men who have won their confidence. They have known only a handful who have had the Indians' best interests at heart. They talk about them often. Lieutenant Hugh Scott, the first military man here, could have been another Chivington or Custer and made a name for himself by killing Indians. But he treated them decently and hounded Washington until Carlisle and the other Indian schools were founded. The Indians talk of him with great reverence. The Quaker agents Lawrie Tatum and Thomas Battey were brave men, and won the lasting respect of the Indians. Colonel Frank Baldwin, the agent who was here when I came, was another. I understand he was awarded the highest decorations possible during the war, so he had nothing to prove here on the frontier. He treated the Indians fairly and criticized Washington severely when the rations were delayed until Indians starved. When he was replaced for his insubordination, the Indians were sad to see him go. Now they have learned to trust Colonel Randlett. But I'm afraid that's the sum of it—only a handful of men who have treated them honorably in their four decades of dealing with the whites."

"It took me ten years to win their confidence," said Dr. Murrow.

"I had it much easier," Isabel said. "The sisters at the Rainy Mountain and Anadarko missions showed the Indians that white women are of a gentler nature than the men. I only followed their example."

"Your modesty becomes you," said Miss Burdette. "We all

know what you have accomplished here. And I can't see why you shouldn't continue with your Jesus talks for a while. The Indians have come so very far in such a short time. Perhaps they need a period of transition."

"They haven't traveled alone," Isabel said. "It seems only yesterday that I thought of them as savages."

In the afternoon, U.S. Indian Agent James F. Randlett spoke from the pulpit. "Today I regret I am not a preacher instead of an agent. I would rather be an honest, sincere preacher who has led a single one of you onto the Jesus road to stay, than to have all the glory that has come to me as a soldier and as an Indian agent."

He paused while Lucius translated.

"You may lose your faith in Indian agents," the colonel went on. "You may even lose your faith in preachers. But you must hold tight to your faith in God and never let go.

"I'm glad your missionaries have taught you that it is a part of Christian life to work. I have seen Indians of many tribes, but never any who built for themselves such a church as this."

Isabel sat listening to Lucius translate, wondering what would become of him. Together with his family, he now held eleven hundred twenty acres of choice land, enough for seven large farms. But she suspected that he was unlikely to find satisfaction as a farmer.

Statehood was bound to come soon to the territory.

Perhaps someday Lucius would represent both whites and Indians in Washington.

"Responsible American citizens, such as you have become, no longer need an Indian agent to serve them," said Colonel Randlett. "The Kiowa-Comanche-Apache Reservation is gone. My job here is done. I may not meet with you again in this world, but I hope someday to see you in the beautiful home where we shall know one another better than we have here. And I promise you this: I shall certainly remember this day to the close of my life."

Next, Captain Parker presented his gift of a large American flag. He then turned to the congregation.

"Some years ago I saw this magnificent valley and mountain for the first time. But I did not know much about the people. Later I heard that you wanted to build a church. I was privileged to help a little. Today I have seen its dedication. You have worked hard, but you will be the better for it."

After translation by Lucius, he pointed to the flag.

"I have brought to your church the flag of our country and yours. The government in Washington the flag represents wishes its Indian children well. The universe is ruled by laws. Through obeying the laws of the Great Spirit, you become strong in body and strong in soul and honor your flag, your country, and your God. When you see this flag, think on these things."

Isabel glanced covertly at the Indians, wondering if they shared her thoughts. The Stars and Stripes so graciously presented by Captain Parker also had flown over the troops who had harassed them in a long series of bloody battles on the High Plains, trapped them in Palo Duro Canyon, and shot all their horses.

Most of the adult Indians now listening to Captain Parker had been there.

It was the flag whose laws had put them into a stone corral and sent their chiefs to prisons in Florida and Texas. Every adult in the congregation had known the shame of seeing his beloved chiefs humiliated. Big Tree, now seated in front of the altar, had been among them. The others were all dead.

It was the same flag that had betrayed a promise and delayed Indian rations week after week until the old and the young starved.

The Indians sat quietly through Captain Parker's well-meaning but thoughtless lecture on the flag. If they saw irony, they were too polite to offer the slightest indication.

After a brief prayer, the afternoon service ended. The congregation walked upstream to the natural baptistery at the foot of the mountain. There six new converts were baptized by Dr. Murrow.

That evening, after another stirring sermon, Dr. Murrow asked the new church deacons to come forward.

Lucius, Gahbein, Akometo, Tonemoh, and Spotted Horse stood before the pulpit.

With his broad right palm, Dr. Murrow seized Lucius by the forehead. "And now, through the laying-on of hands, I do hereby ordain Lucius Ben Aitsan a deacon of this church through God's holy word."

One by one, Dr. Murrow ordained Gahbein, Akometo, Tonemoh, and Spotted Horse as deacons of the new church.

Isabel could not hold back her tears of joy.

In that moment, all of the struggles and disappointments of the past seven years dwindled into insignificance.

The next morning Isabel found a delegation of new deacons waiting on the gallery of the mission house. She was not surprised, but she regretted to see that Lucius was not among them. She was sure the delicate nature of the discussion would be beyond sign language.

Gahbein had been selected as spokesman.

"We are only poor Indians," he signed. "There is much we do not know. We want you to stay here as chief of our church. Now we are told that only a man can be a chief, not a woman. Why? Why? Why?"

Isabel answered the best she could.

"The chiefs who sit at the big Baptist council are men. They say that speaking the word of God is work for a man. They say women have other work. The Baptist chiefs did not send me here. The women in Chicago sent me. The Baptist chiefs told me I could stay here until we made a Jesus house. Now they say only a Jesus man can be chief. That is the Baptist road."

"We do not want to walk this road," Spotted Horse signed. "We Indians made this Jesus house. The big Baptist council did not make it."

The other deacons signed agreement.

Isabel tried again. "All-the-time when we went to Anadarko for the beef rations, the men killed the cattle. The women skinned the hides and cut the meat. The men drove the wagons. The women loaded the meat. No man did woman's work. No woman did man's work. This is the same. Men speak the word of the Great Father. Women do other work. Why, I do not know. In the long-ago time this road was made for us to walk. If you remember, I told you this in my first Jesus talk seven years ago. It is the same today."

The other deacons looked at Gahbein, encouraging him to speak.

Gahbein began to sign, relaying the message they had come to convey.

"If the Baptist council wants a man as pastor, we want that man to be Lucius."

Again the other deacons gestured their agreement.

"Lucius is not a Jesus man," Isabel replied.

Gahbein persisted. "He walks the Jesus road. He is heaped-up smart."

Isabel hesitated, seeking a way to explain. "Before a man becomes a Jesus man, he walks a long, hard road. The Great Father calls him to walk that road. You remember that in our Jesus talks I told you that the Great Father called Samuel four times before he heard. If the Great Father wants Lucius to walk the Jesus-man road, the Great Father will call him and keep on calling him. That is the road for a Jesus man."

The deacons looked at each other.

"Lucius is a good man," Gahbein signed. "The Great Father can hunt all over. He will not find a man half as good."

"I know that. There is not a better man on the face of the earth. But only the Great Father can call him. We cannot make Lucius a Jesus man, no matter how much we want it to happen."

Wearing troubled faces, the Indians walked away.

Sister Bare was still upstairs in her room, writing letters. Not wishing to disturb her, Isabel walked over to the church, amused by her inclination to keep visiting it to confirm that it was really there—the reality that had replaced the dream.

For once, the sanctuary was deserted. She walked behind the pulpit, savoring the richer, warmer tones of the church interior in daylight. The rays of the sun fell through the stained-glass windows, casting colorful patterns on the floor. The deep silence seemed receptive and holy.

Kneeling beneath the cross, Isabel prayed.

"Dear Lord, surely You know that Gahbein is right. You could do far worse than to call Lucius Ben Aitsan into Your ministry."

Chapter Twenty-three

In the wake of the opening, the landscape around Saddle Mountain changed rapidly. Where cattle trails and wagon tracks once crossed open prairie, graded roads suddenly appeared, hastily fenced and ditched. Crude and often illiterate signs went up at every crossroads, pointing the way to towns still under construction. Forty miles to the west, near a new railroad stop called Granite, a homesteader digging a water well struck oil. A plume was erected to burn deadly fumes spewing from the ground. At night the resulting flare could be seen from as far away as Saddle Mountain. The Rock Island Railway Company arranged special excursion cars to convey visitors to see the sight at closer range.

Thrown up within days, most of the buildings in towns throughout the territory remained unpainted, lending them an unfinished aspect. A few boom towns already had become ghost towns. In some instances, the railroad had gone in a contrary direction. A rambunctious mining town collapsed when no market was found for the low-grade ore. After torrential rains, a town named Frazer belatedly discovered that it had been built on a flood plain. The entire populace packed up and moved to higher ground and the city was renamed Altus, apparently in hope the rain god knew Latin.

After completion of God's Light on the Mountain church and mission house, the contractor, Charles C. Cooper, began work on a complete block of structures in a new town fifty miles to the north. He wrote to Sister Bare several times, but Isabel did not know if the correspondence was continuing. She no longer had first crack at the mail.

The application of Saddle Mountain for a post office had been approved, with Sister Bare as postmistress. A downstairs portion of the mission was set aside to receive postal patrons. Once each weekday a mail hack stopped briefly on its circuitous route, leaving the incoming mail, picking up the outgoing.

In making her required "visitations" to Indian families on the former reservation, Isabel saw many changes.

A few of the Indians were beginning to understand that they indeed were "relatively wealthy by white standards"—as they had been told so many times. Every Kiowa, from infant to the most elderly, now owned a 160-acre tract. Most families held titles to six or eight of these "quarter sections"—far more land than even the most industrious could farm. So the Indians became landlords, leasing land to those "unlucky" homesteaders who were not averse to serving as tenant farmers.

Lucius kept his "home place" and the "quarter" allocated to Amos. The land owned by Mabel, Jessie, Leslie, and Richard was leased to tenant farmers.

After discussion among the congregation and a vote of approval, the eighty-acre tract of church land near the graveyard was leased to a white homesteader. The eighty acres upon which the church and mission house stood were covered with boulders and gravel and so were not suitable for leasing.

In addition, the Indians still owned the Big Pasture, a half million acres of grassland along the Red River under lease to Texas cattlemen. Its value grew every day. The distribution of grass money, once little more than a token payment, now financed buggies, fine horses, carpets, and furniture. Slowly the Indians were growing more comfortable with their houses. Isabel and Sister Bare no longer were asked to "fix" them. Some of the Kiowas acquired water wells, fences, work mules, wheeled cultivators, and four-horse plows.

Other Indians were less successful. Inept tenants and indifferent landlords often combined with disastrous results. With the expectation of shares from several farms, many Indians abandoned farming. Others gambled away their money or were fleeced by white sharpers.

Land-rich, many Indians continued to live in poverty.

Yet the poorest Indian often lived in better circumstances than many white families Isabel saw on her visitations. She was appalled by the hovels some homesteaders erected for their families. Sod houses were everywhere—stacked blocks of earth for walls, thin planks, and more sod for a roof. Most "soddies" were windowless, airless horrors. But they were palaces compared with the pervasive dugout. For a dugout, the homesteader scratched a hole in the ground, erected over it a flimsy framework of any material at hand, then covered all with dirt, leaving only a single opening.

Near Cut Throat Gap, Isabel counted fourteen people living in the squalor of a single ten- by twelve-foot dugout. Children, dogs, chickens, pigs, even goats clambered over the filth. Washtubs, buckets, crockery, boxes, and assorted trash littered the landscape.

"The celebrated opening has come and gone," Sister Bare observed. "But it's plain that civilization hasn't hit the country yet."

When Isabel learned that Domot was seriously ill, she immediately summoned Lucius and they drove over for a visit. Domot's number-one wife said he had remained in bed four days but had been sitting up since. She complained that he had quit eating and would do nothing all day long but sit.

"I am tired of this world," Domot said through Lucius. "I think it is time for me to go look at the other one. Most of the people I know are there. I will not be as alone in that world as I am in this one."

Isabel scolded him. "You are not so old you should want to go under. Look at Taboodle. He told me he was a warrior before you were born. He still does much work every day. You have many years ahead of you yet."

Domot remained silent for a time, as if assembling his thoughts. "A little time ago, I tried to go over to Guipago's house the way I have always gone. Now they have put up fences there and I could not get through. Everywhere I want to go is fenced off. We can go from one place to another only between fences, like the chutes we use to move cattle from one corral to another. Who wants to live in a world like this?"

"You can go from anyplace to anyplace, and you can use the good, level roads that the whites have made," Isabel told him. "They are fenced only because the land on each side is now private property. You can go where you want much quicker because of the good roads. You should be thankful for them."

Domot made the "no" sign. "You cannot leave the road and climb a hill to look around. You cannot go to the springs where you have always watered your horses. You cannot go into the river bottoms to pick plums when they are ripe. You cannot go to the trees where you have always found good pecans. White men say they own all this. How can a human being own a tree? He did not plant it. He did not make it grow. He did not tell it to make pecans. It will be alive and growing when he is dead. How can he own it and tell other human beings they cannot pick up the pecans that fall from it? This world has changed. I do not want to live in it anymore."

Two weeks later Domot could not be aroused when wife number two took his breakfast to him. Apparently he had died in his sleep during the night.

Isabel insisted that his funeral be conducted from the church and overrode Sister Bare's objections that Domot was not a member, or even a Christian.

"He fought for this church from the beginning," Isabel said. "No one worked harder for it. And he did not want it for himself. He wanted it for others. That in itself is a Christian thing."

"He was not saved," Sister Bare said.

"I'm not so sure. For a long time I thought the only way to salvation was through strict Baptist orthodoxy. Now I think that may be only one road. My eyes have been opened by the Kiowas. I'm now convinced we whites destroyed a precious thing—a spiritual way of life, a long-standing relationship between these people and God. We have replaced it with something I believe to be better. But I am not as sure of everything as I once was."

Sister Bare made the Indian sign of closing her ears. "The women in Chicago would die of apoplexy if they heard you talk that way."

"I have never hidden my views under a bushel," Isabel said. "I don't intend to start now."

After the funeral, Heenkey announced that he was taking his brother Domot's wives into his own home, in keeping with Kiowa tradition.

"You cannot live with them as man and wives and expect to remain a Christian," Isabel warned him.

Heenkey protested that the women were like sisters to him.

But in the weeks that followed, Heenkey's actions set off a full-fledged scandal.

Paudlekeah recently had become a widower. He let it be known that he looked upon Domot's widow number two with favor and publicly suggested that Heenkey's largess was not as unselfish as he implied.

Both Paudlekeah and Heenkey quit coming to church.

After Heenkey's third absence, Isabel began to assume the worst. She summoned Lucius and drove over to visit Heenkey. Lucius did not want to go, pointing out that Heenkey was his brother-in-law. But Isabel promised that she only wanted him to translate, that he would not be speaking his own words.

"I know you are fighting temptation," she told Heenkey through Lucius. "You need all the help you can get. Don't stay away from the church. We built the church to help each other when the devil tries to make us do wrong."

Heenkey resumed coming to church, but he would not meet Isabel's gaze. She did not intervene further. It was something he would have to work out for himself.

One evening Lucius came to the mission house. "Mabel and I have talked long and hard with Heenkey. He told Mabel the woman now thinks she wants to go and live with Paudlekeah. Heenkey says he will let her go."

The next Sunday morning, Isabel was gratified to see both Heenkey and Paudlekeah among the congregation. She spoke on the Sermon on the Mount. Afterward, she asked for testimonials.

Heenkey spoke first. "You all know that when my brother Domot died, I took his wives into my home. I told myself they were like sisters, but that was not true. The devil made me tell myself that lie. Before long another man wanted to marry one of Domot's wives, and I told him to cut off his thoughts. We had many hot words. Then my sister Mabel came to see me and gave me a wise talk. I did not want to listen to her at first, and I said some bad things. But I love my sister and I am glad she came to see me. She is the one who took away all my bad feelings. I want to tell all you Christians about it. Today I throw away all my bad feelings and I forgive my sister. Now I am thinking right, and I want all of you to be kind to me."

Paudlekeah lumbered to his feet, drawing a huge revolver from beneath his coat. "I have been carrying this pistol with me a long time, expecting trouble," he said. "Heenkey has been giving bad talk about me, and I did not like it. Now it is all over and Jesus has done it. I am very glad. I do not need this pistol now. I will give it to Jesus."

Making his way to the aisle, Paudlekeah solemnly brought the gun to the pulpit and laid it upon the altar.

"Is that thing loaded?" Isabel asked through Lucius.

Paudlekeah nodded that it was.

"Lucius, do something with it," Isabel said.

Lucius came to her side, took the pistol, pointed it at the ceiling, and emptied the cylinder of cartridges. He pocketed them and returned the pistol to the altar.

Isabel led the congregation in the Lord's Prayer and dismissed services.

Afterward, Sister Bare could not stop laughing over the incident. "Did you see Heenkey when Paudlekeah pulled out his big horse pistol? That was the first time I've ever seen an Indian turn into a paleface."

"We have talked and talked, and we all agree," said Lucius. "We do not want a white Jesus man here—not ever."

The deacons sat on the front pew, the congregation arrayed behind them. Isabel stood near the pulpit, beside Lucius. "That is your decision to make," she said. "But I can assure you it will not set well with the Baptist chiefs."

Gahbein stood and responded. "We have your Jesus talks. Now we can have our Jesus eats. We do not need to ask anything from the Baptist chiefs."

As Isabel walked behind the pulpit, she changed en route the theme for her morning Jesus talk.

She had intended to speak on Easter and the Resurrection. But plainly the "Jesus eat" was uppermost in the minds of her congregation. She stood for a moment, gripping the pulpit, gathering her thoughts.

"I want you all to understand this," Isabel began. "Nothing concerning Christianity is more holy than the Jesus eat. It is the fundamental instrument of our worship."

Lucius halted in his translation. "I do not know how to say 'fundamental'."

"Basic. Bedrock. The deepest part of our soul." She made the signs for "deep" and "soul."

Lucius nodded and resumed his translation.

"It is a simple service," she went on. "So simple that any church can observe it, rich or poor, large or small. Jesus wanted to give His children some easy things to do in remembrance of Him. His gospel, life, everything about Him was plain and simple and full of heart. The Jesus eat is the same."

She waited for Lucius to catch up.

"On the night before His crucifixion, Jesus gathered with the apostles for His last supper on earth. After He had eaten, He leaned over, picked up a piece of bread, and breaking it, said, 'This is my body broken for you; eat it and remember me.' The apostles did not understand, but they did what He told them. Then He poured a cup of red grape juice saying, 'This is my blood shed for you.' They did not understand yet, but they drank it and wondered. Then He said, 'Do this often for my sake.'"

As she waited for the translation, Isabel studied the faces of her congregation. Never in any white church had she ever seen such total enrapture.

She resumed her talk. "After Jesus was crucified, the apostles thought quick and understood what He had said at the Last Supper, and they told everyone. Ever since, all over the world, big churches and little churches, with pastors and without pastors, have observed this ceremony that Jesus gave to us, not because the members love one another so much but because they love Jesus more and want to obey His exact commands."

Again waiting, Isabel closed her eyes and searched for the proper words to convey her meaning.

"When your deacons were ordained by Dr. Murrow with the laying-on-of-hands ceremony, it was to empower them to conduct this office. But I must tell you this," she warned. "In the Baptist church, the Jesus eat is almost always served by a Jesus man. The rules are clear. The church deacons may serve the Jesus eat *only* if a Jesus man is not available."

"Are you telling us we must ask a Jesus man to come here?" Heenkey asked.

"That is for you to decide," Isabel replied. "You say you want an Indian church here. There is nothing wrong with that. Black people have black churches. Chinese Christians have Chinese churches. But as Lucius has said better than I, 'Jesus did not come to earth looking for skins.' I must tell you this: There will be much kicking if you keep Jesus men out of this church only because they are white. But I tell you this: No one can say this church is acting on the sly if it *asks* either Brother Hamilton from Lawton or Brother Clouse from Rainy Mountain to come here once each month. They are busy men, and they have other churches. If they do not come here, then the church deacons can go ahead with the Jesus eat."

An argument erupted in Kiowa among the deacons. The debate was long and heated. Odlepaugh, Tonemoh, Lucius, and Kokom did most of the talking.

At last Lucius revealed the result. "We do not want to do it. But we do not want to walk the sly road. We have voted to ask either Brother Hamilton or Brother Clouse to come here once a month for our Jesus eat."

Heenkey added something, and Lucius translated for him. "We hope they do not come."

Isabel's gaze met Sister Bare's. They could not suppress mutual smiles of amusement.

Before the service, Sister Bare had said exactly the same thing.

"I think I can be there," Brother Clouse said. "I will try. We are having a ministerial conference in Guthrie on the eleventh. But I believe I will be back by then."

"I hope so," Isabel said. "We would prefer that you come. But we plan to start communion on a regular basis. If you cannot come, the church plans to go ahead and serve the host."

Clouse stopped in his tracks. His ruddy face turned a shade redder. "You don't mean that!"

His remark took her by surprise. She answered without thinking. "Of course. It is my understanding that Holy Communion is a *church* ordinance."

"But a minister's *office!*" Clouse said emphatically. Little blobs of spittle escaped his mouth and fell through the sunlit air in a silvery shower.

Clouse was walking her from his parsonage to the surrey, where Lucius waited. Isabel had passed the time of day with the Clouses while Lucius visited his children at the Rainy Mountain school. Now they would have to hurry to reach home before dark.

Isabel was sure of her ground. She had been steeped in church work and policies almost from birth. Her father would not have led her astray on this important point.

She met Clouse's furious gaze. "A minister should be present," she conceded. "But if one is not, the deacons may officiate at the table."

"Not according to any church doctrine I've ever heard!"

Isabel glanced toward Lucius. He was waiting patiently and seemed to be paying no attention to the argument. But Isabel knew he was listening.

"Brother Clouse, I'm sure you're wrong," she said. "While I was growing up, my father's seminary students often went out to practice their preaching at small chapels in the rural communities. When they had delivered their sermons, they sat down and the church deacons served the host. That was a common practice."

Purple veins stood out at Clouse's temples. "I don't care how they practice religion in the wilds of Canada. Here the offices of the deacons are purely administrative. The *pastor* is responsible for all spiritual functions. It's out of the question. Those Indians have no concept of Holy Communion."

"They've had six years of careful preparation," Isabel pointed out.

Clouse took another step toward the surrey, then seemed to think better of it. Again he stopped and faced her.

"Unless you promise you will not go ahead without me, or without some minister present, I will wash my hands of the entire matter right here and now."

Isabel fought against her own anger. God's Light on the Mountain had been accorded the lowest position on the circuit pastorage, and now she was being told it could do nothing for itself.

"I'm sorry you feel that way about it. But if I told those Indians they cannot worship God in their own church, I would be going against everything I've ever believed. I will tell the Indians exactly what you have said. I can't speak for the church. If you fail us, the *church* can vote to postpone the ordinance."

"Then I'll not come."

"I thank you for your tea and hospitality," Isabel said. She walked to the surrey without looking back.

Lucius helped her up the steps and climbed into the seat beside her. He gave Clouse an expressionless nod that could have meant anything, then flicked his whip over the rump of the horses. Not until they were more than a mile away from Rainy Mountain did either of them speak.

"You heard?" Isabel asked.

"I heard enough."

"He is not coming. And Brother Hamilton will be going in

the opposite direction that Sunday. So this means we will be without a pastor."

"Heenkey will be happy."

"It isn't right that they should treat us this way. We have worked six years to build our church. The ministers are devoting far more attention to white churches thrown up in six weeks."

"I have not seen any Indians drop dead of surprise."

"I hate it when I allow myself to get this angry. It makes me physically sick."

Lucius glanced at her. "We will have the Jesus eat," he said. "We all watched Brother Murrow carefully when he did it. As you said in your Jesus talk, it is simple."

They rode for a time in comfortable silence. At Big Tree's Crossing, Lucius stopped to water the horses. There she saw that he was wearing what Mabel called his "worry face"—a slight frown, a tightness about the mouth, a narrowing of the eyes.

She had been so wrapped up in her own difficulties that she had not thought to ask about the children, and belatedly made amends, hoping that nothing was wrong.

"Amos and Minnie Goombi told me today they want to get married," Lucius said.

Isabel was aghast. "Oh, Lucius! They're so young! Surely they can wait a while."

"They are almost sixteen. In the long-ago days, Amos would be a warrior. He says he has a hundred sixty acres in his name, and Minnie has another hundred sixty. He says he is ready to start a family."

Isabel thought of the slim little boy standing in the back of the wagon the first day she met the Aitsans.

It hardly seemed possible so many years had passed.

And she could remember Minnie as a sick child during that first terrible winter. She had lifted Minnie in her two hands, and she had seemed as light as a feather. Now she was talking of marriage.

"What will Mabel think?"

Lucius smiled. "She will say it is a good time in their lives, that we should not keep them from it."

Isabel had long known that Mabel was a hopeless romantic. Lucius was right. Mabel would side with the children.

"But how will they live?" she asked. "They have nothing. No house, not a single pot or pan."

Lucius shrugged. "That is the way everybody started out. Young people do not think of those things. If they did, no one would get married. Amos and Minnie will finish at the government school this spring. Amos says it is time for them to move ahead."

"Amos is a level-headed boy," Isabel conceded . "I hope he knows what he is doing."

"He will bring Minnie to Saddle Mountain for a visit in two weeks. He said we should have a big eat for her. We will want you and Miss Bare to be there."

The invitation revealed the true situation.

In reality, no decision was involved. Amos and Minnie had presented their families with the fact that they would soon marry. The formality of parental consent was posed only to allow everyone time to accept the idea.

Isabel vowed to herself that she would say no more. It was a family matter. And who was she to say that it was wrong?

"We'll be there," she said. "In the meantime, I'll be preparing for the first wedding in our new church."

Lucius was named church administrator without a single dissenting vote.

Taking his place at the altar, he arrayed the silver communion service—a gift from Commissioner Jones—and called the Lord's blessings upon it.

The deacons then took their places. Gahbein was now almost blind, so Isabel guided him onto the platform. She then took her seat in a pew beside Sister Bare.

Lucius handed the elements to the deacons. The Indians were served at the communal rail.

It was a scene out of Isabel's dreams. She could not hold back tears. Lucius presided over the ceremony with dignity and reverence. Many Indians were weeping as they accepted the host.

Isabel herself was half blind as she and Sister Bare went forward and knelt with the last celebrants.

Isabel thought back over years of suffering, sickness, and death, hundreds of evenings under brush arbors and Coleman lanterns.

The communion service seemed to be the culmination of a long, arduous journey.

Afterward, when she was alone with Sister Bare, Isabel

spoke the thought that had been lingering in her mind all day: "I only wish my father were alive to see it."

The celebration at the Aitsan compound lasted three days and nights. Two sturdy yearling calves were consumed. The thunder drum and dancing did not stop until the final dawn.

Amos and Minnie were teased so mercilessly that Isabel soon felt the wedding long overdue.

Minnie was a lovely young woman, tall and slim, with wide-set eyes and her father's high cheekbones. Perhaps because of a childhood spent fronting for her white-captive mother, she lacked the shyness common among Indian girls. She handled the confusion of the three-day celebration with quiet self-assurance.

Amos and Minnie demonstrated their independence by choosing to be married in modern clothing and in the white man's way. Isabel described for them the customs and rituals of white weddings. When she reached the part where the groom kisses the bride, the Indians laughed in embarrassment.

They considered the white custom of mouth-to-mouth kisses revolting.

"I wouldn't do that for a hundred dollars," Lucius said.

Brother Hamilton was summoned from Lawton. The bride wore a pink, ruffled blouse, a green skirt, and an orange sash. Her "something old" was an Indian shawl dating from the long-ago times. Its yellow, red, purple, and blue designs harmonized perfectly with her costume. In deference to her family, Minnie used both her "white" and Indian names in the ceremony, even though Brother Hamilton occasionally stumbled in pronouncing "Minnie Kaun-to-dle Goombi."

Amos wore a dark suit, white shirt, and his father's elegant satin bow tie. Isabel and Sister Bare filled the church with wildflowers.

The bride's mother attended, ending much speculation and debate. It was Say-haye-do-hole Goombi's first public appearance among whites since the Indians were driven onto the reservation. She stained her skin with walnut juice, kept her soft, brownish-gray hair covered with a mantle, and sought refuge in the crowd. Although her Anglo features were unmistakable, Brother Hamilton had been taken into Isabel's confidence. No awkward moment occurred.

Amos kissed the bride. It was only a quick peck, but as Sister Bare commented, it was a start.

After the ceremony, gifts were heaped on the young couple during another long celebration at the Aitsan compound.

Isabel gave them the only property of any value she possessed: her wagon and team. Jeremiah and Jonah were no longer colts, but both were still capable of years of moderate work.

In a way, she felt relieved. Either Lucius, the mail hack, or other Indians now took her wherever she needed to go. She no longer needed the wagon and team, and she knew that Amos would treat Jeremiah and Jonah with kindness for the remainder of their lives.

Isabel was alone in the church when Lucius entered. She was cleaning the bin under the pulpit where the communal set was stored.

At first glance she saw that he was wearing his worry face.

"The Kiowas want me to become their Jesus man," he said. "I've told them I don't know enough. But they keep pushing and pushing. I don't know what to do."

Isabel finished arranging the silver and closed the door to the storage space. She sank into a chair behind the pulpit. Lucius remained standing, his back to the altar.

"Have you talked to Brother Hamilton?"

Lucius nodded. "He told me to listen for the call. He told me how it came to him. But I still don't understand exactly. How will I know? I don't want to make a mistake."

Isabel could not decide between what she *wanted* to do and what she knew she *should* do. She felt driven to encourage him. But she remembered how easily she had led the building committee onto the stone road merely by suggesting they study it.

Some decisions the Indians had to make for themselves. This, she knew, was one of them.

"Lucius, I can't help you. I have no experience on this. Maybe you should write to Dr. Burdette."

Lucius paced back and forth on the podium. "When you became a missionary, did you receive the call?"

Isabel spoke carefully. She did not want to say too much. "In a small way, I suppose. I always knew what I wanted to be, but I didn't know how to do it. I was unhappy with what I believed to be a rather shallow life. When I heard Miss Burdette speak, I knew instantly I had found a way to make my life useful. There *was* a thrilling moment when I first knew. Maybe it was a gentle nudge from God. But I'm sure it wasn't like a call to the ministry. I think that is much more profound."

Lucius stepped off the podium and sat in the pew just below the communion rail. "I have prayed hard. I told God I am willing if He wants me. But I also told Him I will not put myself forward. He has said nothing back to my heart yet. I think I can do better work for Him here interpreting. Maybe that is what He wants me to do."

"Perhaps. But Lucius, you must keep listening. God may only be awaiting the proper time."

Lucius glanced toward the altar and to the cross behind it. "What if He *does* call me? What will happen next? No one has told me."

"Several ministers will question you at length. They first will make certain your call is genuine. Then you will understudy a good pastor for a year or two. When he thinks you are ready, you will be questioned again before a Board of Ministers. If the Board finds that you have learned enough, you will be ordained to preach. Your name will be circulated, and some church will call you as the pastor. We both know that church will be this one."

Lucius stared for a time at the floor. "I am so ignorant. How could I ever answer questions asked by someone like Dr. Burdette?"

"Lucius, you know much more than you think you know. You have a good grasp of the Bible, of other books. Your English has improved remarkably. You are very intelligent and a natural-born scholar. If you get the call, you will have no trouble fulfilling it. I am as certain of that as I am of anything in this world."

Lucius frowned. "Will the white pastors teach an Indian?"

Isabel sensed that she should not equivocate. "There may be resistance. I would be surprised if it is otherwise. But God selects His own. St. Paul was a Roman soldier, an enemy. God had no clear reason to choose him, but He did. The Lord chooses the time and place. After He chooses you, He will help you."

"The Indians keep pushing me," Lucius said again. "I don't know what to do."

Isabel left the podium and moved to sit in the pew beside him. "Lucius, I think you should get away from Saddle Mountain for a while and reason it out for yourself. This is between you and God. No one else can help you."

"I am not worthy," Lucius said. "I have watched you year after year, giving all of yourself and asking nothing. I do not know if you are a saint or an angel. But I know I am neither. I am only an ignorant Indian."

Isabel opened her mouth to speak. But before words came, Lucius rose and bolted out the door.

A succession of spring showers was followed by several days of sunshine, and soon both Indian and whites were busy in the fields. Floods in the northern portion of the territory had washed out railroad bridges, and trains were delayed. For a week no mail arrived. Then one afternoon the postal hack brought an entire sackful.

Isabel and Sister Bare sorted the mail, placing their own letters to one side.

Afterward they went into the mission parlor, made tea, and began reading their mail.

Isabel had just opened a letter from her sister Emily when Sister Bare emitted a little yip.

Isabel looked up. Sister Bare's face was pale. The hand holding the letter trembled.

"Mr. Cooper has asked me to marry him!"

Isabel was not surprised. She remembered the way the contractor had followed Sister Bare with his gaze. And Isabel had not forgotten the trips Sister Bare had made to the building sites with cool water and delicacies from the oven.

But Sister Bare had never mentioned him since.

"Congratulations!" Isabel said. "But isn't this all rather sudden?"

Sister Bare ignored the teasing. "Not really. I've known he liked me." She paused thoughtfully. "But he's older."

"How much older?"

"Ten, maybe twelve years."

"I'm sure that will be a terrible chasm for you to breach."

Sister Bare reread a portion of the letter. "He says he has been thinking about me a lot."

"That's rather obvious."

Sister Bare blushed. "I've been thinking about him, too. He wrote several weeks ago that he wants to go back to Michigan, where he is known and respected. He said he likes this country, but it is still too raw and unsettled for his taste. I must admit I have begun to feel the same way. What do you think?"

"How would I know what to think?" Isabel asked. "Obviously it's a tremendous decision to go off with someone you hardly know. I liked Mr. Cooper, and I thought him a good man. But he has been married once—"

"Well, look at me!" Sister Bare interrupted. "I'm no bargain. This is the first proposal of marriage I've received in my whole life!"

"Don't underestimate yourself, Kate. I'd say he would be getting the better of the bargain."

"How in the world can you say that? No one has ever called me pretty. I'm grumpy and bad-natured. I know the Indians call me 'the Bear Woman.' And I know why."

Sister Bare again read the letter from beginning to end. "I must think this over."

She hurried up the stairs to her room.

Isabel smiled over Sister Bare's charade of "thinking over" Mr. Cooper's proposal. Her decision had been obvious from the first.

Isabel had been reading the letters in the chronological order of the postmarks. She opened the last, and most recent. It was from Miss Burdette.

At first the words of the opening paragraphs did not make sense. She sat and studied them until the meaning slowly became clear:

Dearest Belle,

What have you been doing? Several days ago I received a letter expressing grave apprehension and disapproval of the report that you had administered the Lord's Supper in the church at Saddle Mountain. I intended to write to you then but have been so incessantly occupied that I fear I neglected to do so.

Now I have received another letter from another source, a high dignitary of the American Baptist Home Missionary Society, calling attention to it in a way that indicates trouble for you, for the church, and for the society.

Did you do it? I hope not. You certainly would not have made so radical a departure from Baptist usage as that while bearing the commission of the society. Surely not without the approval of the Board. And if you did, it was without their knowledge. I hope you will set yourself right in this matter. I remember your outspoken opinion of the "mannish" woman ministers who made such spectacles of themselves at the World's Congress here years ago. It would seem very strange for you now to assume functions pertaining to the office of pastor.

I shall await with some anxiety but in hope your explanation will suffice to lay these reports to rest immediately.

Yours with love,
Mary Burdette

At first Isabel was too stunned for anger. She took the letter up to her room and studied it line by line, word by word, trying to assess not only what Miss Burdette had written but also all that was left unsaid.

The source of the reports was obvious.

No one had objected to the church conducting Holy Communion except Brother Clouse.

But why had he lied—circulated the outright falsehood that *she* had administered the sacraments?

She had told him plainly that it would be a *church* act and that she would not participate.

Yet Miss Burdette had cited two reports saying *she* performed the office.

Isabel lay on her bed and looked up at the freshly painted ceiling. The window by her bed was open to the pleasant fragrances of spring. Her thoughts drifted back to the beginning of her relationship with Clouse, seeking reasons why he might do such a thing.

Despite this new development, she still had no doubt as to the man's honesty and dedication. Too often she had seen him take the most difficult route, simply because of his convictions.

But she had always known that he had certain limitations. No room existed in his mind for disagreement with his views.

She remembered how he had tried to discourage her from coming to Saddle Mountain. He had made every attempt to keep her at Elk Creek, under his close supervision.

During her first hectic months at Saddle Mountain, he had written repeated letters to her Board, keeping them so concerned for her safety that at one point she was almost recalled.

Now she wondered if his fears had been for her safety, or for the possibility that she might succeed in building her church—winning victory in a province men decreed open only to themselves.

She remembered the "mixup" in Washington over allocation of church land, and her difficulty in setting matters straight.

Commissioner Jones and Colonel Randlett had tried to warn her, saying that there were "Baptists trying to gobble you up."

Now she knew they were right.

Washington had not made a mistake. She was now convinced that Clouse had filed a separate application for Saddle Mountain church land in order to place it under his direct supervision.

The man was capable of great self-delusion. He might have done everything in the belief that he was "protecting" her, never once admitting, even to himself, his deeper motives.

And now, in his eyes, she had trespassed on his most sacred preserve of maleness—his ministry. He had responded by spreading his exaggeration—his falsehood—everywhere that might bring the sky down upon her.

But understanding what he had done, and his motives, did not make her situation less perilous.

Always she had tried to avoid personal conflicts where possible. Now too much was at stake. She must not mince words.

Night had fallen. She lowered the window and lit a lamp. Taking out her writing materials, she penned her reply:

Dear Miss Burdette,

I will make my position clear from the start. If any outside organization rules the Lord's Supper out of the church at Saddle Mountain I will resign at once.

Having said that, I add that the subject of your letter was more than a surprise to me. Your informant is in error. However, for the first time in my life I have gone against the advice of Brother Clouse and no doubt that is the cause of all the busy correspondence.

I remind the Board ladies of the peculiar situation here at Saddle Mountain. When Brother Rainden came years ago for the purpose of organizing a church, he did not succeed. No one can establish a church until the people

themselves ask for it. In that instance, the Indians drove
him away with loaded guns.

When the Indians *asked* for a church, it was a different thing. You all know our long struggle to build a church
and I will not recount it now.

As soon as the church was organized it was not only
the right of the members but also their duty to partake of
the Lord's Supper. I could not tell them otherwise with
an open Bible before me.

Nobody has the right to legislate such a thing for a
Baptist church! That the American Baptist Home Mission
Society or the Woman's American Home Missionary Society would forbid *any* church to partake of the Lord's Supper never entered my head until I read your letter.

I do not understand what you mean when you say, "I
hope you would not make so radical a departure from Baptist usage." Do not Baptist churches that are pastorless
celebrate the Lord's Supper? Is it not their duty to do so?
Does the Bible restrict the ordinances only to churches
that have pastors?

Unless my teachings have been all wrong, I believe I
would be making a radical departure if I said to this organized body of Baptist believers, "You may not celebrate the Lord's Supper till you get a pastor."

This mission is unusual and the ordinary rules and
methods cannot be followed. We are driven to do all the
Bible allows us but I pray God we may never go beyond
its limits. You do not know how it troubles me to feel led
of the Lord as I do and yet be asked to draw back from
what I know is right. Brother Clouse asked me to draw
back, and I did not do so.

I did not conduct the Supper. Lucius conducted it and
all your missionaries did was to shed tears and lead blind
Gahbein by one hand while he passed the elements with
the other. Surely we did nothing wrong in joining with our
poor Indians in obeying the Master's last request to his
disciples.

The whole church and the deacons urged the Supper,
and if we had denied them it would be as if we had set

ourselves up against the church and assumed the right
to rule that God has given it.

Can it be possible that I have misunderstood the teachings I have received? Surely the New Testament teaches
that the church is responsible for the observance and not
the pastor. I will write to Dr. Strong, Dr. Cline, Dr. Murrow, and perhaps others to see what they say. I know
I'm right but there is nothing like having good authority.

Yours in Christ,
Isabel Crawford

Chapter Twenty-four

Two weeks passed and still Lucius had not returned. Hoping
for news of him, Isabel walked over to the Aitsan allotment.

Amos was plowing behind Jonah in the field below the
house. Amos labored along spraddle-legged, striving to keep
the heavy plow upright. His right hand moved constantly
from the reins to the plow and back again. Jessie scurried
along behind him with a hand planter, dropping a kernel of
corn every few inches. As Isabel approached, Amos pulled
Jonah to a stop. Both Amos and Jessie were sweating profusely under the warm sun. Amos removed his wide-brimmed
black hat, wiped his forehead with his sleeve, and grinned at
Isabel.

"You must know the right words," Isabel called to him.
"I've never seen Jonah work so hard."

Jessie raised her head and peeked out from beneath her
slat sunbonnet. "Amos knows the words. He cusses him a
lot."

"I don't," Amos said. He looked at the planted row behind
him. "But I can't keep him going straight."

Isabel laughed. "The farmers in Canada where I grew up

have a saying, 'Better a crooked furrow than an unplowed field.' I think what you and Jessie are doing is wonderful. I know it's hard work now, but just think! All summer you'll be able to watch the corn grow and know it was your doing."

"He's only working because Mama said if he finishes it today he can go fishing tomorrow," Jessie said.

"I'm a married man," Amos told Jessie. "I can go fishing anytime I want. I don't have to ask anybody."

"Nobody but Minnie," Jessie said.

"Where will you go?" Isabel asked.

"Up the Washita. I know a good catfish hole."

"Bait a hook for me. Is your father back yet?"

Amos shook his head. A veil came across his eyes—that familiar, third-eyelid of distancing Isabel had seen so many times.

Amos was truly his father's son.

She wondered briefly if trouble had flared between them. She did not pursue the thought but walked on up the hill to the Aitsan home.

Mabel was out back making lye soap. A small fire burned under a huge, cast-iron pot. Mabel hugged Isabel, then signed that she was waiting for the soap mixture to thicken.

"Have you heard anything from Lucius?"

Mabel made the "no " sign. She stirred the mixture for a moment, then put the wooden paddle aside. "My heart is not quiet," she signed. "All the seed should be in the ground. Amos cannot do all the work. Lucius should be here."

"Did he say when he would be back?"

Mabel made the "no" sign, then added, "His heart is heaped-up troubled. He does not sleep."

Isabel wondered if matters were more serious than she suspected. She decided to ask. "Is Amos angry with him?"

Mabel nodded. "Amos does not want him to become a Jesus man. Amos thinks the other Indians will make funny."

Some probably would. So would many white people. Lucius's burden as an Indian pastor would be heavy.

"Where is Minnie?"

"She has gone to see her mother today."

"Are Amos and Minnie still lovebirds?"

Mabel laughed and made a gesture that might be considered obscene in some cultures. "This summer Amos will build a house on his land. He wants Minnie with him alone."

Isabel smiled to show that she understood.

Another Aitsan generation was in the making.

Mabel tested the soap again with the paddle, but it was not yet ready. She looked up toward the mountain, then toward the east, perhaps hoping to see Lucius returning.

"I do not know where this road is taking us."

Isabel did not understand. She made the "question" sign.

Mabel answered hesitantly. "I cannot see my family in the far-ahead time. We are not Indians now. But we are not white people, either. The reservation is gone. Soon the grass money will be gone. I cannot see the road ahead for Lucius and me, for our children."

"Your children will make their own roads," Isabel said.

"We cannot make their roads for them. No one knows what is coming. The changes we have seen will not stop."

Soon the soap was ready. Isabel helped Mabel pour the mixture to cool.

Afterward Isabel walked home into the sunset.

Day after day passed with no reply from Miss Burdette. Isabel met each mail and went through the incoming sack before Sister Bare could intervene.

She did not know what to think. Miss Burdette had always been prompt in her correspondence.

Sister Bare was no help. She had accepted Mr. Cooper's proposal, and plans were progressing for a Michigan wedding.

"I am genuinely glad for you," Isabel told her. "But I don't know how long I can endure that constant silly grin on your face."

At last a reply arrived from Dr. Augustus H. Strong of the Rochester Seminary in New York. It gave her a much-needed lift.

Dear Miss Crawford,

I refer you to page 541 of my *Theology*.

I have no doubt that you are right in advising the church to celebrate the Lord's Supper even though they have no pastor. The responsibility of observing the Supper is laid by the New Testament upon the body of believers. Neither baptism nor the Lord's Supper is properly the act of the administrator. Baptism is primarily the act of the person baptized, and the Lord's Supper is primarily the act of the church. You are also correct that the church should be taught self-government.

"Dr. Augustus Hopkins Strong is the principal theologian at the Rochester Baptist Theological Seminary," Isabel told Sister Bare. "He also is one of the most conservative Baptist theologians alive today. I wonder what Brother Clouse will say to this letter."

"You plan to show it to him?"

Isabel nodded emphatically. "He should be edified."

Two days later she received a letter from Dr. Cline:

My Dear Sister,

You have done perfectly right under the circumstances and I am surprised that anyone should question the propriety of your course. I think those who have raised objections must be under the impression that you administered the ordinance yourself as pastor of the church. I am glad you did not, but even if you had done so at the request of the church I cannot see who could reasonably find fault. But in having Lucius preside you acted with your customary wisdom and fine thought. It seems to me if your action is correctly understood all adverse criticism must at once cease.

W. H. Cline

"I knew he would remember my father's teachings," Isabel said. "I now have the support of two leading theologians."

"But both Northerners," Sister Bare pointed out. "The Southern ministers may take exception."

"They will listen to Dr. Murrow," Isabel said.

On the following day a letter arrived from Atoka. As Sister Bare had predicted, Brother Murrow's stance was not as supportive:

My Dear Miss Crawford,

The administration of the bread and wine is very much better of course by a regular pastor or by a regularly ordained Baptist preacher. It ought to be an *extreme* case where a church attends to this ordinance without the presence of a preacher . . .

"He doesn't say how extreme," Isabel pointed out.

"But clearly he doesn't approve," said Sister Bare. "I'm afraid that may be the Southern position."

"I'm disappointed," Isabel admitted. "You may be right. Perhaps I should prepare the Indians for trouble."

Lucius had not returned. On Sunday Isabel gave her Jesus talk with the help of John Onko. He was not as adept in translation as Lucius, but he was an intelligent young man and conscientious.

Isabel observed that John and Jessie could not keep their eyes off each other.

Another wedding seemed to be in the offing.

Isabel spoke on Easter and the Resurrection. At the close of her talk, she left the pulpit and walked closer to the congregation.

"I must tell you something," she said. "The big Baptist chiefs are kicking because we had the Jesus eat here. You may hear hot words. Do not let anyone abuse you. No one who knows can say you did wrong. But the big Baptist chiefs will keep on kicking as long as this church does not have a pastor. I want you to think hard about getting one. I cannot take the place of a Jesus man. If you remember, there were no women among the twelve apostles, or among the seventy Jesus sent out everywhere to preach. This is the way it has always been."

Miss Burdette's long-awaited letter arrived the following week. She said she had been ill, did not have strength to write at length, and hoped that the enclosed material would be self-explanatory.

The long document, written in a different hand, was the copy of a letter forwarded to the Rev. Mr. E. E. Chivers at the American Baptist Association at 111 Fifth Avenue in New York. It stated the Mission Board's position and was signed by every member.

Step by step, the document described events leading to the administration of Holy Communion. Several pages of biblical references followed, supporting Isabel's actions.

The Board's statement of policy concluded:

We agree with your observation that this question no doubt again will arise upon application of the Saddle Mountain church for membership in the association. We the Board are very glad that, with a clearer understanding of the circumstances, we can defend this church against the charge. At the same time we recognize the mode of procedure as somewhat unusual and irregular. But none will deny that a blessed work has been done there at Saddle Mountain and none can be blind to the fact that present conditions are critical and require most prayerful management. None feel this more profoundly than the missionaries in the field.

"Amen to that," Isabel said.

Sister Bare had been reading the letter over Isabel's shoulder. "What do they mean by application to the association? I thought the church was already in the association."

"Only provisionally," Isabel explained. "It has to be made formal. A routine matter, I believe. It should be acted upon soon."

"Who rules upon it? New York?"

"No. The territorial ministerial association. They will be meeting either in Guthrie or Oklahoma City."

"They are mostly Southerners," Sister Bare pointed out. "I hope *they* think it is routine."

The remark set Isabel to worrying. Brother Clouse was a member of the association. His mischief might not yet be ended.

Isabel was awakened by a fierce knocking at the front of the mission house. She slipped on a robe, lit a lamp, and went downstairs. A light rain was falling. She walked out the front door to the edge of the gallery.

Lucius sat on his horse in the rain. With the height of the gallery, their heads were at the same level. He guided the horse close to the railing. "It has happened," he said. "I am sure of it."

Water streamed off his hat, onto the faded government blanket draped over his shoulders.

"Lucius, you're soaked to the skin. Come in. I'll build a fire."

"No. I will go on home. I only came here because I wanted you to know."

"I'm glad you did. It's wonderful news."

"Tomorrow I will go to Anadarko and wire Dr. Murrow and Captain Parker. Brother Hamilton asked me to do this. He said they are waiting to hear."

"*Everyone* has been waiting. Can we make the announcement Sunday?"

Lucius did not answer immediately. "Only if you will ask everyone to pray for me. I do not want to do this. But God told me to do it. I will do what He says."

"The Lord has made a wise choice, Lucius. I couldn't be more thrilled. Now you go home and get into some dry clothes."

Isabel went back up the stairs. She blew out the lamp, knelt beside her bed, and spoke softly into the darkness.

"Dear Lord, I thank You for answering this prayer that I have prayed for *such* a long time. I truly believe the call of Lucius Ben Aitsan into Your service may be of even greater importance than the building of the church itself. I pray that You will watch over him and bless him in his blessed work. This I ask in Jesus's name. Amen."

Lucius stood tall and faced the congregation. "Ever since this church was organized, many of you have wanted me to be the pastor. I have only been to school four years. I told you that I did not want you to push me."

He wore his new three-piece black suit. His hair had been trimmed, and overnight his voice had acquired an even deeper, richer tone. He spoke first in Kiowa, then in English.

"I held myself back because I knew that the Great Father would talk to my heart if He wanted me to do this work. I wanted to hear His voice before I did anything. I kept thinking, thinking, and praying hard."

From her seat behind the pulpit Isabel had a complete view of the congregation, and of Lucius in profile. Most of the Indians were on tenterhooks, awaiting Lucius's decision.

"I got on my horse and I rode for two weeks," Lucius went on. "I went to almost every Jesus man in this part of the territory. I asked every one of them to tell me how he knew when the Great Father first spoke to him.

"Every Jesus man told me the same thing: I must pray for guidance and listen hard. They told me how I would know when the time came."

Again he paused with the innate dramatic flair of a born public speaker.

"I heard a whisper first in Watonga. I had been thinking very carefully, and I thought this: 'If I am pastor, all the Kiowas who went to school and are smart will laugh at me.

The Ghost Dance people will laugh at me.' But then my heart said, 'Never mind if they do. You will be a great help to your people.' When I felt this I said, 'No use for me to be afraid to work for Jesus and my people.' "

Lucius lowered his voice and spoke softly.

"It was then that the Great Father spoke to my heart. And this is what He said: 'Lucius, you have worked for Me many years and picked up My words right along. I want you to do this work for Me.' "

Lucius placed both hands on his chest. "When I heard this, my heart shook. It jumped and hit very fast, and then I knew that I had been called."

He spread his hands. "Look at me. I am not fit to be the pastor of this church. But if the Great Father wants me to do it, I am willing. I have spoken."

As Lucius turned and walked back toward his translator's chair, Pope-bah dashed onto the podium and embraced him. Other Indians were close behind. Pandemonium reigned for several minutes.

When order was restored, Isabel glanced toward Lucius. He nodded, signaling that he was prepared to resume translation.

"This is the road we must walk for Lucius to become our pastor," she told the congregation. "Your Board of Deacons must ask that a white Jesus man be sent here for at least a year, so that Lucius may train with him. This request must be approved by the congregation."

The explanation was met by silence and solemn faces.

Odlepaugh rose. He spoke and signed. Isabel understood even before Lucius translated. "Maybe Lucius could go to a white church for a year. The white Jesus man would not have to come here."

"That is another possible road," Isabel agreed. "But I do not believe it is the best one. Lucius is not the only one who needs to be trained. A good Jesus man would put this church onto the Jesus road at a high lope. You all know that Sister Bare is leaving. If Lucius goes away and I am sent elsewhere, you would have nothing here. You must think hard about this. You have built a beautiful church. Now you must use it."

The Indians talked for a time in Kiowa. Lucius did not attempt to translate.

When Tonemoh rose and assumed an oratorical stance,

Isabel understood that she was to hear everyone's position on the matter.

"Before this country was opened to whites there were many wagon roads. We went where we pleased and we did not know about the lines that divide the earth into little pieces. Now we go only on the main roads, and the old ones are all weeds. In the long-ago time the devil was a big chief with us. Now we must learn these new roads. The Jesus women say we should get a white pastor. The Jesus women have done good work here and God's light is shining brightly. I have had this talk in my heart a long time: I stand with the Jesus women. I think we should have a white Jesus man here. Some of the Indians want Lucius to be pastor. I think if one of our boys came to be pastor of this church, after a while some Indians would be pulling one way and some another like a team of horses. Indians are very jealous. I am an Indian and I know. We cannot wait long. We cannot wait for Lucius. We must get a Jesus man here quick. If the Indians do not follow Jesus the light here will get darker and darker like the chimney of the lamp gets black."

Saneco rose. "I want to tell the deacons this. You are not chosen to make funny. The other day I went to the railroad and watched the trains. The engine brings the freight cars behind them straight and strong. I believe the deacons should work like the engine and pull the church straight and strong. Now you are going this way and that way and all over. Get on the straight road quick. I do not like to think hard about it, but I know that I will not live forever. I want to talk to the Great Father here a little bit every day. I want to hear good, strong Jesus talks. I think we should get a white Jesus man here to work with Lucius. I have spoken."

Satezadlebe spoke briefly. "The other day I went to Rainy Mountain to see my grandchildren. While I was there Brother Clouse made a talk. He told us that when we gave the Jesus eat at Saddle Mountain we made a great lie. It turned my heart over and made it very heavy. Brother Clouse said, 'I am a pastor and I have the right. No one else has the right.' I think we should have a white Jesus man here so we can have the Jesus eat and raise up my heart again."

Odlepaugh rose, making the "no" sign. "When we first made the plan to build this church it was under Lucius's arbor. We told Jesus then we would never have a white Jesus man here. We said we would pray for one of our own boys to preach for us. When we built the church we talked about it wisely and we said, 'We are not going to have any white Jesus man.' Our two white sisters understand the Jesus book, and they can teach us what is right. Their Jesus talks have done me much good. You white sisters think the white Jesus men are all right, but we Indians know they are a little bit crooked. We are afraid of this. We want you to write a letter to Miss Burdette and the white Jesus chiefs and tell them this is not their business."

A murmur of agreement swept through the congregation. Isabel and Sister Bare exchanged glances.

Despite support from Tonemoh and a few others, the congregation still opposed seeking a white pastor.

Before Isabel could speak, Loki Mo-keen stood at the back of the church and raised his hands for silence.

"I hear Odlepaugh's words," Mo-keen said. "A long time ago he and I rode many war trails together. We camped together and we talked many nights all the way through. I know what is in his heart. I know it is good. He is right. If a white Jesus man comes here, the first thing he will do is put up fences. He will say the Indian can walk here, but he cannot walk there. He will make rules. He will put himself between the Indian and the Great Father. At Elk Creek, at Rainy Mountain, everywhere there are Jesus men, it has always been so. Only here at Saddle Mountain has the Jesus woman said, 'I will take you straight to the Great Father and we will talk with Him.'"

Again a rustle of agreement came from the congregation. Mo-keen went on as if he had not noticed.

"When Miss Crawford first came here and was still living in her little wagon, on this place where our church now stands, I told her that an Indian lives and breathes his religion with every breath throughout the day, every day. Miss Crawford did not blink an eye before she said, 'That is the way it should be,' and I knew right then that she would do much good here. I stood with her many times and took much abuse for her. She has taught us the Jesus road and never once tried to take away our Kiowa things.

"With the Jesus men it is not so. They think of fences first and then maybe after a while they think about religion. That is the cause of the trouble here at Saddle Mountain about the Jesus eat. The big Baptist chiefs think long and hard about their fences first. An Indian can walk here, he must not walk there. Only after they have thought hard about their rules will they think about the Jesus eat and how the Indian needs it to breathe Jesus. Their road is not for me. I will not walk it."

Again Mo-keen raised his hands to quiet the congregation.

"I say this now to Odlepaugh and those who do not want a white Jesus man here. Maybe the time has come for us to be very smart—smarter than the white man. The Kiowas have always made funny with me, telling me I am sly because I have Mexican blood. Maybe this is so, for this is what I think: We should stand with the Jesus woman. We should bring a Jesus man here to teach my son Lucius. We all know that the Jesus men walk a little crooked. The man we get here probably will be the same. We will be careful and look hard at his roads. You all know that my son Lucius is very smart. He will see what is straight and what is crooked. We can all walk in his steps. Then soon the white Jesus man will be gone and Lucius will be our Jesus man. From that day no one will abuse us to bring a white Jesus man here."

The idea of beating the white man at his own game seemed to hold great appeal. Although other voices were heard, Mo-keen's argument carried the day.

The deacons voted unanimously to make application to the association, requesting a white pastor.

"I suppose that makes moot the question of the Lord's Supper," Sister Bare said later, back at the mission house.

"Not at all," Isabel told her. "I did not mention this, but Saddle Mountain probably will not receive a pastor at least for a year or more. Every new church in the twin territories is hunting a minister—at least a hundred or more. I can't imagine any preacher choosing to come to a church where few among the congregation speak his own language—not when others far less challenging are seeking him."

"Are you saying that nothing has changed—even with application for a pastor?"

"Not at all. The Indians have done what they have asked."

"Then what will happen?"

"I think we will receive a permanent circuit rider—probably Brother Hamilton, or possibly Brother Scott. He will come maybe once a month. More and more, Lucius will assume the role of pastor. After a year or so, he will go before a board and be ordained. He will become our pastor. I seriously doubt a white pastor will ever be assigned here full time."

Sister Bare broke into peals of laughter. "And the Kiowas call Mo-keen sly! Sister Crawford has been *very* smart—smarter than the Indians, smarter than the whites. How long have you had this plan in your head?"

"It isn't my plan," Isabel said. "It's just what I've always felt *should* happen."

Chapter Twenty-five

Isabel came downstairs just as the mail hack arrived. Sister Bare dumped the incoming sack onto her desk and began sorting. "Here's a telegram," she said a few minutes later. "It's for you."

Isabel ripped open the envelope with trepidation, thinking that possibly something had happened to one of her sisters, or to her brother.

But the wire was from Miss Burdette in Chicago:

RECEIVED NOTICE TERRITORIAL ASSOCIATION IN OKLAHOMA CITY VOTED TO REPRIMAND SADDLE MOUNTAIN CHURCH STOP ADMISSION POSTPONED STOP COMMUNION WITHOUT PASTOR SPECIFICALLY FORBIDDEN STOP MISSION BOARD DECREES YOU COMPLY WITH ASSOCIATION RULING STOP

Shaken to the core, Isabel passed the message to Sister Bare.

"Oh, Belle! No!"

Isabel looked out the window. The driver of the mail hack had stopped at the creek to water his horses.

"Give me paper and pen quick," she said.

Hurriedly, she wrote her reply:

THEN I RESIGN STOP I RESIGN STOP I RESIGN STOP

"Belle, you can't," Sister Bare protested.

"I can and I have. Go stop that driver. I must run upstairs and get the money to send it."

"Take what you need from the postal drawer," Sister Bare said. "You can replace it later."

Isabel seized some change from the desk and rushed out to the creek. She gave the man the wire and the money to send it. When she returned to the mission house, Sister Bare was in tears.

"You should have waited. You may think better of it."

"No," Isabel told her. "If I live to be a hundred I will still know I did right."

Sister Bare had finished packing. Her trunk stood on the gallery, ready for her departure. Isabel had not yet started to pack. All afternoon she had dwelled in the purgatory she herself had created. Repeatedly she had begun work, only to remember that she no longer was a missionary.

She had not yet told the Indians.

"Are you hungry?" Sister Bare asked.

"I'm famished. Every woman I know says she can't eat when she's upset. With me it seems to work the other way."

"Odlepaugh brought us a cottontail. I'll put it into the oven and stir up some cornbread. This afternoon I harvested some fresh green onions and a few new potatoes. They're small, but they should be delicious."

While Sister Bare cooked, Isabel went up to her room and packed her books into wooden crates.

Later she and Sister Bare sat down to eat by lamplight.

For a time they spoke as if nothing had happened. But as they lingered over coffee, Sister Bare began to dab at her eyes with the corners of her napkin.

"Do you realize this is our last meal together? After all we went through to build this house, we haven't lived in it long enough to wear off the new."

Isabel's brain seemed to be comatose. She could not yet think of the future.

"Remember Professor Pangloss in Voltaire's *Candide*?" she asked. "When they were taking him out to be hanged, he tried to console his friends by saying that perhaps it was for the best. It could be that *this* is for the best. Maybe it's high time for us to move on. We've done our work here."

"And then some!"

Isabel attempted to make her case. "What would we do if we stayed here? The Indians no longer have Indian problems. Now they have white problems. That's progress, I suppose. Whether or not, they're mostly beyond our help."

"I still don't see how the ministers can say you are in error. I don't see a thing anywhere that you've done wrong. Why did this have to happen? It's so unjust!"

"Looking back, I can see that it was inevitable," Isabel said. "First, I am a woman. As long as I gave my little Jesus talks beneath a brush arbor, no one complained. But the moment we built a church and I began making the same talks from behind a pulpit, they became another thing entirely. I realized this. If you remember, I didn't want a pulpit in the church until we had a pastor. But Mr. Cooper offered to build it free of charge, and I certainly could not refuse."

"It *is* beautiful," said Sister Bare. "I don't think I've ever seen one more beautiful."

Isabel was still assembling her thoughts. "Second, they cannot accept that Holy Communion was served by the same Indians who lifted white scalps not many years ago. Too many people still think of them as savage Indians. If a white church had done the same thing, I doubt anyone would have protested."

"I know it is a common practice elsewhere. I've seen it done."

"Third, there is that book Miss Burdette published, calling me *The Heroine of Saddle Mountain*. That title certainly did not set well with certain men who felt I should have stayed home—or at least remained at Elk Creek. I wish Miss Burdette had not published that book. I knew the effect it would have. But she convinced me it would help the mission work, and I relented. She edited it until the accounts seem exaggerated, and by now it has received wide circulation. I'm sure everyone in the ministry has seen it."

"But Lucius says it is *not* exaggerated. He said it does not say enough."

"Fourth, I came from the North, and I represent a northern organization that was sending abolitionists into black churches in the South twenty years before I was born. There are fifty years and more of bitter feelings behind this I know nothing about—old feuds that have nothing to do with the Indians—or with this church, for that matter. The society still continues work among black churches in the South. *That* is deeply resented. Our poor Indians have harvested all this bitterness. It is so *un-Christian*! How could anyone expect me to do anything other than resign?"

Sister Bare made a brave effort to smile. "What will you do now?"

"I really don't know. I've been accused of running away from life by devoting myself as a missionary. But I've always felt I have been running *toward* life. I'll probably continue work in the church, in some capacity."

"I can't imagine you as anything but a missionary."

"Most of the time I can't, either. I've been tempted to relent enough to accept reassignment. But in my weaker moments I fear I would find myself repeating experiences. And I doubt I could survive reliving what I've gone through here."

Sister Bare nodded emphatically. "I've had enough hard work here to last me a lifetime."

"I don't mind the work," Isabel said. "I'm talking about the emotional drain. All the suffering I've seen. All the Indian babies I've buried . . ."

She fell silent. Much of what she felt could not be put into words. She thought of the endless horror of the elderly Indian men sitting around like fish out of water, too old to take up the new roads. She remembered the terrible winter when entire families starved, froze, or died of illness. And most haunting and vivid of all was the uncertainty on the faces of people who did not know from minute to minute what new injustices would be heaped upon them.

"I never set out to emulate Christ," she went on. "I'm a weak vessel. I can only bear witness to a certain amount of man's inhumanity to man. Beyond that I can't go. I'm not sure I could endure burying one more Indian baby. In ten years I've buried hundreds."

"You will let me know, won't you? You'll write?"

"Of course! But you'll probably be so wrapped up in your man and your new life you'll forget all about me."

"Never!" Sister Bare said. She dabbed at her eyes. "I'm just glad it's you who will be saying good-bye to me. It just wouldn't seem right, your leaving first."

"It doesn't seem right however I do it," Isabel said. "But I must learn to accept it."

*   *   *

Heenkey drove Sister Bare to the railroad station early the next morning. Somewhere en route his buggy passed the mail hack, which arrived at Saddle Mountain before noon.

Mabel had agreed to serve as temporary postmistress until someone could be assigned. Jessie came to help her.

"I've got another telegram for you," the driver said to Isabel as he brought the sack in. "Want me to wait for an answer?"

Isabel opened the envelope. She was not surprised by its contents:

BOARD URGES YOU RECONSIDER STOP SUGGEST INDEFINITE LEAVE OF ABSENCE UNTIL SITUATION RESOLVED STOP LOVE STOP

"My reply will be too long for a telegram," she said. "And it probably would burn Western Union's wires beyond repair."

Welcoming any task to occupy her mind, Isabel went upstairs to her room and set to work on her answer. With the release of emotions long bottled up within her, the words poured onto paper:

My Dear Sisters:

I have considered very carefully your proposition that I change my resignation to an indefinite leave of absence.

Gladly would I do this if it were in my power. I love the work, am perfectly content to live and die in it, but the conditions are such that I am powerless to act other than I have.

I am a Baptist through and through from very strong convictions, and to remain a teacher and guide of a church not "of the same faith and order" is derogatory to the promptings of the Holy Spirit in my heart.

From the very first I have tried to impress upon the minds of the Indians the Divine origin of the Church.

No organization on earth can compare with it. WCTU's, YWCA's, associations, conventions, all are inventions of men for the promotion of good, but none of them is to be compared with the church, nor in any way whatsoever pass any law binding upon the same.

To the *church* has been committed two ordinances. The individual churches, and they alone, are responsible for their observances.

The pastors as the recognized heads of the churches are naturally the administrators, but when a church is pastorless it has no *right* to omit the Lord's Supper.

In obeying the command of the Master, we here at Saddle Mountain supposed that everyone interested would rejoice.

Dark days came upon us unaware. We were denounced from the pulpit and reported to headquarters, threatened with exclusion from the association—and finally voted against.

Brother Clouse, the only minister near enough to be with us regularly, refused to come unless I *promised* that the church would postpone the ordinance if for any reason he failed to appear at the appointed time.

Having no right to speak for the church, I simply said, "If you fail us *the church* can vote to postpone the ordinance."

When asked to postpone the ordinance the church said, "Let it go. We won't vote."

At that moment the Baptist Church at Saddle Mountain ceased to exist. A church without the power to observe the Lord's Supper is not a Baptist church!

A church that bows down to any authority higher than the Holy Scripture is not a Baptist church.

I resign. I cannot stay.

My heart rebels, my whole being rebels against the unjust, unnecessary, *unscriptural* pressure that is being forced upon this church to have a pastor.

May God in His infinite mercy and wisdom bring right out of wrong, peace out of turmoil, and a disposition to let the Holy Spirit rule into every heart related in any way to the work.

> Sincerely,
> Isabel Crawford

Isabel paused and took a deep breath. "Today I make my last Jesus talk at God's Light on the Mountain."

Lucius hesitated, then translated her words. A gasp came from the congregation. Lucius stood with his mouth open, his eyes wide, staring at her in disbelief.

Isabel closed her eyes and did not open them until she had her emotions under control.

"Ten years, eight months, and three days ago I came to this country to live among the Indians," she began. "I did not know what to expect. For three years and more I lived among the Arapaho and Southern Cheyennes. When I went to them, those Indians had been living among whites for four years. Long ago, the great Chief Black Kettle made peace with the whites, and his Cheyennes tried to walk the white man's road. Yet many Cheyennes were killed by the whites, both at Sand Creek and later, when they were in winter camp on the Washita. I pray to the Great Father that through my work I was able in some small way to help amend some of the wrongs that had been done to the Cheyennes.

"While I was among them, I heard much about the Kiowas. I was told that the Kiowas were great warriors. I heard they had never been defeated in battle until the Army trapped them at the Palo Duro Canyon and killed all of their horses. I was told that the Kiowas were very dangerous people and that they would never, never walk the white man's road. But I also was told that some of them had not heard about Jesus. So when Domot invited me, I decided to come here to Saddle Mountain. I was very scared. I cannot tell you how scared. When Red Eagle met me on the edge of the reservation and told me he might scalp me, I did not know he was making funny."

The Indians found partial release for the tension in uneasy laughter. Isabel waited until the interruption ended.

"When I came here only a few of you spoke any words of English. You knew little about the white man. What little you did know was bad. I knew nothing about you. What I had been told was bad. But we worked together. And we performed miracles.

"A few years ago the Kiowa was hungry and cold. His children were dying. He lined up at the agency for his food, and all too often it was not there. The white man treated him as a child. But the Kiowa was not a child. He was—and is—a marvelous human being. He learned new ways. And I can tell you this because no one knows better than I: To this day the Kiowa has never been defeated. The white man killed his horses and drove him onto the reservation. The white man starved him until his children and his old people died. The white man tricked him with strange talk, and now his reservation is gone. But today the Kiowa does not hang his head. Instead, he walks the white man's road as well as any white man. He has built this church, as fine as any in this territory. His sons and daughters are in school, learning all they can. Soon this will be a new state. The Kiowa is ready to take his place in it."

Despite her resolutions, Isabel was forced to stop and fight back tears.

"I pray to God that someday this whole country will know what you Kiowas have done here. I am so *very*, very proud of all of you."

Again she paused to regain control.

The congregation seemed to be sitting in a state of shock. All were staring as if unable to believe their ears. Isabel went on.

"For ten years, eight months, and three days I have been a white missionary to the Indians. I have thought hard and I have prayed hard and now I know what I must do. This I promise you. From this moment on, I will spend the rest of my life as a missionary *from* the Kiowas to the white people. I will write books and magazine articles. I will make speeches. I will do anything and everything I can to tell the world about the most wonderful people I have ever known—the Kiowa Indians."

Pope-bah, Hattie, Sapemah, Ananthy, and other women began to cry. Isabel did not know if she could continue. But she knew she must not stop.

"Now I am leaving Saddle Mountain. Before I go, I will try to give you some wise words. First I want to talk to you young Kiowas who hear me in English even before Lucius does the translation. You have been to school, and everyone is telling you that you are very smart. I will tell you this: If you will keep and use your Kiowa language also, you will be even smarter. Language is not only a way of speaking. It is also a way of thinking. Do not throw away your Kiowa language just because you know English.

"Already some of you make funny of the old people. You love them and you do not do this in meanness, but I want you to stop it. The old people here today have carried the tribe from the long-ago time into the present. There are not enough medals in Washington to honor them for what they have done. They may talk funny to your ears but they are wise. Listen to them. Remember what they say. They have in them the seeds of everything that will flower in you later. Hang onto everything Kiowa. It is a part of you. If you throw it away you will be less of a person."

Isabel paused, gathering her thoughts. The church remained deathly silent except for the soft weeping among the women.

"Now I want to talk to you men," she went on. "The whites have taken this country away from you, but at least they have made you citizens in it. You have the vote. It is one of the most precious things you own. Do not sell it for a side of beef or a jug of whiskey. It is beyond price. It has power. No matter how the whites draw the lines in this part of the territory, there always will be more Indians than whites in the little boxes on their maps. Use your votes wisely, and the Indians will have the power for once."

Isabel looked at the stained-glass windows of her beautiful church. Again she wished fervently that her father could have seen it. Then she forced her attention back to her talk.

"Now I speak to all of you. I want you to remember one thing that I have taught you. Remember it above all else. When you are in trouble, always turn to God. You must never doubt your faith. With faith, you can work wonders. While Jesus was still on this earth, all the apostles were weak men. Thomas was always doubting. Simon Peter denied Jesus three times in one night. All the apostles were jealous of each other. They argued over who was way-ahead and who was way-behind with Jesus. They complained like children. They could not agree on anything. But remember this: *After* the Resurrection, not one ever doubted his faith. Not ever again. Not even Thomas—not after he stuck his finger into the wounds of the Holy Ghost. Those weak men *witnessed* the miracle of the Resurrection, and what they had seen and heard made them the strongest men in the world. They went and preached everywhere. They started something that has not stopped yet. And for it they died terrible deaths. They could have escaped horrible tortures by denying Jesus. Not one did. They spread the word of the Resurrection. It is still spreading today, nineteen hundred years later. All of you here saw it come to Saddle Mountain. It is a precious gift from Jesus, and you must treasure it always. As long as you keep your faith, you will be Christ's disciples and remain strong."

Isabel nodded to Heenkey.

He slipped out the door unnoticed.

"Someday Lucius will make this church a glorious pastor. You must be patient, for he has much work to do before he will be ordained. But he is smart. He will pick up everything quick. He is a wonderful man. I do not know of a finer man on the face of the earth. Treasure him as I have always treasured him."

As her gaze moved from familiar face to familiar face, she dreaded saying what next must be said.

She took a deep breath and let fly.

"I am taking the train to Chicago this very afternoon."

A chorus of loud lamentations, a flurry of "no" signs, and tearful outbursts almost made her reconsider.

But there was no other way to do what had to be done.

She raised her outstretched palms for silence.

"When I came to the reservation, Lucius and Mabel took me into their own home. I have learned to love them. I could not love them more if they were my own brother and sister. I could not love Amos, Jessie, Leslie, and Richard more if they were my own children. I could not love every one of you more if you were my own family."

She paused again for control and made her voice firm. "If I said good-bye to each and every one of you, there would be nothing left of me to put aboard that train this afternoon. I know that. So I want to ask you one last favor. Heenkey has agreed to take me to the railroad in his new surrey. My trunk and bags are already in it. He is waiting at the door of the church. I want you now to bow your heads in silent prayer. I want you to keep on praying until I am out that door and gone. It is the way I want to remember you—praying in the church that we built together."

For a heart-stopping moment, Isabel feared they would not comply.

But they were only taking one last lingering look at her.

The heads went down.

Isabel turned to Lucius. She could barely see him through her tears. She crossed the podium, and her arms seemed to go around him of their own volition. As she felt the strength of his arms and his hot tears on her cheek, all her carefully planned resolutions collapsed. Again she almost relented.

But at the last possible moment, common sense prevailed. She pushed away from him and fled up the aisle and out of the church.

Heenkey helped her into his surrey and they began to move away from God's Light on the Mountain.

By the time she had dried her eyes, Heenkey's two matched grays were moving along the fenced white man's road at a fast trot.

She glanced back.

The church and mission house already were moving into the distance. The day was bright and sunny, but a dark thunderhead boiled behind Saddle Mountain. Rain was moving in from the southwest. A bolt of lightning flashed, and a moment later the voice of the thunder drum reverberated from the depths of the Wichitas. Heenkey urged the horses to a faster pace in an effort to stay ahead of the storm.

Afterword

Isabel Alice Hartley Crawford, Lucius Ben Aitsan, Mary Burdette, Loki Mo-keen, Odlepaugh, *all* the characters in this novel lived at the close of the nineteenth century and the opening years of the twentieth. Their conversations and day-to-day lives were recorded in Isabel's diaries.

She did not view celebrated Indians such as Odlepaugh, Big Tree, and Loki Mo-keen as historical figures but as human beings beset by the almost overwhelming challenges of their times. Her love of the Kiowas and her rage over the injustices done to them cannot be exaggerated.

After overcoming many obstacles, Lucius Ben Aitsan was ordained on June 24, 1913, and at last became pastor of God's Light on the Mountain Baptist Church at Saddle Mountain, Oklahoma. His early death during the Spanish influenza epidemic in 1919 was one among many heartbreaking tragedies for the Kiowas. Today many of his descendants have anglicized their surname to Aitson.

Not long after Isabel Crawford left Saddle Mountain, Loki Mo-keen became a Christian and served later as deacon in his son's church. He remained a keeper of the Tai-may and an honored man of the tribe. He lived out his final years in the home of his adopted son Odlepaugh near Odlepaugh Springs. At the time of his death in 1934, Loki Mo-keen was believed to be more than a hundred years old. The name on his tombstone in Saddle Mountain Cemetery is recorded as "Maukin," assumed to be the proper spelling of his Spanish surname. Although family tradition suggests that he joined the Kiowas in boyhood voluntarily, Isabel records an instance in which older members of the tribe joshed him about how scared he was on the day he was captured. Mo-keen emphatically denied that he was scared.

Say-haye-do-hole Goombi, the white woman captive, was interviewed frequently by newspaper feature writers during the 1920s and early 1930s. She died in 1934 and was buried in Saddle Mountain Cemetery. In 1930, after correspondence between family members and Texans living in the vicinity of Fort Belknap, speculation arose that she may have been Millie Jane Durkin, seized at the age of two during the Elm Creek raid on the upper Brazos in 1864. Certain physical evidence tends to contradict this belief. The debate continues today among historians.

Taboodle, the ancient Kiowa storyteller of Isabel's time, was interviewed by Susan Peters, government field matron, in 1919, when he was adjudged to be "well over" one hundred years of age. Mrs. Peters used the spelling *T'ebodel*. She recorded his oral tradition of the origins of the Kiowas; his account still serves as the principal source concerning the prehistory of the tribe. This tribal tradition was used most effectively in the works of the Pulitzer Prize–winning Kiowa author, N. Scott Momaday, in his books *The Way to Rainy Mountain* and *House Made of Dawn*.

Mrs. Peters first went among the Kiowas in 1917 and served until 1928. After her "retirement," she lived among them until her death in 1965 at age ninety-two. Her collection of recorded interviews remains the most valuable single source of tribal information. Although Isabel was the first, Mrs. Peters also observed the innate artistry of the Kiowas and was instrumental in the training and development of the "five famous Kiowa artists." They were the first of many.

Today Susan Peters and Isabel Crawford are often confused in tribal memories.

Isabel Crawford kept her promise to the Kiowas. After she left Oklahoma Territory, she spent three years among various Indian tribes in upstate New York. Then for the next twenty-three years she traveled throughout the nation, doing "deputation work" for the mission society. She went from town to town, speaking before church and civic groups, telling Indian stories, describing her experiences, and promoting mission work. Newspaper accounts report that the highlight of her program came when, attired in her Kiowa costume, she offered the Twenty-third Psalm in Indian sign language. Kiowas from Saddle Mountain often joined her on the road. Hunting Horse; his wife, Beathomah; Lucius; his son-in-law John Onko; Gahbein; Kokom; his wife, Pope-bah; and several younger Kiowas were among Isabel's traveling troupe.

Before white audiences, Isabel frequently stated a premise first written into the margin of a territorial diary:

"Personally I have never met a 'wild Indian' nor a 'naked savage,' but Indian ladies and gentlemen, rivaling us in good manners and modesty of dress, and outrivaling us in artistic talent in rugs, basketry, beadwork, pottery, and painting, to say nothing of music, prose, poetry, and the universal sign language."

In 1915 she published *Kiowa: The History of a Blanket Indian Mission* (New York: Fleming H. Revell). Containing brief, unconnected excerpts from her voluminous diaries, the book offers a fascinating but confused account of her years on the Kiowa-Comanche-Apache Reservation. She assiduously avoided all public controversy concerning the church.

However, in private life she continued the battle. Her diaries contain correspondence as late as 1930 seeking the views of noted theologians concerning the church and Holy Communion.

An inveterate traveler, she later toured Alaska, England, Ireland, Scotland, France, Italy, Switzerland, Belgium, Holland, Egypt, and Palestine. She seldom missed a Chatauqua conference and, at such events, met such individuals as Thomas A. Edison, Henry Ford, and Franklin D. Roosevelt.

At the age of eighty-six, she published an autobiography, *Joyful Journey* (Philadelphia: The Judson Press). The title is descriptive. Throughout she concentrated on the humorous and enjoyable incidents of her life. She told little concerning her struggles and accomplishments.

Her book was dedicated to Hunting Horse and Beathomah, who were still alive on publication. Hunting Horse died on July 2, 1953, at Saddle Mountain. He was 107. A veteran of at least one revenge raid into Texas, and the Battle of Palo Duro Canyon, Hunting Horse later served as scout under Custer, Sheridan, and Sherman. He was buried in his U.S. Army uniform in an impressive military ceremony rendered by an honor guard from Fort Sill. A twenty-one-gun salute was fired over his grave.

In her later years, Isabel resided with nieces in the town of Grimsby, just west of Niagara Falls on the Canadian side.

There she died in 1961 at the age of ninety-six.

God's Light on the Mountain Baptist Church was moved to Cache Creek in the 1930s and eventually was destroyed. No one recalls what happened to the mission house.

Some towns Isabel saw at birth survived; others did not. Oakdale, Cooperton, Wildman, and Navajoe faded into memory. Lawton—the town Isabel saw born overnight—today is Oklahoma's third-largest city.

Most of the "railroad towns" survive, although the trains that "opened up the country" no longer run. Even the rails and ties have been removed.

Weather, machine agriculture, and decades of shortsighted farm policies have done their work. Today the landscape of southwestern Oklahoma is scarcely more populated than when Isabel first saw it. Deer, wolves, and wild turkey have returned. The Wichita Mountain Wildlife Refuge today serves as pasture for foundation herds of buffalo and Longhorns. The Fort Sill Military Reservation, an artillery center through two world wars, is today a missile range.

As brooding and haunting as ever, Saddle and Rainy mountains still lure the Kiowas back to their ancestral home. Families often gather there from throughout Oklahoma and surrounding states for powwows.

It is well worth the trip. On those occasions, the thunder drum is heard once again in the Wichitas.

About the Author

Leonard Sanders, called by James Leo Herlihy "one of the most gifted storytelling spellbinders alive," and by Sidney Sheldon "one of my favorite authors," has been a book critic and columnist in the Southwest for more than a decade. He is the author of several novels, including *The Hamlet Warning*, *Sonoma*, and *Fort Worth*. He was reared in southwest Oklahoma, not far from Saddle Mountain, and spent much time roaming the Wichitas during his boyhood. Sanders and his wife reside in Fort Worth, Texas.

The Carolina Chronicles

by Inglis Fletcher

A rich, historical saga reaching from Colonial days to the Revolutionary War, Inglis Fletcher's classic series of novels dramatizes the pioneering lives of the men and women whose courage claimed a new nation, and a monumental dream. From their first steps into a barbarous Eden to the nation they forge from that wilderness, Fletcher follows the lives, passions and dreams of these, the first Carolinians.

Read all of Inglis Fletcher's CAROLINA CHRONICLES series

Romantic Favorites

Eugenia Price

☐ 26559	MARGARET'S STORY	$4.50
☐ 25618	BELOVED INVADER	$3.95
☐ 26362	MARIA	$4.50
☐ 25017	NEW MOON RISING	$3.95
☐ 24137	LIGHTHOUSE	$3.95

Grace Livingston Hill

☐ 24736	AN UNWILLING GUEST	$2.50
☐ 24799	GIRL FROM MONTANA	$2.50
☐ 26364	A DAILY RATE	$2.75
☐ 24981	THE STORY OF A WHIM	$2.50
☐ 26389	ACCORDING TO THE PATTERN	$2.75
☐ 25253	IN THE WAY	$2.95
☐ 25806	LO, MICHAEL	$2.95
☐ 25930	THE WITNESS	$2.95
☐ 26104	THE CITY OF FIRE	$2.95

Buy these books at your local bookstore or use this handy coupon for ordering:

Bantam Books, Inc., Dept. PL, 414 East Golf Road, Des Plaines, Ill. 60016

Please send me the books I have checked above. I am enclosing $_____ (please add $1.50 to cover postage and handling.) Send check or money order—no cash or C.O.D.s please.

Mr/Ms _____

Address _____

City/State _____ Zip _____

PL—1/87

Please allow four to six weeks for delivery. This offer expires 6/87. Prices and availability subject to change without notice.

BANTAM
SHOP-AT-HOME
C·A·T·A·L·O·G

Special Offer
Buy a Bantam Book
for only 50¢.

Now you can have Bantam's catalog filled with hundreds of titles plus take advantage of our unique and exciting bonus book offer. A special offer which gives you the opportunity to purchase a Bantam book for only 50¢. Here's how!

By ordering any five books at the regular price per order, you can also choose any other single book listed (up to a $4.95 value) for just 50¢. Some restrictions do apply, but for further details why not send for Bantam's catalog of titles today!

Just send us your name and address and we will send you a catalog!